Charlotte

The Halversons: Book #5

By

KIMBERLY RAE
JORDAN

THREE**STRAND**
P R E S S

A CORD OF THREE STRANDS IS NOT EASILY BROKEN.

A man, a woman & their God.
Three Strand Press publishes Christian Romance stories
that intertwine love, faith and family. Always clean.
Always heartwarming. Always uplifting.

Charlotte/ Kimberly Rae Jordan. -- 1st ed.
ISBN-13: 978-1-988409-77-1

*He has made everything
beautiful in its time.*

Ecclesiastes 3:11

CHAPTER ONE

Charlotte Halverson turned in a slow circle, casting a critical eye over the room she'd just finished decorating. She'd been working for the past few hours to get her classroom ready, using brightly colored posters to transform the room from dreary to warm and welcoming for her students.

It was hard to believe that the first day of school was almost upon them, so Charli cherished these quiet moments as she prepared her room for her students and the school year ahead.

The summer holidays had been busy. She'd spent most of it with Layla and Peyton and whatever family members had been available to hang out with them as they went to movies, bowled, and even traveled to Seattle for a few days to do some activities there.

Though she was excited about the upcoming school year, Charli was also apprehensive about it since her daughter, Layla, wouldn't be in the same school where Charli was teaching. Layla would be in grade six, which meant she'd be starting at the Serenity Point Middle School.

For the first time, Charli had some trepidation about the first day of school, as it related to Layla. From the day Layla had started kindergarten, Charli had been within a few steps of her if she'd needed her. And now that would no longer be the case.

Not wanting to get bogged down by the emotions of how fast her baby was growing up, Charli focused on making sure that she'd done everything she wanted to in the classroom. She took a few minutes to walk past the desks, running her fingers over each name-tag as she said a prayer for the child.

She knew many of the children who were in her class that year. Some had older siblings who Charli had previously taught. Others were children of families who attended the same church as Charli. There would also be some who were new to the school.

A knock on her open door had Charli turning toward it. The secretary from the office stepped into the classroom, a piece of paper in her hand.

She was a young woman who had been in the position for just a year, having taken over for the previous secretary when she'd retired after working at the school for almost forty years. That woman had been in the position since before Charli or any of her siblings had even started to attend the elementary school.

"We've got another student for you," Rachel said as she approached Charli and held out the paper. "She was just registered this morning, and since you still had room in your class, you get her."

"That's fine," Charli told her as she took the paper. "I'll do up a name tag for her desk."

Rachel glanced around the room. "This looks so fun."

Charli spent the next couple of minutes chatting with the woman as she took her on a tour of the room. When Rachel left, Charli went back to her desk and sat down to make another name tag.

She'd shift a few of the names around to make room for the new student, making sure that the little girl was seated next to someone who would be friendly to her.

Opening the drawer where she kept the thick card stock she used for the name tags, Charli pulled out a sheet along with some markers and set them on the desk. Uncapping a marker, she glanced at the info on her newest student, and her gaze snagged on the name.

Amelia... Madden?

Charli stared at the paper for a long moment.

It wasn't the first time she'd come across that last name in the past twelve years. However, each time she heard or saw it, there was always a small pulse of pain.

It wasn't unique enough that she could assume that anyone with that last name was related to *him*, but it also wasn't a super common last name. Which was why it always gave her a moment's pause when she came across it.

The information Rachel had given her about Amelia contained only her name and birthday, so she couldn't see who her parents were. Though she had no idea what had happened to Blake Madden after he'd left Serenity Point all those years ago, she was pretty sure he wouldn't have moved back, even if he did have family in the area.

She hated that thoughts of Blake had interjected themselves into her day. Everything had been going great, but now she was thinking about him when she'd rather think about pretty much anything else.

Resolutely pushing those thoughts aside, Charli wrote out a colorful and playful nametag for her newest student. After it was done, she took it to the desk she'd chosen for Amelia and taped it in place.

After everything was done to her satisfaction, Charli gathered up her things and left the school.

When she stepped into her house a few minutes later, she heard the murmurs of conversation. She'd left Layla at the house with Denise, her brother Jay's mother-in-law, who came every Friday to clean the large house. As she had throughout the summer, Denise had brought Peyton and Ciara, Jay and Misha's kids, with her.

"Hi, Mom," Layla called out when Charli walked into the kitchen.

She and Peyton were kneeling on stools at the island, leaning forward on their elbows, watching as Denise transferred cookies from a baking sheet to a cooling rack.

"We made chocolate chip cookies," Layla told her. "And Miss Denise let me help her measure things, then Peyton scooped them onto the pan."

Denise smiled at Charli. "How did it go?"

"Everything is ready," Charli told her as she set her bag on the stool next to Layla. "Just need the kiddos."

"Are you excited?" she asked. "Layla seems to be more excited about school starting than I remember my kids being."

Charli leaned a hip against the counter. "I'll be glad to be back in school."

"I just want to see all my friends," Layla said. "Lots of them have been away."

"You're such a little social butterfly," Denise told her with a smile.

Layla smiled back. "I love butterflies."

Charli got herself some water as Layla went on to tell Denise why she liked butterflies.

The older woman had been such a blessing to them, not just because she helped keep Charli's home clean, but mainly because she brought another loving relationship into Layla's life. She treated Layla like one of her grandchildren, and Charli appreciated that.

"Did you want to stay for pizza?" Charli asked.

"Thank you for the invite, but I'm meeting some women from my craft group for a potluck dinner."

"Oooh. What are you making?"

"I was asked to bring my fried chicken."

"Good choice," Charli said. "It's amazing."

Denise beamed. "It was my nana's recipe, so I'm glad people like it."

"Thank you for making those cookies and keeping an eye on Layla for me. I really appreciate it."

"Anytime." Denise gave her a hug. "You know I love spending time with her."

Since Jay and Misha would be coming for dinner, Denise left their kids with Charli, so she had the older two keep an eye on Ciara for a couple of minutes while she went to her room. She set her bag on her desk, then used the bathroom and freshened up a bit before heading back to the living room.

Scooping Ciara up, Charli sat down in the comfy rocker-recliner that was tucked into the corner of the room near the fireplace. She didn't have a lot of time to relax before she needed to prepare for the influx of guests for their semi-regular pizza night, but she loved cuddling with the toddler.

Layla came over and snuggled up next to Charli in the chair. It was getting more difficult to do that, as Layla was growing so fast. Still, neither of them minded being squished.

There was no room for Peyton on the chair, but he knelt on the floor in front of them. As fast as Layla was growing, Peyton was growing even faster. He might be younger than Layla, but he was already taller than her, obviously having inherited Jay's height.

His brown eyes sparkled as he smiled and tickled Ciara. The toddler's delighted laugh was contagious and soon they were all laughing.

These three represented the next generation of Halversons, and Charli loved each of them with all her heart. The only one missing was darling Timothy, Gareth and Aria's son, who was just a couple of months shy of his first birthday.

"Can we watch a movie while we wait for everyone to arrive?" Layla asked.

"Do you have one in mind?" Charli asked as she ran her hand over Layla's long, dark hair.

They spent a few minutes discussing the options, then they left to go to the basement. Since she kept toddler toys down there, the kids took Ciara with them, and Charli made her way to the kitchen.

She got out the ingredients to make a salad to go with the pizza. Normally that would be Layla's task, but since she was downstairs with the other two, Charli tackled it herself.

She'd just finished the salad when she heard the garage door open, which meant that Will and Janessa were home. They'd continued to live at the house after their marriage a few months earlier, which had made Charli happy.

The house would have been way too big for just her and Layla. She knew that eventually, Will and Janessa would move into a home of their own, but Charli wasn't going to dwell on that eventuality just yet.

The couple greeted her as they came in from the garage, then Janessa went upstairs to change out of her work clothes. Meanwhile, Will sat down on a stool at the island.

"What can I do to help?"

"I think everything is basically ready. Just need the people and the pizza."

Over the next half hour, people straggled in, with Gareth and Aria bringing the pizza that week.

Kayleigh and Hudson showed up as well. Prior to getting into a relationship, Kayleigh hadn't always come to the pizza nights. But somehow, Hudson's presence in her life had resulted in more frequent attendance.

Jackson, one of Gareth's best friends, was also there, as was their friend Wade. They didn't always include friends, but Jackson and Wade had been a part of their lives for so long they might as well have been family.

After Jay said a prayer for the meal, people began to load up their plates. Charli waited until everyone else had their food before she took a couple of slices and some salad. The large table was full with so many of them there, and that made Charli happy.

Her gaze swept around the table as the meal progressed, settling on Kayleigh and Hudson. Kayleigh was laughing and smiling more than she usually did, and Charli knew it was because of the man at her side.

Not that Kayleigh had been an unhappy person. She'd just been serious. Focused on her job. Hudson's arrival in her life had been because of work, but it had turned personal, and now Kayleigh's focus was split between Hudson and her job.

Hudson had his arm around Kayleigh's shoulders, his hand lazily stroking her upper arm, as if he wasn't even aware he was doing it but needing the connection. Kayleigh leaned against him, seeming to not desire any sort of personal space from him, which was also a change for her.

Growing up and even as an adult, Kayleigh had always wanted her space. There had been enough space in the house that she could have lived with Charli and Janessa, but she'd chosen to buy her own home and live by herself. Apparently, all it had taken was the right person to get past the aloofness she had used to keep almost everyone at arm's length.

A familiar jealousy wound its way through Charli.

For as long as she could remember, she'd struggled with jealousy towards Kayleigh. Her older sister had seemed to have everything. She was petite and beautiful, smart, and determined to achieve her goals. If she wanted something, she went after it, and it was rare that she didn't attain whatever she wanted.

In high school, though she could have had any guy, Kayleigh had only rarely dated, not all that interested in pursuing marriage or a family. Meanwhile, that had been *all* Charli had wanted. But she hadn't been what teenage boys had been looking for. Too often, guys would befriend Charli only because they'd hoped for an in with Kayleigh.

And why wouldn't they? Next to Kayleigh, Charli had always felt oversized and awkward. No doubt boys had seen her that way, too.

"Has your cousin settled in, Jackson?" Gareth asked.

The question took a moment to sink through Charli's dour thoughts about her sister, and when it did, her hand tightened around her glass, so much so that she was surprised that it didn't break. She opened her mouth to ask what Gareth meant, but then snapped it shut, remembering that she wasn't supposed to know much of anything about Jackson's cousin.

"Yep. Mom and Dad are renting Blake one of the suites in the four-plex on Maple, and the moving truck with all his stuff arrives tomorrow, so we'll be there to help him with that."

Charli was going to be sick. Every bite she'd taken of her meal threatened to reappear at the thought that her past was returning, bringing with it the possibility of totally wrecking her life.

For every month, then every year, that passed without Blake coming back to Serenity, she'd started to think it would never happen. To hope it would never happen.

But now it *had* happened, and she felt sick at what it might mean for the secret she'd kept close to her heart.

A million questions tumbled through her mind, but Charli knew she couldn't ask any of them. Not without raising suspicions, at least.

"Why'd he decide to move here?" Jay asked. "Isn't he from California?"

Jackson shrugged. "I haven't really had a chance to ask him. I just know he decided not to re-enlist in the army, and then he asked my folks if they'd be able to help him find a place to live for him and his daughter."

Daughter.

Charli didn't really believe in coincidences, so she was pretty sure that the new student in her class was Blake's daughter.

How had this become her life? Not only had the man she'd once loved, and who had broken her heart, returned, she now had to teach his child.

Why had God allowed this to happen?

She knew she'd made mistakes in her past, but she'd asked God for forgiveness, and she'd been more committed to her Christian walk since everything that had happened with Blake. Being faced with Blake's return, her first instinct was to panic and try to figure out how to keep him from torpedoing her life.

She had to protect the person most important to her.

"You haven't kept in contact with him?" Gareth asked.

"Not really. When he left here, he just kind of disappeared. No one knew where he went. My aunt told my mom that Blake's dad had been livid when Blake refused to take a position in their family business. I guess he decided to enlist in the army instead, but we didn't know about that until recently."

She was feeling so overwhelmed by all she'd learned that Charli was glad when Layla asked if she and Peyton could finish watching the movie. After giving her permission, Charli took the opportunity to escape the conversation at the table and went into the kitchen to start the coffee and put some cookies and brownies on a plate.

But avoiding the conversation certainly didn't mean that she wasn't thinking about Blake and the fact that he had *finally* come back to Serenity.

She just hoped that Gareth wouldn't decide that his best friend's cousin needed to be part of their gatherings. It wasn't a stretch to think he might, especially since Blake had a child, and Gareth would likely think that Layla and Peyton might be good friends for her.

Charli wasn't sure how she could keep that from happening, but she was going to try her best. The last thing she wanted was for Blake to find out about Layla. She'd never told her family who Layla's father was, and when Blake had disappeared, she hadn't been able to tell him either.

Now, she had no interest in sharing parenting responsibilities with anyone, but most of all, not with the man who'd promised her everything she'd ever wanted and then walked away.

CHAPTER TWO

Blake Madden dropped onto his couch, a can of soda in his hand. He popped the tab, then took a long swallow.

The day had been long, and he was glad for the opportunity to sit down. There were still boxes to empty, but they could wait. The most important things that needed to be unpacked had been Amelia's, and with his aunt's help, they'd managed to get her whole room set up.

"Thanks for your help, Jackson," he said, glancing over to where his cousin sat sprawled on the overstuffed loveseat that matched the couch. "I really appreciate it. I doubt I could have made this move without all the help you and your parents have given me."

Jackson lifted his can of soda in a cheers motion. "We're happy to help. It'll be nice to have you around again."

When Blake had realized that the career he'd planned for himself in the army wasn't going to work out, he hadn't been sure where to go. He'd known he needed a good place for Amelia. A place where he would have support as he raised her by himself.

Since his own family wouldn't offer him that, he'd had to look elsewhere. His aunt and uncle had always been warm and welcoming towards him, so Blake had decided that he had no option other than to return to Serenity.

He really hoped he hadn't made a mistake.

"What do you plan to do for work?" Jackson asked.

"I'm hoping to get work as a mechanic," he said.

"You've always liked cars, but don't you need special training to do that?"

"I worked as a mechanic in the army. They offered me a lot of training, so I have that experience now."

"No interest in furniture, huh?"

"Not unless I need to buy something to sit on."

Jackson gave a huff of laughter. "Do you own *any* Madden furniture?"

"Nope. And I don't plan to. If they're not going to support me, I'm not going to support them. Plus, it's a little out of my price range these days."

"When was the last time you talked to your family?"

"I haven't talked to Dad or Mom since I left Serenity last time. When Dad realized I was serious about not taking a role in the company like he wanted me to, he cut me off and told me I had to make my own way in the world."

"Harsh," Jackson said with a grimace.

"Yeah. I think he thought the threat would pull me back in line."

"Guess that backfired, huh?"

"Yeah. But it left me with no options. I'd been getting a pretty healthy monthly allowance from my dad throughout college. Stupid me, I assumed that even though I didn't want to join the company, he'd keep giving me the money after I graduated. Thinking that way meant I'd saved up nothing."

"You could've come back here," Jackson told him. "We would have helped you out."

Except that he had felt like he couldn't return to Serenity. Not when he could no longer follow through on what he'd promised Charli. How could he help her achieve her dreams when he no longer had an income and no prospect of being able to earn what he'd need to give her the life she deserved?

He'd made promises based on what he'd thought was going to happen, only for the rug to be pulled out from under him by his dad's ultimatum. Rather than taking the time to deal with the situation like an adult, he'd allowed his dad's rejection of his plans to morph into a fear that Charli would reject him because he couldn't follow through on the promises he'd made.

Blake had always planned to get a job while he figured out how to get the training and experience he'd need to work as a mechanic. However, he'd counted on continuing to receive the substantial allowance from his dad to supplement whatever he earned while he tried to get his own dreams off the ground. It would have been enough to support himself and Charli.

Looking back, Blake could see that even though he'd been twenty-two at the time, he had been somewhat naïve and, yes, spoiled. His dad had provided everything for him, and he'd mistakenly assumed it was because he loved him and wanted him to be happy as he pursued his dreams.

What that meant, however, was that he'd been very dependent on his dad and had no idea what it was like to have to work hard for what he wanted without a safety net in place. That was when his fear of failing Charli had taken over, robbing him of common sense.

So, without the training he needed or any job prospects, he'd somehow decided that the army recruiter who'd come to his high school years earlier had presented him with an option that he could seriously consider. He'd made the snap decision to join the army, and, in the process, he'd run away from everything.

It had been impulsive and a stupid move, catering more to his fear and pride than anything else, but once that commitment was made, there was no turning back. He'd grabbed onto the idea that he could get the training he wanted, along with a guaranteed salary, and hadn't looked back.

If he'd faced that situation now, things would have turned out much, much differently.

Though his decision had broken his heart, he'd felt it was for the best for Charli. He'd thought he'd freed her to find the man who would help her realize her dreams and spared her from dealing with the failure he'd felt he was back then.

"Being in the army helped me acquire the skills I needed to do what I really wanted," Blake said, remembering how convincing the recruiter had been about that in their first conversation, offering him everything he'd felt like he'd just lost. A job. An income. A home. A future.

"I never considered there were mechanics in the army, but I suppose it makes sense."

Blake nodded. "I was responsible for keeping the wheeled vehicles in good running order."

"And you were deployed?"

"Not the whole time, but for quite a bit of it."

"Where's Amelia's mom?" Jackson asked.

Blake's gaze went to the closed door of Amelia's room. He'd put her to bed a short time ago, but there was no guarantee she was already asleep. She knew that her mom was no longer around, but not the gritty details that had led to her death.

"She passed away." Though their relationship hadn't lasted long, it still hurt to think about what had happened.

"Oh." Jackson frowned. "I'm sorry to hear that."

Blake had no idea how to respond to that. He had been deployed when it happened, and because she hadn't been his wife or even his girlfriend, he hadn't qualified for leave to attend her funeral. Thankfully, Lauren's sister had stepped in to take care of Amelia until he could get back Stateside.

"Do you mind me asking what happened?"

He looked at the closed door again. "She was killed in a car accident."

The surprise on Jackson's face wasn't unexpected. Blake thought he'd probably ask a bunch more questions, but apparently, he'd picked up on Blake's reluctance to talk about it.

"Sorry... yeah, sorry to hear about that, too."

Blake took another swallow of his soda, then wrapped both hands around the can as he leaned back into the couch. "Do you still hang out with the Halversons?"

Jackson looked relieved at the change of subject as he nodded. "Yep. Was just with a bunch of them last night for dinner."

"How're they doing?" Blake was most interested in one person, but he didn't mind hearing about them all.

"Good. Gareth is married and has a kid. Janessa is married to Gareth's best friend, Will. Kayleigh is engaged to some guy she works with. Jay is also married with two kids."

Blake told himself it was a bad idea to ask for more specific information, but he couldn't seem to help himself. "How's Charli?"

"She's fine." Jackson stared at him for a long moment. "Why do you ask?"

Figuring there would be no harm in disclosing what had happened so many years ago, or maybe just assuming that Jackson wouldn't answer his question in more detail if he didn't give him a reason to, Blake said, "She and I had a bit of a... thing when I was last here."

Jackson's eyes narrowed. "A bit of a *thing*? What does that mean, exactly?"

"We got... close."

"Like, physically close? Or just spending time together?"

"Physically close. I even gave her a promise ring. It was my plan to return after I told my dad I wasn't going to work for him. We'd even talked about getting married."

Jackson's eyes went impossibly wide, then his brows drew close as he frowned. "How on earth did you manage to spend that much time with her?"

"We actually connected at the end of the summer before that last one. During the school year, we kept in touch through calls and texting."

"That's why you wanted to come back here again for the summer," Jackson said.

Blake nodded. "Charli scheduled a lot of her shifts so she was off when most of you were at work. And since I wasn't working, it meant that we had plenty of time together."

"I am just dumbfounded," Jackson said. "Like... wow... I never would have guessed. And obviously no one else did either."

"We worked very hard to make sure that was the case."

"Her family would have objected to your relationship," Jackson said.

"I'm aware."

"You weren't a Christian then. That would have been an issue for them. They would have been super protective of her," Jackson said. "They still will be. I'd recommend keeping your distance from her. If her siblings find out about how things went back then, you'll wish you'd moved somewhere else in this country."

Charli had said something similar back when they'd been spending so much time together. They'd been sneaking around because she'd said that her parents might not approve of them dating. It hadn't made sense to him, since they were both adults, but he hadn't argued because he wasn't sure his parents would have approved either.

His plan had been to go back to California to inform his parents of his plan to become a mechanic, then return to Serenity, where they'd then make their relationship public. It had just felt better to wait, since he was sure that his parents would blame Charli for his change of heart, and he hadn't wanted that to happen.

"They'd come after me, even though it's so far in the past?" Blake asked, thinking it was a bit of an extreme reaction, given how much time had passed.

"Maybe not, but better safe than sorry."

"Is Charli in a relationship?" He remembered how much she'd wanted to get married and have children, so he was prepared to hear that she was.

It didn't hurt as much as it once had to imagine her moving on and finding love with another man. But the regret that *had* lingered had become stronger since returning to Serenity, and it was edged in pain.

For some reason, Jackson seemed to give his response some thought. Blake could only assume it was because he felt some sense of protectiveness over Charli, given Blake's revelation.

"Not at the moment," Jackson said slowly. "But that doesn't mean she'd be receptive to you trying to rekindle something. She's very particular about who she dates these days."

Was he even interested in that? Or had too much water passed under the bridge?

Way too much water had passed under the bridge, Blake decided. And there was so much baggage between them. Namely, his abrupt text message ending things, followed by his disappearance.

"Not trying to rekindle anything," Blake said. "I was just curious."

Jackson's phone made a sound, and he stretched out his leg to work it free from his pocket. After staring at the screen, he said, "Mom wants me to remind you to send her the school supply list for Amelia."

The school secretary had emailed him the list the previous afternoon, but he hadn't even looked at it yet. Thankfully, Jackson's mom, Julia, had offered to get the supplies and anything else Amelia might need before school started. He was very grateful for her help.

He pulled out his phone to bring up the email, then, after having Jackson recite his mom's email address, forwarded it to Julia. Since he had the email open, he tapped on the attachment to see how big the list was. Hopefully, it wasn't too long, though Julia had assured him that she liked to shop, so getting the supplies wouldn't be an issue.

The heading at the top of the document grabbed his attention. "Looks like I'm not going to be able to avoid seeing Charli, even if I'm not interested in rekindling a relationship."

"Amelia's in her class?" Jackson said with a frown.

"Yep. Looks like it."

Jackson continued to frown. "She's a great teacher, from what I've heard, so that's good for Amelia."

After all that had happened between them, Blake wondered how Charli might feel about teaching his daughter. He didn't think she'd take any negative feelings she had for him out on Amelia. Back then, she'd loved kids, and he doubted that had changed if she was now teaching them.

"Charli is an amazing woman," Jackson said. "She didn't deserve for you to break up with her."

Jackson's passionate tone drew Blake's attention. "Did you and she...?"

"No. She's just become a good friend over the years."

Blake had no right to feel any sort of way about Charli dating other men, but being back in Serenity had brought out all kinds of thoughts and memories of the last time he'd been there. It had been a time filled with so much happiness and promise.

"I get that you'll have to interact with her as Amelia's teacher, but I hope you'll steer clear of her otherwise."

"What if she doesn't want that?" Blake asked, a bit ticked at Jackson's determination to keep him out of Charli's life.

Jackson gave a huff of laughter. "Oh, I'm pretty sure that won't be the case. Hearing about what happened between the two of you has explained a lot about how she's approached men and relationships over the years."

"What does that mean?"

"Let's just say that if a guy wants to get close to Charli as more than a friend, he's really going to have to work for it. There haven't been a lot who've been willing to put in the effort. Especially recently. Early on, I'm guessing that perhaps she had a rebound relationship, but these days, if she's dating, she's not talking much about it."

It had taken a while before Blake had been interested in another woman, which had been fine, since he'd been tied up with basic training and then the training he'd had to take to work as an army mechanic. He'd dated a few women before meeting Lauren, but after they'd broken up, he hadn't dated anyone.

"I'd better go," Jackson said, pushing up to his feet. "Let me know if you need more help."

Blake stood up and followed him to the door of the apartment. "I think we're probably good. Thank you for all your help today. I couldn't have done it without you."

Jackson flashed him a quick smile, then stepped out the door onto the landing they shared with one other apartment. The building only had four apartments, two on each floor. The apartment wasn't very big, but Blake was grateful to his aunt and uncle for renting it to them for a very reasonable rate.

He would have loved to have a small house with a yard for Amelia and a garage for himself. However, his current budget didn't stretch that far. With no income, he was having to live on the money he'd managed to save. Thankfully, he'd learned his lesson about not saving money and had lived as frugally as possible on his army salary, which meant he had a bit of a cushion.

Once he'd closed the door on Jackson's retreating figure, Blake took a moment to survey the space. The furniture he'd purchased for their apartment in Texas was almost too big for this place. He probably should have just tried to sell it before they moved, but it had been fairly new, since he'd originally thought they'd be able to stay there.

After working through the figures, he'd determined it would be cheaper to ship everything than to pay to replace it all. Plus, he'd worked hard to find good quality things at a reasonable price, and if he'd had to replace them, it would probably have been with even cheaper quality things.

He gathered up the empty soda cans and tossed them in the recycling bin, then made sure everything was cleared away. Waking up to a messy space was the last thing he wanted. Being in the army for so long had ingrained in him the need to keep his space tidy.

Amelia made it a challenge at times, so Blake tried to be more relaxed about it. But if he had the choice, he wanted things neat. And not just in his physical surroundings. He liked his life to be that way, especially after the turn his life had taken when he'd made that snap decision that had changed the direction of his life.

Unfortunately, getting involved with Lauren meant his personal life had been anything but neat and tidy.

Even after they'd broken up, they'd had to continue to be in each other's lives because of Amelia. He didn't regret having Amelia, but he wished that she'd been born into a different type of relationship between her parents.

His career, which had demanded his absence for long stretches, combined with Lauren's addiction struggles and subsequent death, had led to Amelia being exposed to upheaval throughout much of her short life. It was his hope that now that he was out of the army and able to be with her on a daily basis, she could heal from her mom's death and enjoy some stability in her life.

Stability was something he wanted for himself too, and he needed it in order to be the best father he could be to Amelia.

He prayed that Serenity Point would be the fresh start they needed, even though he'd chosen to return to a place that was loaded with baggage.

CHAPTER THREE

As she sat with the other teachers for a quick meeting before the school day started, Charli's emotions were all over the place. She was excited about meeting her students, but also nervous about possibly coming face to face with the man who'd broken her heart and left her a single mother.

Charli was also sad that she couldn't be with Layla on her first day of middle school. Thankfully, Janessa had stepped up to take her place.

The first day of school usually only brought excitement and anticipation. Nervousness hadn't been a part of it since her first couple of years of teaching, and sadness had never been present on a first day before. But both were there that morning.

"Let's head out and have a great day," the principal said with a smile. "I'm looking forward to seeing what the year holds for all of us and our students."

With that, they were dismissed to return to their classrooms. Charli walked with her fellow grade three teacher that year. It was her second year at the school, and she and Charli got along really well.

"Here's to surviving the first day," Junie said as they reached their classrooms. She held out her hand for a fist bump, and Charli obliged her before heading into her room.

Though parents weren't generally allowed to wander the halls of the elementary school, on the first day, the principal made an exception and allowed parents to come and drop off their kids in their classrooms. It meant things were a bit chaotic, but it usually settled down pretty quickly.

The secretary's voice came over the PA system to let them know that the doors were opening to let the students and parents into the building. Pressing a hand to her stomach to try to quell her nerves, Charli stood up from her desk.

The prospect of seeing Blake again was dominating her thoughts, as it had since realizing that his daughter was going to be in her class. She'd told herself not to think about it as she'd dressed that morning, but that had been a lost cause.

Thankfully, because she wore mainly pants while teaching, her choices weren't too vast, or it might have taken her forever to decide what to wear. In the end, she'd chosen a soft pink blouse that she knew was a flattering color and fit, and paired it with black slacks.

A large part of her wished that she'd been more proactive about exercising and losing the weight she'd added from her pregnancy with Layla, because she wanted to look good when Blake saw her again after twelve years. But there was nothing she could do about that now.

And it didn't matter, she reminded herself.

Blake was a part of her past, and seeing him again meant nothing. She had zero intention of spending any time with the man because she had zero intention of letting him meet Layla. That might be wishful thinking, considering Jackson was his cousin and spent a lot of time with her family.

Charli just had to hope that Blake would think that Layla was too young to be his daughter. She was a bit small for her age, so it was possible she might get away with it. Her family wouldn't put two and two together, since they didn't know what had happened between her and Blake.

She just needed Blake to focus on his own daughter and leave hers alone.

"Good morning, Miss H!" a little girl called out as she skipped over to where Charli stood in the doorway of the classroom.

Charli greeted her with a smile, then spoke to her mom, who she knew from church. The pair then headed into the classroom to find her desk and get her settled. After that, there was a steady stream of students with their parents.

For a short time, focusing on the children meant she didn't dwell on Blake's imminent arrival. Sort of... However, there was really no way to keep that thought completely out of her mind.

Then, she happened to glance up between greeting students and caught sight of his tall figure walking down the hall toward her classroom. His head was angled down, so for a brief moment, she had a chance to take in the sight of him without his awareness.

His blond hair, which he'd worn long the last time she'd seen him, was now cut short, and though he'd been tall and fit before, he seemed even more so now. He wore a simple white T-shirt tucked into a pair of blue jeans.

Her gaze wanted to stay on him. To continue to categorize all the things that had changed since she'd last seen him. Each stride he took toward her made her heart rate increase, just like it had when they'd been together before.

As Blake neared, their eyes met for a moment, but then another student reached Charli and took her attention, for which she was grateful. She didn't want her heart to race for any reason when it came to Blake. But here she was, heart pounding so hard she was sure everyone could hear it, even as she tried to keep her attention on the student in front of her.

As the mother and son she'd been speaking with moved past her into the classroom, Charli braced herself for the coming interaction with Blake and his daughter. When they reached her, she chose to focus on the little girl instead of her father.

"Hi there," Charli said, her smile feeling a little forced as she held out her hand. "I'm Miss Halverson. What's your name?"

The little girl regarded her with big blue eyes that looked very much like her father's. Her blonde hair was pulled back into a ponytail, and she was dressed in a pleated blue skirt and pink T-shirt with a unicorn on the front.

"I'm Amelia," she said, her voice soft as she put her hand in Charli's.

"It's nice to meet you, Amelia. Would you like to take your dad into the classroom to find your desk?"

Amelia glanced up at Blake, as did Charli, because she just couldn't help it. Blake was watching her, but his expression was unreadable. Charli forced her gaze back to the little girl in time to see her nod.

"Perfect. You can look for your desk and put your supplies there, and then you have a cubicle where you can put your backpack. Both have your name on them."

Amelia nodded, then pulled Blake toward the doorway. Charli offered them both a smile, then turned her attention to the next student waiting to speak with her.

When the bell rang to start their day, Charli made her way to the front of the room.

"If I could have your attention," she called out, waiting for a moment before continuing. "Parents, please help your child find their seat, then say your goodbyes."

As she waited for the parents to do as she'd requested, Charli let her gaze drift around the room, making note of which children seemed to be having a bit of difficulty with the goodbyes. There were always a few who were fine to wave their parents out the door, but most were a little apprehensive. A few were teary, reluctant to let their parents go.

Amelia appeared to be one of the latter, and Blake was on a knee next to her desk, speaking to her quietly.

Soon, the majority of the parents had said their goodbyes and exited the room, leaving just three parents.

Charli made her way to one of them, assuring the parent that it was okay for them to go. Some parents were reluctant to leave their child when they were upset, but most of the time, the child settled once they were gone.

She left Blake and Amelia to last, giving them some extra time together. As she approached Amelia's desk, Blake looked up at her. Charli tried not to acknowledge the flutter of nerves in her stomach as his gaze focused on her again.

"She'll be okay," Charli said, then turned her attention to Amelia. "We're going to do some fun stuff today. Coloring, crafts, and reading some stories. Maybe even some about unicorns. Your dad will be back to pick you up before you know it."

"Give me a hug, Berry," Blake said, drawing Amelia into his arms. "You're going to have fun, I'm sure of it. I can't wait to hear about everything you do."

Amelia's brows drew together, but when Blake set her down in her chair, she didn't protest. Charli returned to the front of the room, watching as Blake made his way to the door, glancing in her direction once before disappearing into the hallway.

With all the parents gone, Charli began her day by having each child share their name and what their favorite thing was.

When she'd prayed for the students that morning as part of her devotions, most had just been a name to her. This exercise was the first step in getting to know these children who were her responsibility for several hours every school day. As the year progressed, her prayer for each child would become more detailed.

She couldn't help but keep an eye on Amelia as the day progressed. The little girl didn't shed any tears, but she also didn't smile. She had a very serious demeanor as she watched everything going on around her.

Amelia answered any question she was asked, but she didn't initiate any conversation. At lunch, they ate at their desks, and while normally, Charli would have left them in the care of a teaching assistant and gone to the teacher's lounge to eat her own lunch, since it was the first day, she stayed with them.

When the bell rang to end the day, Charli felt a rush of relief. She was pleased with how everything had gone, and she had a good feeling about the class and how the year would go. There were some kids who would clearly require more guidance and understanding, but that was always the case.

Charli stood at the doorway as the kids lined up to follow the TA out of the room. The young woman would make sure that the students got to where they needed to be. Some had parents waiting for them. Others would be climbing onto buses to go home.

Since the parents weren't coming to the classroom to pick up their kids, Charli didn't see Blake again, which was a good thing. It was distracting enough to have his child in her class. She didn't want to have to come face to face with him every single day at work.

It wasn't that she cared about him—she really, really, really, really didn't—but she didn't necessarily want to be reminded of the bad decisions she'd made the last time he'd been in her life. Nor did she necessarily want to see him in the role of father, given that he'd never been that for Layla. She didn't want to think what Layla might have missed out on by not having him in her life.

But speaking of Layla, Charli was eager to hear how her day had gone. Thankfully, Denise had offered to pick Layla up from the middle school, then bring her to the elementary school to drop her off when she came to pick up Peyton.

When Layla appeared in the doorway of her classroom, Charli hurried to pull her into a hug. "How was your day, sweetheart?"

"It was great!" Layla's smile helped to ease the worry Charli had been trying to ignore throughout the day.

As Charli gathered up her things and headed out to the car, Layla continued to tell her all about her first day. Listening to her, Charli couldn't help but wonder what Amelia was telling her dad... and maybe her mom. She still wasn't sure if the woman was present in Amelia's life, since so far, she had only seen Blake with Amelia.

Over the years, Charli had pushed thoughts of Blake as Layla's father out of her mind. Whenever Layla had asked about him, Charli had simply said that he hadn't been able to be a dad.

Her family had pressed harder for the man's name, but Charli was nothing if not stubborn. Eventually the questions had fallen away, and now she was more glad than ever that she'd never named Blake as Layla's father.

Now all she had to do was try to keep their paths from crossing.

Normally, she wouldn't be too worried about that, but the same connection that had brought them together the first time could bring them together again. Jackson...

There was just no way she wanted to welcome Blake into her home the way she'd welcomed Jackson and Wade. Unfortunately, it might be difficult to keep him out without giving an explanation.

By the time they made it home, Layla had finished giving a thorough recounting of her day. Charli sent her off to get changed, while she did the same.

As she started on supper, her thoughts kept returning to Blake and what it had been like to see him again after so many years. He definitely carried a more serious air than he had twelve years ago. Since he'd been in the military, it was possible he'd seen some things that had left their mark on him.

When she found herself wondering what those things might be, Charli reminded herself that she didn't want anything to do with the man. Blake had proven himself to be a man she couldn't trust. He'd said all the things she'd wanted to hear, drawing her in to the point where she'd been willing to compromise her convictions to be with him.

And then he'd abandoned her. She didn't need a man like him in her life, and she certainly didn't want that sort of man around Layla.

Her daughter wanted a father, but Charli couldn't take the chance that Blake would walk away from them again. Especially since he had a daughter who was clearly important to him. Layla might come in a distant second, and Charli just couldn't handle seeing that.

There was only one person in the world who knew the circumstances of Layla's parentage, and Charlotte was feeling a strong need to talk to her. It was just too bad that her best friend had left Serenity Point for college and never returned. Unfortunately, their friendship had weakened, and she didn't think they were close enough anymore for the conversation she needed to have.

Settling back into their normal schedule should have left Charli with contentment humming through her, but that was definitely not the case. Instead, her thoughts were tied up in the past.

The only good thing was that seeing Blake again hadn't dragged forth all the love she'd had for him before he'd abandoned her. And even the hurt from that time hadn't surged up to completely eclipse everything else.

The emotion that kept rising to the surface was anxiousness and fear. More than anything else, she feared that he'd meet Layla and realize who she was to him. That was the absolute last thing that Charli wanted.

She didn't think she'd be able to keep him from meeting Layla, so all she could do was hope and pray he wouldn't suspect anything. Hopefully, the fact that Amelia and Layla looked *nothing* alike would keep him from being suspicious.

Later, as she prepared for bed, Charli thought again of her first glimpse of Blake in twelve years. Over the years since he'd left, Blake had taken on attributes that supported what he had done to her. In her mind, he was a user. He was shallow and uncaring.

Those thoughts made it easier for Charli to accept what had happened.

But all of those supposed attributes were swept away as she'd watched him deal with his daughter. His gentleness. His protectiveness. The security he offered Amelia.

Charli remembered him being that way with *her*. How he'd treated her had been one of the reasons she'd fallen in love with him. He'd made her feel special. So loved. To the point where she was absolutely able to picture a future with him.

Even during the time when they'd only been able to communicate via phone or email, he'd been so caring of her.

Blake could have been with any girl. He'd been surrounded by plenty of beautiful young women at his college. But for some reason, he'd focused on her and had done his best to assure Charli that he was fully committed to her.

Everything she'd felt for him began to resurface now that her emotions weren't weighed down by the negative attributes she'd assigned him because of the breakup.

Blinking, Charli blew out a long breath, trying to push aside her feelings and the *what might have beens.* They weren't productive and would only lead to heartache.

She couldn't let that happen for a second time.

CHAPTER FOUR

Blake walked to the steps leading to the front doors of the elementary school, Amelia's little hand tightly gripping his. It was day five of school, and Amelia still wasn't sure what she thought of it. Thankfully, they were almost at the weekend, and once this day was over, she'd have two days off.

Moving off to the side of the main door leading into the school, Blake lowered himself to one knee so he could look her in the eye. "Have a good day, okay, Berry?"

Amelia sighed with a frown. "Can't I just stay with you?"

"School is where you need to be," Blake said. "Plus, I have an interview today for a job. If I get it, then we'll both have places to be each day."

"Can we have ice cream tonight?" Amelia asked.

"Strawberry sundae?"

Amelia nodded. "And blueberries too."

Blake smiled. "I'll go to the store after my interview to pick up berries and ice cream."

"And maybe we could make pancakes with berries tomorrow morning?"

"Sure. We can do that."

That seemed to be enough to help her face the day. She wrapped her arms around his neck and gave him a tight hug, then kissed his cheek.

"Love you, Berry. I'll be here when school is over."

Straightening, Blake led Amelia to the doors, then turned her care over to the people standing at the entrance who made sure the kids got to their classrooms. He stood, watching as her tiny figure disappeared inside, taking his heart with her.

Though Charli's interaction with him on the first day had been that of a stranger, knowing that she was there for Amelia made it a little easier to let her out of his sight.

Once Amelia disappeared, Blake turned and left the building, jogging down the steps, dodging other parents and students who were making their way up to the door.

Since that first day, he hadn't even gotten a glimpse of Charli, and Blake had mixed feelings about that. Seeing her again had reminded him of all the things he'd loved about her. Things he'd somehow managed to push to the back of his mind over the years.

She'd been a great listener, and the first person to really encourage him to forge ahead with a future different from what his parents wanted for him. Talking with her had been easy, and she'd opened up as well, giving him the opportunity to encourage her.

Their moments together hadn't all been serious, however. Charli had a bit of a dry sense of humor, and there had been plenty of times when laughter had burst out of him unexpectedly because of something she said.

If things had unfolded the way they'd planned while sitting together at the edge of the nearby lake, he wondered where they'd be now. How many kids would they have? Charli had wanted a lot.

Jackson had said she wasn't currently in a relationship, but that didn't mean she didn't have children. From what Jackson had said, it sounded like she'd been dating again fairly quickly after he'd broken up with her.

Regardless, it was really none of his business. He kept reminding himself of that, but it still didn't stop him from wondering.

Once he was behind the wheel of his truck, Blake put the address for his next destination into the GPS. He wasn't thrilled about having to work for someone when his dream was to have his own business. Unfortunately, he wasn't in a position to do that just yet.

There were only two mechanic garages in Serenity, so he hoped that at least one of them would have a job for him. Though he really wanted to work in the field he had training in and loved, Blake knew he might have to accept a different job if neither of those places would hire him.

He needed to do whatever was necessary to provide a stable life for Amelia.

As he pulled into the parking lot of the garage, Blake took a moment to look over the building. It was painted gray with red trim, and it appeared to be in good shape. There were actually flowers in cement planters along the front wall of the building.

There were three roll-up doors—one of which was already open—as well as a regular door that was next to a large picture window. He got out of the truck and headed for the door that he assumed led to the office.

If he wanted to be able to stay here in Serenity, he really needed a job, so he prayed that the conversation he was about to have would result in an offer of work.

A bell jangled over his head as he pushed open the door. There was a faint scent of cleaning supplies in the air, but there was no disguising the familiar scents of oil and rubber.

The room held a comfortable-looking couch, as well as three armchairs and a television on the opposite wall. A small desk with an office chair behind it faced the room, though it was currently empty. It was all clean and tidy, a welcoming space.

A middle-aged man appeared in the doorway with a smile on his face. He was a tall man who appeared to be fairly physically fit. His head was bald. Whether by choice or nature, Blake couldn't tell.

"Blake Madden?" the man said, approaching him with his hand out.

Blake took his hand and gave it a firm shake. "Yes."

"I'm Stan Wilson." He released Blake's hand. "Let's go into my office."

Blake followed him through the doorway into a small office. A desk and chair dominated the room, but there was still room for a filing cabinet and a couple of smaller chairs in front of the desk.

"Have a seat," Stan said, gesturing to the chairs as he walked around the desk to his seat.

Once they were both seated, Stan gave him a smile. "Tell me a little about yourself."

Blake took a moment to gather his thoughts. "Uh... I've just left the army, where I worked as a wheeled vehicle mechanic."

"How long were you in the army?"

"Twelve years."

Stan settled back in his chair, steepling his fingers in front of him. "You weren't interested in making a career of it?"

"Initially, I was," Blake told him. "However, my daughter's mother recently passed away, and I didn't think I'd be able to care for her properly while still being in the army, so I didn't re-enlist."

"What brought you to Serenity?"

"I have some family here," he said. "And I was here before I enlisted and really loved it. I thought Serenity would be a good place to raise my daughter."

"It is a great place to raise a family," Stan agreed.

The conversation then turned to the practical side of things, with Stan asking him specifics about what qualified him to work in his garage. Blake felt more at ease discussing that part of his life. He was confident in his ability to fix vehicles, whether it was on a military base or in a civilian garage.

"It sounds like you could be a real asset to the garage," Stan said. "And I've actually just had a guy hand in his notice because he's decided to move out of Serenity, so I do have a position coming available."

Hope bloomed in Blake. He'd been confident in his abilities, but if there was no opening for him, all his experience wouldn't matter. When he'd phoned to see if there was a job available, Stan hadn't said one way or another, but rather had invited him to come by the garage for a chat.

"The thing is, though, before I hire someone, I need them to understand a few things about me and how I run my business." Stan leaned forward, bracing his arms on the desk. "First and foremost, I'm a Christian. For me, that means I run my business in a way that I believe honors God. I try to reflect that in how I relate to my employees and how I deal with my customers."

Blake didn't know for sure what that would look like, but if it meant Stan was honorable in his dealings, Blake was on board with that.

"We do the work that's needed, without adding anything on. You're responsible for the work, I'm responsible for the billing. There are times when we'll do work for reduced costs or even for free. You'll always get paid, regardless of what we bill a customer."

It didn't seem the most practical way to run a business. "How long have you had this garage?"

"Coming up on twenty years," Stan said, then lifted his brows, bringing wrinkles to his forehead. "Are you worried that the way I do business isn't profitable?"

"It did cross my mind," Blake admitted, deciding that the man would probably prefer honesty.

"I understand that." Stan smiled. "But while this is definitely a business, it's also always been a ministry, and I feel that God has blessed us operating the business this way."

"I don't have a problem with the way you choose to run your business. Working on vehicles is my passion, so if you offer me that opportunity, I'll do things however you want."

Stan gave a nod. "Oh yes. One more thing. There are times I take on apprentices from the high school. Do you think you'd be able to work with them?"

Blake wasn't a stranger to training people, especially over the past three years. Some of the people he'd trained had been... difficult, at times. He thought he'd be able to work with teenagers.

"I believe I could manage teaching," Blake told him, then shared his experience with that in the army.

"You said you have a daughter?" At Blake's nod, he said, "Is she in school?"

"Yes. Grade three."

"Will you need to work within the school hours?"

"If possible." His aunt had offered to pick Amelia up and watch her, and while Blake appreciated that, he didn't want her to have to do it every day.

After a brief discussion about the hours at the school, Stan said, "I can work with that if you can."

"You're offering me the job?"

"I am," Stan said with a nod. "You'll have a three-month probation period."

"I am fine with that."

Stan pulled out a file and handed a thin stack of papers to him. "We're not a big company or anything, but I like to make sure you have all the information on how things work here, so there are no misunderstandings. But if you have any questions at all, don't hesitate to ask. My door is always open for anything. Work related or not."

"Thanks. I appreciate that." And he really did. Having everything laid out was a bonus, and it made him feel confident that this could work out well.

"How soon can you start?"

"Monday?"

"Perfect. You can work alongside Frank, the guy who's leaving. He'll teach you how we do the repair side of things here."

Blake felt a keen sense of relief that this job had fallen into place. If nothing else, he'd be able to pay his bills without having to dip into his savings too much more. He'd be making less than he had in the army, but such was life.

He wouldn't be able to add a lot to his savings, but there would be a roof over their heads, food on their table, and clothes for Amelia, who seemed to grow out of stuff on a regular basis.

"Let me introduce you to the guys who are here already," Stan said as he got to his feet.

Blake followed him out of the office and through another doorway that led to the garage. There were a couple of cars up on lifts, and three men in coveralls were working on them.

One man looked to be in his mid-forties, while the other two looked to be closer to Blake's age. They were friendly, and Blake felt like he could work with them.

After a quick tour of the garage, he and Stan went back to the waiting room.

"I'll see you Monday morning," Stan said, holding out his hand.

"Yes, sir," Blake said as he shook it.

"I was going to ask who your family is here."

"My aunt and uncle are Julia and Robert Scott."

Stan smiled. "Oh. I know them. We attend the same church."

Blake wasn't really surprised to hear that. Serenity wasn't a super small town, but as soon as Stan had said he was a Christian, Blake figured he might know his aunt and uncle.

As he pulled out of the parking lot a couple of minutes later, Blake smiled, happy with how things had turned out that morning. When he'd called the garage the previous day to see if he could talk to someone about a position there, he hadn't dared hope that he'd walk away from the conversation with a job.

But he had, and it reinforced the feeling that he'd made the right decision in coming back to Serenity. Now he just had to hope that Amelia would find her place there as well.

What he really wanted with regards to Amelia was to talk to Charli to see how she was doing in school. Whenever he asked Amelia how her day had been, she would just say fine.

He wanted details.

If she was really struggling, he assumed Charli would let him know. Or at least he hoped she would.

By the time he got back to the apartment, Blake had decided to send Charli an email. There had been one on the papers that Amelia had brought home the first day. A work email address.

He still had her personal one, although it was possible that she didn't use it anymore. Plus, he felt that she wouldn't appreciate him contacting her that way. She'd interacted with him in a very professional way on Monday, so he didn't think it would be right to contact her using her personal email.

Finding the file where he'd put the papers earlier that week, Blake sat down at the table and opened the email program on his laptop. He added Charli's work address to his contacts, then brought up a blank email.

Right off the bat, how to address her stumped him. Had Amelia's teacher been anyone else, he would have used a formal style of address. However, it was hard to consider doing that with Charli, someone he'd known intimately.

Blake hated feeling so uncertain, though he knew he had no one but himself to blame. Finally, he figured he'd just start the email with *hi* and go from there.

Part of him wanted to share all the details of his and Amelia's life to give Charli an idea of what Amelia was dealing with. In the end, though, he just told her what she likely already knew, that they'd just moved there, so everything was new to Amelia.

He then asked her to please contact him if she had any concerns about how Amelia was doing in her class. After reading through it a couple of times, he finally hit send.

Sitting back in his chair, he stared blankly at his laptop. In the quiet of the apartment, with Amelia gone, Blake could let his doubts rise to the surface. He'd never imagined that he'd be solely responsible for a child.

Even with Lauren struggling with her addictions, he'd always assumed she'd be around, and during the times she'd been in rehab, her sister, Callie, had stepped up to help out. But Lauren's death had changed everything.

And then, Callie had told him that she wouldn't help him anymore. If he'd still had her help, he could've stayed in the area, even after leaving the army. But without her help, he'd known he needed to go somewhere he would have support.

He was certain now that he'd made the right decision, because already Julia and Robert had stepped up to help him, and he couldn't be more thankful.

At the end of the day, however, he was responsible for Amelia's physical and emotional well-being. He was her father, and even though he didn't feel very confident in his ability to be what she needed, he was going to have to just do his best and hope it would be enough.

And weird though it might be, he hoped that having Charli as her teacher would help him and Amelia. He knew from the conversations he and Charli had had that she loved kids, and even though she hadn't had any kids yet, she'd had lots of experience with them. Babysitting had been something she'd done plenty of, and he was sure that her experience had only grown since then.

Though Blake doubted she actually wanted to be a partner with him in raising his daughter, he trusted that she'd care for Amelia during the hours she was in her care, just like she would any other student in her class.

And Blake was certain that Amelia would be all the better for having Charli in her life.

CHAPTER FIVE

Charli set her plate of pizza down on the table, then settled into her seat beside Janessa. It was once again a full table, and there was plenty of conversation going on around her.

She'd survived the first week of classes, but she was tired. It was always a bit of an adjustment when she first went back to school after the summer. Though she appreciated being back on a schedule, at the same time, the lazy days of summer had been enjoyable.

"You should invite your cousin and his daughter to our next pizza night, Jackson," Jay said. "I'm sure it's a challenge being a single dad in a new place."

Jay's words grabbed Charli's attention, and her stomach knotted. She couldn't let Blake into her personal life again. She just couldn't.

But how was she supposed to make sure that didn't happen?

When Charli glanced over at Jackson to see how he was going to respond, she was surprised to find him looking at her. There was an uncharacteristic frown on his face, his brows drawn low over his eyes.

His expression cleared as he looked away from her and said, "I don't know if that's the best idea right now. So far, he's settling in okay with Amelia. Maybe we can include them later."

Charli stared at him and as she listened to his nonsense response, she came to a chilling realization. Jackson *knew*. He *knew* about her connection to Blake, and in his own clumsy way, he was trying to keep her from having to be around him.

How much did he really know? Had he mentioned something about Layla to Blake?

She was going to have to have a conversation with him to figure out what exactly he knew and what he was going to do with that information.

For the first time since hearing that Blake was back, Charli accepted that the secret she'd held for years was at a high risk of being revealed. In fact, if Blake planned to make Serenity his home for the foreseeable future, there was absolutely no way his and Layla's paths wouldn't cross.

Charli's appetite fled at the very idea of Blake learning he was Layla's father. It seemed inevitable, and she knew that she should have accepted that when she heard that he was back in Serenity.

Instead, she'd stuck her head in the sand, believing she could keep Layla hidden from him.

But maybe she didn't need to hide Layla. Blake had ended up going on to have a child with someone else, so it wasn't out of the realm of possibility that he would think the same had happened with Charli. Especially since she'd made it clear to Blake how much she wanted children.

"You okay?" Janessa asked, jostling her elbow.

Charli glanced over at her as she lifted a piece of pizza from her plate. "Yep. Why?"

"You just kind of spaced out."

"Just daydreaming," she said.

"You always did like to drift off to another place."

Charli couldn't deny that. And when she hadn't been escaping into a daydream, she'd been doing it through books. She liked to think that her imagination allowed her to relate to the children she taught, since at that age, most kids loved to dream up things.

"So, any teacher's pets yet?"

For some reason, her thoughts went immediately to Amelia. The little girl hadn't really warmed up to anyone, preferring to be on the edge of the group, watching everything with her big blue eyes. The air of sadness and reserve hadn't lessened at all, and even after a week, she still only spoke when directly addressed.

"I try not to favor any of the kids, but there are a few that I will probably come to really enjoy having in the class."

"The best-behaved ones, right?"

"Not necessarily. There's one boy who is likely going to drive me a little batty with his boundless energy, but he also has such a sweet and funny personality that he makes me laugh. Then there's the boy who we know from previous years has a real struggle academically, but he tries so hard."

"You love them all already."

Charli gave a small huff of laughter. "Of course. Each of them is amazing in their own right. What's not to love?"

"Twenty plus kids all in one place? That would pretty much be my idea of a nightmare."

"Well, there are parts of your job that would be my idea of a nightmare."

Charli was thankful for the distraction Janessa provided, even though her sister had no idea what was going on with her.

On top of the realization she'd come to about Jackson, Charli was also trying not to think about the email she'd found in her work inbox earlier. She had yet to answer it because she needed to think about her response.

"What's for dessert, Charli?" Aria asked. "I hope it's chocolate."

Janessa gave a snort. "Do you miss not being able to blame what you crave on the baby?"

"Everything I wanted to eat while pregnant *was* because I was pregnant."

"But you're still wanting weird stuff at eleven o'clock at night," Gareth said. "And there's no pregnancy to blame."

Aria leaned against Gareth, looking up at him, love clear on her face. "And you're so good to always get it for me, even though I'm not pregnant anymore."

Gareth pressed a kiss to Aria's hair. "Even when you were, I didn't get it for the baby, sweetheart. I got it for you."

Emotion clogged Charli's throat, and she picked up her glass to take a drink. Once again, jealousy swirled through her as she remembered what her pregnancy with Layla had been like.

She'd had such a tumult of emotions back then.

Worry. Anger. Love for the baby, but also a whole lot of anxiety.

And she'd felt very alone during those months. There had been no one there to get her pregnancy cravings or massage her sore back and feet. Sure, she'd been surrounded by her family, but the one person who should have been there had been absent.

Knowing that her situation had disappointed her parents, she'd felt like she needed to shoulder all parts of the pregnancy by herself. So, whether it had been the wretched morning sickness through far too many months or feeling the baby kick, she'd experienced it all on her own.

Before he'd left and not come back, Charli had been certain that Blake would be the perfect husband and father. She'd imagined what it would be like to be pregnant with his child. But when she'd gotten pregnant, the reality had been very different.

Charli hated that she was feeling so much jealousy lately. Though she'd struggled with it a lot as a teen, it had faded over the years as she'd focused on Layla and her career.

Blake's return, however, had brought with it a reminder of how things had ended between them. Of how absent he'd been during her pregnancy and all the years since. And now she was feeling jealous over the relationships and pregnancies of her siblings.

She knew that was not what she should allow into her heart. But lately, it had become a big battle that she struggled to win.

Needing to escape for a moment, Charli got to her feet and went to the kitchen to get coffee and dessert, which was once again cookies and brownies. It seemed to be their go-to dessert on Friday nights. An easy final course to an easy meal.

Charli took some cookies to Layla and Peyton, who were playing video games in the basement. In no rush to rejoin the others, she hung out with them for several minutes before going back up to the dining room.

Eventually, people began to leave. Even Janessa left, heading out with Will to go to a late movie. Layla had come up with Peyton, but she'd gone to her room once he'd left with Misha and Jay.

Charli was still in the kitchen when the doorbell rang. Frowning, she dried her hands on a dishtowel and headed for the front door. When she opened it, she found Jackson on the porch.

"Forget something?"

"Can I talk to you for a minute?" Jackson asked.

"No." Though she suspected why he was there and she knew she should talk to him about it, Charli felt too confused to deal with him. Still, she sighed, then stepped back as she waved toward the kitchen. "Fine."

Once there, Jackson settled onto a stool at the island. "Given that response, I'm going to assume you know what I want to talk to you about."

"I have an idea."

"Why didn't you tell anyone?" Jackson asked. "This means that Layla's my *cousin*."

Charli glanced at the door leading out of the kitchen. "Precisely because of that. I didn't want you to know because you would have told Blake."

Jackson frowned. "You didn't want him to know?"

"I did. At first. But then I got a text from him saying that didn't want to be with me. So I figured if he didn't want to be with me, he wouldn't want to be with my baby."

"I'm sorry that he made you feel that way," Jackson said, leaning his arms on the counter. "It's crazy to think we've been family this whole time, and I didn't know."

"There are only two people in the world who know the truth now," Charli said. "You and Missy."

"Missy knows?"

"Of course. She was my best friend, and she was the first person I told when I found out I was pregnant."

"Where is she these days?"

"I'm not sure where she is right at the moment, since her job has her flying all over the world, but she lives in New York."

"Did she think you should tell Blake back then?"

"No. After the way he treated me, she didn't think Blake deserved to know."

Jackson grimaced. "Yeah. Can't say I'm impressed by what he did."

"I have his daughter in my class."

He nodded. "Blake mentioned that."

"She seems to be a sad little girl."

"She is." Jackson hesitated, then said, "She lost her mom not too long ago."

"I'm sorry to hear that. It must be a difficult thing for her to deal with."

Charli wanted to ask for more details, but for once, Jackson didn't seem inclined to chat about it. It was probably just as well. Charli didn't want to feel sorry for Blake, and learning how he'd lost his wife or girlfriend would probably make her feel that way.

Unfortunately, Jackson's revelation about Amelia's mother had made it clear that Charli was going to have to respond to Blake. She'd known that she'd have to as Amelia's teacher, but now she felt obligated on an emotional level. Amelia would need more than just educational instruction.

"Well, I'd better go," Jackson said as he got to his feet.

"You're not going to say anything to anyone, right?"

Jackson stared at her for a long moment before he shook his head. "I'll keep your secret, even though I do think that Blake would like to know he has another daughter."

"He already has a daughter," Charli said. "He doesn't need mine."

"But Layla might benefit from having him in her life."

"She doesn't need another male role model. She's got plenty of good ones already."

"She does," Jackson agreed. "It's not my decision, of course, so I'll leave it up to you."

As Jackson headed out of the kitchen, Charli said, "How did you figure it out?"

He turned back around. "He asked about you."

Charli froze at his words. "He did?"

"Yep. So I asked him why he was interested in you and he mentioned that you'd gotten... close the last time he was here. I may not be a math whiz like Will, but even I get four when I add two and two."

"I appreciate you not spilling that answer to him."

"I wouldn't do that," Jackson said. "You're like a sister to me, and honestly, I know you better than I know him at this point. So I'd always side with you."

"Thank you. I appreciate that."

"By the way, he also wanted to know if you were married."

Charli wasn't sure how hearing that made her feel. "What did you tell him?"

"That you weren't currently in a relationship."

"I haven't been in a serious relationship ever, never mind currently."

"True," Jackson said with a shrug. "But he doesn't need to know that. Although I did hint at you rebound dating someone during the time after he left. That might be enough to make him think Layla was the result of that."

"Thank you for not telling him about Layla." Charli would never have thought she'd be appreciative of Jackson, but she was glad that underneath his flippant personality, he'd had the sense not to blurt out her secret.

"You're welcome. See you around," Jackson said, then with a wave of his hand, he left the kitchen and let himself out the front door.

Charli leaned over the counter, resting on her arms as she played over her conversation with Jackson. It was definitely an unexpected turn of events, and she hoped that Jackson wouldn't inadvertently spill anything.

But now that she'd had this conversation with Jackson, she needed to reply to Blake's email. It was important to approach him the way she'd approach any parent who contacted her, concerned about their child.

Straightening, she grabbed her phone and pulled up the email from Blake. It wasn't long, but she could read the worry in his words, which made even more sense after talking to Jackson.

It would be normal for her to assure a parent with similar concerns that she'd be on the lookout for any issues that might arise with their child. But for some reason, it felt weird to write those assurances to Blake.

It was important to view him as Blake, Amelia's father, not Blake, the man who had gotten her pregnant and walked away. Or the man she had once loved with all her heart.

No matter how she might feel about Blake, Amelia deserved her best efforts to make sure she felt safe and supported in Charli's classroom.

After checking on Layla, who was curled up on her beanbag chair reading a book, Charli went to her room and changed into her pajamas, then sat down in her favorite chair. The only light in the room came from the lamp on the small table next to her.

By that point, she had a pretty good idea of what she wanted to say, keeping it short and to the point.

Amelia has been quiet and reserved this week, but she has done her work without any issues. I will certainly keep an eye on her, and let you know if I have any concerns.

Normally, she would tell a parent to feel free to contact her if they had any further concerns, but she just couldn't bring herself to offer that to Blake. She had a feeling that he'd email her again if he was worried, whether she asked him to or not.

So she was going to go with the *or not* for now.

Before she could dwell too much on what she'd written, Charli hit send, then clutched her phone in her lap as thoughts of Blake tumbled through her mind.

Before he'd returned, it had been awhile since she'd last thought all that much about him. Over the years, she'd been able to separate Layla from the man who fathered her. She'd even been able to separate Jackson from his cousin.

Blake existed as a solitary entity in her mind, disconnected from her, Layla, and Jackson. But now that he was back, his connection to Jackson had solidified once again. She didn't want that to happen with Layla.

As she sat in her chair, her gaze went to the door leading into her walk-in closet. Tucked in the back was a small wooden chest. She hadn't opened it in years, but it contained all the things that had touched her heart back when she and Blake had dated.

She'd pressed and preserved some of the flowers he'd given her. Then there were all the cards and notes he'd written her. But the thing she'd valued most, at the time, was a gold ring with a slender band and a small diamond.

A promise ring, he'd said.

Even though her feelings for Blake had died years ago, she'd kept everything. Maybe she'd give them to Layla someday and tell her about the man Charli had fallen in love with. She'd had doubts that that man had actually existed, but in her heart, back then, he had.

Charli had wanted to be able to tell her daughter that her father was a loving and caring man, but his actions after he'd left Serenity hadn't backed that up. So for years, the chest had stayed in the closet. And it would continue to stay there for the foreseeable future.

With a sigh, Charli set her phone aside, then got up and headed out of her room. Layla's bedroom was right next to hers on the main floor. They had their own secluded set of rooms in the house, with the rest of the bedrooms being on the second floor, which was where Janessa and Will had their room. For the time being.

"You need to get ready for bed, sweets," she said.

Layla looked up, then glanced at the digital clock on her nightstand. "But I can still stay up and read, right? Because I'm at a really good spot in my book."

"Yep. It's the weekend, so you can stay up. You just need to be in bed."

Getting up from the beanbag, Layla put her book on the bed, then changed into her pajamas, chatting about the book as she did so.

She hadn't always been a huge fan of reading, but over the past year, she'd begun reading longer books, and discovered how very much she enjoyed them. She'd read through the *Little House on the Prairie* series, and while she'd liked them, she'd fallen in love with the *Narnia* series.

Charli had always loved reading, so she was glad that her daughter shared that with her now. They'd both spend the evening reading, though Charli would be staying up even later than Layla.

When Layla returned from brushing her teeth, she jumped on the bed that Charli had turned down, making it bounce and shift. "How late can I stay up, Momma?"

Charli laughed as she sat down beside her on the bed. "Same as every Friday. Ten-thirty."

As she snuggled under her comforter, Layla grinned. "Just checking."

Layla held out her hand, which Charli took, then they prayed together.

"Have you got your verse for the week memorized?" Charli asked.

"Yep." Layla's brow furrowed, then she took a breath and said, "Set your mind on things above, not on things on the earth. Colossians chapter three, verse two."

"Good job." Charli held up her hand for a high five. "Do you remember what we talked about it meaning?"

For the next few minutes, they discussed the verse. When they were done, Charli leaned forward to press a kiss to her forehead.

"Love you, Momma," Layla whispered. "More than all the candy in the world."

As she looked at her daughter, Charli was glad that she was basically a mini version of herself. That had probably been what had helped the memory of Blake slip away. If Layla had looked more like her father, it would have been a lot more difficult to forget him.

And the fact that she didn't look like Blake would hopefully also help keep him from suspecting that Layla was his. For a little while anyway. She knew that the pair would cross paths, sooner than later, most likely.

If it was inevitable, maybe she needed to approach it with a confidence that said she wasn't worried about Blake thinking Layla was his. Even though the thought really did terrify her.

"Love you too, sweetie. More than all the books in the world."

Blake's reappearance might have shaken her up a bit, but Charli would absolutely make sure that Layla never saw that. Protecting her had always been Charli's top priority, and that hadn't changed.

Would never change.

CHAPTER SIX

Blake helped Amelia into her booster seat in the back row of his truck, then climbed behind the wheel. As he started the engine, Blake looked into the rearview mirror to see Amelia staring out the window at the school.

"How was school today?"

She turned to briefly meet his gaze in the mirror. "It was fine."

"And you still like your teacher?" Blake wasn't sure why he kept asking her that. Maybe he was trying to get a feel for the type of person Charli was now, and Amelia was his only connection to her at the moment.

"Yeah. She's nice."

Charli's email in response to his had been short, and he hadn't heard from her since. Which was fine, except that he really wanted a daily update on how Amelia was doing. He needed to know that Amelia hadn't been negatively affected by his decision to move her to Serenity.

But honestly, it didn't matter if it was the right decision or not, because it had really been the only one he could make. Hopefully, in time, Amelia would find some joy in their life in Serenity.

Perhaps starting that night.

The school had sent home information at the start of the week that they were having a back-to-school carnival that evening. He'd seen some bouncy castles and slides in the large field behind the school when he'd picked Amelia up, so it looked like it would be a fun event.

He would have been fine to give it a pass, but when he'd asked Amelia if she wanted to go, she'd said yes. And if she actually wanted to do something associated with school, he was going to make sure she was there.

When they got to their apartment, he pulled out the strawberries and blueberries he'd bought at the grocery store the night before, then quickly prepared them for Amelia's snack. He could run out of pretty much everything else, but as long as he had berries of any kind, Amelia was happy.

"Here you go," he said as he set the berries on the coffee table in front of Amelia. "I'm going to go take a shower. Do you want to watch some television?"

After he had her set up with one of her favorite shows, he went to take a quick shower. The last thing he wanted to do was wander around with Amelia smelling like sweat, grease, and oil. He loved his job, but he didn't like the way he smelled after a day at work.

After he'd showered and dressed in a pair of jeans and a T-shirt, he joined Amelia in the living room.

"Finished your snack?" he asked.

She held up her empty bowl. "All gone."

He took the bowl from her and carried it back to the kitchen. "Do you want to change before we go to the carnival?"

Getting to her feet, she looked down at herself. "I can change?"

"Sure. If you want to wear something else, you can. But make sure your outfit has pants."

She had a tendency to prefer skirts, especially ones that had little shorts attached to them. However, that night, if she wanted to go on the slides, pants would be a better choice.

"If you need help, let me know," Blake called as Amelia headed to her room.

It had taken some time and trial and error to get the hang of helping a little girl with her clothes and hair. Where he would have picked practical items to dress her in, she'd wanted ruffles, lace, and bows. Thankfully, she wasn't as picky about her hairstyles. She was happy with a ponytail most of the time, as long as it had a bow or ribbon attached to it.

When she reappeared a few minutes later, she was wearing a pair of dark blue leggings and a long-sleeved T-shirt with a sparkly unicorn on it. He had no idea what drew her to the mythical animal, but if it was on anything, she wanted it.

And who was he to deny her something that made her happy? She'd dealt with a lot of sadness and upheaval in her short life, and his goal now was to bring some peace and joy to her life.

"Can you put this ribbon around my ponytail, Daddy?" Amelia asked as she held out a ribbon that matched her shirt.

"Sure thing." He sat down on a chair at the table, then drew her between his knees and turned her to face the television. "Did you bring your brush?"

When she held it over her shoulder, he took it, then carefully slid the previous bow and elastic from her hair. With gentle strokes, he smoothed the fine wayward strands of hair.

"So, what did you do in school today?"

He tried a different version of the question he'd asked her earlier, hoping one of these days, she'd answer him with a torrent of words. Even though he also wasn't a chatty person, he lived for the day when Amelia would shower him with details about what had happened in school.

She might take after him and always be more on the reserved side. Or maybe, once her life had settled down, she'd begin to open up a bit more.

All he wanted was for her to feel comfortable and secure. It was his goal to give her the stability she really hadn't had much of in her life so far.

"Miss H told me that my shirt was pretty today, and that she liked it."

"Did she?" Blake worked her hair into the hair elastic. "That was nice of her."

"Yes. She's nice."

Blake of twelve years ago wouldn't have been surprised to hear that. Actually, he wasn't really surprised now, either. It was more that he was relieved. Relieved that Amelia had ended up in Charli's class, and that Charli was still the nice person she'd been all those years ago.

"There you go," he said as he finished attaching the ribbon to her ponytail.

She stepped away, then turned to face him. "Do I look okay?"

"You look beautiful, Berry."

A quick smile flitted across her face, and for a moment, emotion choked Blake. Her smiles were a special gift, and he was grateful for each one she gave him, no matter how small.

"Can we go now?" she asked.

Blake glanced at his watch. The carnival was supposed to open at four, so if they left right then, they'd be there when it started. He didn't know how long Amelia would want to stay. This was the first time they'd been at an event like the carnival, so he had no idea if she'd want to hang around the whole time or leave after a little while.

Either was fine. He was just glad to be out of the apartment.

They tended to spend a lot of time at home when they weren't working or at school, though he did try to make sure that they got out for a walk every couple of days. It seemed to be something she enjoyed, and he was always up for getting some fresh air and exercise.

Previously, he'd worked out nearly every day of the week, but he wasn't able to do that now. Thankfully, his aunt had stepped in to take care of Amelia a couple of times a week, so Blake was able to go to the gym on those nights. It was definitely better than nothing.

"Once you get your shoes on, we can go."

Amelia ran to the door and stared at the shoe rack for a moment before choosing a pair of purple slip-on runners. Blake shoved his feet into his favorite black Chelsea boots, then gathered up his keys, wallet, and phone and followed Amelia out of the apartment.

When they reached the school, it was clear that they weren't the only ones who had wanted to be there right at the start. Thankfully, he found a spot to park on the street not too far from the school, then helped Amelia out of the truck. She kept a tight grip on his hand as they headed down the sidewalk toward the school.

The towering shade trees that lined the street cast dappled shadows on them. Their leaves were already turning yellow and orange, and Blake found himself looking forward to autumn in Serenity Point.

He was still a bit on the fence about winter. Since he'd never lived anywhere that had a significant amount of snow, it was going to be an adjustment.

But given the adjustments he and Amelia had had to make over the past year, this one would be the least significant.

They followed a small meandering line of people around to the field behind the school. Kids' songs were being played over a sound system, a lively background to the excited screams and chatter of the children already there.

Several large inflatables were positioned around the outside of the field, while the interior held a bunch of carnival-style games. He also spotted popcorn and cotton candy machines, and to the left of the entrance, there were a bunch of barbecues set up.

They were really going all out on this event for the kids. He'd never heard of something similar happening at Amelia's old school. Of course, he hadn't always been around or as actively involved in her life as he was now, so it was possible it had.

As they wandered further into the field, a group of children ran past them. Amelia bumped into his leg, her grip tightening on his hand as the kids laughed and yelled.

Blake turned to look down at her. "Want me to carry you, Berry?"

She nodded, then lifted her arms. At almost eight, she was probably too old to be carried, but she was pretty slight, so he had no problem lifting her. Once she was secure in his arms, she hooked her arm around his neck.

"Where would you like to go?" he asked. "Do you want popcorn?"

Amelia nodded. There were a few popcorn stands around the field, so he looked for the one with the fewest people around it, then headed in that direction.

"Hey there." The teenage girl gave them a friendly smile. "Would you like some popcorn?"

"Yes, please," Amelia said as Blake set her down.

"What grade are you in?" the girl asked.

"Three."

"Who's your teacher?"

"Miss H."

The teen's smile grew as she scooped popcorn into a paper bag. "Do you like her?"

"Yep."

"That's good." She held the popcorn out to Amelia. "Her little sister Skylar is my good friend."

"Hi, Beth!"

Blake shifted to look at the young girl who'd just run up to the popcorn machine. She gave the teen a hug, then stepped back as a young boy came to a stop beside her.

"Do you two want popcorn?"

"Yes!"

"Did you run away from your parents?" she asked.

"Mom said I could come see you," the little girl said. She had long dark hair that was pulled back in a ponytail, hazel eyes, and was dressed in a pair of jeans and a T-shirt with flowers in the shape of a heart on the front of it.

Blake glanced back in the direction the pair had come from and spotted Charli and her brother Jay approaching them.

"Mom!" the girl called toward them. "Did you want popcorn?"

"I'll just share yours," Charli said as she joined her daughter.

Jay's gaze landed on Blake, then he smiled. "You're Jackson's cousin, right?"

"Yep," he said with a nod. "I'm Blake."

Jay held out his hand. "Nice to see you again."

The little girl sitting in the crook of his arm grinned at Blake, and he realized that she and the little boy must be Jay's kids. His mind was still kind of stuck on the fact that the little girl was Charli's.

"This is my daughter, Amelia," Blake said.

"Hi, Amelia." Jay rested a hand on the boy's shoulder. "This is my son, Peyton, my daughter, Ciara, and that's Charli's daughter, Layla."

"Amelia's in my class," Charli said.

Jay smiled at Amelia. "You have a great teacher then."

Blake watched as Layla held out her bag of popcorn so Charli could take some. He was curious about Layla. Jackson had said that Charli wasn't currently in a relationship, so he wondered what had happened to Layla's father. Was she the result of the rebound relationship Jackson had hinted at? Or was she... his?

That didn't seem likely since Jay hadn't had a son when Blake had been there last time, and given his size, he appeared to be older than Charli's daughter. He also couldn't see anything of himself in Layla the way he could in Amelia.

Though regret over what might have been flared up again, he ignored it, determined to not let it overshadow what was supposed to be a fun time for Amelia. Instead, he focused on Charli, taking the opportunity to observe her in a way he hadn't been able to on the first day of school.

She wore a pair of fitted denim capris and a floaty blouse with a pink floral pattern that ended a little below her hips. The loose sleeves went to her elbows. And her hair—which had been long when he'd last seen her—was now cut in layers to frame her face, just reaching past her shoulders.

Her physical softness had been what had drawn him to her initially when they'd first met. Though he'd worked out regularly to hone his own body, he'd found her curves appealing. But it hadn't just been her body that had drawn him in. It had also been the genuineness and gentleness of her personality.

As they'd spent time together online and later, in person, she'd quickly become the most comfortable and important part of his life. With the demands constantly put on him by his parents, to have a relationship in his life that wasn't demanding had been new and so appealing.

He should have found a way to keep in contact with her. To keep their relationship alive. If only he'd been able to stand strong. If only he'd valued their relationship the way he should have. The little girl sharing popcorn with Charli could have been his, and maybe they'd have had even more children.

The very moment he thought that, however, his heart rebelled. He couldn't wish away Amelia. His precious daughter had given him purpose and direction, and now that he was her sole caregiver, he couldn't imagine his life without her.

Charli's face lit with laughter as Layla jerked the popcorn bag away from her when she reached for more. "Brat."

"Beth would give you your *own* bag," Layla retorted.

"So how are you settling into life here in Serenity?" Jay asked, drawing Blake's attention away from Charli.

"Pretty good. Jackson and his parents have been a big help."

"Have you got a job?"

Blake nodded, bending to put Amelia down when she wiggled in his arms. "I'm working at Stan Wilson's garage."

"So you like cars?"

"I do. It wasn't what I went to college for, but I got extensive vehicle maintenance training and experience in the army."

"You enlisted?"

"Yep. I was in for twelve years."

"Momma, can we go on the slide?" Layla asked. "You can have the rest of my popcorn."

Charli chuckled as she took the half-eaten bag. "Sure."

Layla turned to Peyton. "Want to go, Pey?"

Peyton's mouth was full of popcorn, so he nodded.

"Do you want to go too, Amelia?" Layla asked.

Amelia looked at Blake, a tentative question on her face. He could see that she wanted to, but she was also uncertain because she didn't know the two kids.

"Why don't we all go to the slide?" Jay suggested.

Relief crossed Amelia's face as she reached out to take Blake's hand. They moved as a group to the nearest slide.

"I'll go up with you, Amelia," Layla offered.

Blake watched as the two girls made their way to where they'd climb up the bouncy slide. Peyton trailed behind them.

He could see some of the traits in Layla that he'd loved in Charli in the gentle way she helped Amelia up onto the inflatable.

"You can't go with them, baby girl," Jay said as the little girl wriggled to get down.

"Here, let me take her." Charli held her hands out, and the toddler didn't hesitate to go from Jay's arms into her aunt's.

The love on Charli's face for the little girl brought an ache to Blake's heart. How different would things have been for Amelia if she'd had that type of love directed at her from her mom when she'd been Ciara's age?

From what he remembered of the Halversons, Blake had no doubt that all three of those kids were surrounded with lots of love all the time. That Layla and Peyton were sharing even a little of the love they'd experienced with Amelia made Blake grateful.

Jackson and his parents were good about loving on her. But if there were more people to interact with her in a kind and gentle way, she would definitely benefit from it.

"Is Misha coming here after work?" Charli asked as she took little dance steps with Ciara, making the toddler grin.

"Yep. She should be here soon."

Blake watched Amelia come down the slide ahead of Layla, relieved to see that she had the biggest smile he'd seen on her face in a long time. When she reached the bottom, she gave him a wave, but stayed at the slide as she waited for Layla and Peyton. Once they'd joined her at the bottom, the trio headed for the steps to go again.

There were more kids around now, and Amelia glanced at Blake. For a moment, he wanted to go over and rescue her, but he stood his ground when Layla and Peyton stayed close to her.

"I really appreciate the kids helping Amelia," Blake said. "I don't think she's made any friends yet."

Jay looked at Charli. "She isn't making friends?"

"She's quite reserved in class," Charli said. "And she'd prefer to read or color rather than play with the other kids."

Blake nodded. "Those are her favorite things to do."

"Peyton took a while to settle when he first came to live with me," Jay said. "He had a difficult adjustment."

"He's adopted?" Blake asked.

Jay shook his head. "No. I just didn't know about him until recently."

"Wow. That must have been... interesting, and a big adjustment for you, too."

"It was for sure," Jay agreed. "But it's one of the best things that's ever happened to me."

Charli moved away from them toward the slide as the kids came down again.

"Hey there, sweetheart," Jay said, his gaze going past Blake.

He turned to see a beautiful Black woman heading for Jay. She stepped into his arms and lifted her face for his kiss.

"Blake, this is my wife, Misha," Jay said after he'd kissed her. "Blake is Jackson's cousin."

Misha gave him a friendly smile. "It's nice to meet you."

"Mama!"

Charli returned with Ciara, who practically threw herself out of Charli's arms to reach Misha.

"Hello, baby," Misha said as she took the little girl. She nuzzled Ciara's neck, making her giggle.

"Can we go somewhere else, Mom?" Layla asked as the trio ran over. "I want to try some games."

"Sure," Charli said.

Somehow, Blake found himself part of the Halverson group as they trailed the kids around the field. Given how she kept her distance from him, Blake didn't think Charli was all that happy about the development, and he couldn't blame her for that.

It was a bittersweet experience being this close to her again. After he'd walked away, Blake had never imaged seeing Charli at this stage in her life. Before that, he'd assumed he'd be with her during these years.

Since his return to Serenity, the acceptance of the direction his life had taken because of his own decisions had become sharply edged with regret. He should probably not hang around the Halversons—particularly Charli—if he wanted to avoid the painful reminders.

However, Blake knew that making connections would help them put down roots in their new hometown, and he definitely wanted that. Especially for Amelia.

CHAPTER SEVEN

Charli wished she could tell Jay she didn't want to spend their time at the carnival with Blake. But how could she do that without raising suspicions?

Simple answer? She couldn't.

Plus, she could see how much Amelia was enjoying herself with Layla and Peyton. The little girl was smiling more than Charli had seen her smile in all the hours they'd spent together. It would be wrong to deprive her of this simple joy.

So instead, Charli tried to keep control of her emotions and not think about how her daughter was hanging out with her little sister. She was having a hard time accepting that this was her reality, and not a nightmare that she couldn't wake up from.

For some reason, she'd never considered that Blake would return to Serenity. A visit, maybe. But to live? That likelihood had never crossed her mind.

In the first few years, she'd braced herself for Blake coming back to visit Jackson and his family. But when four years passed with no sign of him, she'd figured that he'd never return.

But boy, had she been wrong.

He was back... with a vengeance. And her family was proving to be their usual welcoming selves by befriending him and Amelia, and she knew it was only a matter of time before someone—likely Jay—would invite them to their Friday night pizza dinner.

She wondered if Jackson would try to subvert the invitation, or if he, like her, would accept that it was inevitable.

"I'm hungry," Layla said after they'd spent some time at the games that had been set up for the kids.

Blake had helped Amelia with the games, showing remarkable patience with her. It was an odd feeling to see him in the role of father.

During their many conversations, he'd said he wanted to be a father after she'd revealed that she wanted nothing more than to have several kids, much like her own parents had. Maybe not ten, but more than two.

Charli hadn't known for sure what type of father he'd be—Blake hadn't even known that—but he'd been so caring with her that she'd been able to easily imagine raising children with him.

It was because he'd been so loving and caring that she'd compromised her beliefs and slept with him. She'd known that they'd have to be apart for awhile, and she'd wanted to have that closeness... that connection with him before he left.

All the while believing that he'd return to her. That she'd given her virginity to the man she'd be spending the rest of her life with.

But that hadn't been the case. And now, as she spent time with him in the present, it was hard not to remember those times together.

She watched as Blake swung Amelia up into his arms, seeing again the strength that had been part of what had drawn her to him. He'd had a strong build back in the day, and it looked like he'd spent a lot of time working out in the years he'd been gone from Serenity.

Meanwhile, just like he had more pronounced muscles, Charli had more pronounced curves.

When they'd been together before, he'd been able to convince her he actually liked her curviness. He wouldn't be able to do that now, even if he wanted to.

She wasn't sure she'd believe a word he said to her now, particularly as it applied to anything personal.

If she was going to survive having Blake around, Charli knew that she needed to separate *then* and *now* in her mind. She couldn't look at Blake as the man she'd fallen in love with. He couldn't be her former love, and he certainly couldn't be Layla's father.

He needed to be the father of one of her students and Jackson's cousin.

And absolutely nothing more.

When they reached the area where the food was, a couple of food trucks had joined the barbecues. There were line-ups for every truck, but they weren't too long.

Charli was glad that the school hadn't required the teachers to be part of running the carnival. They'd gotten volunteers from the community as well as from the high school, where they'd offered an extra credit mark to each student who helped. There were quite a few teens manning the different areas, so apparently, it had worked.

"Can I have a hotdog and a bag of chips?" Layla asked as she leaned against Charli's side while they waited in line.

Charli wrapped her arm around Layla's shoulders. "Yep. What juice do you want?"

"Apple, please."

The school had brought in a bunch of picnic tables, and after giving her order to Jay, Misha took Ciara over to see if she could find one for them.

Jay was ahead of them in line, and after he placed his order, he motioned for Charli to give hers. "My treat tonight."

"You don't have to do that," Charli said.

"I know, but I want to." He looked past her to Blake. "You and Amelia too."

Blake protested as well, but Jay was nothing if not stubborn, and in the end, he prevailed. Once they gave their orders, it didn't take long to get their food.

Layla carried their bags of chips and her juice box, while Charli carried the rest, trailing behind her on the way to the table where

Misha waited. When it became clear that she and Blake would be sitting on the same side of the table, Charli maneuvered things so Layla and Amelia were between them.

Jay had Peyton and Layla pray for the food, then they began to eat. As they did, Charli had to take a moment to consider how she'd ended up there, sitting at the same table as the man who'd abandoned her, his daughter, and the daughter they shared—but that he didn't know about.

Her relatively uncomplicated life had suddenly become very, very complicated.

But a kids' carnival wasn't a great place to contemplate the sharp left hand turn her life had taken. Since Misha was seated across from her, Charli tried to focus on her instead, leaving Jay to interact with Blake.

"How was your day?" Charli asked. "Busy at the clinic?"

"It wasn't too bad," Misha said as she handed a piece of her hamburger to Ciara. "But it looks like tomorrow is going to be busy."

Saturday was the day Misha operated the free clinic for people who might not have access to insurance, for whatever reason. It had previously been a half-day, and the doctors had rotated shifts each week, but since Misha had become part of the clinic, she'd taken it to a full day on Saturdays and assumed full responsibility for it.

"We all ended up with treats from the coffee shop because Aria was craving a chocolate croissant."

"Oh, nice. Funny how she's continued to have these cravings even though she's not pregnant anymore."

Misha chuckled. "Well, the sweet cravings have always been my favorite because whoever goes to pick something up for her usually gets treats for all of us."

Since Gareth and Aria had decided to wait until their baby was born to find out the gender, they'd all been eager for the baby's arrival. Charli understood why they might want to build the suspense until the baby was born, but it had driven the rest of them a little crazy. Her mom, especially, had wanted to find out what they were having, so she'd know what to buy the baby.

Though she didn't have the big family she'd always dreamed of, Charli had Layla and all the nieces and nephews to love on. She had no idea if or when Jay and Misha might have a baby, given they already had two. Janessa and Will were still in the newlywed stage, and Charli doubted they'd want to have a baby until they moved into a place of their own.

Hudson and Kayleigh weren't married yet, but that would change in a few weeks. Though Kayleigh had never really expressed an interest in having kids, she might have changed her mind now that she had Hudson in her life.

As far as Charli was concerned however, Layla was probably going to be her one and only.

She didn't necessarily feel that what Blake had done had spoiled her for every other man. But after Layla had been born, her focus had been on raising her. Getting to know a man well enough to feel comfortable with them being around Layla had felt like too much effort.

So she'd just lived her life focused on Layla and her job, and she'd continue to do that. Blake's reappearance in her life had changed *nothing*.

"You should bring Amelia to church," Jay said. "She might find it easier to get to know kids in a Sunday school class. Some of them are probably in her grade at school, so if she has a chance to interact with them at church, it might make her more able to connect with them at school."

Charli fought the urge to sigh and roll her eyes. Was Jay just going to include the man in every part of their lives? She couldn't even object without revealing why.

Her family had long since stopped asking who Layla's father was, for which Charli was glad. But that also meant that she didn't want to do anything to rouse their suspicions.

She knew her siblings. She knew what would trigger them to start inquiring about it again. And she wasn't that stupid.

"My aunt said she teaches the class that Amelia would be in," Blake said. "She suggested the same thing."

"Well, there you have it." Jay grinned. "It must be a great idea if Julia came up with it too."

Blake gave a huff of laughter. "I have a feeling she'd say the same if she knew you'd suggested it as well."

Charli's stomach clenched at the sound of his laughter. They had spent a lot of time laughing together, and she'd loved it.

She'd initially met Blake when he'd come to Serenity to visit Jackson and his family. At first, he'd seemed rather reserved and serious. She'd thought he was handsome, for sure, and she'd soon found herself hoping that he might be interested in her. A little subtle flirtation at the end of that first summer had led to them connecting initially on social media before moving to texts and video chats.

Since it had all been long distance, it had been a great way for them to get to know each other, out of the sight of their families.

She'd still been in college, and her parents had wanted her to focus on her schooling. Though she'd agreed with them, for the most part, there was just something about Blake that made her want to throw caution to the wind.

At first, she'd thought he was a Christian because he'd attended church with Jackson and his parents. Later on, she'd learned that he wasn't, but by that point, it hadn't mattered. None of the things that should have kept her from getting involved with Blake had mattered.

All he had to do was smile at her, and she was a goner. His smiles and laughs became things she'd cherished.

He carried a more serious air now, but Charli was no longer going to try to make him smile. Nor were his laughs or smiles something she'd try to remember when they were apart. Not anymore.

Amelia, however, was a different story. If Charli could prompt smiles and laughs from the little girl, she was definitely on board with that. Amelia's seriousness reminded Charli a lot of Blake's. He'd always been more reserved than Jackson, so she still wasn't sure if that was the little girl's personality, inherited from Blake, or if it was because she was someplace new.

"Everybody done eating?" Jay asked a short time later.

"Yep!" Layla replied enthusiastically. "Can we get cotton candy now?"

"I suppose," Charli said. "I did say you could after we ate supper."

"Yes, you can too, Peyton," Jay said before his son could even ask.

"Can I too, Daddy?" Amelia asked, looking up at Blake.

"Sure thing, Berry."

"Why do you call her Berry?" Layla asked. "I thought her name is Amelia?"

"It is Amelia," Blake told her. "But ever since she was little, she's loved berries. Blueberries and strawberries are her favorite, so we started to call her Berry."

"Oh! That's cool. My favorite fruit right now is a... banana." She grimaced. "That wouldn't be a fun nickname, I don't think. Berry is fun and pretty."

"You could be popcorn," Charli said as she gathered up the remnants of their meal. "You love that a lot."

"That's not much better," Layla muttered.

"Your name is pretty," Amelia told her. "You don't need a nickname."

"You're lucky to have a pretty name *and* a nickname."

Charli didn't know how she felt about the interactions between Layla and Amelia. As much as she wanted to ignore the fact that they were half-sisters, seeing them together made it impossible to do that.

"Let's go get some cotton candy," Charli suggested. "Maybe we could call you cotton candy."

"At least that would be pretty," Layla told her as she swung her legs over the bench and stood up.

"Layla always makes me smile," Misha said as they followed the kids to the nearest cotton candy machine.

"I have a feeling that Ciara is going to be like her, then you might not smile at everything she says."

Misha laughed. "I'm quite sure you're right. But I'll enjoy the years between now and then by smiling at Layla."

Jay and Blake were walking ahead of them, with Jay carrying Ciara. It had been so interesting to watch Jay grow into being a great father. And now, a great husband. Charli was proud of him, and the things he'd accomplished in his personal life over the past few years.

Charli had helped Jay when Peyton had first arrived to live with him, but he didn't need her help now. He and Misha had created a stable home for both of their children.

"Do you want some, Mom?" Layla asked as she held out the mound of cotton candy on a stick.

"Sure." Charli had a bit of a sweet tooth, but the cotton candy was almost too sweet. Even for her. Still, she took a small bite, enjoying the way it melted on her tongue. "Thanks, sweetie."

While the kids ate their cotton candy, they continued to walk around the field. They paused to talk to other kids and their parents. It wasn't just Charli they talked to, though she knew them all from having taught their kids at one time or another. Many spent a few minutes speaking with Jay and Misha, too. Until their kids pulled them away from the conversation.

Blake stuck with them, likely because Amelia seemed happy to hang with Layla and Peyton. It was too bad that one of them wasn't in her grade, but at least Peyton was still at the school so he could maybe look out for her at recess.

Layla had voiced more than once that she missed being at the elementary school. Not because she missed Charli, however. Nope. She missed hanging out with Peyton and a couple of other friends who were in the lower grades.

"Thanks a lot for letting us stick with you guys," Blake said when they finally decided it was time to leave. "This is the happiest I've seen Amelia since moving here."

"It was great to have you both around. Maybe we'll see you on Sunday."

"We'll probably be there," Blake said.

Charli was torn about how she felt about that prospect. She agreed with Jay that attending Sunday school might be good for Amelia. However, she'd rather not have Blake at yet another place where she regularly spent time.

Jay insisted on exchanging numbers with Blake. "Give me a call if you need anything."

Charli didn't feel inclined to do the same. Blake already had a way to contact her. He didn't need her phone number on top of that. As she watched him talk with Jay, she knew that she really needed to have less contact with the man, not more.

As Blake took Amelia's hand after she said goodbye to Layla and Peyton, he glanced at Charli. That brief meeting of gazes made her heart race, and her breath caught in her chest in anticipation of Blake addressing her directly.

But he didn't.

After what felt like a long, drawn-out moment, Blake gave her a quick nod, then turned his attention to Amelia as they walked away. The tightness in her chest eased, but completely unwanted disappointment filled her.

"Do you have Layla's stuff with you?" Misha asked. "Or should we swing by the house?"

Charli had given permission for Layla to spend the night at Jay and Misha's. Denise would be watching the kids the next day while the couple went to work at the clinic.

"Yep. Everything is in the car," Charli said as they made their way from the carnival area to where they'd parked.

When school had ended earlier, Denise had picked up Layla and Peyton from their schools, then gone to the house with all three kids. Charli had swung by the clinic to get Jay, since Misha needed to stay a bit later, then they'd gone to the house to grab the kids.

At the car, Charli handed Jay the small suitcase that contained Layla's things, then hugged Layla. "See you tomorrow, sweetheart. Be good for Uncle Jay and Aunt Misha."

"I will. Love you."

"I love you too."

When she let herself into her house a few minutes later, quiet greeted her. Usually Friday evenings meant guests for pizza night, but since she, Jay, and Misha had planned to go to the carnival with the kids, everyone who usually came had made other plans.

She assumed that Janessa and Will had gone on a date somewhere, which normally would have been fine. Except that evening, without them there, she had nothing to distract her from her thoughts as she puttered around the kitchen, unloading the dishwasher.

At one point, all her tangled emotions surged to the surface, and Charli was horrified to find tears pricking at her eyes. It had been a long time since she'd cried over something that wasn't in a book or a movie.

Crying over Blake, though? That had been even longer. She'd decided not long after Layla was born that Blake didn't deserve her tears. After how he'd treated her, he wasn't entitled to them.

That was still true.

However, the time at the carnival had given her a glimpse of what things might have been like had they ended up together.

For a moment that evening, her past hopes and dreams had smacked her in the face in the most painful way. Seeing Blake with his daughter, showing her the gentleness he'd once had for Charli, had brought with it a sharp pain, along with some anger.

The worst part was the doubts and insecurities that being around Blake had resurrected. For too long after he'd sent the message breaking up with her, she'd wondered if the reason he'd left her like that had been because he'd realized he could do better than her. Or maybe his family had convinced him he could do better than a chubby girl whose main goals in life had been to become a teacher and have a large family.

He'd taken her virginity, got her pregnant, then left her behind.

It was pretty clear from Amelia's presence, however, that at some point, he'd found a woman he was willing to stick with.

Charli decided she didn't want to chance Janessa coming home and finding her in such an emotional state. So, after she finished emptying the dishwasher, she made herself a cup of hot chocolate and grabbed a couple of cookies to take to her room.

Normally, she enjoyed the rare evenings when Layla stayed overnight with Jay and Misha or her parents. That night, though, she would have loved for her to be at the house to offer Charli a distraction.

Once in her room, Charli changed into her pajamas, then settled into her chair with a book, hoping to escape the mess of emotions the evening at the carnival with Blake had stirred up.

If a good story couldn't distract her, then nothing could.

CHAPTER EIGHT

When Blake pulled into the parking lot of the church, he found a spot that wasn't too close to the building. He shut off the truck, but then just sat there.

It wasn't that he didn't want to go to church. It was more that he wasn't thrilled to be walking into a new situation yet again. He'd let himself be convinced by his aunt and Jay Halverson that Sunday School would be a good thing for Amelia, and he really hoped that was going to be the case.

When he'd first come to visit Jackson and his parents, he'd attended church with them. At first, he'd gone because he hadn't really had anything better to do on a Sunday morning.

But later, he'd gone because Charli had caught his attention. It wasn't until the summer was nearly over that he'd finally reached out to her on social media, and they'd begun to talk.

The next summer, he'd continued to go to church because he'd wanted to see Charli and spend some time around her. They hadn't been able to acknowledge what they were to each other during that time. However, what he'd felt for her had been enough for him to attend church regularly, even though he'd really had no interest in spiritual things at that point.

In the first few years following his enlistment, he hadn't gone to church at all. But then on a deployment he'd made friends with a man who was a Christian, and after they'd faced a tragic event on their base, Blake had been open to the Gospel message in a way he hadn't been before.

It had been an amazing time for Blake, one that had changed his life in surprising ways. And as he'd attended services and Bible studies with an openness to learn about God that he hadn't previously had, he'd also gained a new insight into Charli and her family, and the importance faith had played in their lives.

Now, he felt like he needed to apologize to Charli for not respecting her faith more. But in his defense, he just hadn't *known* what it all meant. He had a much better understanding now, having learned and grown in his own faith.

And now he wanted that for Amelia. They hadn't gone to church in Texas because he hadn't been sure about introducing Amelia to another new situation, especially knowing they wouldn't be staying there.

But Serenity was going to be their home, so it was time to venture into this part of their lives.

"Are we going in, Daddy?" Amelia asked from her seat. "I want to see Layla and Peyton again."

Blake angled his rearview mirror so that he could see her in the back seat. "You realize they might not be in your class, right?"

"Yeah. I know. But Aunt Julia said she teaches the class I'll be in."

It was Amelia's bravery and her willingness to actually go into a new situation that finally got him out of the truck. Once Amelia was beside him, he took her hand, and they walked across the parking lot to the doors of the church.

As they stepped into the foyer, he looked around, immediately spotting his aunt as she walked toward him with a big smile on her face.

"Oh, my darlings," she said as she approached them. "I'm so glad to see you here."

She bent to hug Amelia, then gave Blake one as well, holding him a little longer than she had Amelia. He appreciated her affection, especially since he'd had precious little of it over the past several years.

Even before he'd enlisted, his mom had never been exactly free with her affections, so the way Julia interacted with them was welcome. If she didn't look so much like his mom, he would never have believed they were sisters.

Where his aunt was full of smiles, willingly giving out hugs and kind words, his mom was much more reserved. Her words were more likely to be ones of criticism than encouragement.

Blake wondered if the differences between them were partly because of the men they'd married. His dad had high expectations for those in his family, and it seemed that no one ever achieved them to his satisfaction.

Jackson's dad was pretty much the opposite. The man had found success with his business, and Jackson worked alongside him, apparently fine with being in the family business.

Unlike Blake's dad, Robert was content for his business to remain small. He didn't spend all day at his job, only to retreat to his office in the evenings. He seemed to feel that his wife deserved his time and attention at the end of the day.

"I'll take her down to the classrooms," Julia said. "The adults are meeting in the sanctuary. Jackson and Rob are already there."

Blake watched Amelia walk away with Julia, not even looking back at him. His feelings about that were a mix of pride and worry.

When they disappeared down the stairs, Blake sighed and turned toward the doors leading to the sanctuary. The part of him that didn't enjoy going into new situations wanted to leave the church and go to a coffee shop until it was time for the service. But before he could even consider putting that plan into action, he saw Jay and his wife coming through the doors with their kids.

When Jay spotted him, he grinned, then said something to Misha. Nodding, she took Ciara from him, then headed to the stairs with Peyton.

"Good to see you here," Jay said as he approached Blake, his hand out.

Blake took his hand in a firm shake. "Amelia was quite insistent that she wanted to come."

"Sometimes children will be the ones to lead us." Jay tilted his head toward the doors to the sanctuary. "Want to head in?"

So much for an escape. "Sure."

They walked into the sanctuary, then Jay led him over to where Jackson stood talking with Wade.

"Hey, cuz," Jackson said with a grin. "Fancy meeting you here."

"Yeah. Fancy that."

Blake listened as the men talked, not entering the conversation, since he still didn't really feel comfortable with any of them but Jackson. The camaraderie of the men reminded him of his buddies in the army. He missed them, but they were in different parts of their lives now. His focus had to be on Amelia, while theirs was still on their positions in the army.

As he settled on a pew with Jackson and the others, Blake reflected on the path that had brought him there. A path he'd vowed he'd never take because he'd thought returning to Serenity wasn't an option considering how things had ended between him and Charli.

Yet, here he was, having put the needs of his daughter above his reluctance to face Charli again.

A few minutes after Blake sat down, Charli slid into the pew in front of him with Janessa and Will.

Charli glanced over her shoulder, and their gazes met for a moment before she turned her attention to the front of the sanctuary. A man took his place behind a small podium that stood on the floor in front of the section where they sat, greeting them with a smile.

Blake had gotten to the point where days—even weeks—could go by without him thinking about Charli. He'd accepted that, because of his own bad decisions, he'd have to carry on his life without her.

But now, every day, he was thinking about her again. Maybe if Amelia hadn't ended up in Charli's class, that wouldn't be the case.

Or maybe she still would have dominated his thoughts, just because he was back in the place where they'd made so many memories. Where they'd made plans for a future together.

After the man said a brief prayer, he began the lesson. Blake unzipped his Bible cover and slid out the notebook and pen he kept there. As the man spoke, he handed a woman in the front row a stack of papers to pass among the attendees.

For most of the class, Blake's attention was split between Charli and the man leading the class. She didn't seem to have a similar issue. It was as if his presence there didn't impact her at all.

Which shouldn't matter to him. But for some reason, there was an ache inside him as his heart remembered all the promises they'd made to each other.

Promises that had shriveled up and died when he'd made a snap decision and run away from his future instead of trying to figure out how to reach for the life he wanted with Charli.

His gaze drifted to Charli again, taking in the gentle curves of her profile. He'd once had the right to cup her cheek in his hand. To kiss her soft lips. To hold her in his arms.

Realizing that thinking about their previous relationship wasn't productive or appropriate, Blake forced his gaze away from Charli to the man at the podium. Blake really hoped that no one gave him a pop quiz on what the man had taught that day, because he'd get an F for sure.

He had to try harder to keep that from happening in the future.

"Do the kids join us up here?" Blake asked Jay when the class ended. "Or do I need to go down and get Amelia?"

"I'm sure Julia will bring Amelia to you," Jay said.

"I guess I should have asked her." Blake glanced toward the entrance of the sanctuary. "Just to make sure."

"We can head out to the foyer to see if they've come upstairs yet."

Because he was eager to make sure that Amelia was still okay, Blake didn't object to heading out of the sanctuary, even knowing they'd be coming right back in.

"Daddy!" Blake smiled when Amelia ran up to him.

He scooped her up. "Did you have a good time?"

"The best," she told him. Her blue eyes sparkled, even if she didn't have a big smile on her face. She held a couple of papers up. "We learned about Jonah."

"Did you?"

"Yep. And Aunt Julia gave us a paper with the story, so I can read it to you later."

"That's great, Berry."

"She did really well," Julia said as she joined them. "A couple of little girls she knew from school were in the class."

"Did she seem to connect with them?"

Julia nodded. "I think so. Though she clearly has a preference for Layla and Peyton."

"Is there a kids' activity for her during the service?"

"Yes. There's a junior worship for kids in grade six and under. They are with us for the first part of the service, then they're dismissed before the sermon."

"Hi, Layla!" Amelia waved at the young girl who was walking with her mom and Peyton across the foyer.

Layla darted over to them, her dark brown hair swinging in its ponytail. Her big smile was friendly as she came to a stop in front of them. "Hi, Amelia Berry!"

Blake set Amelia down, watching as the girls hugged. Glancing up, he saw that Charli was also watching them. However, she didn't seem to be as happy about their interactions. It wasn't that she looked mad, just... not entirely happy.

Although, after twelve years, what did he know? He was definitely out of practice reading her expressions. That was assuming her expressions even meant what they once had.

She was a woman with twelve more years of life experience, just like he was a man with all that additional experience, too. Not all of it had been good for him, and he thought that perhaps, since she was raising her daughter by herself, it hadn't been all good for her either.

He just hoped that she'd let their daughters continue to build a friendship. He could see a gentleness in Layla that Amelia needed, because Amelia hadn't known a lot of that in her life.

Lauren and her sister, who had been the most influential people in Amelia's life, had frequently fought like cats and dogs. Blake hadn't seen any of that until after he and Lauren had been together for awhile. Since it took awhile for her to introduce him to Callie, he'd only figured out why after he'd finally met her.

Callie had flirted with him every time they were around each other. He hadn't been interested in her, not even after he and Lauren had broken up. She'd tried again after Lauren had died, but when she'd realized that he *still* wasn't interested, she'd washed her hands of him and Amelia completely.

Now, though, Amelia was coming into contact with people who seemed to actually enjoy being around her. Who offered her that gentleness that Blake wanted Amelia to experience in her life.

"Can we sit together, Mom?" Layla asked Charli.

It took a moment for Charli to respond, but thankfully, when she did, she agreed.

"Why don't we go find seats?" Jay suggested, having been joined by Misha and Peyton.

They headed back into the sanctuary, and this time, they settled into a row closer to the back. Jay and Misha stepped into the row and shuffled all the way to the end, followed by Charli, Peyton,

Layla, and Amelia. Blake ended up on the aisle on the end opposite to Jay.

When he felt a touch on his shoulder, Blake glanced up and saw his aunt walk past him, pausing briefly to give him a warm smile. She had turned out to be such a huge support for both him and Amelia since they'd arrived back in Serenity. There had been no judgment from her. Just a desire to do what she could to help him and Amelia adjust.

The three kids were chatting softly as the sanctuary slowly filled. Blake kept his attention on the large screen at the front, reading through the announcements that appeared on it. He wasn't particularly interested in them, but he didn't want to make eye contact with anyone right then.

And he didn't need to find himself staring at Charli yet again.

For the first time, Blake wondered if she'd be willing to have a conversation with him. He owed her an apology. However, it was possible that she'd feel it was too little, too late. And he couldn't blame her if that was the case.

She didn't owe him the opportunity to explain or apologize.

The service started right at eleven, and though Amelia hadn't attended church before, Blake wasn't worried about her not being able to sit still. She'd never had a problem sitting quietly.

She watched everything going on with big eyes, glancing over at Layla and Peyton whenever they stood up or sat down, then followed suit.

"As we stand for this song, the children can make their way downstairs for their time of worship."

Blake stood along with everyone else, then as children scooted out of the surrounding rows, he stepped into the aisle. He stayed out of the way of the other kids as he waited for Layla, Peyton, and Amelia to leave their row. Amelia glanced up at him, worry on her face.

Bending down, Blake said, "You'll be with Layla and Peyton. Everything will be okay. But if you need me, you just quietly come back here. Okay?"

She nodded, then gave him a quick hug. He turned to watch the trio, grateful to see that Layla had taken Amelia's hand.

Once they'd disappeared from view, Blake stepped back into the row. He tried to ignore the large gap that existed between him and Charli, now that the kids had left the pew. While a part of him wanted to step closer to her, he remained firmly in his place.

For the rest of the service, Blake tried his best to focus on what the pastor was saying, but he found his thoughts bouncing between Amelia and if she was doing okay, and Charli. His mind was making up for lost time, mulling over all the things he could have done differently and all the things he'd missed with Charli.

He didn't normally have an issue paying attention during sermons, but even twelve years ago, Charli had been a distraction for him at church. If it continued to be an issue, he'd have to make sure he sat in a row in front of Charli so he couldn't see her. He was too old to be having this struggle, but Charli had always been his weakness.

When the service ended, Blake got to his feet and joined the other worshippers as they moved toward the foyer. His plan was to grab lunch for him and Amelia from somewhere, then head home and spend the afternoon watching kids' movies. Not his idea of an ideal way to spend an afternoon, but he'd do it for Amelia.

Maybe they'd take a walk since the weather was so nice. They'd gone to a nearby park one afternoon not long after they'd moved there, but Amelia hadn't wanted to join the other kids on the playground equipment. Walks seemed to be the thing she enjoyed the most.

"Hey, Blake."

Blake turned at the sound of his name to see Jay headed his way, with Misha, Janessa, and Will trailing behind him.

"What's up?" he asked.

"We're all going to the park after the service for a picnic lunch, and we usually play some volleyball. You should join us."

Though it sounded a lot better than watching kids' movies, he wasn't sure if he should go, given it would probably bring him into close proximity to Charli. She wouldn't like that, he was sure.

However, Amelia would probably love it.

"I don't really have anything to contribute to a picnic," he said, because that was also a concern.

Jay waved a hand dismissively. "Don't worry about that. We always have more than enough food."

"Let me see how Amelia feels about it."

Blake wished he could ask Charli how she might feel about him joining them, but he wasn't sure how to do that without raising questions about why he was talking to her. It was clear she'd never shared anything about their secret relationship with her siblings. If she had, he wasn't sure that they'd be all that welcoming to him.

Before they could converse further, the kids came running up to them. Amelia's smile was a little bigger than it had been earlier.

He went down on one knee, so he was at her level. "Did you have fun, Berry?"

Nodding, her smile grew. "We sang songs, and then they acted out some stuff. I liked it."

"That's great." He leaned forward to press a quick kiss to her forehead. "Do you want to go to the park? Or would you rather go home and watch some movies?"

Her little brow furrowed. "Go to the park by ourselves?"

"You could come with us," Layla said. "We're going to the park."

"Can we?" Amelia asked, her expression pleading.

He could hardly fight against that. "Sure."

"Yay!" Layla cheered, holding her hand up for Amelia to smack in a high five.

"We'll go home first so you can change," he told her.

"I'm gonna change too," Layla said. "And my mom bought some hula hoops. I'll bring those so we can try to use them."

Blake straightened to his full height, glancing over to see that Charli had joined them. She'd obviously heard the conversation, and her expression this time was resigned.

Part of him felt like he should change his mind and tell Amelia they'd just stick to his original plan. But one look at Amelia's face had him accepting Jay's offer to join them.

Though he would have liked to spare Charli his presence, right then, it was more important to do something that made Amelia happy and allowed her to spend time with a couple of kids who had connected with her when she hadn't really connected with anyone else yet.

If he could avoid Charli for her sake, without affecting Amelia, he certainly would. It was just that his daughter had no one else to provide these opportunities for her, so he had to do that for her.

Blake couldn't deny that there was also a small part of him that accepted these opportunities because he wanted to be around Charli, even though it was clear she didn't welcome his presence.

CHAPTER NINE

"Isn't it great that Amelia and her dad are coming to the picnic?" Layla asked as she twirled around the kitchen.

No. It most definitely was *not* great that Blake was bringing Amelia to their picnic. But instead of saying that, Charli gave a non-committal hum in response.

"I'm going to bring my hula hoops. It'll be fun to see if Amelia can do it."

Charli put the rolls she'd baked the previous day into the plastic bin she was preparing to take to the park. Already in the bin were the cookies and brownies she had on hand from Denise.

Baking goodies wasn't part of Denise's job description when she came on Fridays, but when they'd told her that, she'd just waved their objections aside. Denise loved to cook and bake, and they all appreciated her efforts.

"Are we taking juice boxes?" Layla asked as she peered into the bin.

"If you'd like." Charli went to the pantry and pulled out an insulated freezer bag. "Put some in there."

"Just the juice boxes? There's room for more stuff."

Opening the fridge, Charli added a tub of butter and the potato salad she'd prepared the day before. Layla wanted to take popsicles, but it was warm enough that day that Charli didn't think they'd stay frozen.

"Can't we put ice in the bag to keep them cold?"

She checked the freezer and saw a bag of ice there, so she nodded. "Pick a few of each flavor and put them in a plastic bag."

While Charli repacked the bag with the ice, Layla got a plastic bag and loaded a bunch of popsicles into it. Charli still wasn't convinced they'd stay frozen, but Layla seemed certain that the ice would work its magic.

Once it was all ready, Charli began to carry the stuff out to her car. She had to make a couple of trips since she couldn't handle everything they were taking in one go. In addition to the food, she and Layla put the hula hoops and some folding lawn chairs into the back of the car.

After they'd gotten home from church, Charli had changed into a pair of mid-thigh length cuffed denim shorts and a loose pink blouse with short ruffle sleeves. Her shoes were her favorite flat sandals.

Layla also wore a pair of shorts, but she had paired them with a sleeveless tank top. She'd put on a pair of runners since she was more likely to be playing while Charli was relaxing. Or at least trying to. The likelihood of truly relaxing with Blake around was actually quite slim.

"Ready?" Charli asked as she closed the back hatch.

"Yep!"

Janessa and Will had already come and gone, since they'd been assigned the task of saving their group a spot at the park since it was likely to be busy. That day was warm and sunny. Soon enough, however, the warmth of summer would shift into fall, bringing with it cool and rainy days, before finally settling into the cold and snow that would be with them for a few months.

Charli slid behind the wheel, then quickly checked her phone to make sure she hadn't missed a message from anyone, asking her to bring something that had been forgotten. There was nothing on her phone, so she started up the car and headed for the park.

Once there, Charli pulled to a stop behind Jay's vehicle. Layla clambered out the passenger side door, waving at Peyton.

Letting out a sigh, Charli got out of the car and went to where Layla waited impatiently at the rear of the car. Charli had just opened the back hatch when she heard another vehicle pull up behind them.

Glancing over her shoulder, Charli saw that it was Blake. She tried to ignore the jump of her pulse and the way the air seemed to momentarily vanish from her lungs.

Why were her reactions when she saw Blake the same as they'd been twelve years ago? Where was her hurt and anger? She needed them to keep these other emotions at bay.

She focused back on the contents of the trunk as she heard the truck door open. And after she'd handed Layla the hula hoops, she heard her enthusiastically greet Amelia.

"Do you need a hand?" Blake asked after the girls had run off to greet Peyton.

Charli wanted to tell him no, but that would clearly be a lie since she'd then have to either struggle to carry everything herself in one go or make two trips. "Sure. That would be great."

"What do you want me to carry?" he asked.

"The cooler bag is the heavier one." She stepped back, watching as Blake leaned into the back of her car and lifted the bag out, his T-shirt stretching across his shoulders. "Thanks. You can just set it on the picnic table."

Charli grabbed the bin, then shut the hatch. When she turned, she realized that Blake had waited for her.

What was she supposed to do? Tell him to go on without her and then stand there for a minute like an idiot before following him?

Looking like an idiot was out of the question, so Charli fell into step beside Blake as they walked across the grass to where the others were.

"Would I be able to talk to you?"

No... "About Amelia?"

"Well, if you think we need to talk about her, then definitely," Blake said. "But I'd also like to speak to you about what happened... before."

"That's in the past," she told him, her heart pounding. The last thing she wanted was to talk about that time because she was afraid that he might ask about Layla. "I don't think we need to have a conversation about it."

"If that's your decision, I'll respect it." Charli felt a swell of relief at his words. "But if you change your mind, I'd be very grateful for the opportunity to talk about everything."

Since they were just steps away from the picnic table, Charli didn't say anything further. However, the conversation continued to play in her head, and not all of the versions her brain came up with were her saying no to what Blake wanted.

"Everything okay?" Janessa asked as she came to stand next to Charli at the picnic table.

Thankfully, Blake had set the bag down, then moved on to where Jay and Will were standing.

"Yep. Why?"

"It looked like you and Blake were having an intense conversation."

"Intense?" She supposed that from a distance it hadn't looked like a friendly interaction. But that's because it hadn't been.

"Was it about Amelia?"

"He is concerned about her making friends in my class."

"And she isn't?"

"Not really. Not yet. Perhaps after this weekend, that might change since I'm sure she had a couple of my students with her in Julia's Sunday school class."

"Layla seems to have taken her under her wing," Janessa said, turning her gaze to where the girls and Peyton were trying to make the hula hoops work. "Too bad they aren't in the same grade."

"Yeah." Only that would have been impossible.

"Maybe she could at least hang out with Peyton at recess."

Charli nodded as she opened the freezer bag and set the potato salad and the tub of butter on the picnic table. Then she zipped the bag back up and set it under the table, out of the sun, in hopes that the popsicles wouldn't melt.

"I think he might be interested in you," Janessa murmured.

Charli frowned as she looked up from the bin, her grip tightening on the bag of rolls she'd just picked up. "What are you talking about?"

"Blake keeps looking at you."

"I doubt he's interested in *me*," Charli said. "And even if he is, that doesn't mean I'm interested in *him*."

Janessa gave a snort of laughter. "You're never interested in *anyone* these days."

"This is true. I don't see any reason to change things up now."

"Except he's cute, and it seems like he's going to be a part of our group. Plus, he's got a little girl who already meshes really well with Layla."

And Charli didn't want to think about why that might be. She knew from experience that having a biological connection to a sister didn't necessarily mean they'd get along. In fact, she got along better with the sister she *wasn't* biologically related to.

Still... there was no denying that the girls had connected for whatever reason. Perhaps it was just Layla's big heart that allowed her to see someone else's need. She'd done the same with Peyton when he'd arrived, uprooted from everything he had known.

Charli was proud of that quality in her precious daughter, and she hoped that never changed.

"Are we ready to eat?" Jackson asked as he approached the table, his gaze taking in all the food that was laid out. "I'm starving."

"You're always starving," Janessa said.

"Yep. Especially when there's good food around." Jackson glanced over at her. "How're you doing?"

"I'm fine. You?"

He shrugged. "Hungry, but otherwise, good."

"Gone on any dates lately?"

That got a grimace out of him. "Nope. I think I'm going to take a break for a bit."

"Really?" Jackson was pretty much Charli's opposite when it came to dating, so she was surprised that he would take a break from it. "Why?"

"I don't know. I'm just getting tired of going on these dates, only for them to leave me no closer to finding someone I actually want to be with."

Charli wished she had some advice for the guy, but she had no clue what to say. He wasn't a bad person. His joking, lighthearted personality wasn't really her thing, but Charli was sure that there was a woman out there somewhere who would appreciate it.

"Let's pray, then we can dig in," Jay said as everyone gathered around the table.

Once he said amen, Misha passed out paper plates. The adults waited while the kids filled their plates, then carried them to the large blanket that had been spread out on the grass.

While the others got their food, Charli returned to her car to retrieve the lawn chairs she'd brought. When she returned, Jay said, "You should have asked me to get those for you."

Charli gave him a quick smile. "It wasn't a big deal."

"Go get your food," he said as he took the chairs from her. "I'll get these set up."

Glancing around, Charli saw that Blake was at the picnic table with Will. She hesitated a moment before walking over to join them. Avoiding him was just not possible and would only make people wonder what was going on.

Blake looked over as she joined them at the table. The stack of paper plates was on his side of the table, and without her having to ask, Blake picked one up and held it out to her.

"Thanks." His consideration was a reminder of how he'd treated her when they'd been together.

Growing up in such a large family with some bold personalities, it had been rare for anyone to focus on her. There were times she'd longed for more attention, especially her parents, and in Blake, she'd found someone who had given that to her. Even when they hadn't been public about their relationship, he'd still managed to let her know that he was watching her. That he saw her.

"You're welcome." Why the deep timber of his voice sent shivers down her spine with just those two words, she didn't know. But it did.

"So, where do you work, Blake?" Will asked.

"At Stan Wilson's garage. I'm a mechanic."

"Oh nice," Will said. "That's where I take my and Janessa's cars whenever we need work done on them."

It was where Charli took hers as well. Would she continue to in the future, knowing she might have to deal with him if she did? Probably.

He'd always been passionate about cars. In the time they'd spent together—when they'd meet up at a nearby lake—he'd talk about his hope to be able to open his own garage in the future and how he dreamed of restoring an old car one day.

Looking back, Charli couldn't help but remember how they'd connected. It was a connection she hadn't experienced before Blake. Or since. She had no idea why that was. It made her think that perhaps what they'd shared might have gone the distance. If they'd had the chance.

Back then, she'd thought that after the months of long distance they'd had to endure, it would be strong enough. But then things had ended the way they had, and Charli had been left to wonder about everything.

Like if the times he'd been unavailable to chat during their period of long distance had been because he'd been with someone else. She wondered if she'd only imagined how much they'd connected.

But then, thoughts of how they'd been together during the next summer would take over, reminding her of how devoted Blake had been to her. Unfortunately, that just left her confused and hurting because she'd loved him *so much*.

Of all the decisions she'd made twelve years ago, Charli thought that keeping things quiet was the best one. Especially since Blake was connected to her family through Jackson.

It was bad enough that Jackson was aware of who exactly Blake was to her and Layla. There was no way she wanted the rest of her family to know.

What was a bit... perplexing was that Blake seemed to not even suspect that Layla might be his. Maybe that was because they'd only slept together once, and she'd assured him that they were safe because she was on the pill.

Of course, since she'd been taking it to help with her cycles and not as birth control, she hadn't been the best at taking the pill regularly like she was supposed to. Given that she had been raised in such a medically oriented family, she absolutely should have known better. She'd just never imagined that she'd be one of those people who got pregnant after only one time—while she was on birth control.

But she'd wanted to be with Blake, so she'd thrown all caution—as well as her morals—to the wind. Regret had only shown up when Blake had stopped communicating, and it had only gotten worse when she'd found out she was pregnant.

She assumed that Blake had dismissed the possibility of Layla being his for the same reason she had been in disbelief when the pregnancy test first showed she was pregnant. And Charli was fine with Blake not even considering that Layla might be his. She really was, as it meant she didn't have to deal with whatever would have resulted if he realized the truth.

As she put some potato salad on her plate, Charli glanced over to where the kids sat, her gaze lingering on the girls as it often did when they were together. It was a constant search for the similarities between them, which, thankfully, she had, as yet, not seen.

Leaving Blake and Will to continue their conversation, Charli walked over to the lawn chairs and sat down. Jay had set them up next to the blanket, which meant the kids were in front of her. It also meant that when Blake sat down next to Amelia, he was in her view.

"Can I have another pickle, Daddy?" Amelia asked, scooting over to settle next to him.

Blake gestured to his plate. "I figured you might want more, so I took extra."

Reaching out, she plucked a pickle from his plate, then smiled up at him. "Thank you."

"You're welcome, Beautiful Berry." He leaned forward and kissed the top of her head.

Charli's breath caught in her chest at the exchange. Forcing herself to look down at her plate, she scooped up a forkful of potato salad and put it in her mouth.

She didn't taste it as she chewed. All she could focus on was the fact that she was depriving Layla of a relationship like that.

"Are you done, Lia?" Layla asked.

Charli glanced at Blake to see if he minded Layla shortening his daughter's name. There was a small smile on his face as he watched Amelia scramble to her feet, popping the last of her pickle into her mouth.

Would he be the same way with Layla? Or had whatever he and Amelia been through given them a bond that he wouldn't be able to form with another child?

Charli wasn't sure that she could take that chance with Layla's feelings. At her age, she was old enough to understand if she was being treated differently. It was hard to be tempted to expose her to that possibility because Charli had always tried her best to protect Layla. She'd never willingly place her in a position where she'd be hurt in any way.

For the time being—and possibly forever—things would have to stay as they were.

"Look at me, Mom!" Layla called.

Charli watched as she held the hoop around her waist, and then started it spinning, wiggling her hips in an attempt to keep it going. She got about two revolutions in before it dropped to the ground.

"Good job, sweetheart. Keep practicing."

Layla beamed at her and bent to pick it up and try again. Amelia and Peyton were also trying their hoops out, with limited success.

The guys were slow to get up to play volleyball, but eventually, Jay rallied them to split up into teams. Charli rarely played, but Misha and Janessa sometimes did.

Though they'd arrived later than the rest, Kayleigh and Hudson had shown up, and Hudson happily joined in the game as well. After sending him off with a kiss, Kayleigh dropped down into the chair beside Charli.

"How's life?" Kayleigh asked as she crossed her legs, keeping her gaze on Hudson.

"It's good." Relatively speaking. "How about for you?"

"Busy. Hudson was away for most of the week."

There were times Charli found it hard to believe how attached Kayleigh had gotten to Hudson. Her older sister was fiercely independent, so it was weird to see how much she liked having Hudson around. Apparently love did that to a person.

Charli fell quiet as Misha and Janessa joined in the conversation. She split her attention between the kids and the volleyball game, trying to find some semblance of calm.

Unfortunately, calm had been hard to come by since Blake's reappearance in her life. But maybe if he wasn't going to come after her about Layla, she could relax and not be so tense whenever he was around them.

As she watched the volleyball game, memories of how she'd once imagined her and Blake being part of family gatherings assaulted her. Of them hanging out with her siblings. Of their wedding in the presence of her family.

Because they'd kept things secret, she'd dreamed of the day they'd be able to be public about their relationship. Only they'd never had the chance.

So there she sat, watching her siblings with their significant others and trying not to let her jealousy grow.

Twelve years ago, Jay had been the only one in a serious relationship—and that had been with someone none of them liked—so it hadn't been as hard to be around her siblings.

Blake had hung out with them a lot back then, but it hadn't really been fun since they'd had to keep their distance and pretend they were nothing more than friendly acquaintances.

And now they were once again pretending that nothing existed between them. Except that this time, there really wasn't anything between them but a painful past.

Charli couldn't let on that they'd previously been involved because the whole family would know the truth about Layla's paternity. It was bad enough that Jackson had put the pieces together.

"Are you interested?" Kayleigh asked.

Charli looked at her sister, wondering what she'd missed while she'd been lost in the wasteland of her memories once again. "Interested in what?"

"Not *what*. *Who*."

"Who?"

Kayleigh rolled her eyes. "Are you interested in Jackson's cousin?"

"Not in the way you're probably thinking." Over the years, Charli had gotten used to her family trying to sus out her interest in different men.

"How *are* you interested?"

"Well, he's the father of one of my students. I'm always curious about the home lives of the kids in my class. How they interact with their parents."

"He seems like a good dad, from the little I've seen."

Charli just nodded, then looked to where Amelia was playing with Layla and Peyton. They'd moved on from trying to use the hula hoops properly, to trying to throw them over each other.

"Layla and Peyton have been good with her, too," Kayleigh added.

"Yep. They've taken her under their wing the way Layla did with Peyton when he first arrived."

Charli was glad that Layla had such a sweet and friendly personality, but it definitely was adding a complication to her life. Now that Amelia had made the connection, she would likely be included in anything where Layla and Peyton were present. Which meant that Blake would be where Charli was.

How had this become her life?

CHAPTER TEN

After they'd played a couple of games, Blake dropped down onto the edge of the blanket where the kids were sitting. He leaned back on his hands as he stretched his legs out onto the grass.

The games had been more fun than he'd thought they'd be. He'd played plenty of volleyball and basketball over the years. It was also something he'd played with his buddies while deployed, and sometimes they'd gotten together to play even while stateside.

Janessa and Misha had joined for the second game, but no one asked Charli if she wanted to play. She remained in her lawn chair, talking with her sister, Kayleigh, who also hadn't been asked to join. Kayleigh's husband, Hudson, had been on Blake's team.

So much had changed since he'd last hung out with the Halversons. Back then, Jay had been dating a tall blonde, who'd looked like a model, but had been nowhere near as friendly as Misha. Kayleigh hadn't spent much time with them, though when she had, she'd never had a guy with her.

There had been no children, but now there were four. Would there have been more if he and Charli had been able to continue their relationship?

Given everything that had happened between them twelve years ago and in his life since then, Blake hadn't thought that he'd harbor any sort of interest in Charli. However, the more he was around her, the more he was discovering he did.

She was as beautiful as he'd remembered, and all the things he'd appreciated about her were still there. Seeing her in action as a parent and a teacher was a reminder of all they'd hoped for, and everything he'd lost.

"Thanks for coming," Jay said as he lowered himself to the ground beside Blake. "It was nice to have another person who can actually play the game."

"Hey now," Janessa said with a scowl at her brother. "We can all play this game. It's not our fault that you take it so seriously."

Jay tilted his head to look up at her as she stood beside him. "You think that's seriously? You need to come to one of my practices. Then you'll see seriously."

"He's right, Nessa," Will said as he slipped his arm around her waist. "Those practices are intense."

"Still. We're trying our best. Well, Misha and I are trying our best." She glanced over at her sisters. "Charli and Kayleigh rarely ever hit a single ball."

"I'm height challenged," Kayleigh called over. "I refuse to be anyone's handicap."

"You could play the game on Hudson's shoulders," Janessa said. "That would make you tall enough."

Everyone, including Blake, chuckled at the suggestion, while Kayleigh said, "I'm not a *child*, Janessa. I don't need to ride on my fiancé's shoulders."

By this time, the kids had the ball and were tossing it back and forth over the net. It was the first time that he'd seen Amelia having so much fun. To see her blossoming like this validated yet again his decision to come to Serenity.

He glanced over at Charli, surprised to find her watching him. Back when they'd been together, catching her looking at him like that would have made his heart race. And it didn't leave him unaffected right then, either.

However, she didn't give him a small smile or a wink like she had in the past. Meeting her gaze now brought an ache to his heart.

After a moment, Charli blinked and looked away from him to the kids. He happened to glance in Kayleigh's direction and was a bit surprised to find her gaze on him, too. She watched him with an intensity that made Blake wish he could read her mind.

Had Charli told any of her sisters about their relationship?

From what he remembered, Charli hadn't been close to Kayleigh, but perhaps that had changed over the years.

"Anyone want dessert?" Misha asked as she gestured to the table. "I think we've got a bunch of cookies and brownies, so plenty for everyone."

Hudson walked over to Kayleigh and bent to kiss her. "Do you want something?"

"A brownie, please."

"Your wish is my command," Hudson said as he rubbed the back of his fingers against Kayleigh's cheek, then headed for the picnic table.

"Finally, someone who lets you boss them around without complaining," Charli said with a laugh.

"That's because he's nicer than you guys. Love makes us servants to each other."

"It's a joy to do things for Kayleigh," Hudson said as he returned with a brownie in hand. "And she does plenty for me. Coming home from a trip to find she's made me my favorite meal is a true joy."

The love the couple shared was hard to miss, and it left Blake with an ache for what he'd missed out on. Blake wondered if he even had the ability to be part of a successful relationship. So far, he hadn't managed it.

Would he have been able to have one with Charli if he'd returned to Serenity instead of running off in another direction when things hadn't worked out exactly as he'd wanted?

Blake realized in that moment that he wanted a second chance.

The love he'd thought long gone was still there, buried deep beneath years of pain and regret. But being back in Serenity and seeing Charli again had caused his feelings to surface, demanding his attention and making sure he couldn't just ignore them any longer.

Unfortunately, he wasn't the only one to be considered in this situation. From what he'd seen so far, Charli most definitely wouldn't be on board with what he wanted.

She wasn't interested in spending time with him. She wasn't even willing to have a conversation with him. And he couldn't even blame her for feeling that way.

"Can I have a cookie, Daddy?" Amelia asked as she ran over from the volleyball court.

"Sure thing."

"Do you want me to get one for you, too?"

"That would be great."

She flashed him a smile, then dashed off to the table, joining Layla and Peyton, who were looking over the dessert selection. Misha was there to help them out, and soon Amelia headed back with two cookies in hand.

"Chocolate chip or peanut butter chocolate chip?" Amelia asked as she held them both out to him.

"You pick which one you want, and I'll eat the other one."

She stared at them for a moment before offering him the chocolate chip cookie. "I want to try the peanut butter one."

"Let me know if you like it."

After taking a bite, she grinned. "It's yummy!"

"My mom made those." Layla plopped down on the blanket next to Amelia. "I like them because they taste like Reese's Pieces."

Amelia nodded. "They do."

Blake watched as the two girls chatted about cookies, wondering again where Layla's father was. If things had been different, she might have been his daughter.

But they'd only been together once, and Charli had been on birth control. It hurt a bit to realize that she had moved on so quickly after he'd left. However, he couldn't hold it against her be-cause it was his choice to walk away.

Still, it hurt.

"I wish you were in my class," Amelia said.

"Since my mom's your teacher, I couldn't be in your class even if we were in the same grade. They don't let her teach me."

"She wasn't your teacher?"

"Nope. I had to be in the other class for that grade."

"I like her as my teacher."

Layla smiled. "Everyone does."

Blake was glad to hear Amelia tell Layla that. She'd told him that she liked Charli, but hearing her tell others that made him happy. Now, if she could just make some friends in her own grade.

"Anyone up for another game?" Jay asked as he got to his feet.

Blake stood up and walked across the grass to join Jay and the other men at the volleyball net. He wasn't ready for the afternoon to end just yet, and he was quite sure that Amelia agreed.

"Come play, Charli," Janessa yelled.

Charli didn't move from her seat. "I think not."

"You don't even have watching Ciara as an excuse this after-noon, since Denise is keeping an eye on her," Jay said.

"I don't need an excuse," Charli told him, completely unphased by her siblings' ribbing.

"Just get on with it," Kayleigh told them. "You're not going to be able to convince either of us to play."

"One of these days..." Jay said as he caught the ball Peyton tossed him. "Let's play."

Blake was on Jay's team that time, along with Misha, and they were a bit more aggressive in their playing. Jackson, Will, Hudson, and Janessa were on the other team. It was a fun game, and when victory was theirs, Blake high-fived Jay and Misha.

That seemed to be the last game, since after chatting for a bit, Hudson and Kayleigh said goodbye and headed off for a walk.

Jackson, Janessa, and Will also said goodbye before they piled into their cars and left.

Misha and Jay were a little slower as they gathered up their stuff, and Blake picked up the two lawn chairs and freezer bag, carrying them over to Charli's car. The girls were still playing with the hula hoops, though Jay had told Peyton to get in the car.

"See you guys around," Jay called out once they were ready to go. He and Misha got into the vehicle, then they pulled away from the curb.

Charli opened the hatch of her car so he could put the things inside. Once his hands were free, he shoved them into the pockets of his jeans.

"It's been good seeing you again," he said, needing to see if there was some way they could get past the awkwardness.

The look Charli gave him went from incredulous to angry. "How is that possible?"

"What?"

"How is it possible that it's good to see me again?" she demanded, her dark eyes flashing. "You couldn't wait to see the last of me twelve years ago."

"That's not how I felt back then." Blake knew he deserved her anger, but he was just hoping that they could at least talk about the situation.

"You seemed more than happy to end things," she reminded him, her voice sharp with anger. "And you did it by text, without any explanation. Not to mention that you also changed your number. How was I supposed to think that you weren't happy to just walk away?"

"I felt like I had no choice," Blake said. "Things changed when I got back to California."

"And I didn't deserve a conversation about that? I didn't deserve an explanation?"

Blake's heart ached at the hurt that edged the anger of her words. "You did. You absolutely did. I was just..." He lowered his gaze to the ground. "Scared. And I guess I was upset that I couldn't do what I promised I'd do for you... for us."

"Why couldn't you? What happened?"

Now that she was giving him this opportunity, Blake felt a little sick at the idea of revealing why he'd made such bad decisions. "When I got home, I told my dad I didn't want to work for the furniture company. That I wanted to become a mechanic and open my own garage one day. He was livid and said he'd never support that. That meant he wouldn't give me the money for any training I might need, and on top of all that, he stopped my monthly allowance."

"So why didn't you just come back to Serenity?" Charli said. "We could have made it work, even without your dad's help."

Looking back now, he could see that there might have been other paths. Even back then, he had tried to look for options. However, he'd quickly realized that the training he needed would cost him money he didn't have. He'd also had no income to tide him over.

Every promise he'd made to Charli had felt like a crushing weight, and he hadn't known how to achieve his own dreams, let alone help her reach hers. Which meant he might stand in the way of her being able to accomplish what she wanted in life. It felt like he'd be disappointing Charli before they'd even managed to take their relationship public.

"I didn't feel like that was possible."

Blake ran a hand through his hair. It was so hard to find the words to explain his mindset back then. Twelve years of maturity gave him a completely different outlook on the situation.

"I would do things differently now." He met her gaze. "But back then, I had a real sense of hopelessness. Joining the army gave me the opportunity to support myself and to get the training I needed without me having to pay for it."

"The only cost was our relationship and the dreams we had," Charli said bitterly.

"I'm sorry, Charli," Blake told her, relieved to finally be able to say those words to her. "I'm sorry for hurting you the way I did. I was wrong, and I made some horrible decisions."

She stared at him, emotion brimming in her eyes. Silence stretched between them, and Blake realized the acceptance of his apology that he wanted might not be coming.

He cleared his throat. "That's all I wanted to say. I won't bother you about this again."

Turning, he looked for the girls and found them still playing around with the hula hoops. After a last glance at Charli, Blake walked across the grass toward them.

"We need to leave, Amelia," Blake said, trying to keep his voice gentle and free of the emotion he was feeling.

"Okay." Amelia handed the hoop she was using to Layla. "Thank you for letting me play with your hula hoops."

Layla gave her a quick smile. "You can play with them anytime." The girl slid the hoops over her shoulder. "I had fun today."

The pair headed across the grass to where the vehicles were parked. Blake trailed behind them, watching as Charli took the hoops from Layla and put them in the car. She opened the back door, then smiled at Amelia.

"I'll see you tomorrow," Charli said to her without looking at Blake.

Amelia nodded, then turned to Blake. He took her hand as they walked to the truck, struggling to keep his emotions under control.

The relief he'd felt at being able to apologize to Charli had evaporated. He hadn't realized how much he'd wanted her forgiveness for what he'd done. And now that she'd denied him that, he was struggling to know how to feel.

Frustration and anger wanted to win out, but Blake knew that those emotions weren't fair unless they were directed at himself. Unfortunately, some of his frustration *was* aimed at Charli.

He'd hoped that she would be able to understand that he'd been young and stupid and had made a bad decision. Since it didn't seem that she understood or accepted that explanation, Blake didn't know what else to tell her.

She'd been so focused on the future back then. So determined to make everything she wanted come true. It was like she didn't have a moment's doubt that what she wanted would become a reality.

Her confidence had been infectious, making him feel like he could achieve his dreams as well. Only, at the first sign of trouble, he'd run in the opposite direction, upset by the lack of support from his parents and scared of returning to Serenity and failing Charli.

He'd been naïve and selfish.

Blake liked to think he'd grown and matured to become a man who wouldn't be as easily swayed by his emotions and fears. If presented with the same scenario with Charli now, he'd definitely deal with it differently.

However, Charli didn't care about those changes in him, and she didn't need that from him now. Amelia, on the other hand, absolutely did.

"Did you have fun, Daddy?" Amelia asked from the back seat.

He glanced into the mirror and nodded. "I enjoyed playing volleyball."

"That's good. I had fun too."

Her gaze went out the window, a small smile on her face. He might not have gotten what he wanted for himself that day, but seeing Amelia happy was a very good thing.

Back at the apartment, they still had enough time to watch a movie. It was Amelia's favorite princess movie, so she was distracted by it, but Blake was not.

His thoughts were still on the afternoon at the park and the conversation with Charli. He replayed everything he'd said, wondering if he could have phrased things differently. If there was anything more he could have shared with her, that might have changed her reaction.

Maybe he just needed to give her time.

Obviously, he'd known the details of why he'd broken up with her for years. This was all news to Charli, and it was likely that no matter what he'd said, she'd still need time to let his explanation sink in.

But Blake knew that he had to be prepared for the possibility that she would never accept his apology. She might never forgive him for what he'd done.

Would he be able to live with that?

But it wouldn't matter if he could live with it or not, he would have no choice. With his decision to end things the way he had, he'd forced his will on Charli once already. He couldn't force her to accept his apology and move on from their painful past.

And he needed to make peace with that.

CHAPTER ELEVEN

"I'm not sure how to dissuade Blake from accepting the invitations that your brothers keep extending to him," Jackson muttered. "Not without raising some questions about why I don't want him joining."

Charli hadn't known why Jackson was calling her, but as she listened to his explanation, she appreciated his concern. "Yeah. I haven't been able to figure that out either. Especially because Layla enjoys spending time with Amelia."

"Isn't that a bit... weird?" Jackson asked.

"A bit," Charli admitted. "But I can't exactly forbid Layla from being friends with Amelia. If I did that, everyone would definitely be questioning why."

"Yeah." Jackson sighed. "Anyway, I just wanted you to know that he'll probably be there tonight with Amelia."

"I suspected as much," Charli said. "But thanks for the head's up."

"Yep. See you later, because I'll be there too."

Charli said goodbye, then tossed her phone onto the bed. With a sigh, she went to her closet to swap the black slacks and green blouse she'd worn to school for a pair of jeans and a long-sleeved T-shirt.

She emptied her school bag onto her desk, then picked up her phone again. As she left the bedroom, she met Layla coming out of hers.

"How long until Peyton gets here?"

"About an hour, most likely."

"Will we be able to watch a movie?"

"Probably. We'll have to see what his parents say about the options."

"Okay." Layla went into the kitchen ahead of her. "Did Grandma Dee make more cookies?"

"I think so. She usually does," Charli said, smiling at Layla's name for Denise.

Layla may have missed out on knowing Blake's parents, but she didn't lack for grandparental figures in her life. *Positive* grandparental figures. It didn't sound like Blake's parents would have been that, even if they'd known about Layla.

Climbing up on a stool, Layla pulled the cookie container toward her on the counter. She cracked the lid open, then grinned. "Yep. Lots of cookies."

For a moment, Charli saw a resemblance to Blake in Layla's grin. There had been plenty of times when he'd smiled at her like that, but the memory of his smile had faded over time. Because of that, she hadn't registered that resemblance until recently, thanks to his return.

"Is Amelia coming too?" Layla asked as she settled back on the stool.

"I think so." Charli began to pull out the things they used when they had the large group there for pizza.

"That's good. I think she likes me and Peyton."

"You don't mind that she's younger than you? Younger even than Peyton."

Layla shrugged. "She doesn't act like a baby."

"And she does what you say," Charli said. "You like to boss her around."

That got a laugh out of Layla. "Maybe a bit. But I don't *force* her to do anything. I'm not mean."

"No. You're not."

"Want me to cut lettuce for the salad?" Layla asked, apparently done with the subject of her bossiness.

Since it was the task Layla usually took on for the pizza nights, Charli nodded. While Layla got the salad fixings from the fridge, Charli set out the plates, cups, napkins, and plasticware. They were just finishing up the salad when Will and Janessa arrived home.

Charli had been very glad when the couple had made the decision to continue to live in the large house, even after they were married. It wasn't going to be a long-term thing, but at least it delayed the emptiness of the house for a bit longer.

After a quick hello, the pair headed upstairs to change. Charli set Layla to making some juice, while she tried to prepare herself for Blake's arrival.

The week had gone well for Amelia. She appeared to have made a couple of friends, both of whom had been in her Sunday school class.

Because of that, there had been no need for Charli to contact Blake. Which meant that the last conversation they'd had, had been one of anger. Well, anger on her part.

She'd spent a lot of time over the past week—usually late at night, as she struggled to fall asleep—thinking about what Blake had said before they'd parted ways the previous Sunday.

In the months following his disappearance from her life, she had dreamed of a moment like that. Of having him explain what had happened and apologizing.

And asking for a second chance.

She hadn't wanted any of that during their conversation, and his explanation hadn't given her any sense of peace. It had just made her angry, which was a completely different reaction than she'd imagined she'd have.

However, the more she thought about it, the more sense her anger made. If he'd really been sorry about what he'd done, he would have tried to reach out to her sooner to explain and apologize.

Instead, he hadn't attempted that until he returned to Serenity... without even giving her a head's up. He'd crashed into her life again, helped along by her brothers' welcoming gestures. And then, he'd wanted to explain away the horrible wound he'd inflicted on her heart when he'd just walked away from her without a second thought. Like she'd never meant anything to him.

Because she wanted to believe that if he'd really loved her, he would have thought twice about leaving her behind. And he'd have realized that he loved her enough to come back and fight for the future they'd been planning.

But now, she really wished that he'd had the decency to stay out of her life. To refuse invitations when he knew she'd be there. Like pizza night at *her house*.

Charli heard the front door open, then Peyton ran into the kitchen, a big smile on his face.

"Hey, Aunt Charli. Hey, Layla."

"Hi, sweetie." Charli gave him a hug, then he went to climb up on a stool beside Layla.

Not long after, Jay and Misha appeared with Ciara and the pizza, which smelled deliciously spicy and greasy. When Misha set Ciara down, she made a beeline for Charli. Smiling, Charli scooped her up.

"Hey, baby girl," Charli said. "How're you?"

"Good!"

Ciara had started talking several months ago, and her vocabulary was astounding. She could talk in sentence lengths that Charli wouldn't have expected from someone under three.

"Are you ready for pizza?"

"Yep. And cookies."

"You're in luck," Charli said. "Grandma made cookies today."

She held up three fingers. "I want four cookies."

"That's three, Ci," Peyton said as he came over to them. He gently took her hand and lifted one more finger. "Now it's four."

Careful to keep her four fingers in place, she held them up in front of Charli's face. "I want four cookies."

"You'll have to ask your mom and dad, sweetie," Charli said.

Ciara wiggled, so Charli put her down. She ran over to Jay, where he stood next to where he'd put the stack of pizza boxes on the counter. Holding up her hand, she said, "Four cookies, Daddy. Please."

"We'll see, baby," he said as he picked her up. "You have to eat supper first."

She nodded. "Then cookies."

"Are Kayleigh and Hudson coming?" Charli asked.

"Not tonight," Jay said. "But Gareth thought Aria would be ready to get out of the house for a bit."

Their baby boy, Timothy, had been born earlier that year, and his arrival had been a bit of an adjustment for his parents. But now that he was sleeping through the night, they all seemed to be doing better.

Aria had gone back to work part-time recently, and Charli's mom was watching Timothy during the hours Aria was at the office. If she wasn't available, Denise stepped in to help them out.

Charli heard the door open again, smiling when Aria came in, followed by Gareth carrying a car seat. After Gareth set the car seat on the floor, Charli knelt in front of it to free Timothy from his straps.

When the doorbell rang, Jay said he'd get it, so Charli didn't have to abandon her task. As she lifted Timothy up, Charli got to her feet, just as Jay returned with Amelia, Blake, and Jackson.

Amelia had changed since school, but once again wore a T-shirt with a unicorn on the front. Blake had on a pair of faded jeans and a dark green T-shirt. Like his daughter, he had a style that he definitely favored. It suited his physique, though Charli didn't want to dwell on that.

Dragging her attention from Blake, she said hi to Amelia, then introduced her to Timothy. Amelia was very interested in the baby, and she smiled when he grasped the finger she held out to him.

The little girl stayed close to Charli as Gareth prayed, then she joined Layla and Peyton to get some pizza. Charli bounced Timothy on her hip as she waited while the others got their food. She had two highchairs permanently in the dining room now. One for Ciara and the other for Timothy.

Once Aria had taken her food to the dining room table, she came back and took Timothy so Charli could get her food. "He sure loves you. Lately, he's been fussy when anyone but me, Gareth, or your mom tries to hold him."

"Well, the feeling is mutual," Charli assured her. "I love him too."

Aria gave her a hug, then headed back to the table. Charli picked up a plate and put a couple of slices of her favorite pizza on it before adding some salad and dressing. Since she was in no rush to join the others at the table, she took her time, straightening up a little in the kitchen before starting the coffee maker.

Finally, she took her plate into the dining room, glad to see that there was an empty seat next to Aria, though it was across from Blake, which made it a little less appealing.

Still, as she sat down, she couldn't help but glance over at him.

Blake was watching her, and for a moment, Charli couldn't look away. This was how it had been before. Stolen glances whenever they'd been around people they'd needed to hide their relationship from.

Back then, glances like that would have made her heart race. Now, however, they made her chest ache. And unfortunately, her heart still raced.

Charli looked away from Blake and took a deep breath before picking up a piece of her pizza. The conversation they'd had a few days earlier hadn't helped to ease the awkwardness between them. In fact, on her side, it had probably made things worse.

"How's work been going for you, Blake?" Gareth asked.

"Really well. I'm fortunate that Stan had an opening for me."

"You're working at a place that has a great reputation, so the garage is always busy. I imagine Stan knew a good thing when he saw it," Jay said. "We all take our vehicles there."

"So the other garage isn't as good?" Blake asked. "I had planned to apply there if Wilsons hadn't offered me a job."

"It seems to be hit or miss," Jay said.

"For me, the worst part is that the guys who work there can be... creepy around females," Janessa added with a grimace. "Stan would never let a guy like that work for him."

"Yeah. All the guys at Wilsons seem to be pretty decent," Blake said.

This could have been their life. Each of them working at a job they loved. A couple of kids. Maybe more.

Charli picked up her glass to take a drink, hoping she'd be able to swallow past the tightness in her throat.

Why did she keep thinking about what might have been? It had been ages since she'd been so caught up in that mindset.

She hadn't spent the past twelve years pining after Blake. Or rather, she hadn't spent the past *ten* years pining after him.

The first two years after his abrupt departure had been rough, and she definitely would have taken him back if he'd shown up during that time. Once it became obvious that he wasn't coming back, she knew she had no choice but to let her love for him go and move on.

So she had.

But now that he'd come back a more mature version of himself, she was having a hard time not thinking about all the *what-ifs*. And she hated herself for that weakness.

In between bites of her pizza, it took all of Charli's attention to make sure that her focus seemed natural. That she didn't completely ignore Blake, but that when she did look at him, she didn't stare like she wanted to. It was hard, but she hoped that she had pulled it off.

However, it quickly became clear that she hadn't succeeded when Janessa cornered her in the kitchen once everyone had gone home.

"*What* is going on between you and Blake?" she demanded.

Charli sealed the bag containing some leftover pizza as she said, "What do you mean?"

She definitely needed clarification before she responded.

"He couldn't stop looking at you, and you seemed to be trying very hard not to look at him."

At first, Charli was frustrated that her sister knew her so well. However, then her mind latched on to what Janessa had said first. Blake hadn't been able to stop looking at her? Warmth rushed through her, and her heart thudded in her chest.

"So? Spill it," Janessa demanded. "What's going on? Is there something between the two of you?"

"Not now," Charli said as she opened the fridge to put the leftover pizza inside. "But when he was here before, I had a bit of a crush on him."

"Really? Did he know?"

She hesitated a moment before nodding. "But nothing came of it because he left and joined the army."

"Wow. Why didn't you say something about it back then?"

Charli walked over to the sink and grabbed a cloth to wet it under the water. "It didn't seem significant."

Looking back now, in the light of all that had transpired, her feelings for Blake really didn't seem significant. She was so glad she hadn't told anyone about her love for him, given how everything had ended.

Janessa pulled herself up to sit on the counter. "And now?"

"Now what?" Charli glanced at her. "Are you asking me if I have a crush on a man I haven't seen in over twelve years?"

Giving a shrug, Janessa said, "Maybe?"

"That's a bit ridiculous," Charli told her.

"Well, to my knowledge, you've never dated anyone seriously, so maybe you're hung up on him."

Charli wiped down the sink, then rinsed the cloth out and hung it over the tap. "You don't know everything about my dating life."

"That's an understatement," Janessa scoffed. "I mean, we *still* don't know who Layla's dad is."

Given that she still didn't plan to clue her in, Charli turned to face her, leaning back against the counter, crossing her arms but not saying anything.

Janessa leaned forward, her dark brown eyes going wide. "Is *Blake* her father?"

Layla had gone to her room to read, but thankfully, Janessa kept her voice down. Charli's heart began to race a bit, though not as bad as when she caught Blake staring at Layla. But still...

"Do I strike you as someone who would sleep with a guy I had a *crush* on?"

She hoped that Janessa didn't wise up to the fact that she hadn't exactly answered her question. Or that she'd answered her question with a question.

The truth was that she absolutely wouldn't have slept with Blake if she'd just had a crush on him. The other truth was that she shouldn't have slept with Blake, even with how determined they'd been to build a future together. But it was hard to regret what they'd done because she had Layla, and she wouldn't give her up for anything.

So she'd asked God for forgiveness for what she'd done, then thanked Him for blessing her with Layla. It had still been a long process to get to the place where she was free of the guilt that had filled her during the months of her pregnancy.

"I suppose not," Janessa conceded, leaning back on her hands. "But I really don't understand why you don't just tell us who he is."

"It's irrelevant." Charli had been over this plenty of times, but of all her siblings, Janessa was the one who still periodically ask about Layla's dad. "He chose to walk out my life, so everyone knowing who he is won't matter."

"Will you ever tell Layla?"

It was a question she'd thought a lot about, and until Blake had shown back up in their lives, she'd had a pretty set answer. "Since she's really the only one entitled to know that information, I'll tell her when she needs to know."

"And her father?" Janessa prompted. "Does he deserve to know?"

"Not at the moment. I tried to let him know when I got pregnant, but he'd disappeared."

"You are crazy if you think this isn't all going to come around and bite you at some point in the future."

In the past, Charli would have brushed that statement off. However, this time, she could see that it was entirely possible.

Both the situation with Layla being his child and her previous relationship with Blake were confusing her.

In the past, she'd felt like he didn't deserve to know. He'd left her without a backward glance, and when she'd asked him to explain what was going on, to have a conversation about everything, he'd ignored her.

What if she told Blake about Layla, and then, at some point in the future, Blake decided to leave Serenity again? He'd take Amelia, of course. But if he knew about Layla, would he want to take her too? Would he want to share custody with her?

Charli didn't think she could handle that. She didn't want to share custody with *anyone*. Even Layla's father.

Was it a control issue? Probably. But she wasn't convinced that anyone but her would know what was best for Layla.

"Well, it's possible that Blake is interested in you now," Janessa said. "Perhaps your crush might develop into something more."

Charli rolled her eyes. "My crush has been long over."

"So you two are going to be a weird version of star-crossed lovers?"

"What?"

"You loved him back then, but he couldn't stay. Now he's back and has feelings for you, but your love for him has died."

"A crush isn't love."

"True. But it can turn into love."

"What are we talking about?" Will asked as he walked into the kitchen. "Love?"

Janessa grinned at him as he came to stand next to her at the counter. "Yep. Charli has a crush on Blake."

Will's brows rose, making Charli scowl at her sister. "*Had.* I *had* a crush on Blake. Like many, many years ago."

"Oh, dear," Will said. "Janessa isn't going to let up on that."

"Tell me about it," Charli groused. "You can entertain her now, Will. I'm going to my room."

With that, she left the two of them, rolling her eyes as Janessa's laughter followed her out of the kitchen.

Charli poked her head into Layla's room. Unsurprisingly, her daughter was once again curled up on her beanbag, her nose buried in a book. She'd changed into a pair of pajamas and looked very cozy under a fluffy blanket.

Layla looked up and smiled at her. "Can I have popcorn, Mom?"

Though Charli didn't want to have to go back to the kitchen, she nodded. "Do you want milk or apple juice?"

"Milk."

"Okay. I'll be back in a few."

She went to change into her favorite loungewear first, hoping by the time she went to make the popcorn, Will and Janessa would have gone upstairs.

Thankfully, when she stepped into the kitchen a short time later, it was empty.

While the bag of popcorn was in the microwave, Charli poured Layla some milk into a cup with a lid and straw. She also grabbed a can of diet soda for herself.

Once the popcorn was done, she dumped it into two bowls, then carried everything back to Layla's room. She got her settled with the snack before heading to her own bedroom.

Charli set her popcorn and drink on the table next to her chair, then settled into it, drawing the blanket she kept there over her legs. She picked up her tablet to read, wanting to be lost in a world that wasn't her own. But instead, she just stared at its dark screen.

She had no idea if Janessa was right about Blake's interest in her, but even just the thought of it had her stomach in knots. There was a far bigger part of her than she was comfortable with that was excited at the idea of Blake wanting to be with her again.

Even though she hadn't dated anyone seriously since breaking up with Blake, it hadn't been because she was pining for him or worried that another man might hurt her like he had. It had just been her resolving to be more careful about relationships after feeling like she'd misjudged things with Blake.

Also, she'd been focused on her career and being a single mom. And to top it all off, she just hadn't met a man she'd felt was worth exposing Layla to.

But now, she wasn't sure any of that was the whole truth. All it had taken was Blake's reappearance in her life for her to question all of it.

The biggest question, however, was what she'd do if Blake was, in fact, interested in her and in rekindling what they'd once had. It was a complicated question that she wasn't sure she had any sort of answer to.

Unfortunately, it felt like it was important enough that she had to give it some thought and consideration. If for no other reason than she didn't want to be caught off-guard, should what Janessa suspected be true.

CHAPTER TWELVE

Blake had a hard time believing that he and Amelia had been back in Serenity for almost two months. They were in the middle of October, and fall was in full swing in the area. It was a beautiful time of year, though he wasn't sure if he was ready for winter to arrive.

"Are we going to pizza night?" Amelia asked from the back seat of the truck.

He glanced into the mirror to find her watching him with an eager expression. Honestly, he'd been thinking of skipping it, mainly because he was pretty sure that Charli would prefer he not be there.

It wasn't his desire to make her uncomfortable, but it was hard to know how Charli truly felt about the situation. She hadn't said she didn't want him around, but she also kept her distance from him.

There hadn't been a pizza night every Friday since that first one, though he—and he was sure Amelia—would have loved it if there had been. Charli, however, was probably relieved that they hadn't been around more.

He'd hoped that Charli would come around to acknowledging his presence in her life, and maybe even accept his apology. But neither of those things had happened, and he had finally accepted that they probably wouldn't.

If he'd just been meeting her, he might have asked her out on a date. Just like when they'd met the first time thirteen years ago, there was something about her that drew him in. They'd had a year together, and that draw hadn't lessened over that time.

"Do you want to go?" he asked.

It was a dumb question. He already knew the answer.

"Yep. Peyton said he'd be there, and, of course, Layla lives there. She's got a really cool room."

"Better than your room?"

"No, I like my room."

He was glad to hear that, as he'd made sure she liked everything they'd bought for her. It was the one room in their apartment that actually had some personality and wasn't just set up with practicality and comfort in mind.

For the first time in his life, he was making a home for someone. He'd never focused much on that in the places he'd lived in over the years. All he'd cared about was a comfortable bed, a comfortable chair in the living room, and a large screen TV. A strictly practical approach, but it had been good enough for him.

That was still true about the majority of their apartment in Serenity. His mom would have a heart attack if she saw it.

Because the family business was designing and selling furniture, their family home had always been a showcase. Even as a teen, his room had been immaculately decorated with nothing that reflected his own personality. There had definitely been no posters of his favorite cars on the wall.

When he'd come to visit Serenity, he'd been jealous of Jackson because his room truly reflected who he was. The only thing his aunt had asked was that Jackson keep it relatively clean.

Everything had been so much more relaxed at Jackson's family's home. And that was the environment Blake wanted to provide for Amelia. Which was why he'd let her have a say in everything they'd purchased for her room. The only thing he'd decided on was the mattress for her bed.

Another of his goals since coming to Serenity had been to provide Amelia with opportunities to be around people who would treat her with care. And he knew without a doubt that was the case whenever they were with the Halversons. So they'd go, and he'd hope that his decision wouldn't give Charli more reason to hate him.

"I guess we'll go."

"Yay!" Amelia cheered. "Peyton said that there's a basketball game tonight. Can we go to that, too?"

Jay had also mentioned the game to him. When he'd first talked about it, Blake hadn't been sure about going. But then the man had revealed that he was the coach for the Serenity high school team, so supporting him seemed to be a good reason to go.

Though Jackson was closest to Gareth, Jay and Will had been the two—aside from Jackson—that Blake had interacted with the most. He was grateful for their friendship, and they definitely had helped him feel more connected to his new hometown. And he knew Amelia felt the same way about Layla and Peyton.

"I think we can go to the game," Blake said. "At least this time."

After they got home, Blake got her a snack of strawberries, then went to shower and change. He'd told her to change once she finished her berries, leaving her outfit choice up to her. She didn't have a ton of clothes, but she had her favorites that she tended to wear frequently.

He didn't have a lot of clothes either, and what he did have consisted mainly of jeans and T-shirts, though he'd needed to buy them both a couple of sweatshirts recently since the weather had turned cool. The evening temperatures had started to dip into the *jackets are necessary* zone.

There was no rush to head out because he didn't want to be the first person to arrive at Charli's. If they were on better terms, he definitely would have shown up as soon as he could. Since they weren't, he usually waited until he was sure at least a couple of other people had arrived before them.

After Amelia was dressed in warm enough clothes, Blake redid her ponytail, since it had gotten messy during her day at school.

"Can we go now?" she asked when he was done.

"In a few minutes," he told her. "Do you have homework this weekend?"

She brought her backpack over to the table and together they went through it. He set her lunch box on the counter to clean out when they got home from the game, then looked through her folder. Charli had sent home a new reader, along with a laminated bookmark that she'd use to mark off what stories Amelia completed.

He was very glad that Amelia enjoyed reading, and she picked up new words quickly. He wasn't as much of a reader, so it was good she hadn't taken after him.

Charli had proven to be a great teacher for Amelia. Amelia hadn't been all that excited about school the previous year, but she was definitely enjoying school in Serenity. She'd gotten to where she happily shared what was going on in her class, and she never complained about doing the little bits of homework Charli gave her.

"Go ahead and get your shoes and jacket on," Blake said once the backpack was empty.

"Yay!" Amelia ran to the closet by the front door to do as he asked.

Blake couldn't believe the changes the past several weeks had brought about in Amelia. Her excitement for things made him smile, simply because she'd never shown much excitement about anything before.

It was like she'd finally realized that she was allowed to be excited. To be happy.

So far, since coming to Serenity, the only thing that concerned him a bit was that she very rarely spoke about her mom.

Not that she'd talked a lot about Lauren even before coming to Serenity. She'd definitely internalized whatever she thought or felt about her mom. It was unfortunate that most memories she had of Lauren were likely of her struggles with addictions.

As they left the apartment building, Amelia skipped beside him and happily scrambled up into the back seat of the truck. Blake watched her as she buckled herself in, then shut the door.

The drive to Charli's didn't take long, and soon, he was pulling to a stop behind Jay's SUV. Amelia was out of her seat and standing on the sidewalk by the time Blake got out and rounded the hood of the truck.

"Can I ring the doorbell?" Amelia asked as they climbed the stairs.

"Go for it," he told her.

Not long after she did, the door swung open to reveal Will. The man greeted them with a smile, then held his hand up for a high five from Amelia.

Blake appreciated that the adults in this group didn't just dismiss Amelia. Each of them had been caring to her during their time together.

"Are you ready to eat fast tonight?" Will asked as they followed him through the foyer. "We've got a game to go to. Are you coming?"

"That's the plan," Blake said.

As they stepped into the kitchen, Blake's heart gave a thump in his chest at his first glimpse of Charli. It happened every time he saw her.

Over the past few weeks, he'd gotten used to the reaction... and even welcomed it.

Unfortunately, he was pretty sure that Charli didn't feel the same way when she saw him. And he didn't blame her for that.

The kids greeted each other enthusiastically, reminding Blake of why he'd braved Charli's displeasure.

The connections Amelia was making with Layla and Peyton were so important. She had a couple of friends at school now, who were also in her Sunday school class. However, even after two months, Layla and Peyton remained the most important to Amelia, likely because they were the first to have reached out to her.

"Let's pray so we can get to eating," Jay said. "I'm going to have to leave pretty soon here."

Once he'd prayed, they let Jay go first, then the kids filled their plates. As usual, Charli waited for everyone else to get their food, though Blake had no idea why she did that.

Eventually, she settled into a seat across the table and down a seat from him. She was wearing a burgundy-colored T-shirt, similar to the ones the others were wearing. It had the high school logo on it, so he assumed they were all going to the game as well.

"How was school this week, Charli?" Misha asked.

"It was fine. Nothing too exciting."

"Really? I can't believe that a room full of young kids isn't exciting."

Charli chuckled. "Well, I guess that depends on your idea of exciting."

"Zachary threw up today," Amelia volunteered.

"Was that exciting?" Misha asked her with a smile.

"Nope. Just gross."

"I agree with Amelia," Charli said. "It was definitely gross. More up your alley than mine, Misha."

Blake waited for someone to comment on how that wasn't appropriate conversation for the table—his mom *definitely* would have said something. But then he realized that since they were a medically oriented family, Amelia's comment probably wasn't as off-putting as his mom would have found it.

He didn't necessarily enjoy discussing kids throwing up, but he sure did like the relaxed atmosphere. It was reminiscent of hanging with his buddies in the army.

Though he missed his friends, most hadn't understood his decision to walk away from his career in the army for Amelia's sake.

That meant he hadn't had a lot of contact with them since leaving Texas.

So finding some friends who offered him and Amelia a similar environment was hard to resist. And if it allowed him to be close to Charli, that was just gravy.

"Okay, folks," Jay said as he pushed back from the table. "I'm off. See you in a bit. Cheer loudly."

He bent to give Misha a kiss, then did the same to their kids before leaving the dining room.

"What type of team are we playing tonight, Will?" Jackson asked.

"A pretty decent one. But Jay's guys still have a good chance."

"As good as when Cole was on the team?" Janessa asked.

Will grimaced. "Well, no. I'm not sure the team will ever be that good again. Cole and the other guys on that team were just a stellar combination."

"I guess it doesn't really matter," Jackson said. "We're going to cheer them on, regardless."

"I'll be bringing cookies to the game," Charli announced. "So don't worry about not having dessert here."

They didn't linger over their meal, and when they were done eating, everyone pitched in to clear the table. Blake gathered up his and Amelia's disposable dishes and carried them into the kitchen.

"You can put those in the garbage can under the sink," Charli said when he stepped around the island. "Thank you."

"Thank *you* for letting us join you for these evenings."

It was probably iffy to thank her for that, given that she hadn't invited them herself.

Charli nodded, her expression revealing nothing of how she might really feel about his presence.

"Do you know where the high school is, Blake?" Will asked.

"No. I haven't been there yet."

Will pulled out his phone. "I'll send you the address so you can put it into your GPS, but it's not too difficult to find."

When the text arrived, Blake checked the message and copied the address into his map app, then studied the route. It didn't appear to be too far from the elementary school, so he had a good idea of how to get there.

"I'm going to swing by and leave Ciara with my mom," Misha said. "So I'll see you all there."

After Peyton followed his mom out, the rest of them got ready to leave. Charli bumped into Blake as she turned from the closet where she'd pulled her jacket out. They exchanged a glance as he stepped back to give her more room.

Dragging his attention from Charli, Blake checked to make sure that Amelia was ready. As he shrugged into his jacket, he looked around at the others, meeting Janessa's curious gaze. Blake waited for her to say something. However, Janessa just gave him a quick smile before turning her attention to Charli.

"Let's just go," Charli muttered as she finished buttoning her jacket.

Will chuckled as he opened the door, waiting as everyone paraded past him before stepping out onto the porch and pulling it closed. They each went to their own cars, then headed to the high school.

Blake had no trouble finding the place, mainly because he followed Will. But he was glad to have the address just in case he lost sight of him. The town wasn't huge, but it was large enough that Blake still didn't have all the street names and locations memorized.

After parking next to Will, he and Amelia joined him and Janessa to walk to the doors of the gym. When Layla ran up to them, they paused to wait for Charli to also join them.

"No frowny faces allowed at a basketball game, Charli," Janessa said as she poked her sister's cheek. "So turn that frown upside down."

Charli gave a huff and batted Janessa's hand away. "Then stop annoying me."

Blake reached out to open the door, then held it for the others. Charli glanced up as she walked past him. "Thanks."

How was it possible for a single word to make him so happy? It shouldn't be possible, but he couldn't deny that it did.

"You're welcome."

Janessa also smiled up at him. "You're a gentleman, just like my Will."

"I try." His mom had been insistent that he always be polite and respectful, especially around women.

Once everyone was through the doorway, Blake followed them down a wide hallway. Even before they reached the gym, he could hear the sound of shouts and multiple balls bouncing.

When they stepped into the gym, Blake was thrown back in time to his teen years. He hadn't played any indoor sport at that time—his dad had preferred he play football—but he'd attended plenty of basketball games in the gym of his private high school.

The sights, sounds, and even the smells took him back to those years. And it wasn't the worst memory. School hadn't been bad for him, even though his dad had a lot of expectations of him. Thankfully, he hadn't struggled scholastically, so his dad hadn't ragged on him too hard about his grades.

For the most part, he'd enjoyed those years, and Blake really didn't mind the memory of them. Of course, those memories were also closer to the time he'd spent with Charli, and he liked those memories as well.

He continued to follow the group as they walked in front of the bleachers until they reached a section where they climbed up the steps to the top. Layla led Amelia into the row in front of where Jackson, Will, Janessa, and Charli filed in and took seats.

Blake found himself on the end of the row, with Charli next to him. He purposefully kept some space between the two of them, guessing that she wouldn't appreciate him getting too close.

If their relationship had continued as it should have, they would have had lots of nights like that one. Sitting together at basketball games would have been commonplace.

Blake felt a pulse of pain in his heart at the realization of yet another loss.

"Daddy." Amelia stepped up on the bench in front of Blake, which brought her pretty much eye to eye with him. "Am I allowed to have a sleepover?"

Blake had a feeling he knew where this was going, and in order to preserve what little tolerance Charli had of him, he knew he needed to nip it in the bud. "Not yet, Berry. I think you're still a little too young."

He hated to disappoint her, but he did actually feel that she was a little young for a sleepover. And disappoint her, he did. Her expression saddened, as her shoulders slumped.

"How old do I have to be?" she asked, her eyes wide.

"I'm not sure. Maybe ten."

"That's so long."

"I know, Berry." He reached out and took her hands. "But I'd rather have you sleeping at home in your own bed. I would worry if you weren't there."

"You would?"

"Definitely," he said. "You're very important to me, and I want to be able to check on you at night."

She gave him a small smile, then leaned forward to wrap her arms around his neck. He returned her hug, holding her until she pulled back.

"Can I have blueberry pancakes tomorrow?" she asked. "With blueberry syrup?"

Blake chuckled. "Sure thing."

That got him a bigger smile before she returned to sit next to Layla. Soon enough, she wouldn't be so easily placated, so he'd take these wins whenever he could get them.

Though he wanted to turn to Charli and talk to her, Blake leaned forward and rested his elbows on his thighs as he watched the teams warm up. Jay stood tall behind a bench that was scattered with water bottles and warm-up jackets, arms crossed as he kept a close eye on his team, periodically calling out instructions and encouragement.

Thankfully, the game started not long after they sat down, which helped ease the temptation to speak to Charli. The noise level rose as the teams gathered at center court for the jump ball to start the game.

Though he didn't know anyone on the team aside from Jay, Blake cheered along with the rest of the people in the stands each time the team scored a basket. Even Amelia was getting into the game, though she seemed to look to Layla and Peyton for guidance on when she should cheer.

When half time arrived, Jay's team was trailing by four points. That didn't seem to put any kind of damper on the enthusiasm of the fans, however.

Once the teams had left the court, people in the stands began to get to their feet. Blake glanced over to see if any of the people he'd come with were getting up so that he could get out of their way if they wanted to exit the row.

Charli was digging through the bag she'd brought with her, while Janessa and Will were talking to someone sitting in front of them. Jackson stepped down a couple of rows, then walked over and back up to where Blake sat.

His cousin gave him a frown before focusing on Charli. "Did you say you were bringing cookies?"

"Yep." Charli pulled a container from her bag. "I brought a couple of different kinds."

Blake leaned back against the wall behind their row, trying to figure out what had Jackson frowning at him. He knew that his cousin hadn't been happy when Blake had revealed that he'd been involved with Charli the last time he'd been in Serenity. And Jackson had been less than impressed to keep running into him at places where Charli was also present.

But since Charli had made it clear that day at the park that she didn't want anything to do with him, he hadn't sought her out for another private conversation. Yes, they'd shown up at her church, at pizza nights and the park, and now at a basketball game, but he'd done it for Amelia.

Mainly for Amelia.

Blake looked away from Charli and Jackson to where Amelia sat with Layla and Peyton. He couldn't deny that he'd put Amelia's desires and needs above Charli's.

That revelation made his stomach knot a little. It wasn't his desire to cause Charli any additional pain through his presence.

But Amelia...

It was hard to regret his decision to spend time with the Halversons when he saw Amelia smiling and laughing, opening up more and more.

The Charli he'd known twelve years ago would have understood the importance of creating positive experiences for a child. He was sure that this Charli also understood that. She just might not like how it was impacting her.

A container of cookies appeared in his line of sight, dragging his gaze from the kids. "Did you want a cookie?"

He glanced at Charli to find her watching him as she held out the container. "Uh. Sure." Looking into the container, he picked out a cookie, then said, "Thanks."

When Charli offered cookies to the others, Jackson thumped Blake on the knee. "Why don't you come get some drinks with me?"

"Drinks?"

"Yeah. There's a canteen where they sell hot dogs, chips, and drinks."

"Alright."

"Text me if you want a drink," Jackson called out to the others.

Blake finished his cookie as he followed Jackson down the steps to the floor. He had a feeling Jackson was just wanting to get him away from Charli.

He followed his cousin willingly enough because he was curious, and hard as it was to accept, Charli probably wanted him away from her, too.

CHAPTER THIRTEEN

"Want a drink, Charli?" Janessa said. "I'm texting Jackson."

Charli put the lid on the container of cookies. "Sure. Diet Coke, please, and apple juice for Layla."

Staring out at the court, she watched the people taking advantage of a break in the game to stretch their legs.

There were many familiar faces there that evening, but she made no move to speak to anyone in her vicinity, choosing instead to sit there with a container of cookies on her lap. She didn't want to have to put on a happy face. Not when she was feeling confused and conflicted.

Her gaze fell on Kayleigh and Hudson as they walked up the stairs to where she sat. Hudson had a hand on Kayleigh's waist and bent down to say something to her as they neared Charli.

Jealousy surged through Charli once again, but it wasn't the only emotion she was dealing with. Sadness and longing had come along for the ride. As tears pricked her eyes, all she could think of was what a ride it had been.

Crying couldn't happen, so she looked away from her sister and Hudson, trying to pull up a different emotion. One that didn't make her feel so vulnerable.

"You guys are late," Janessa said as the couple filed into the row in front of them.

"Yeah. Work stuff," Kayleigh told her. "We were actually here earlier but didn't feel like traipsing in front of everyone in the middle of the game to get to you guys."

Janessa reached out and tapped the container. "Charli brought cookies."

Charli opened the lid and held it out. Kayleigh took one, but Hudson snagged a couple of his favorite before giving her a smile and thanking her.

Though she battled with her jealousy of Kayleigh, Charli couldn't be mad at Hudson. He was a genuinely nice guy and had always treated all of them with friendliness and respect.

Really, she couldn't stay mad at her sister either.

Kayleigh wasn't rubbing the situation into the wound in Charli's heart. She didn't know what Charli was struggling with. She and Hudson were just living the life God had led them into.

Charli stayed mired in her thoughts while Janessa grilled Kayleigh over the last-minute things that still needed to be done for their upcoming wedding. It was going to be a smaller event than Janessa and Will's wedding had been, but Charli wouldn't be surprised if it was more expensive, given who Hudson's family was.

Janessa was going to be Kayleigh's matron of honor. People might assume that Charli would be upset she hadn't been asked to be in the wedding party, but frankly, she was relieved. Layla was going to be a junior bridesmaid, so it wasn't as if Charli's little family wasn't represented.

Layla was over the moon, and Charli was happy about that. With the number of weddings that had happened lately, she'd been a flower girl a few times already. However, her dress for Kayleigh's wedding was truly amazing, and Layla loved it.

Charli only half-listened to the discussion between Kayleigh and Janessa. Her attention kept drifting to the large doorway of the gym, which was annoying, but she couldn't seem to help herself.

"What are Jackson and Blake arguing about?" Kayleigh asked, her topic of conversation finally grabbing Charli's focus.

Janessa glanced at Charli. "Are they arguing?"

Charli shrugged. "No clue."

"How did you know they were arguing?" Janessa asked Kayleigh.

"We saw them out near the canteen, and it looked like they were arguing."

"Well, hopefully they remember to get our drinks," Janessa said, clearly focusing on what was most important.

Charli looked over at the doorway again, wondering why the cousins might be arguing. Did it have something to do with her and Layla? It shouldn't. There was no reason for them to be the focus of any argument, especially where Jackson and Blake were concerned.

She frowned when she spotted the cousins coming back into the gym. Jackson led the way, with Blake following behind him, his gaze on his phone while he carried several soda cans in the crook of his arm.

As Jackson climbed the stairs to where they sat, Charli could see that his face was tense, which was in direct contrast to his normal expression. She looked past him to Blake and found that he looked tense as well.

Something clearly had happened after they'd left to get the drinks.

"Hey, Kayleigh," Jackson said as he stepped into the row next to her. He held out a couple of sodas to Janessa and Will. "For you guys."

As Janessa took the cans and handed one to Will, she said, "Thanks."

"The Diet Coke is for Charli," Jackson said, directing his comment to Blake.

Blake held out one of the cans he held. "Here you go."

Charli's fingers brushed his as she wrapped them around the cold can. "Thank you."

"Did you ask for apple juice for Layla, Charli?" Jackson asked, holding up a couple of juice boxes.

"Yes."

"And for Amelia?" When Blake nodded, Jackson held up the remaining box and looked at Misha. "Orange juice for Peyton?"

"Yep. He likes apples, but not in juice form."

"Oranges are already juicy," Peyton said as he took the box. "So it tastes the same as the juice."

"Makes sense to me, buddy," Jackson told him.

Whatever had upset Jackson had apparently passed, but Blake remained a silent presence at Charli's side. He'd opened his soda and taken a drink, but now he just held it between his hands, head bent.

Against her will, Charli's curiosity was roused. It seemed that whatever argument they'd had, Jackson had recovered from it already. Or maybe it was just that he was able to hide whatever had annoyed him better than Blake.

She really, really wanted to ask Blake what had happened, but took a sip of her soda instead. It was getting harder to stay distant from him, especially since they'd had a conversation about what had happened twelve years ago.

Charli still wasn't sure how she felt about what he'd revealed, and she hadn't told him that she forgave him. That was mainly because she wasn't sure that she had. She was also hesitant to do so because of what forgiving him would signify.

Would it mean she wanted him back in her life?

If it weren't for Layla, she might... *might*... have been willing to consider that. But she did have Layla, and she wasn't ready to share her. She might never be.

It still surprised her that Blake had apparently not figured out that Layla was his. If he suspected that she was, he certainly wasn't sharing those suspicions with her or with Jackson.

Blake wasn't dumb, but perhaps he was clueless. At the very least, he should have known that she wouldn't run out and sleep with another guy so soon after he'd left her.

He'd known she was a virgin, and she'd told him why she wasn't sexually active when a lot of girls her age were. So, in a way, it hurt that he thought she'd move on that quickly. It was like he hadn't known her at all.

Or maybe he'd just forgotten that about her. So when Jackson hinted that Charli had had a relationship after he'd broken up with her, Blake hadn't even questioned Layla's parentage.

"You have more cookies, Charli?" Will asked, leaning past Janessa to eye the container in Charli's lap.

"Yep." She handed the container to him, then watched as the kids turned around to beg for more.

"Am I going to be the favorite uncle if I let you have some?" Will asked.

Layla looked over at Charli, a questioning look on her face. Charli nodded, though normally she didn't like Layla having too many sweets.

"Can I have more cookies too, Daddy?" Amelia asked.

"Sure, Berry," Blake said.

Amelia gave Blake a big smile, then waited for Will to hold the container out to her before taking a cookie. When she'd made her choice, she thanked him, her shyness showing in the tiny smile that accompanied her words.

The teams were filing back onto the court, and soon the noise level rose again. Blake kept his attention on the game, but Charli could sense that he wasn't really paying attention. She hated that she knew him well enough to be able to tell that. Even after all these years.

Had they still been together, she would have laid her hand on his back, connecting physically with him, then asked him what was going on. And he'd tell her, because until everything had fallen apart, they'd been great at communicating. Being in a long-distance relationship had meant they'd spent a *lot* of time talking or texting.

But had it just been her imagination that they'd communicated so well? Had she done too much of the talking and not enough listening? Was that why she hadn't seen that he wasn't as committed to their future as she'd been?

Charli sighed, frustrated that all she did when Blake was around was try to dissect everything that had happened. And she never came to a different conclusion. Never gained any further insight. All she did was upset herself.

By the time the game ended—which the home team ended up losing—Charli had come to understand that this was her new reality. Blake was once again part of her life, whether she wanted that or not. Even if he didn't show up at things like the pizza night or church, she was still teaching his daughter.

So she could either continue to let his presence tie her up in knots, or she could somehow make peace with the situation. She'd gotten to the point where the heartache no longer held her captive. Unfortunately, his return to Serenity had resurrected some of the hurt, but more than that, it had brought with it a fear that he'd realize that Layla was his daughter.

But since he apparently didn't suspect anything, maybe she could relax.

Maybe...

As they got to their feet, Misha called her name. "Do you want to go for ice cream with us?"

"Ice cream!" Layla exclaimed. "Yes! Let's go for ice cream, Mom."

Charli frowned at Misha. Her sister-in-law should have known better than to ask about something like that in front of the kids.

"Pleeeeeease, Momma!" Layla begged. "I want ice cream so bad."

"But you had cookies," Charli reminded her.

"I know, but cookies and ice cream go together. Cookies and cream! They go together peeeerfectly!"

Charli gave her head a shake of exasperation, then sighed. "Okay. Fine."

"Do you want to join us as well, Blake?" Misha asked.

Amelia turned her pleading gaze to her dad as she folded her hands beneath her chin. "Can we please go too, Daddy?"

When Charli looked at Blake, she could see the battle in his expression. And she realized that his presence at events with her family might not be about him. He wanted this for Amelia. He knew that her family offered a safe place for his daughter.

Charli didn't know what all the father and daughter had gone through, but it had left a mark on both of them.

As her gaze moved from Amelia to the tense expression on her dad's face. Charli found herself wanting to tell Blake that it would be fine if he and Amelia joined them.

It surprised her, but seeing the pleading on Amelia's face made Charli want to welcome them to yet one more gathering where she and Layla would also be.

Blake looked at Charli, clearly understanding that she wouldn't want him there. Him giving deference to what she might want led her to look at Amelia and say, "I'm sure Layla and Peyton would enjoy having you come if it's okay with your dad."

Amelia grinned, then looked at her dad again. "Is it okay, Daddy?"

Charli heard Blake sigh, then say, "Sure. It's fine."

"Yay!" Layla cheered as she hugged Amelia. "There are lots of flavors to pick from. It's amazing."

"We can go ahead," Misha said. "Jay will meet us there."

"Are you guys coming too?" Charli asked, glancing at the others there.

Kayleigh shook her head. "Not me. I'm exhausted."

"Since I'm her driver, I'll need to pass as well," Hudson said as he slipped his arm around her waist.

"You can go if you want," Kayleigh told him.

"It's fine, sweetheart. I'd rather you be there, too."

"We'll go," Will said. "I never turn down ice cream."

"What if I want to go home?" Janessa asked.

"I wouldn't believe you." Will grinned. "You never turn down ice cream either."

"Okay. Fine."

"Are you coming too, Jackson?" Will asked.

Jackson glanced at Blake, then said, "Yep. Ice cream for the win."

With that, they made their way down the bleachers. The majority of people had already exited the gym. The few who lingered were most likely the parents of the players who were still gathered around Jay.

"I'll send you the address, Blake," Will said as they reached the parking lot. "It's not too far from here."

"Nothing is too far from anywhere here," Blake replied.

Will laughed. "Yeah. True."

Charli headed for her car with Layla, hoping that agreeing to go to the ice cream parlor hadn't been a mistake. But she needed to stop thinking just about herself. Going for ice cream clearly meant a lot to Amelia, and Charli was pretty sure that it wasn't just because she wanted another treat.

She wasn't blind to how Amelia seemed to blossom when she was around Layla and Peyton. Though the little girl was finally finding that connection with a couple of the girls in their class, she still seemed most at ease with Layla and Peyton. Her smiles came more quickly and were bigger when she was around them.

"I wish Skylar was still here," Layla said as Charli drove to the ice cream parlor. "I miss her cheering."

"I'm sure she misses cheering, too."

Skylar had graduated the previous spring, and she was now off at college. Surprisingly, she hadn't chosen to go to the same college as her boyfriend and Cole.

Though Skylar hadn't said it yet, Charli thought that maybe they'd broken up. She just hoped that if they had, it was Skylar's choice, and that Adrian hadn't ghosted her like Blake had done to her.

Not that Adrian could get away with that the way Blake had been able to. Since he was best friends with Cole, it was likely that Cole would always know where Adrian was. Plus, Adrian's immediate family still lived in Serenity and went to the same church as the Halversons. He wouldn't be able to slip out of Skylar's life as easily as Blake had slipped out of hers.

The ice cream parlor wasn't full, so they had no problem snagging enough seats for all of them after pulling together a couple of tables. There were a few other people there, but since the temperatures had turned more autumnal, ice cream didn't appear to be as popular.

The next little while was spent getting everyone settled with their choice of ice cream. The kids chose to sit at the counter, while the rest of them gathered around the tables. Jay had arrived right as they were sitting down, and once he had his ice cream, he sat down beside Misha.

Charli was trying to ignore the fact that she and Blake had ended up sitting next to each other. Jackson was on her other side, while Janessa and Will sat opposite her.

When Jay glanced at her, then Blake, and smiled, Charli realized that perhaps Misha had set this up—with the stamp of approval from her husband. That was probably the reason for asking in front of the kids, knowing the parents wouldn't be able to say no to them. She narrowed her gaze at Jay, but he just lifted his brows.

What on earth were Jay and Misha thinking?

She knew that Jay and Will had been getting close to Blake, which was fine. However, she wasn't on board with the matchmaking. Several of her siblings had tried to set her up over the years—

though not so much recently. None of those attempts had been successful.

Jay had never tried before, so she wondered how much was him, or if Misha had decided that it was time for Charli to have a chance at a relationship. Regardless of who or why they had gotten to this point, this attempt wasn't going to be successful either.

"How do you feel Amelia is adjusting to life in Serenity, Blake?" Misha asked.

Blake scooped up a spoonful of his ice cream—chocolate peanut butter, which is what she remembered him liking twelve years ago—and took his time answering. Charli wished she could read his mind.

"She seems happy here," Blake finally said.

"That's wonderful," Misha told him.

"It is. I don't think I've ever seen her as happy as she's been over the past few weeks."

"Serenity has a way of doing that," Jay said. "It took awhile, but Peyton will also tell you that he's super happy here now, even though he wasn't when he first came to Serenity."

"I wasn't super happy when I came here either," Misha confessed. "But I'm thankful that God led me, my mom, and Ciara here."

"You're not Ciara's dad?" Blake asked Jay.

"Nope. He's not," Misha said. "In fact, I'm not her biological mom."

"Oh, wow. I didn't realize that."

"It's not something we talk about a lot because Ciara and Peyton are both our kids now. However, Ciara is my late brother's daughter. After he passed away, his pregnant girlfriend was going to abort their baby, but I told her I'd adopt the baby if she carried it to term. Thankfully, she agreed."

Charli had had some intense feelings when she'd heard Ciara's story for the first time. It was a blessing that Misha and her mom had been there to take over the little girl's care.

When Charli had realized she was pregnant and then abandoned by Blake, abortion could have been an option for some, but it wasn't for her. It might have made her life less complicated if she'd had that option, but Charli was glad that she hadn't. And because she believed a baby's life was to be valued from conception, she'd been blessed with Layla.

She knew Misha felt the same way about Ciara.

"I didn't know about Peyton until a couple of years ago," Jay said. "But I'm grateful that even though his mother didn't tell me she was pregnant, she didn't abort him. Learning about him was a shock, but having him in my life has been amazing."

When Jay had returned with Peyton, Charli had had feelings about that situation, too. That had a lot to do with not understanding the decision Peyton's mom had made to give him away.

But regardless of how people ended up as part of their family, Charli was glad to have each of them there.

As Jay shared more about his and Peyton's journey, Charli came to the stark realization that, in her situation, Blake filled the same role that Jay had as the unknowing father. She didn't like the comparison, because she didn't want to be cast in the role of Peyton's mom.

However, unlike her, Charli *had* tried to tell Blake about Layla. Perhaps she could have tried harder. However, when he'd abruptly ended things and then ignored her requests for a conversation, she'd decided if he didn't want Charli in his life, she didn't want him in her child's.

"I wasn't in Amelia's life as much as I should have been." Blake used his spoon to dig into his ice cream but didn't lift any out. "Her mom got primary custody because I was deployed a lot."

"How did you end up with her now?" Jay asked. "If you don't mind sharing."

Blake's shoulders slumped. "Lauren—Amelia's mom—had trouble with addiction. She was clean when we met and throughout her pregnancy. We broke up when Amelia was about a year old, and a couple of years later, for whatever reason, she started to struggle with her addiction again. Since we weren't together then, and I was deployed for a good chunk of that time, I wasn't aware of what was going on until recently."

Charli felt a pang of sorrow for Amelia. She'd had students who came from homes where addiction was an issue. An environment like that was confusing for children so young, and ofttimes, hurtful.

However, she also felt bad for Blake, which surprised her.

"So you were able to get custody?" Misha asked.

Charli's gaze followed Blake's as he glanced over to where Amelia sat with the other kids, her feet swinging as she ate her ice cream. "I got custody because Lauren was killed in a car accident, resulting from driving under the influence. After that happened, I knew that I needed to leave the army in order to take care of Amelia."

Charli stared at Blake for a moment, then focused on her ice cream as she let what he'd said sink it. Blake's revelations explained so much about Amelia's sadness. And even Blake's.

They might not have still been in a relationship, but Charli was sure that Blake would never have wished something bad like that to happen to the mother of his child.

"I'm sorry to hear what you've been through," Jay said. "What brought you back to Serenity? Your family doesn't live around here, do they?"

Blake shook his head. "They're all in California, but I've been estranged from them since just before I joined the army. I decided to come back because I knew I'd need support, and Jackson's family had always been so good to me. Plus, from what I'd remembered of Serenity, it seemed like it might be a great place to raise a child."

"It definitely is that," Jay agreed. "And Jackson's parents are amazing. Jackson, however..." He seesawed his hand back and forth.

A smile flitted across Blake's face as Jackson sputtered in protest.

Jackson scowled. "Not cool, man."

Jay grinned at him, and the mood lightened a bit.

Charli, however, had a lot of thoughts and feelings about Blake and what had happened to him and Amelia over the past few years. She looked over at the counter where the kids were sitting, Amelia between the two older ones.

While she was glad for the understanding she'd gained about a student's past, Charli wasn't sure that she wanted to feel sympathy for Blake. He'd hurt her *so* much that she just wanted to feel *nothing* where he was concerned. Not hate. Not love. Not sympathy. Nothing.

And yet there was a part of her that was softening toward him.

What was she supposed to do about that?

CHAPTER FOURTEEN

Blake wasn't sure what had prompted him to share so much about his past with Lauren, especially with Charli there. It was a reminder to her that he'd had another relationship, and he didn't really want that.

However, it was out there now, and there was nothing he could do about that. If it made her even more angry at him than she'd already been, so be it.

Even though he had picked his favorite ice cream flavor, he didn't manage to finish it before it became soupy. Pushing the bowl away, he folded his arms on the table, listening as the conversation moved away from him, for which he was glad.

Though he didn't know why they'd included him and Amelia in their plans to get ice cream, he was glad they had. Amelia looked like she was having fun, and it beat going back to the quiet of their apartment.

Somehow, he'd once again ended up sitting next to Charli, whose nearness pierced him with a familiar double-edged sword. Since he'd returned to Serenity, the pain of what he'd lost was nearly always present. And even though being close to Charli also increased that pain, he never turned down the opportunity to see her.

"Peyton has been bugging us to go bowling," Jay said. "Any chance you guys would like to make a night of it?"

"Is that why Layla asked me about it?" Charli asked. "Where did Peyton get the bowling idea from?"

"He was invited to a birthday party where they bowled, and he really enjoyed it."

"I haven't bowled in a very long time," Charli said.

Jay nodded. "Me neither."

It sounded like Blake had been bowling more recently than anyone there. He and some of his buddies had gone bowling on occasion, and for some reason, they'd been more competitive at bowling than when they played basketball or volleyball.

"We could go next Friday after pizza," Jay said.

"No game?" Jackson asked.

"Not on Friday. We're out of town for a game on Saturday."

"I'm sure that would be fine for me and Layla," Charli said.

"How about you, Blake?" Jay asked. "Interested in going bowling."

"I'm not sure Amelia could handle the heavy balls."

"The place we go to has Duckpin style the smaller balls without finger holes. So it might not be as exciting for us adults, but the kids will probably have a blast."

"I prefer bowling with the small balls myself," Charli said. "Less chance of ruining nails, and they're lighter."

"I'm with Charli," Janessa said.

"I'll check to see if Kayleigh and Hudson want to join us."

"Too bad Mom and Dad aren't around," Jay said. "They'd probably come."

"Where are they?" Blake asked.

"They're with Wilder in Asia at the moment, visiting some orphanages to offer their medical services as needed," Janessa said. "They'll all be back soon, since Kayleigh's wedding is coming up."

Blake had been surprised when Kayleigh and Hudson had let him know that he and Amelia were welcome to attend the ceremony and reception. Though he'd had some conversations with Hudson, he hadn't thought their friendship warranted an invitation to their wedding.

"It's weird not to have to look after Skylar or the dog when Mom and Dad go away now," Charli said.

"Is Layla still asking for a dog?" Jay asked.

Charli shook her head. "She took it really hard when Bella died. I think that made her think twice about having a dog."

Blake had considered getting a dog once they moved to Serenity. Though Amelia probably would love one, Blake had decided to wait until they had a house with a yard.

"Peyton has started asking for a cat."

"A cat?" Charli asked. "None of us have cats. Why does he want a cat?"

"He says it gets too cold in winter to have to walk a dog," Misha said with a laugh.

"Oh, well, I'd have to agree with him on that," Charli said.

This was the most Blake had heard Charli talk. She'd always been reserved during the pizza nights at her place. That night, she seemed more relaxed as she sat beside him, eating ice cream.

He wasn't complaining. These moments gave him glimpses of the young woman he'd known all those years ago. And they were a reminder of why he'd fallen in love with her.

Laughter flowed around the table as the siblings and Jackson continued to talk. Blake didn't contribute much. He'd spoken enough earlier. He'd much rather listen right then. Plus, he'd always been more on the reserved side when he was in a group.

His more reserved nature had bugged his parents—especially his dad—who wanted Blake to be able to charm people the way he did when dealing with them in the business world. His two sisters had been much more outgoing. They'd also been able to read people quickly and cater their conversation to the person they were talking with.

Lauren had been very gregarious, drawing people to her. Blake being one of them. It had only been after they'd been together for awhile that he'd realized that she wasn't always so upbeat and outgoing.

It wasn't that he'd expected her to constantly be up, but rather than just withdraw a bit, Lauren seemed to swing in the complete opposite direction. As often as she was up, she had moments when she was down—very down—where her withdrawal into herself had been concerning.

And it was during one of those times that Blake had become aware of her drug and alcohol use. He'd come to realize that she preferred to medicate herself that way than to take the prescriptions she'd been given.

Amelia had been so withdrawn when he'd taken custody of her that he'd worried she had similar tendencies as her mom. She'd always been a bit reserved during the times he had visitation with her. But after her mom's death, her withdrawal had seemed to deepen.

On the surface, it had made sense. She'd lost her mom, after all. But when he considered what Lauren had struggled with, Blake felt like he had a right to be concerned.

Thankfully, since being in Serenity, he'd seen Amelia come out of her shell, and he was grateful to Charli and Jay's kids for helping make that happen. He thought that the stability of their home life had also helped.

Did he believe she'd come through everything unscathed? No. Unfortunately, she'd had a front-row seat to her mom's struggles. But so far, she resisted any attempt to be drawn into a conversation about it. She may have been a quiet child, but she was also a stubborn one when she wanted to be.

So, he kept an eye on her, and hopefully, if Charli, as her teacher, had any concerns, she'd let him know.

He was so glad that she was Amelia's teacher, even though the situation had made things awkward. Blake knew that he could trust Charli to care for Amelia while she was in her classroom, and that Charli would understand the importance of communicating any worries she might have to him.

That was a real blessing and an answer to prayer. At least for him. He was aware that Charli might not feel the same way.

As they sat there, more people came into the ice cream parlor, some of them greeting the Halversons or Jackson. There weren't a lot of tables in the space, and they'd tied up a couple of them, but most customers just came in, got their ice cream, then left.

"We should probably get home," Jay said after they'd been there for about an hour. "We have to be up early for the clinic tomorrow."

When Jay and Misha got up, Blake prepared to stand as well, but no one else moved. Well, no one except the girls. Layla and Amelia abandoned the counter and slid onto the chairs left empty by Jay and Misha.

"Mom, can we play games on your phone?" Layla asked as she smiled at Charli.

Charli pulled her phone out of her purse and handed it to Layla. The girl clearly knew her mom's password because she tapped on the screen without hesitation. Then she motioned for Amelia to come closer, and the girls bent their heads together over the phone.

Blake stared at them for a moment, then glanced at Charli to find her watching them too. He was glad that whatever feelings she might have toward him, she didn't carry them over to Amelia.

"Are you going to the gym these days, Blake?" Will asked.

"Not very often," Blake said as he leaned back, crossing his arms over his chest.

It was something he missed, but getting to the gym while having Amelia was a challenge. His aunt had volunteered to watch her in the evening once or twice a week, but when a guy was used to working out daily, it didn't feel like enough.

"Don't feel bad," Janessa said. "Not all of you can be buff gym bunnies like me."

"Buff?" Will asked incredulously.

"Gym bunny?" Charli asked with a healthy dose of skepticism in her voice. "Not sure that's what *I'd* call you."

"You're just jealous because you don't go to the gym like I do," Janessa told her.

"I'm jealous because you go to the gym once a *month* these days?"

"Well, it's more than your *never*," Janessa retorted.

"The never-ending gym battle," Will said with a laugh.

"Never-ending?" Blake asked, wondering about the inside joke.

"A few people in the Halverson family don't share Jay's passion for fitness," Will said. "In particular, Janessa and Charli."

"Hey." Janessa leaned into her husband. "You didn't like going to the gym *either,* darling."

"Yeah. I know. But I've been converted."

"Do you miss not being able to workout more, Blake?" Janessa asked.

Blake had tried not to think of everything he'd had to give up, everything he missed, after having to take on the full-time responsibility of raising Amelia. After all, it was what a parent did, and he was the only parent Amelia had left, so he would do whatever he had to for her. Even if it meant giving up some things he enjoyed.

"I do." He shrugged. "But it's not like I don't get a bit of a workout at my job. I'm not sitting at a desk."

"You're not?" Will asked. "You can't fix a car sitting on your butt?"

Blake chuckled. "Not really. I mean, you could try, but it would be a challenge."

"Well, if you want to work out some time, you can drop Amelia off at the house," Janessa said.

Blake appreciated the offer, but he wasn't sure that Charli would back it up. That was why he was surprised when she said, "Layla would probably love that."

"Uh. Okay. Well, thank you. I might take you up on that."

Janessa grinned at him. "You make sure you do. If you don't, I'll have Will show up on your doorstep and drag you to the gym."

"Uh, babe..." Will said. "I don't think I could drag Blake anywhere."

When Janessa looked between Will and him with a narrowed gaze, Blake lifted his brows.

"Okay. I'll come with you, and both of us will drag him."

Blake couldn't help but grin at Janessa. He hadn't spent a lot of time with her before, though he knew that of all her siblings, Charli was closest to Janessa. He wondered if Charli had talked to her about their previous relationship.

No, actually, he didn't wonder. There was no way Charli had told Janessa anything. Janessa might have a great sense of humor, but he was pretty sure that she was also fiercely loyal when it came to her sister.

"You won't have to drag me anywhere," Blake said.

"Whew." Janessa wiped her forehead. "Such a relief."

Blake glanced at Jackson since his cousin hadn't been participating in the joking, which was unusual for him. Jackson definitely didn't look like he was into the fun. When their gazes met, he narrowed his eyes at him, which infuriated Blake. He regretted ever sharing about him and Charli with Jackson.

Earlier, Jackson had been upset with him for sitting beside Charli. Which was ridiculous because it hadn't been his maneuvering that had made that happen. His cousin's reaction seemed over the top and made him wonder again if there was something more there on Jackson's part.

His cousin had become protective of Charli, though Blake didn't recall Jackson caring about her like that twelve years ago. He hadn't even seemed to interact with her back then, so it bugged Blake that he was taking on this protector role.

"Well, with that being settled, we should probably head out," Will said. "I think they're closing soon." He looked over at the counter. "Are you closing soon, Izzy?"

The teen looked up from where she was cleaning the counters. "In about fifteen minutes, Mr. K."

"Guess we'd better go then," Janessa said as she got to her feet. "But this was fun. We'll have to do it again."

Blake agreed, and he hoped that they'd include him and Amelia.

Everyone got up from the table and cleared off their ice cream containers and napkins. It didn't take long, and soon they were headed for the door. Blake reached it first and held it open for the others.

Charli was the last to walk out, following after Layla and Amelia. When she passed him, she glanced up, smiling briefly as she thanked him once again. It was definitely better than a dagger in his stomach.

Blake fell into step behind her, feeling lighter than he had in a long time. Amelia's happiness, along with his own feeling of finally being settled, combined to ease the tension he'd been carrying for a very, very long time.

Even considering the things he'd had to give up, the discontent he'd anticipated feeling wasn't as strong as he'd thought it might be. Returning to Serenity had definitely helped with that, even though it had meant dealing with his past.

"See you at church on Sunday," Will said as he clapped Blake on his shoulder.

"Yep."

They'd settled into the church more quickly than he might have thought they would. Amelia loved it, and not once had she balked at going. Yet one more thing to be thankful for.

He also enjoyed attending the services, but his enjoyment was a bit more complicated. Though he might want to deny it, Blake had to admit—at least to himself—that much like it had been when he was younger, seeing Charli was part of the appeal of attending church. Just not as much as it once was.

With the spiritual maturity he'd gained over the past couple of years, he now understood the value of paying attention to the sermons and lessons. He even enjoyed listening to Christian podcasts, usually having been recommended by someone he trusted.

So, they'd go to church come Sunday, and he'd enjoy the sermon *and* the opportunity to see Charli once again.

When Sunday rolled around, it did indeed give him the opportunity to see Charli again. Not just see her, but to once again sit next to her during Sunday school.

Though he hadn't maneuvered anything to make that happen, he was starting to get the feeling that someone else *was.*

Blake hadn't protested their manipulations, but he doubted Charli felt the same. He was pretty sure she wasn't the one doing the maneuvering.

It seemed that perhaps her siblings—particularly Jay and Janessa—were the ones creating situations to bring them into closer contact.

Was she aware of what they were doing?

And if she was, why wasn't she protesting it?

He didn't think for a minute that, if given a choice, she'd choose to spend time with him. However, he was no longer getting the feeling that she hated his guts.

Progress, he supposed.

Moving from hate to indifference? Some might say that apathy, not hate, was the opposite of love. But in Blake's estimation, if they were going to co-exist in the same space, hate would have made that impossible.

So, if she felt apathetic about his presence, he'd accept that. If he couldn't have love, indifference felt better than hate.

Sunday had dawned rainy and chilly. So rather than hanging out at the park with the Halversons like they'd gotten into the habit of doing after church, he and Amelia had gone home to watch some movies and color.

Though Amelia would get to see Charli during the week, Blake was probably going to have to wait until Friday. Thankfully, the garage was busy, so the week wouldn't drag by.

As he sat eating lunch with another mechanic in the small lunch-room at the garage on Friday, Stan appeared in the doorway.

"Hey, Blake," Stan said as he approached the table, pulled out a chair and sat down. "Any chance you can stay until closing to-day?"

"I'm not sure. I'll have to check if my aunt is available to pick Amelia up."

"I'd really appreciate it if you could do that. Matt had to leave because he really wasn't feeling well, and I need to make sure we get the Anderson car finished up before closing."

Blake nodded and pulled his phone out. When Julia answered, he chatted with her for a minute before explaining what he needed that afternoon.

"Oh, sweetie, I have an appointment in Coeur d'Alene at three," Julia said. "But I could try to reschedule."

"No. Don't worry about it. I think Charli would probably be willing to keep an eye on her until I'm able to get her." If not, he might have to run and pick Amelia up and then have her sit in the garage office while he finished out his workday.

After he ended the call with his aunt, Blake looked up the in-formation for the school. He didn't know if Charli checked her email throughout the day, so he decided he'd better contact the office.

When the receptionist answered, Blake said, "Hi. I have a child in Charli Halverson's class, and I was wondering if I could have a message passed to her. It's rather time sensitive."

"She's on her lunch at the moment, but I'll see if I can get her for you."

He was on hold for a minute, then Charli came on the line.

"Hi Charli, it's Blake," he said after she answered. "I'm sorry to disturb your lunch hour, but I'm wondering if you'd be able to take Amelia home with you after school."

"That shouldn't be a problem," she

"Thank you so much. I really appreciate that," Blake told her. "Stan asked if I could stay until closing since one of the guys here got sick. We have a couple of cars we're trying to finish up before the weekend."

"I'm sure the owners will be happy about that. I can meet you at the bowling alley with her, if you want."

The plan was to grab dinner at the bowling alley. Jessica had texted him for his pizza order to place ahead of time since they were going to be a fairly sizeable group.

"That would be great. Once I'm done here, I'll need to run home and change, then I'll meet you all at the bowling alley."

"Sounds good. I'll see you there."

"Yep. Thanks again."

Once the call ended, Blake lowered his phone from his ear, then stared at it. Their interaction had felt so... normal. The awkwardness of previous interactions had been missing. Most likely because it centered on her job in relation to Amelia.

Whatever the reason, he was grateful.

"Everything okay?" Stan asked.

"Oh." Blake looked up from his phone. "Yep. Amelia's teacher said she'd take Amelia home with her since we're meeting up at the same place later for supper."

"You're friends with the Halversons, eh?" Stan said.

"Yep. Charli's daughter and Jay's son have befriended Amelia, so we've been spending quite a bit of time with them. Jackson is also a good friend of Gareth's, so they've been good about including us in various activities. Tonight, we're going bowling."

"Have fun," Stan said with a laugh. "I haven't been bowling in a long time. Not since my boys were young."

Because they had a lot of work still to do, they quickly wrapped up their lunch, then returned to the cars they had to finish before the end of the day.

When five o'clock rolled around, the cars had been repaired and picked up, and Blake was free to go. He didn't linger, heading right to the apartment so he could take a quick shower and change.

He hoped that Amelia was doing okay.

There was no reason she shouldn't be, but he usually prepared her for any change to their plans, which he hadn't been able to do this time. Also, he hoped she was okay wearing what she'd worn to school that day since she hadn't had the chance to come home and change her clothes.

His anticipation of the evening had been relatively high, given that it meant being able to spend more time with Charli and the others. After their positive conversation earlier that day, he was looking forward to their evening together even more.

Which probably wasn't a good thing. However, he hoped that perhaps, in time, he and Charli would get to the point of being friendly acquaintances, if not friends.

Blake didn't dare extend that hope for anything more, though. He might be a lot of things, but he'd like to think he wasn't stupid enough to get his hopes up about something that was unlikely to ever happen.

CHAPTER FIFTEEN

Charli held hands with both Layla and Amelia as they walked across the parking lot toward the doors of the bowling alley. The large building stood alone in a parking lot on the edge of town. Though there was another bowling alley in the town, this was the one they'd frequented the most as teenagers.

When they reached the door, Layla let go of Charli to grab the handle and pull it open. Amelia, however, kept a tight hold of Charli's hand as they walked into the building.

The interior of the bowling alley wasn't the most modern, with the carpet and décor on the walls looking like it had been last updated in the eighties. However, it was clean and didn't have a musty smell that one might expect of an outdated building.

They climbed a short set of wide stairs to the main area of the business. Charli looked around and spotted a few others of the family there. They were gathered by the three lanes at the far end of the space.

Layla spotted them at the same time and grabbed Amelia's hand. "C'mon. I see Peyton."

The pair ran ahead of Charli, and as they reached the others, she noticed that Blake wasn't there yet. It wasn't surprising, since he'd said he needed to work until five and then planned to go home to change his clothes.

Charli greeted her family as she joined them. "Who else is still coming?"

"Well, Blake," Janessa began. "Jackson, for sure. Maybe Wade, depending on his work. Kayleigh said she and Hudson would try to make it but might be a bit late."

"No Gareth and Aria?"

"Gareth wasn't sure," Jay said. "He was going to see how Aria was feeling."

"Also depends on what sort of day Timmy had," Janessa added. "He's been teething."

Charli loved kids, but she didn't miss those more challenging moments of early childhood. She had found teething to be such an extremely difficult time as Lyla had been so fussy, which resulted in sleep deprivation for Charli.

"Why did Amelia come with you?" Misha asked.

"Blake phoned me earlier and asked if I could take her home with me after school, since Stan had asked him to work until five."

"That's good that you were able to help him out," Jay said.

Charli shrugged. "It wasn't as if it was a hardship since we were all going to end up at the same place anyway. The girls were thrilled to have some extra time to hang out."

She'd been more than a little surprised when she'd taken the call and heard Blake's voice on the other end of the line. The last time she'd spoken to him had been over the phone, the day after he'd arrived back in California.

As usual, that memory had brought other memories to the surface, along with emotions she would have happily gone without recalling, if she'd been given a choice.

Though hearing his voice like that had been difficult, she'd managed to keep her calm as she'd listened to what he'd asked of her. And there was no way she could have said no. Even if she'd wanted to.

"It's good that he felt comfortable enough to do that," Janessa said with a bright smile. "Don't you think?"

"Sure," Charli agreed, though she doubted that he'd called because he was comfortable. She was fairly sure that Blake would do whatever he had to in order to make sure Amelia was taken care of. "It just made sense."

"Hey, everyone," Jackson greeted them enthusiastically as he joined the group, holding up his hands for high fives from the guys. "How's it going?"

They chatted for a few minutes, then he glanced around and said, "I see Amelia, but where's Blake?"

When everyone turned to look at Charli, Jackson's brows rose.

"He called me at school to ask if I could take Amelia home with me and then here to the bowling alley. Stan had asked him if he'd work until five because one of the other guys was sick, and they had work they needed to get done."

"I bet Amelia enjoyed that."

"Yep. Both she and Layla did."

Speaking of the pair, the girls approached them with Peyton, who said, "Can we bowl, Dad?"

"Yep. Let's get you some shoes."

Charli went with Jay and the kids to get their shoes. She had to get Amelia to take off one of her shoes so that she could check her size.

"Are you going to get your shoes now?" Jay asked as they waited for the bowling alley employee to bring back shoes for the kids.

"I suppose I might as well," she said, resting her arms on the high counter.

As the man set the shoes on the countertop, Charli gave him her size, then Jay did as well. After she'd handed the kids' shoes to them, the trio ran back to the lanes where the other adults waited. She turned back around to wait for her shoes, trying not to think about how the evening might unfold.

"Hey there, Blake," Jay said.

Butterflies erupted in her stomach as Charli turned to watch Blake approach them. His hair looked slightly damp, and he wore a pair of jeans and a denim jacket over a white T-shirt.

"Was Amelia okay for you?" Blake asked Charli after greeting them.

Blake's concern for his daughter touched Charli, reminding her of the man she'd thought he was.

"She was just fine," Charli assured him. "She's over there putting on her shoes."

Blake glanced in the direction Charli indicated before looking at her again. "Thanks for helping me out. I really appreciate it."

"You're welcome."

"Here are your shoes."

Charli turned her attention back to the employee and took the shoes. "Thanks. Do we pay for this now?"

"Nope. Janessa made arrangements to just pay for everything at the end. You have those three lanes for unlimited games. Just tell people in your group to let me know that they're part of the Halverson party."

"Okay. Great."

"Do you want to get your shoes now?" Jay asked Blake as he picked up his shoes.

"Might as well."

Though she knew she shouldn't, Charli lingered around the counter with the men, then walked back with them to the rest of the group.

There was some discussion over whether people wanted to bowl a game first or if they wanted to eat. The pizza was going to be ready in about twenty minutes, so most opted to wait.

Janessa had definitely set this up to be more than just bowling a couple of games and eating a couple of slices of pizza. There were two long tables set up on the same level as the shoe counter, which looked out over the lanes. Most of the adults sat down at the table, while Charli went down to the lower level.

She sat down to swap out her shoes, then put them in the cubbies behind the lanes.

The kids already had their shoes on, ready to bowl. The gutter guards were up on the lane against the far wall, so that was clearly the kids' lane. And for whichever adults felt the need for added help while bowling. Which might be her, depending on the path of the first few balls she threw.

Amelia turned from where they were looking at the balls in the ball return, her face lighting up when she spotted Blake. "Daddy!"

"Hey, Berry," Blake said as he joined them at the lane.

After setting his shoes on the ground, he picked Amelia up. She wrapped her arms around his neck and kissed his cheek. Clearly, Blake was doing something right as a single dad, because Amelia adored him.

It was in those moments, when she saw the two of them together, that Charli saw so much of the man she'd fallen in love with. He might have changed since then, but there were still parts of him that she recognized.

When Charli's gaze moved to Layla, she found her daughter watching the pair. Her heart clenched at the expression on Layla's face. She wasn't asking about her dad anymore, but it was clear that it was something she still wanted in her life.

Charli wished she could give her a stepfather. She hadn't set out to avoid getting married, but the pressure of making sure that any man she dated wouldn't just make a good partner for her, but also a good father for Layla, had discouraged her. The last thing she'd wanted was for Layla to get attached to someone and then have them walk away.

If she told Blake who Layla was, he might want to have a say in her life. And she wasn't sure that she could handle that. He didn't know Layla, and he certainly didn't love her. So the idea of him taking on a co-parenting role made Charli panic.

Looking away from Layla, Charli tried to push down the pain her daughter's longing caused her.

Was she being selfish?

Possibly.

Probably.

But how was she supposed to know if Blake would stay in Serenity? She didn't have any guarantee that he wouldn't decide to leave again. Especially since his immediate family—his wealthy immediate family—lived in California.

The thought of her daughter having to spend any significant amount of time away from her gave Charli palpitations.

She couldn't do it. She just couldn't do it.

Thankfully, it didn't seem like she'd have to since Blake still hadn't put the pieces together, and Jackson had—so far—kept her secret. She was actually kind of surprised about that, but definitely very, very grateful.

"Mom, are you going to bowl now?" Layla asked.

"Yep. I'll bowl with you."

"I'm going to assume you three want to play in the lane with the gutter guards," Jay said. "I'll go put in the names at the counter. How about you, Blake? Want to bowl with the kids?"

"Sure. I might have a chance at winning with the gutter guards in place."

"Are you going to bowl with us, Dad?" Peyton asked.

"Nope. Are you kidding me? My ego won't be able to take it if one of you beat me, and I wouldn't even have the excuse of gutter balls."

Peyton laughed as he punched the air. "*I'm* going to win!"

After he gave Peyton a high five, Jay left them, and within a couple of minutes, their names flashed up on the screen above the lane. Amelia was up first, followed by Peyton, Layla, Charli, and Blake.

Charli settled on one of the hard plastic seats that were connected in a curve behind the set of chairs at the scoring machine, which she'd thought was kind of obsolete since everything was automated nowadays. Layla was sitting in one of the seats at the scoring machine, while Peyton hovered by her shoulder, watching as Blake and Amelia approached the ball return area.

Blake helped Amelia choose a ball, then walked her to the line. He lowered himself to a knee so he was closer to her height, then gave her some pointers. She nodded, pausing for a moment before throwing the ball.

It hit the lane floor with a thud, then slowly made its way toward the pins. Peyton and Layla yelled encouragement while Blake slipped his arm around Amelia and stayed down on his knee beside her.

The ball collided with one of the gutter guards, then rebounded enough to hit a couple of pins when it finally reached them.

"Good job, Amelia!" Layla called out.

Blake helped Amelia with the final two balls of her turn, giving her a high five when she knocked down four of the ten pins. As Peyton went up for his turn, Amelia took his spot next to Layla.

Blake came and perched on the end of the curve of chairs opposite Charli, leaning forward to brace his elbows on his thighs as he watched Peyton.

Charli tried not to feel disappointed that he didn't talk to her. After all, she hadn't been thrilled when he'd started hanging out with them. So why on earth was she hoping for a conversation with him?

Besides, what did they have to talk about?

The only thing they had in common was Amelia, and they shouldn't be discussing anything pertaining to her in a casual setting like the bowling alley, anyway. Especially with her and other little ears around.

"Good job, son," Jay called out to Peyton at the end of his turn when his balls had managed to knock down six pins.

"Do you need help, sweetie?" Charli asked as Layla got out of her seat.

Layla turned toward her and gave Charli a big grin. "Nope. I'm good."

Amelia came over to stand with Blake, who straightened and slid his arm around her as she leaned against him. Charli kept her gaze on Layla as she threw her first ball.

When the ball reached the pins without hitting the gutter guard and took down three pins, Layla jumped up and down, waving her hands in the air. With no hesitation, she went to get her second ball, then waited for the lane to clear before she threw it.

The second and third balls left two standing, which meant Layla was at the top. Rather than get upset about losing the lead, Peyton gave her a fist bump.

"Your turn, Mom."

Charli got up and moved past Blake and Amelia to pick up a ball. As she positioned herself to throw her first ball, Charli was acutely aware of Blake's presence behind her. Probably watching her.

At one time, she would have enjoyed knowing his gaze was on her. It would have made her happy to have a hold of his attention.

However, without a relationship to make their situation more comfortable, Charli hurriedly threw her three balls, ending her frame tied with Layla.

As she left the lane approach area, Layla gave her a hug. "Yay, Mom! We got the same score!"

Charli bent to kiss her forehead, then straightened to see Blake had gotten to his feet. She gave him a nod and a quick smile as she passed him on her way to her seat.

After Blake picked up a ball, he tossed it into the air a couple of times as he stared at the pins. Charli had no idea how he'd play this. Would he be competitive and bowl to win? Or would he take it easy and give the rest of them a chance?

Regardless, at least she had an excuse to be watching him.

When he threw his first ball, it absolutely flew toward the pins. Faster than any ball thrown in their lane so far.

The ball hit the pins with a crack. Well, the *pin* apparently, as only one went flying. There was a moment of silence, and the kids stared at Blake with their mouths open.

"Uncle Blake..." Peyton began, giving him the title that he also gave Jackson and Wade. "You only got *one* pin with that super fast ball."

Blake turned to face him, a grin on his face. "Guess I need to do better than that, huh?"

"Still really cool to be able to throw *that fast*," Peyton said, his eyes wide.

"Well, let's see if I can get more than one down this time." Blake turned to pick up another ball, then lined himself up with the pins again.

Charli leaned back against the thin padding of the seat, watching as Blake threw the ball. It didn't blaze its way down the lane this time, showing that Blake knew how to control the ball better than she did.

Pins went flying, knocking down all but one. The kids cheered, and even Jay called out encouragement.

No surprise, they ended the first frame with Blake in the lead. Charli thought Amelia would be upset that she was last, but it didn't seem to bother her at all. She was just excited that it was her turn again.

"Do you want me to help you again?" Blake asked as she picked up a ball.

"Nope. I got it."

Charli couldn't help but smile at the little girl's confident response. Blake didn't return to his seat, choosing instead to stand back with his arms crossed and his feet braced. He and Amelia presented a dichotomy as he watched her bowl. His strength and size as opposed to hers.

He stood like a sentinel behind Amelia, ready to protect her. Although, from what, Charli wasn't sure.

Though he held himself with a more military bearing now, even back when they'd been together, she'd always felt safe with him. And he'd been protective of her, too.

It was something she had missed.

After Amelia was done, Blake returned to where he'd been sitting. If Charli needed to be reminded that he had well and truly moved on from her, it was there in the way he didn't look at her. Didn't interact with her. Just kept his focus on the kids.

Why did it hurt so much?

It shouldn't. They'd been broken up for years.

However, their breakup back then—his rejection of her—had happened while they were apart from each other. Now, having him sit so close and yet not say anything to her—to not even acknowledge her—felt like a repeat of the rejection she'd experienced twelve years ago, only up close and personal. Like a slap in the face.

But maybe she only had herself to blame. She hadn't exactly been welcoming or friendly to him. She could hardly act that way, then expect him to pursue interactions with her.

"It's your turn, Mom!" Layla called out to her.

Charli looked up to find that Layla had finished her turn. "Thanks, sweetie."

She hated that she'd let her emotions rob her of the joy of the moment. Getting up, she focused on picking up a ball, then sending it down the lane.

Charli didn't give in to the temptation to look over at Blake to see if he was watching her. Her crazy emotions wouldn't be able to take it if she realized he was focused on his phone or even just staring at the floor rather than watching her.

Which was ridiculous since just a few days ago, she'd been annoyed that he was popping up everywhere in her life. She'd even ignored *him* at times.

Clearly, the conflict of her head and heart was a mess.

"Good job, Auntie," Peyton called out when she knocked down five pins with her first ball. "Only five more to go."

Charli gave him a smile as she picked up another ball. Standing there, she took a couple of deep breaths and told herself to get out of the emotional gutter she'd ended up in. Too bad there weren't gutter guards for her emotions to help her stay focused on the moment.

As she threw her final two balls, she pulled her emotions deep inside to deal with later.

It was something she had a lot of experience with. She'd had to hide her sheer joy at being with Blake back when they'd been dating. Then, when he'd disappeared and she'd realized she was pregnant, she'd had to hide her heartache.

If she could keep her emotions under wraps during all that, she could do it through an evening of pizza and bowling.

Their game hadn't ended by the time the pizza was brought out to the tables, but the kids abandoned it to go eat. It was Charli's turn to bowl, so she watched them go, then picked up her second ball.

"Think you can get a spare?"

The sound of Blake's voice drew her from her preparations to throw the ball. She turned to find him watching her with raised brows, as if to challenge her.

"Probably not."

"You've gotta have more confidence in yourself than that."

Butterflies fluttered madly in her stomach at his words. Trying to keep her calm, she shrugged and said, "It's bowling. Winning or losing this particular game isn't worth too much introspection, but I'll try my best."

She turned back around and took a deep breath, exhaling before she sent the ball down the lane. Normally, she would have walked over to pick up her third and final ball for the frame, but instead, she watched as her throw made its way to the pins.

There were only three pins left, and they were all clumped together. So it was really no surprise when her ball clipped one and it was enough to drop the other two as well.

"Yay, Mom!" Layla yelled down at her from the food table.

Charli turned around and smiled up at her, before dropping her gaze to Blake. He was still seated on the bench, leaning forward with a smile on his face.

Her heart gave a hard thump before it began to race, taking her breath with it for a moment. She hated that his smile could still affect her like that. But at the same time, she had missed the breathlessness that his attention could create in her.

"You did it," he said as he got to his feet. Gesturing, he motioned for her to precede him up the small flight of stairs to the pizza table.

Charli took the empty seat between Layla and Janessa, not letting herself even look to see where Blake sat.

"Did you have fun?" Janessa asked as she handed her a paper plate with a couple of slices of pizza on it.

"Yep. Are you going to bowl at all tonight?"

"I plan too. I just wanted to eat first," Janessa said. "It looked like Blake was having fun."

"The kids were too, which is good, since this is for them."

Kayleigh and Hudson had arrived, which surprised Charli a bit. She had a hard time imagining either of them wearing shoes that had been previously worn by a stranger. Knowing them, they'd probably bought a couple pairs of designer bowling shoes to use.

"Are you going to bowl, Kayleigh?" Janessa asked as she sat down across from them.

"Yep. I brought a pair of thick socks for the multi-person use shoes."

"I would have thought you'd have bought your own shoes to bring," Charli said.

Kayleigh laughed. "I did consider it, but Hudson told me no."

Hudson slipped his arm around her and said, "You're not that out of touch, babe."

It wasn't long before the kids were done eating and ready to bowl some more. Since she'd played with them already, Charli didn't rush to join them again. Jay figured out who wanted to bowl next, then went up to put the names in for the scoreboard.

This time, Jay had names for two lanes, and soon it was just her, Blake, Kayleigh, and Hudson at the food table. Charli shifted so she could watch the bowlers while she finished her pizza. She also listened to Kayleigh and Hudson chat with Blake, though his attention was also split between their conversation and Amelia as she bowled with the other kids.

For some reason, she rarely remembered that Blake also came from a wealthy family—though probably not quite as rich as Hudson's. Still, they were both from that world.

"Are you going to bowl, Charli?" Kayleigh asked.

"I already bowled with the kids," Charli said as she wadded up her napkin and put it on her empty plate.

"Did you win?"

"We didn't finish the game. The kids ran off to eat before we were done."

"You played with the gutter guards?" Kayleigh asked.

"Yep. Pretty much the only reason I ended up with the score I did was because of that."

"Maybe I'd better play with them, too."

"The kids make it quite fun, to be honest. They're not as competitive as the adults."

"Definitely the people I want to bowl with then."

When the games finished up, Charli and the others left the food table and joined the rest at the lanes to play another game. Kayleigh and Misha decided to bowl with the kids, then the rest of them were split between the other two lanes.

Charli wasn't surprised that when Jay told the guy the names for the display, she and Blake ended up on the same team. It seemed her siblings were determined to put her and Blake in close proximity to each other.

A few weeks ago, she would have been adamantly opposed to that.

Now? She wasn't sure how she felt.

Blake wasn't the same man she'd fallen in love with, and she certainly hadn't pined after that man all these years. But there was still enough of the guy she'd loved back then in who Blake seemed to be now to draw her to him.

But she could resist the draw, right?

Surely she could resist falling in love yet again with the man who'd once promised her the future she'd always wanted, then left her behind.

Right?

For the first time since Blake's arrival back in Serenity, Charli wasn't one hundred percent certain about that.

CHAPTER SIXTEEN

Blake had tried to give Charli space as they bowled, but it got harder and harder as the evening went on. He was already enjoying himself, because seeing Amelia having a blast made him happy. Being there with Charli was like icing on the cake.

"Should we have people pair up for this next game, so that their combined scores determines the winner and losers?" Jay asked after he'd won their first game with the adults. "That way it's not just the best player winning."

"How're we going to decide the pairs?" Janessa stared up at the monitor. "Maybe Jay should be paired up with the person who got the worst score."

"Lucky me," Misha said with a laugh.

Jay slipped his arms around Misha. "I won't argue with that setup."

"That means that Will gets Charli, Blake gets Hudson, and Jackson and Janessa are paired together." Kayleigh said, having already declared she wasn't going to bowl again unless it was with the kids.

"I don't like that," Janessa announced. "I want to be with Will, and I think Hudson and Blake both need handicaps more than each other. Blake should get the worst between Charli and Jackson, since he was better than Hudson, then Hudson gets the other."

"Sounds good," Jay said, looking up at the monitors. "Jackson, you're with Hudson, and Charli, you're with Blake. I'll put me, Misha, Jackson, and Hudson on one lane, and the rest of you will be on the other one."

Before anyone could protest, Jay headed for the counter. Blake glanced at Charli, but she wasn't reacting visually to what her siblings had decided.

"Hope you're prepared to lose," she said as they walked to their lane.

As far as Blake was concerned, win or lose, he was just happy to be playing on her team. "Don't worry. I'm pretty sure we have a chance. Jackson seems to live up to the role of professional handicap in every activity we choose, so I think we'll be okay."

A quick smile crossed Charli's face. "I think he likes having such a low expectation to live up to. Every once in a while, he surprises us."

Not for the first time, Blake wondered if Charli or Jackson had an interest in each other. He really hoped not. He might not have a chance to recapture what he'd once had with Charli, but he wasn't sure he could stand by and watch Jackson connect with her on a romantic level.

All he could hope was that Charli and Jackson had already had enough time to get to know each other, so if they'd wanted to be together, they would have been by this point. He wasn't sure he could witness the two of them dating.

"Alright," Jay said when he came back. "We're ready to go."

Will and Janessa joined Blake and Charli at the lane closest to the one the kids were playing on. Blake appreciated that, since he liked being able to keep an eye on Amelia.

So far, the kids seemed to be having a blast, and Blake had a feeling that Amelia was going to be exhausted when they got home that night. He was also certain that she'd ask to go bowling again soon. Although, if Peyton and Layla weren't able to join them, she might not be as excited to bowl again with just him.

"You're up first, Charli," Janessa said. "Show us how it's done."

Charli laughed as she stood up and went to grab a ball. "About all I can really show you is how to hit the gutter. It's a challenge for me to consistently keep the ball in the middle of the lane for some reason."

Blake got up and took a couple of steps toward Charli. "Can I give you a couple of tips?"

After a brief hesitation, Charli nodded, so Blake joined her on the approach area.

Standing next to her, Blake gestured to the lane. "You tend to pull a bit to the left. If you want your ball to stay more central, either turn your hand a bit more to the right or position yourself more to the right of center."

"Do I need to do both?" Charli asked.

"I think you just need to do one. Try each of them to see which one works best for you."

Blake stepped back off the approach area, crossing his arms as he watched her step toward the foul line and release the ball. She had lined herself up with the middle still, so it seemed she was working on the position of her hand first.

The ball didn't seem to pull as far to the left and made it to the pins without hitting the gutter. Unfortunately, it only managed to hit the two pins on the far left.

"Well, at least it wasn't the gutter," Charli muttered as she turned to pick up another ball. "I'll try moving off to the right this time."

She had more success with that, and the ball hit the middle pins and left only one pin on the right standing.

Turning around, the smile she gave Blake made him smile back. "That worked out great. We might just win this."

Blake chuckled. "We just might."

"Will, are you going to give *me* tips?" Janessa asked her husband, when it was her turn, Charli having not been able to get the remaining pin with her last ball.

"I give you tips all the time," Will said. "But you never listen to me."

Janessa considered his response for a moment. "I suppose that's true. I listen when it's important, though."

"Maybe this will be important."

"Possibly." Janessa gave her husband a broad smile and a quick kiss before going to pick up a ball.

Janessa didn't do as well as Charli had, but she managed to keep two of her three balls out of the gutter. Blake got all ten pins with two of his balls, and Will did the same.

At the end of the first frame, Will did the math, then announced that Blake and Charli were in the lead. Charli came over to where Blake sat and gave him a high five before she went to pick up a ball to start the next frame.

Janessa and Charli developed a friendly rivalry, and soon they were trash talking each other. Will just sat back and let the sisters go at it, so Blake did the same.

"If I get a strike," Janessa said, turning to face Charli with a ball in her hand. "You have to go on a date."

Charli gave a huff of laughter. "Okay. Sure."

Blake glanced at Charli in surprise. From what he'd heard, Charli wasn't one to date. So the fact that she was willing to commit to that was a bit surprising. Although, he supposed that there wasn't much risk to Charli agreeing as Janessa hadn't managed to throw a strike yet that night.

"Hey, everyone." Janessa had raised her voice enough that the others in the next lane turned toward her. "Charli has agreed to go on a date if I get a strike."

Misha laughed. "I'm guessing she figures that's a pretty safe thing to agree to."

"Hey, sometimes getting a strike is as much luck as it is skill," Janessa protested.

"Good luck, then," Jay said. "And I really mean that."

Charli sat on a seat in the curved row behind the lanes, legs and arms crossed. She didn't appear to be worried at all as she watched Janessa prepare to throw her ball.

Pretty quickly, it became apparent that Charli's lack of concern wasn't misplaced. Janessa's first ball ended up in the gutter, leaving Blake feeling a strange mixture of disappointment and relief.

"Nice try, Nessa," Charli called out.

"Oh, I might have missed this one, but I still have a few more frames."

Charli uncrossed her arms and legs as she popped up on her feet. "Hang on a second."

Janessa turned around, an innocent look on her face. "What's the problem?"

"I didn't agree to you getting a strike whenever during this game. It was just for this frame."

After throwing her second ball, Janessa turned around. "You didn't specify that."

"You didn't specify it was for the whole game."

"All I said was that if I threw a strike, and you agreed."

Charli groaned as she slumped back in her seat. "Siblings suck."

Blake managed not to laugh, assuming that Charli wouldn't appreciate it if he did. The tension she showed every time Janessa's turn came, made it pretty evident that she actually didn't want Janessa to get that strike.

The odds were still pretty much in Charli's favor, but Janessa wasn't completely wrong either. Sometimes luck played a role even when skill was absent.

Janessa was down to two frames, and as she prepared to bowl the second to last frame, she paused for longer than usual before throwing her ball. Apparently, whatever she did to prepare served her well because, shock of all shocks, she got a strike.

As the display flashed STRIKE above her, Janessa stood there for a moment, just staring, and then she slowly turned around. Instead of looking at Charli, Janessa stared at Jay with wide eyes.

"Congrats, Nessa," Jay said with a broad grin.

"Nope. No congrats," Charli announced.

Janessa looked at her then, a smile growing on her face. "And that's how you do it."

"Nope."

"Okay. Here's a deal for you," Janessa said as she sauntered toward her sister. "If *you* get a strike, it will cancel out mine."

Charli glared at her sister, then stalked over to the ball return and stared down at the balls. Blake wondered if she was trying to find a lucky ball or something.

Finally, she grabbed a ball, then walked over to the foul line. She took a small step to the right, clearly planning to do all she could to improve her chances of getting a strike.

Though she'd been bowling better than Janessa throughout the game, Blake still didn't hold out much hope for Charli getting a strike.

Her turn was right after Janessa's strike, and unfortunately for her, she didn't get her strike and was definitely not happy. Charli's mood did not improve when both he and Will each managed to do what she had failed at.

When Blake joined Charli at the chairs, she sighed. "Janessa, since Blake's my partner, can his strike count as mine?"

Blake chuckled, but then pinched his lips together when Charli turned to glare at him. No one seemed to be taking Charli's upset too seriously, but Blake could see that their flippancy was really bugging her.

He wasn't a fan of set-up dates himself, so he could understand why Charli was upset about it. Her siblings' determination to send her on this date seemed over the top, however. Blake knew he was missing something.

When the game was over, Charli still hadn't gotten her strike, but they had come out on top. She tried to use that to cancel the strike, but Janessa wasn't having it.

"You are so manipulative," Charli told her. "Doing whatever you can to get your own way."

"Only in order to help you out."

"I don't *need* your help."

"Your single status says otherwise."

"Okay, you two," Jay said, stepping in to wrap an arm around the shoulders of each of his arguing sisters. "Fight this out at home."

Charli glared at both of her siblings. "I know what you two are doing, and it's not going to work."

"Time will tell," Jay said.

With that, Charli stalked over to where Layla was bowling with the other kids and dropped down on a seat next to Kayleigh. Blake watched her for a moment, before looking back at the others.

"Do I want to know?" he asked.

Jay chuckled. "Probably. Are you interested in going on a date?"

Blake was momentarily struck speechless, but not for long. "Depends on the circumstances."

Jay nodded. "We'll talk about it later."

"So, do we get a prize for coming in first?" Blake asked.

"Yep." Janessa grinned at him. "You two have won dinner at the restaurant of your choice."

"Ah. Do we have to go together?"

Janessa frowned at him as she crossed her arms. "You don't want to go for dinner with Charli?"

"I'm fine with that," he assured her. "I'm just not sure Charli feels the same way."

"She doesn't," Janessa agreed readily enough. "But I think she'll come around."

"Let the two of us talk about it and let you know."

"I can deal with that."

Blake had no idea what they were hoping to accomplish, and he was pretty sure Charli wasn't on board with the plan. He still didn't think they were aware of what had transpired between them twelve years ago.

If he'd been in their position, and he'd learned that a guy had been secretly dating his sister, had slept with her, and then disappeared, he wouldn't be trying to set them up. And he most definitely wouldn't be inviting the guy to their family gatherings.

Whatever the Halverson siblings were concocting with regards to him and Charli, it most definitely was being done in ignorance of the relationship they'd once had.

Blake didn't know exactly how to handle things. If Charli would agree to talk to him, maybe together they could figure out what to do. And maybe—if he was lucky—she'd agree that they should just go on the date.

The more he was around Charli and the more she relaxed around him, the more Blake saw of the woman he'd once loved. The memory of that love was stronger than it had been in years, making him wonder if perhaps it hadn't died completely.

As he watched Charli talk with the kids, Blake wondered if there was even a remote possibility that she'd give him a chance to show her the type of man he was now. He wanted to show her that he was stronger now. More capable of standing beside her as she reached for her dreams.

Except that she'd already achieved most of what she'd dreamed of having. She had the job she'd hoped to get. She had a daughter she doted on. She had a lovely home.

And she'd done it all without him.

When he'd left, Charli hadn't let his desertion stop her from moving forward—moving on—and reaching for the things she desired for her life.

The only thing she didn't have was the marriage she'd wanted, though he wasn't sure that she hadn't been married and divorced. And there was still the question of who Layla's father was.

Blake looked over at the young girl, searching for signs of her father in her looks. But all he saw was Charli. Though her hazel eyes were a couple of shades lighter than her mom's, Layla had her dark hair, and even her mannerisms and personality were so much like Charli's.

Was there a chance she was his?

He couldn't tell for sure just from looking at her. Knowing her birthday might help figure that out, but there was no guarantee that Charli hadn't gotten involved with someone else as soon as she realized they were actually, really done.

Jackson had basically admitted that she'd had what sounded like a rebound fling... with a guy she had apparently not minded her family knowing about. He didn't want to think about that situation, particularly because it meant another man had helped Charli achieve her dream of being a mom.

Short of asking Charli directly, Blake had no way to know for sure who Layla's father was. Not that she would tell him. After all, from what Jackson had said, she hadn't told anyone.

Would Charli keep it from him if Layla was his?

She hadn't tried to keep him from being around Layla. He would have thought that if Layla being his was a secret Charli was keeping from him, she would have kept them apart.

Blake sighed, thoughts of the possibilities cramping his brain.

He had to believe that Charli would tell him if Layla was his. If for no other reason than for him to share the financial responsibility of raising her.

Watching Charli, Blake could see that she was still ticked off. Even though she was speaking with the kids, her usual smile was missing. This wasn't the first time Blake had seen Charli angry. She had a bit of a temper, and he'd witnessed it occasionally during their relationship. Even back then, it had mainly been her siblings that made her mad.

It took a lot to set Charli off, but when she went off, she went *off.* Thankfully, most of the time, she didn't stay mad for very long, and Blake had always enjoyed cajoling her out of her bad mood. Somehow, he doubted he'd have that same luck this time around.

As soon as the kids finished their game, everyone began to get ready to leave. Blake swapped out his bowling shoes, then helped Amelia with hers, and carried both pairs up to the counter. Jay was there already, settling the bill for the evening.

When Blake tried to pay for his and Amelia's part, Jay waved him off.

"We're happy that you both could be here," Jay said.

"It was more fun than I thought it would be, and it looks like Amelia really had a good time, too."

Jay smiled. "It's always great to see the kids enjoying life."

The others joined them to return their shoes, then they all left the bowling alley. Amelia skipped ahead with Layla and Peyton, while Blake followed after them. Charli must have still been avoiding her siblings because she ended up walking alongside Blake. Not too close, but closer to him than to any of the people who had annoyed her.

The sky was dark, with the sun having set while they'd been inside, but the parking lot had plenty of lights that illuminated the area. There were quite a few cars in the lot, which wasn't a surprise since the lanes had slowly filled during the time they'd been there.

The bowlers had consisted mainly of families and teens. Despite its somewhat run-down appearance, it was apparently still a favorite destination for people looking for something to do on a Friday night in Serenity.

As they neared their cars, Blake said, "Hey, Charli, would you mind giving me your phone number?"

She stared at him, and for a moment, he thought she was going to outright refuse him. "Why?"

"After tonight, I think your siblings have something on their minds. I thought maybe we should talk about it."

She sighed, then held out her hand. Blake unlocked his phone and opened his contacts before handing it to her. It took her only a minute to enter her name and number into his phone and give it back to him.

"Thanks," he said.

Charli narrowed her gaze at him. "Don't make me regret this."

"I won't."

After twelve years, he had her phone number again.

Last time, he'd ended up blocking her number, then deleting it, because he hadn't wanted to be tempted to contact her, especially after he'd tied his life to the US army. Changing his number had been the final step in the severing of their relationship and the connection with his old life.

He understood Charli's reluctance to give him the information again, so he'd be mindful of how he used it.

Blake had to practically drag Amelia away from the other two. Thankfully, Jay and Charli also told their kids to get to their cars, so Amelia had no choice but to go with him to the truck.

As he waited to exit the parking lot, Amelia said, "Does Layla have a daddy?"

"I don't know," Blake said, wondering where the conversation was going.

"Maybe her daddy is gone like my mommy."

"Maybe."

"I wish we were sisters. Then Miss H could be my mom and you could be Layla's dad."

Blake didn't know how to respond to that. In another world where he'd made different decisions, that might have been the case.

In a way, he was a bit surprised that it had taken her this long to come up with these observations, although she'd never really been one to jump into things. This might be the first time she was voicing these thoughts, but it was entirely possible they'd been percolating in her brain for much longer.

Blake tried to come up with a response that wasn't dismissive, but he also didn't want to encourage her in this line of thinking.

"I'm going to pray for it," Amelia announced before Blake had sorted out his answer.

"What?"

"Aunt Julia said that we can pray and ask God for things," she told him. "So I'm going to pray and ask God to make Layla my sister."

Now Blake really didn't know what to say. He didn't want to tell her not to pray, or that God wasn't going to answer her prayers. But how would she feel when God didn't answer her prayer the way she wanted? Because that was probably going to be the case.

Thinking back over the sermons he'd heard, Blake tried to come up with something to help her understand that *no* was also an answer.

"You need to realize that God might have other plans for them and for us," Blake said gently. "But you can always pray about it, so God knows what you'd like."

Amelia remained quiet for the rest of their drive home, and Blake was worried about it. However, she didn't seem upset by what he'd said. And when he went to put her to bed that night, she prayed with more faith than he had about the situation. He couldn't help but admire her for that.

Though he left Amelia in her room a few minutes later, Blake couldn't leave behind her comments on Charli and Layla. She might have enough confidence to pray for what she wanted in this situation, but Blake didn't. Mainly because it felt selfish to pray for something he'd already had once and handled badly.

Was it fair to ask God for a second chance with Charli when he messed up so terribly the first time around?

Blake wasn't sure that it was. No matter what he might want.

CHAPTER SEVENTEEN

For some reason, Charli had expected Blake to contact her right away after asking for her number. However, he didn't. And—as had become too common of late—she wasn't sure how she felt about that.

He'd obviously picked up on the antics at the bowling alley and wanted to discuss what had happened. Her siblings—Jay and Janessa especially—were determined to play matchmaker, and short of telling them everything that had happened years earlier between her and Blake, she wasn't sure how to discourage them.

Would Blake have any ideas? Maybe if he made it clear to Jay and Janessa that he wasn't interested in her, they'd back off.

But was Charli strong enough to ask him to reject her for a second time?

At least this time, she wouldn't be left in the dark, wondering what had happened. She'd be giving him permission to reject her.

And since her heart wasn't caught up in him anymore, it wouldn't hurt.

Right?

It was Saturday afternoon when a text finally showed up from Blake. It came from an unknown number, but as soon as she read the text, it was clear it was from him.

Hey Charli. This is Blake. Would now be a good time to text or call?

While she contemplated how to answer that, Charli put his info into her contacts. She preferred texts from pretty much everyone.

However, a call would probably be easier than trying to type everything out.

We can call.

Almost immediately, her phone rang. Taking a deep breath, Charli answered it, bracing herself for the sound of Blake's voice. They'd spent a lot of time on phone calls back in the day since they'd been trying to keep their relationship on the down low, so she'd gotten used to hearing his voice over the phone.

"How are you doing?" Blake asked when she answered.

"I'm doing okay. How about you?"

"I'm fine. I would have contacted you sooner, but I needed to get Amelia settled with something distracting."

Charli thought of Layla playing games with Janessa and Will in the kitchen and wondered if Blake ever had a break or if he was always around Amelia when he wasn't at work.

"That's fine."

"I don't want to take up too much of your time, so I'll get right to the point," Blake said. "Am I right in assuming that you never told your family about us?"

"That would be correct. There wasn't any reason to after things ended. Plus, it would have been awkward because of your relationship with Jackson. No one had suspected anything, so I just left it and moved on."

"I'm sorry again for how things ended."

"That was a long time ago," she said, though it actually felt closer than ever.

"Is Layla mine?"

The unexpected question hit Charli in the gut, robbing her of breath for a moment, but she managed to pull herself together enough to say, "Why would you think that? We were only together once."

Though she'd rehearsed for the possibility of this conversation, now that it was there, fear filled her heart. She couldn't let him hear how his question had twisted her up inside. Protecting her secret was the most important thing in that moment, so she needed to pull herself together and hold a normal conversation with Blake in response to his question.

"True, but it only takes one time."

"However, I was on birth control. I told you that."

She didn't want to outright lie and say no to him, so she gave him all the reasonings she'd given herself when she'd first realized she was pregnant. Once she'd accepted that Blake had disappeared, he'd ceased to be Layla's father in her mind. She'd needed to squash the memory of his involvement in her life in order to survive.

Layla was hers and hers alone.

Even as she thought that, Charli felt a tug of conviction in her heart. She was lying to Blake. She might not have lied outright, but she was definitely leading him to believe a lie.

It was wrong, but it was for a good reason. Though she could see Blake was a good dad to Amelia, she still wasn't sure about sharing parenting responsibilities with him. She needed to be sure that he really was putting down deep roots in Serenity. And even then...

"Anyway, like I said, there was no reason to tell my siblings what had gone on between us," Charli said, anxious to drag the conversation focus off Layla.

"So that's why they think matching us up now is a good idea?"

"I guess. They've tried to set me up a few times in the past, but now that they've found love in their own lives, they seem even more determined for each of us to experience it."

There was a moment of silence before Blake said, "How do you want me to handle this situation?"

And wasn't that the question?

"I think maybe you need to tell them that you're not interested in what they're trying to do," Charli said. "Just tell them the truth."

More silence. "Well, to be honest, that wouldn't entirely be the truth."

Blake's words took a second to sink in. Was he saying...?

Charli wasn't sure what she wanted him to say, but she needed clarity. "What wouldn't be the truth?"

"That I'm not interested in what they want."

"I don't understand."

"I didn't disappear twelve years ago because I didn't love you." Blake let out a heavy sigh. "Seeing you again has made me so mad at myself for the decisions I made back then."

Charli scoffed. "There is no way on earth you'll ever convince me that you still love me."

"That's not exactly what I'm saying."

Of course it wasn't. But hearing him say that still hurt.

"Being around you again has reminded me of all the reasons I fell in love with you in the first place."

"I've changed," Charli informed him. "I'm not the same as I was twelve years ago."

"I understand because I've changed, too."

Charli had seen that. Though some of what she'd observed hadn't necessarily been outward changes in him, but more of a maturing, a strengthening, of the qualities she'd once loved.

"So what are you suggesting?" she asked.

"Let's go on the one date you owe your sister," Blake said. "If, after we spend that time together, we don't feel like we want to pursue anything further, we tell your siblings we tried, and it isn't going to work. Chances are they'll be more willing to accept that after we at least give it a shot."

"You don't know my siblings," Charli muttered.

"So you don't think they'd back off then?"

"They might, but there is no guarantee."

"Let's give it a shot," Blake said.

Charli had a hard time believing that Blake really wanted to spend time with her. And honestly, though part of her did want to spend time with him, she was scared. It felt like doing so would just put herself out there for hurt once again.

However, it was just one date. Just one evening.

It might be the most awkward time she'd ever had, but it would be just one evening. And if it got her siblings off her back, maybe it would be worth the awkwardness.

"Okay. We'll give it a shot." Charli knew that she didn't sound super excited about it, but she couldn't afford to be. The excitement she felt about spending time with Blake had disappeared a long time ago.

Maybe.

The beat of silence following her words told her that Blake hadn't really thought she'd agree. Had he been hoping she wouldn't?

She had to stop thinking like that or she'd end up with a headache. The Blake she knew before hadn't been one to say things he didn't mean. Of course, he'd said he loved her, then disappeared. So what did she know?

"Okay. Great." He cleared his throat. "Janessa said that our prize for winning was dinner at the restaurant of our choice. So, do you have somewhere you'd like to go?"

She wasn't going to suggest her favorite restaurant, because if the evening didn't go well, she didn't want to have to avoid it. "I'll think about it and let you know. But if you have somewhere in particular that you'd like to go, I'm fine with that."

"I don't really know many places around here," Blake said. "At least none that aren't kid friendly."

"We have time to figure it out."

Charli had once dreamed about being able to go on a date to a restaurant where they wouldn't have to worry about someone seeing them and revealing their relationship before they were ready to. Now, she was getting one "date" with no promise of anything more.

"Yep. We do."

Needing the conversation to be over, Charli said, "I'd better go."

"Thanks for talking to me. I'm sure you didn't want to, so I appreciate that you did."

She didn't bother to dispute his comment, because while it wasn't one hundred percent true, there was some truth to his assumption.

After saying goodbye, Charli flopped back onto her bed beside the pile of laundry she was supposed to be folding. She stared up at the ceiling, trying to figure out what had just happened.

Charli was still trying to figure that out the following Saturday as she got dressed for their dinner.

"Why are you wearing that on your date?" Janessa asked from where she was sitting against Charli's headboard.

Charli looked at herself in the mirror next to her walk-in closet. Though she might have taken offense any other time, that day, she didn't. It had taken her a long time to decide what to wear because it was so hard to shut down the little voice in her head that was trying to convince her to choose something she'd know for certain that Blake would like.

"I mean, it's not a bad color," Janessa said as she regarded the red, long-sleeved silky blouse Charli wore. "But I would have thought you'd go with purple or that soft pink that looks so nice on you."

Normally, she would have, but she happened to know that Blake liked both those colors on her, and she didn't want to be dressing with him in mind. Regardless of what Janessa might be calling it, she was choosing to think of it as just *dinner* and not a *date.*

"I like the style of this blouse." Charli smoothed her hands down her sides. "And it's comfortable."

Janessa sat forward, drawing her legs up to cross them on the bed. "You don't think anything is going to come of this, do you?"

"Not really," Charli said with a shrug. "I mean, we're going out because you guys basically held a gun to our heads."

"That doesn't mean you can't enjoy yourselves and get to know each other."

"Just remember that this is a one-time thing," Charli said as she went into her bathroom to make sure her hair was okay.

Janessa followed and leaned against the doorjamb, her arms crossed. "But you should at least keep an open mind for this evening."

"I will."

Janessa gave a huff. "You never keep an open mind where men are concerned, so honestly, I'm not holding out much hope that you will for Blake."

"Then why are you forcing me to go out with him?"

"Because every once in a while, you need to be reminded that you don't have to be alone. That decent men still exist."

Charli finished brushing her hair and set the brush on the counter. Would Janessa still think Blake was decent if she knew everything?

"We'll see how it goes," Charli said, picking up the bottle of her favorite perfume and lightly spritzing herself.

Janessa followed her back into the bedroom, standing there as Charli pulled on the ankle boots she'd decided to pair with her pleated black slacks. They would give her a couple more inches of height, though she'd still be a few inches shorter than Blake.

When Janessa's phone chirped, she looked at the screen. "Will says Blake is here."

A swarm of butterflies erupted inside Charli's stomach, and for a moment, she wanted to call it all off. Nothing good could come from them spending time together.

"Let's go," Janessa said as she slipped her arm through Charli's. It was like she didn't trust Charli to make it downstairs without supervision.

Charli grabbed her purse, which already had her phone in it, then allowed Janessa to drag her out of her room. The murmur of male voices in the distance did nothing to quell the nervous fluttering in her stomach.

As she and Janessa walked into the living room, both men turned in their direction. Blake's gaze landed on her, and after a moment's hesitation, he gave her a smile. When her stomach knotted with even more nerves, Charli wasn't sure she was going to have an appetite once they got to the restaurant.

Janessa let go of Charli and went over to where Will stood. "Doesn't Charli look beautiful?"

Will looked down at his wife. "Am I allowed to agree with that?"

With a laugh, Janessa said, "I wasn't asking you, but yes, you can agree. And so can Blake."

The smile on Blake's face grew. "Yes, she does look beautiful."

Charli wanted to shake her head at him. This dinner was supposed to get her siblings off their backs. Blake agreeing that she looked beautiful did not support that goal, especially when Janessa was there to witness his words.

"We'd better go," Charli said. "We can't be out too late."

Charli had dropped Layla off at Jay and Misha's earlier, and Blake had taken Amelia there as well, so the three kids were getting to hang out.

Part of her agreement to go out for dinner was that the girls not know what was going on. The last thing she needed was for Layla to get wind of things and think that she might be getting a step-dad. Thankfully, everyone had agreed.

Her siblings weren't unreasonable. Just extremely stubborn and crazy.

"See you guys later," Janessa called out as they left the living room. "Have fun!"

Fun wasn't exactly what Charli had assumed the evening would be. Awkward was more in line with her expectation. She would rather have gone to a movie so they wouldn't have to talk, but Janessa had insisted they go for dinner.

They were both quiet as they walked out of the house and down the sidewalk to where Blake's truck was parked at the curb. He opened the front passenger door and waited for her to settle in the seat.

Glancing around, she took in the clean interior of his Truck. He'd always prided himself on taking care of his vehicle. Back in the day, Blake had driven a fully loaded truck, and it looked like he still had it.

There was a mixture of scents in the cab, all of them centering on Blake. There was a light scent of oil and rubber, but stronger was the scent of cedar and sandalwood, which she assumed was his cologne. It was kind of like getting a hug from him.

Her reaction to that was mixed, which was pretty much a reflection of her feelings about everything in this situation she'd found herself in.

Blake climbed behind the wheel and turned on the engine. The dashboard lit up, and the radio began to play softly, filling the interior with jazz. That was a bit of a surprise as previously, he'd been more of a country or soft-rock listener.

Was he trying to set the scene for romance?

"How was your week?" Blake asked as he pulled away from the curb of the quiet street she lived on.

"Well, the kids had a good week, which meant I had a good week. How about you?"

"It's been busy at the garage. Lots of people coming in to get their vehicles prepared for winter. That's a new one for me, to be honest."

"Are you ready to deal with winter here?"

"Yep. Amelia's excited about it. She's never seen snow in person."

"Where did you live before you came here?" Charli asked the question without thinking. She'd had no plans to delve into the time since he'd last been in Serenity, but the question was definitely heading in that direction.

"Texas."

"Oh, yeah, that's going to be a bit of an adjustment. Have you got winter wear for Amelia?"

"Not yet, though Aunt Julia mentioned something about it earlier this week."

"Don't leave it until the last minute. The selection can get picked over, plus the cold can come up on us really quickly."

"Okay. I'll chat with Julia again about helping us out."

Charli bit her tongue to keep from offering to help. If the girls were closer in size, she would have been able to offer Amelia some of Layla's hand-me-downs. However, because she didn't have any friends or family with kids the right size to pass clothes down to, she tended to donate most of Layla's outgrown clothes to the local shelter.

Even if she did have more kids in the future, there would be too big of an age gap to make keeping the clothes a practical thing. At most, she had the previous year's stuff, but Amelia was at least two sizes behind Layla.

She hadn't given away everything, having chosen to keep some of the baby furniture she'd had for Layla, but she was beginning to lose hope that she'd have any more children. Misha had used some of it when she'd first arrived with Ciara, but since then, it had all just sat in the storage area in the basement. Gareth and Aria had chosen to buy most of

"Does Layla ice skate at all?"

Charli's first response was to not want to share anything with him about Layla. But she knew she couldn't do that without raising his suspicions. "Yes. She takes lessons every year."

"Amelia has mentioned that she'd like to learn. If you could recommend a teacher, I'd really appreciate it."

"Does she have aspirations to skate in the Olympics?"

Blake chuckled. "Not exactly. But I think she'd love to be able to wear pretty costumes."

"Layla does ballet as well," Charli said, even as she lectured herself that answering questions was different than volunteering information about Layla. "That might give Amelia more of a chance to wear pretty outfits, as Layla usually does her skating lessons bundled up in warmer clothes."

"Oh, she's mentioned ballet as well."

"Lessons will start up soon for the ice skating. They've already started for ballet, but she should still be able to join the lessons."

For a moment, the surrealness of the situation sank in. Never in her wildest dreams had she imagined that she'd be having a conversation with the man she'd once loved about their daughters. Daughters that they weren't parenting together.

"It was nice of Kayleigh to make a reservation for us," Blake said as they left Serenity and headed in the direction of the resort where Kayleigh and Hudson worked.

"Yep. It's good to have connections."

They'd needed to choose a restaurant not too far from Serenity, since their time together was limited because of the girls. That meant that restaurants in Coeur d'Alene had been out of the question.

When Kayleigh had offered to set up a reservation for them at a restaurant in the resort, Charli had presented that option to

Blake. He'd liked the sound of The Steakhouse, and Charli had always enjoyed the food whenever she'd eaten there, which wasn't too often as she didn't want to take advantage of her sister's generosity. Plus, it was kind of pricey.

They didn't have to worry about paying for their meal that night, as her siblings were footing the bill. Normally, Charli would have protested that and taken care of the cost herself. However, since Jay and Janessa had been so insistent about the dinner, Charli was happy to let them pay for it.

"Do you eat at the resort often?"

"No. Usually the only time I do is if others in the family are going."

"Hudson said he really likes The Steakhouse."

"I think that's where they eat lunch quite often."

"So Hudson works at the resort too?"

"He has an office there, but he doesn't work for the resort. His job is with Remington, the company that owns the resort. So while they work for the same company, they don't work together."

Blake asked about her other siblings, having met most of them when he'd been there twelve years ago, even the ones who were currently away from Serenity. Charli was glad for a topic of conversation that wasn't too personal and happily divulged all the details on everyone else.

When they reached the resort, Blake parked the truck, then they got out into the cool fall evening air. As they reached the door to the restaurant, Blake pulled it open and waited for Charli to precede him inside.

Blake had always had impeccable manners, and when she'd commented on them previously, he'd said that they were the result of his mom demanding he act a certain way. It looked like none of that had been lost in the years he'd been in the army.

The hostess greeted them with a smile that grew when Blake gave his name. "Oh, you're Kayleigh's family."

Blake glanced at Charli, then said, "Yep. Charli is her sister."

Charli waited for the woman to stare at her, searching for the similarities between Kayleigh and Charli, beyond their dark hair and eyes. The woman's expression didn't change at all as she turned her smile on Charli.

She picked up a couple of menus, then asked them to follow her. The restaurant was filled with soft music and dim lighting. There were tables scattered around the room, as well as booths along the outside wall.

The hostess led them to one of the booths in the far back corner of the restaurant. A Tiffany lamp suspended above the table cast a soft circle of light. After they'd settled into opposite sides of the booth, the hostess handed them each a menu.

"Your server will be with you in a moment."

For the next little while, their attention was focused on ordering their meals. But once the waitress had left to put their order in at the kitchen, silence filled the space between them.

"So, uh, Amelia's doing okay at school?" Blake asked. "I assume that you'd let me know if that wasn't the case."

"Yes. I definitely would," Charli assured him. "She's doing just fine. I appreciate the time you've taken to read with her each night. It really shows in how quickly she's progressing."

Blake smiled. "It hasn't been a problem to spend time each day reading, as she never fights me when I say it's time to do it. She likes to read."

"That's not the case with all my students, and I know it can be a strain on the parents to have to force their child to read."

"Does Layla enjoy reading like you do?"

With another question from Blake about Layla, Charli realized that she was going to have no choice but to share bits of information about her daughter with the man who didn't know he was her father.

CHAPTER EIGHTEEN

Blake could hardly believe that they'd actually made it to their dinner date. From the conversations they'd had leading up to the evening, Charli had definitely not been as excited about it as he was, though he'd tried to rein in his enthusiasm whenever they talked. Janessa was still in the doghouse with her sister, but she didn't seem bothered by that.

The previous night, when he'd been at their place for another pizza dinner before going to a game at the high school, Blake had expected her to come up with a reason to put off their dinner. However, there had been no discussion of their plans because the kids had been present, and Charli had insisted that the girls not know what was going on.

She'd made it clear that if anyone let slip that she and Blake were going for dinner together, everything was off. Blake had kept his fingers crossed that no one would slip up because he had really hoped to have this time with her. The only thing that would have made it better would have been if she'd actually been happy about the evening.

Unfortunately, he didn't think that was going to be the case. Though Janessa had continued to refer to their time together as a date, Charli had only ever referred to it as them *having dinner.*

It was his hope that even if she was going under duress, the evening would help to lessen the tension between them. He could see Serenity as a long-term home for him and Amelia, and since she'd already forged a friendship with Layla, it would be best for everyone if there was no awkwardness between him and Charli.

Even though their time together might ease the tension, Blake was aware it could also make things worse. But since that definitely wasn't his goal, he would do what he could to avoid that outcome.

"How was Amelia doing in school where you were before?" Charli asked after she'd shared that Layla did, in fact, love to read.

"To be honest, I wasn't involved in her day-to-day life until recently, so I really can't tell you."

Blake hated to reveal that, since it didn't reflect well on him. When Charli frowned, he wished he'd just given a surface answer. But since he'd shared that much, he might as well give her more information about their life in Texas.

"Since Lauren had primary custody, she took care of all that. And when she passed away, her sister took over Amelia's care until I could get back from my deployment and out of the army."

"Did Lauren's sister mind that you moved so far away with Amelia?" Charli asked.

Blake sat back as the waitress approached their table with their food. She set their plates in front of them, then left them alone.

After spending so much time with the Halversons, Blake knew that Charli would pray for her meal, so he wasn't surprised when she bent her head. Blake also bowed his head, silently thanking God for his food, but also asking God to bless their conversation and that the evening would be a pathway to peace between them.

Once they'd finished praying, Blake picked up his knife and fork and cut off a piece of his steak. It cut so smoothly that Blake knew he was in for a real treat.

From that single bite, Blake figured it was probably the best steak he'd ever eaten. But then, considering the price of the meal, it should be.

"So... about Lauren's sister?" Charli prompted.

Right. Even a good meal wasn't going to distract her, though Blake would rather not talk about that part of his past. He'd give her the answers she asked for, however, because he felt he owed her that much.

"After Lauren died, her sister told me that she'd be willing to continue to care for Amelia if I financially supported her. So I sent her the payments I'd been giving Lauren. It felt like the best thing to do, since Amelia had already spent a lot of time with Callie. I finished out my deployment and when I got home, she told me that I needed to pay her more or make other arrangements." He didn't mention how she'd also said that if he married her, that would work, too. "That was when I decided not to re-enlist."

Charli frowned, pausing in the cutting of her steak. "She was doing it for the money?"

"It certainly felt that way at the time." Blake recalled the sick feeling he'd had when he'd come to that realization. "And it made me wonder if Amelia had been mistreated."

"Oh, no," Charli said softly. "That's horrible. Did you ask Amelia about it?"

"I did, and from what she told me, it seemed like perhaps more than mistreatment, she'd been neglected. Which, of course, is also mistreatment."

Charli's expression showed that his revelation had impacted her, which really didn't surprise him. She'd always had a love for children that would make it difficult for her to hear about a child being hurt in any way.

"I knew then that I had to make her my priority," Blake said, recalling how, in the end, the decision to leave the army and Texas had felt like the right one. "But I also knew that I couldn't raise Amelia on my own. So I contacted Aunt Julia, and she said to come to Serenity."

"You didn't consider going back to California?"

"Not even for a moment. I needed support, and I definitely wouldn't get that in California."

"Even your mom wouldn't help you?"

Blake shrugged. "She agreed with my dad's decision to disown me when I went there twelve years ago. I've never told her or any of my family about Amelia. My dad would not be impressed."

"It's weird how different your aunt is from your mom."

"Tell me about it," Blake said with a grimace. "I'm very grateful for that, though, because Julia and Robert have been a huge help to me and Amelia."

"Amelia has certainly blossomed in the past several weeks," Charli said. "So being here seems to have really benefitted her."

"I think so too. I'm thankful to everyone who has welcomed her, especially you and your family. You could have kept Layla from becoming friends with her, but I'm so glad you didn't."

"I never would have done that," Charli said. "You should know that."

"After how things ended for us, I wasn't sure how you'd feel about me and my daughter coming back into your life."

"It has been... weird," Charli admitted.

Blake was sure it had been more than weird, but he appreciated her not making it sound worse.

"If I didn't feel so strongly that Amelia needed what Serenity offered, I never would have crashed into your life again."

Charli stared at him for a moment before she focused on her meal. Maybe he shouldn't have said that. It made it sound like he hadn't actually wanted to see her, which hadn't been the case at all. But the truth was that if it hadn't been for Amelia, he might not have had the courage to return and face Charli again.

"Not that I didn't want to come back here and see you," he tried to clarify. "But after what I'd done, I figured you wouldn't want me around."

Charli lifted her gaze to his. "You would have been correct."

Though her words hurt, he definitely deserved them. "I am sorry for how my coming back has impacted you."

"It was difficult at first," she said, dropping her gaze to her plate. "But it's gotten easier."

Blake should have been glad to hear that, but he feared it was because she just didn't care. But what he felt didn't matter. He'd messed with her life twelve years ago, and if she needed to not care about him in order for her to be able to deal with him coming back, that was... fine.

"If you'd prefer me not to come around as much, just say the word. But even though I don't have the right, I would love it if you'd still let Amelia hang around Layla and Peyton."

"I'm not going to tell you to stop coming around. For one thing, that would raise suspicions in my family. Second, like I said, it's gotten... easier."

"And then your siblings finagled this situation."

Charli shrugged. "It's been okay."

Suddenly, a ton of words pressed against his tongue. All the things that he wanted to tell her. That he hadn't been able to say to her in so many years.

But she'd just said that it was getting easier to be around him. Did he want to ruin that by telling her that he wished he could have a second chance?

"I want to tell you again how sorry I am for what I did. I've regretted it countless times, and I really wish I'd handled things differently." He hesitated, then said, "But I can't focus on what I would have done differently because now I have Amelia and you have Layla. I wouldn't wish them away."

"I wouldn't either," Charli said. "I wasn't happy at the time. But finishing college, getting a new job, along with having Layla, all helped me move forward."

Again, he wanted to ask about Layla's father. However, it seemed like a subject she wasn't keen to discuss with him, aside from telling him that he wasn't her father. But maybe now that she'd heard about Amelia's mom, she'd be more forthcoming.

They were quiet for a few minutes, focusing on their meals. As the silence stretched on, Blake found it weighty and unlike anything he'd ever experienced with her before. He didn't like it because it was a silence that spoke loudly of broken promises, fractured hearts, and so much hurt. "So, how's your steak?"

Charli looked up at him and smiled. "Pretty good. Tastes like an expensive steak."

"Where do they get such tender steaks? The ones I've cooked never tasted this good."

"Mine either," Charli said. "I have no idea where they get their steaks, but I could probably ask Kayleigh. My guess is that you'll need to sell an arm or leg to afford them."

Blake chuckled. "Think I'll keep my limbs, thanks. If it takes a little more effort to chew my food, such is life."

When the corners of Charli's mouth tipped up, his heart gave a hard thump. He'd always loved to make her smile. She'd smiled easily enough. But still, it felt like such a treasure to say or do something that made her gaze soften as her face transformed with happiness.

Even though their time together that evening had been forced on them—well, on Charli, anyway—it was going better than he had dared hope.

He'd always enjoyed his time with Charli, and it seemed that perhaps twelve years hadn't dimmed that.

For the remainder of the meal, their conversation stayed light. Most of it centered once again around Charli's siblings and the lives they'd lived while he'd been away. She was far more at ease speaking about their lives than about her own.

"So you like Misha better than Casey?" Blake said, remembering how often she'd expressed her displeasure over the woman Jay was dating and how she'd treated Jay.

"Oh, most definitely. Misha, from the moment we met her, has proven herself to be a very sweet and kind woman. The patients at the clinic love her, which is so important."

"Jay does seem a lot happier than I remember him being the last time I was here."

"He is. Even after what he went through to get Peyton."

"I'm sure that was a shock."

Blake wasn't sure how he would have felt if he'd discovered years after the fact that he had a child. If Layla had been his.

"I think more of a shock for him was the fact that Peyton's mother wanted to give up custody of him, especially after having raised him for the first several years of his life. If she'd given him up right at birth, Jay would probably have had an easier time understanding her decision."

The one thing he'd always liked about—maybe had even been a little jealous of—the Halverson family was how, even though they didn't always get along, they pulled together when one of them needed support.

His sisters had tended to stick together, but they'd never included him. Probably because their dad had clearly favored him. Not that he'd spoiled Blake. No. His favor had been clear in the way he'd constantly brushed aside the girls' attempts to have input in the business, while asking Blake for his opinion.

The total dismissal of them had infuriated his sisters, especially the oldest one, which meant that when his dad had disowned him, he'd had nowhere to turn.

When the server came to clear away their empty plates, she asked if they wanted coffee and dessert.

"What do you think?" Blake asked, deferring to Charli.

She looked at the time on her phone. "I suppose we have time."

"Would you like decaf or regular coffee?" the server asked as she held out two small menus.

"Decaf for me," Charli said.

"For me too."

The server nodded as she took a step away from their table. "I'll be right back with your coffee."

Blake perused the dessert options. "I'm going to assume that the apple crisp isn't going to just be a run-of-the-mill apple crisp."

"Probably not. It's most likely an elevated version, though don't ask me what that might be."

"Well, I think I'm going to see if that's true."

"I'm going to go with the lava cake."

That didn't surprise Blake at all since she'd always been partial to chocolate.

When their desserts arrived, Blake was glad he'd made the decision to order the apple crisp. The apple mixture was the perfect blend of sweet and tart, the crisp tasty, and the ice cream served with it was creamy and vanilla-y.

"Oh, the center is perfect," Charli said as she cut into the small cake on her plate.

In the past, they would have shared bites of their desserts with each other, but that wouldn't happen that night.

His thoughts went to the last meal they'd shared, just the two of them. Knowing that they were going to be apart for awhile, Blake had arranged a special evening for them.

He'd reserved a suite at a nice hotel in Coeur d'Alene. It hadn't been his plan for them to sleep together, since he knew about her stance on pre-marital sex and respected her conviction. He had booked the room so that they could share a romantic dinner away from the chance of someone seeing them.

The room had a nice table next to a large window that looked out over the city, and he'd ordered a lavish meal from room service with several courses.

The evening had started out according to plan, and they'd enjoyed their time together, making plans for the future they hoped to have. However, after he'd given her the promise ring he'd bought, things had taken a physical turn.

It had been tempting to just go with the flow, but he didn't want Charli to regret what might happen. So, though it had been difficult, he had managed to pull back so they could talk.

As they talked about the future they wanted together, along with their upcoming separation, Charli had told him that since things were so serious between them, she wanted that physical closeness, too. He'd been hesitant, but also very tempted.

In the end, together, they'd made the decision to move forward physically.

Blake remembered Charli holding up her hand to show him the ring he'd given her that night. A promise ring. A promise he'd intended to keep... until life had taken an unexpected turn.

And now, there they were, sharing a meal fully supported by her family, but with a huge chasm between them.

Still, it could have been a lot worse. The evening had turned out better than it might have. Charli was just stubborn enough that it had been entirely possible that she'd choose to not speak the whole time they were together.

That she chose, instead, to interact with him in a relatively friendly manner was a better outcome than Blake had even dared to consider. He hoped that it might bode well for building some sort of friendship in the future.

"I guess we'd better head out," Charli said once they'd finished their desserts.

Though Blake would have liked to linger over a second cup of coffee, Charli was right. They needed to pick up the girls. But first, he had to take Charli to her house to pick up her car.

There was a definite chill in the air as they left the restaurant, and they both hurried to where he'd parked the truck. The cold was taking some getting used to, and it hadn't even gotten cold enough for it to snow yet.

Thankfully, it didn't take long before heat was pouring from the vents. "Can't imagine how much colder it's still going to get."

"Won't be left to your imagination much longer," Charli assured him. "Plenty more cold and snow on the way."

The drive to Charli's seemed to pass in the blink of an eye. Far quicker than Blake would have liked. He knew that the likelihood of another evening like this happening was pretty much nil.

As soon as he came to a stop at the curb in front of Charli's house, she reached for the door handle. Before opening, she turned to him. Her face was cast in shadows as she said, "That went better than I thought. Thanks for making it less awkward than it might have been."

"Thank you as well. I appreciate you also making it easier than you had to."

She pulled the door handle, and light flooded the cab of the truck. "I guess I'll see you in a few minutes."

"Yep."

After giving him a quick smile, she slid out of the truck and closed the door. Blake watched until she disappeared into the house, then he put the truck in gear and headed to Jay's.

Jay and Misha's home was large, and light glowed warmly from its windows. As he walked up to the front door, Blake wondered if he'd ever be able to afford a home like that.

Twelve years ago, he hadn't even questioned what type of home he'd be able to provide for Charli and the family they hoped to have. He'd assumed that his dad would continue to give him a monthly allowance since he'd continued to give it to his sisters, even though the oldest one was closer to thirty than twenty. So even if he hadn't made a lot in his career as a mechanic, he'd thought he'd have enough money to give Charli a nice home.

Jay greeted him with a broad smile when he opened the door. Stepping back, he motioned for him to come into the foyer.

"How did it go?" Jay asked, closing the door and blocking off the flow of cold air.

"It went fine," Blake said as he put his hands into the pockets of his jacket. "The food was amazing."

"Yeah. The resort's restaurants have a great menu."

Blake glanced around the open floor plan of the home, taking in the comfortable living room with large, overstuffed furniture and the spacious kitchen and dining room area. "How was Amelia?"

"She was just fine," Jay assured him. "She ate a whole bowl of spaghetti with a piece of garlic bread and had a cookie for dessert."

"Oh, that's good. She doesn't always eat well, so I'm glad she ate what you gave her."

"They're downstairs watching a movie," Jay said. "Misha just went down to get them. It might take a minute for her to get them corralled and up here."

The kids still weren't upstairs by the time Charli arrived. Jay greeted her with a hug, then asked how she'd enjoyed the evening. After a quick glance at Blake, she basically said the same thing he had when Jay had asked him.

"I'm glad it went so well," Jay said with a big smile. "So, where are you going next?"

"We didn't discuss that," Charli said. "And we might not."

That made Jay frown. "If this evening went well, why wouldn't you plan to do it again?"

Before either of them could reply, the kids came running up the stairs from the basement and through the kitchen. Amelia came right to him and readily accepted the hug he bent to give her.

"Did you have a good time?" he asked her, though the smile on her face answered his question.

"It was great! Can we do it again?"

"Maybe." He didn't want to commit one way or another. "But for now, we need to go home."

208 · KIMBERLY RAE JORDAN

"Did you and Amelia's dad come here together, Mom?" Layla asked as she looked between them.

"Nope. I drove my own car."

"Oh." Layla seemed a bit disappointed, which made Blake realize that Charli had been wise to keep their plans from the girls.

"I don't suppose I have to ask if you had fun," Charli said as she cupped Layla's face and leaned forward to kiss her forehead.

Layla laughed. "Yeah. I always have fun here."

"Well, say goodnight to everyone," Charli told her.

Before long, the four of them were walking out of Jay's house. Layla gave Amelia a hug, then skipped over to their car.

"Have a good night, Amelia," Charli said as she rested her hand briefly on Amelia's shoulder. "You too, Blake."

After they said goodnight, Blake helped Amelia up into the truck.

"What did you do while I was with Layla and Peyton?" Amelia asked.

"Not much," he said. "Just ate dinner, mainly."

"That's boring."

If only she knew. "I'm sure you had a lot more fun than I did."

"We had supper, then we played some games and watched a movie. I really liked being with Layla and Peyton."

Blake was glad to hear she'd enjoyed herself. These days, it wasn't often that he left her with anyone except Julia outside of school hours. Realizing how neglected she'd been in Lauren's sister's care, Blake had resolved to never expose her to something like that again.

Thankfully, he was confident that Charli and her family would always take good care of Amelia. Too bad he wasn't likely to need to use their babysitting services again for a date with Charli anytime soon.

CHAPTER NINETEEN

Charli sat on the bed in one of the bedrooms at the family home, watching as the hairstylist fixed her daughter's hair.

Layla had woken up with a smile, and it hadn't dimmed at all over the past few hours. Now she sat bundled up in a white robe that had her name embroidered on it, which matched the ones worn by Kayleigh and the two bridesmaids.

The hairstylist who'd come to do Kayleigh's hair had also done their mom's, the bridesmaids', and now, Layla's. The makeup artist and her assistant had worked their magic on each of them as well. Charli hadn't been sure about letting Layla wear makeup, but thankfully, Kayleigh had left the decision up to her.

After making sure that Layla understood it was a one-time thing, Charli had agreed to let her wear a little bit of natural-looking makeup. That had included a soft eyeshadow with some mascara and lip gloss.

Layla had been thrilled with the results. Charli had been less so because it was a reminder that her little girl was growing up.

All the pampering didn't make Charli wish that Kayleigh had included her in her wedding party, but she was so glad that her sister had asked Layla to be a junior bridesmaid. Ciara was the official flower girl, and Sabrina, Hudson's half-sister, was a bridesmaid, while Janessa was the matron of honor.

Layla had loved all the pampering over the last couple of days, which had included a manicure, pedicure, and a facial the day before. Charli hoped her daughter didn't develop a taste for spa days quite yet. She was already growing up so fast.

The photographer that Kayleigh had hired circled the room, taking a bunch of shots of the primping process. Charli stayed out of the way as she wasn't quite ready for camera time.

Her heart ached a little as she watched her mom interact with Kayleigh, her pride clear on her face. It had been the same on Janessa's wedding day.

Charli didn't begrudge her sisters their love and relationships. However, it was hard not to think about the fact that if things had unfolded the way she'd hoped they would, she would have been the first child to get married.

Instead, she was watching sibling after sibling fall in love and get married. It was... hard. Especially now that the man she'd planned to marry was back on the scene, bringing to the forefront of her thoughts and emotions everything she'd missed out on.

"Do I look pretty, Mom?" Layla asked as she came to spin in front of Charli. Her dark hair was gathered up in a pile of curls, with a ribbon with curling ends wrapped around her head.

"You look absolutely beautiful, sweetheart," Charli assured her, emotion clogging her throat at the joy flooding Layla's face.

Because she was getting married in the fall, Kayleigh had chosen burnt orange and burgundy as her colors. Layla's dress was burgundy, with a burnt orange band around her waist, which matched the ribbon in her hair.

Janessa's dress was burnt orange, which looked gorgeous with her skin tone. Sabrina wore a burgundy dress in the same shade and material as Layla's, but the style was a little more mature to suit the fifteen-year-old. The bouquets they would carry had a mixture of all the autumnal colors.

Charli had decided on a dark green for her own dress, and it was a much simpler style than the dresses the bridal attendants wore.

"Knock, knock!"

Charli turned to see Misha come in with Ciara on her hip. The little girl was the flower girl, and she'd be walking down the aisle with Peyton. Her dress was the same color as Janessa's, but the style matched Layla's, just shorter.

"You look so pretty, Ciara," Layla said as Misha put the little girl down.

"You wook pretty too," Ciara replied with a beaming grin.

Charli smiled at the cute pronunciation of Ciara's words. She was also growing up so quickly, as was Peyton.

Once Kayleigh and her bridal party were all ready, the photographer wanted them outside in the backyard of Charli's parents' home for pictures. Charli planned to get herself prepared, now that Layla was ready to go.

"Charli," Kayleigh called out from where she stood near the door. When Charli approached her, she said, "I want you and Skylar to get your hair and makeup done too. I'm paying the hair stylist and make-up artists for you two as well, so don't argue about it."

Charli frowned, but then she nodded. It would save her having to do it, so if Kayleigh insisted, she'd take her up on the offer. "Okay. Thank you."

"You're very welcome." Kayleigh leaned forward and brushed a kiss on Charli's cheek. "Love you."

"Love you too." They had an up and down relationship, but at the end of the day, they were sisters, and that mattered.

Once the wedding party, along with her mom and Misha, had left the room to go outside for pictures, Charli told the waiting hair and makeup people that she'd be right back. She went down the hallway and rapped on the door of Skylar's room.

Skylar had arrived the night before, but she'd been rather quiet amidst all the preparations. Kayleigh had asked her to be a bridesmaid, but Skylar had—surprisingly—turned her down. Charli didn't know what reason she'd given to Kayleigh, but Kayleigh hadn't talked about her refusal beyond saying Skylar wasn't going to be a member of the wedding party.

When Skylar opened the door, she looked exhausted.

"Are you okay?" Charli asked.

"Yeah. Just didn't sleep very well."

"Well, Kayleigh has arranged for you and me to have our hair and makeup done, too. They're all finished with the wedding party, so now it's our turn."

Skylar hesitated, then shrugged. "It would be nice to have someone else do it for me."

"That's what I thought too."

Together, they went back into the room that had once been Kayleigh and Charli's and happily submitted themselves to the skills of the trio waiting there.

"How's school going?" Charli asked as they settled into chairs so the women could do their makeup.

Skylar was currently away at college, having left Serenity a few months earlier. The last Halverson child had flown the nest.

"It's fine. I'm still getting used to living in a dorm and finding my way around the much larger campus."

"Are you liking your classes?"

Charli was glad for the opportunity to chat with her sister, all while having someone else do her hair and makeup. She'd never had her makeup done professionally, and she didn't have a lot of skill herself, so this was a real treat.

By the time they were done and dressed, the photographer had finished with the bridal party, and everyone was preparing to head out. A stretch limo waited in the driveway to take them to the church.

The vehicle was large enough for all of them. However, Charli decided to take her car so that she'd have the option of leaving when she wanted. Skylar opted to go with her, and they left ahead of the limo so they'd be at the church already when the bridal party arrived.

"Is this supposed to be a big wedding?" Skylar asked.

"You'd think it would be, given the money they've laid out for wedding attire and the décor at the church, but it's not. I think Kayleigh said around a hundred or so."

"Hudson's family didn't want to bring a lot of guests?"

"Hudson had even fewer guests on the list than Kayleigh."

"For some reason, I assumed they'd be having a huge wedding."

"I'm pretty sure we all thought that," Charli said. "Kayleigh did say that they were stopping by New York on their way back from their honeymoon because Alexander wanted to throw a party in celebration recognition of their marriage."

Once Charli had parked at the church, the two of them headed for the front door. It was still early, but Kayleigh had wanted a few quiet minutes in a room at the church while she waited for the ceremony to start.

Hudson and his groomsmen were already at the church but were currently nowhere to be seen. Hudson had gotten close to Gareth over the past year, so he had asked him to be his best man. Both of Hudson's brothers were also part of the wedding party, and Peyton had been designated as the ring bearer.

She was braced to see Blake that day, since she knew Kayleigh and Hudson had invited him and Amelia. It had been a week since their... dinner, and Jay and Janessa kept asking her when she was going to go out with him again. She hoped that for that one day, they'd forego the matchmaking and keep the focus on Kayleigh and Hudson.

It had been her hope that going out with Blake once would allow her to brush off future attempts by her siblings to pair them together. Clearly, she underestimated the tenacity of her siblings. Since their dinner had turned out reasonably well, her siblings seemed to think they should do it again.

Though she would never admit it to them, she kind of agreed. But she didn't think more one-on-one time with Blake could lead anywhere, so what was the sense?

"You two look great," Cole said as he strode up to them.

Everyone had come back to Serenity for the wedding, so her parents' home had been full for a couple of nights. Although the guys had come to her place earlier that day to get ready, since the ladies had all gathered at the family home.

Charli gave him a hug. "Thanks."

Cole and Skylar's interaction was a little more reserved than Charli was used to seeing between the two.

"How's school going, sis?" Cole asked. "Regretting not joining me?"

"Not at all." The words had an edge to them that Charli got stuck on for a moment. "I'm enjoying being on my own, making new friends that don't know me as somebody's little sister."

"Yeah. I liked that too," Cole agreed, apparently not picking up on Skylar's testiness.

"So I think I'll stick to my school, and you can stay at yours."

The one person neither mentioned was Aiden, which just made Charli think her assumption was correct that something had happened between Aiden and Skylar.

They were joined by their other two brothers, Lee and Zane, who greeted her and Skylar with hugs.

"Hey, Lee. Did I hear right?" Cole began as he thumped Lee on the shoulder. "You're thinking of coming back to Serenity?"

"It's possible," Lee said. "Dr. Jensen asked me to stop by to see him yesterday. He said that he's thinking of retiring."

"Wow. I didn't think you wanted to move back here," Skylar said.

"It's not that I didn't want to, but more that I wasn't sure that I could have a career here. Now it sounds like maybe I can."

"So it's not a for sure thing yet?" Charli asked.

"No. Not yet. But we've opened communication about the possibility of me working at the vet clinic."

Charli knew that her parents would be thrilled if Lee moved back, so for their sake, she hoped it worked out. For all of them who lived there, really. It would be good to have more family close by.

"Will you be moving back next, Zane?" Cole asked.

"Nope. Nope. Nope." Zane shook his head. "I'm happy where I am. I've even started dating someone, so I'm not interested in uprooting my life."

"There's the limo," Skylar said, gesturing to the large glass windows by the doors.

"They took their time," Charli commented.

"Probably," Skylar agreed. "But you also *didn't* take your time."

Charli rolled her eyes at her sister. "I didn't speed or run any red lights."

Lee chuckled as he headed for the doors. "Come help me, Cole."

The two of them pushed the doors open and stepped outside to hold them as the wedding party made their way inside. Their parents led the way with Kayleigh and headed down the hallway to the room that had been set aside for the bridal party.

Layla waved as she went by, her face beaming with happiness.

Once Kayleigh and the others had come inside, the limo pulled away. Soon, other cars began to pull into the parking lot.

"I'm going to go check on Layla," Charli said.

Skylar fell into step with her as they made their way to the room. Neither of them spoke as they walked. Skylar appeared as lost in her thoughts as Charli was in hers.

Once she was sure that Layla was doing okay, they left the room. Layla had been very adamant that Charli didn't need to wait at the back with her, so Charli planned to go into the sanctuary to find a seat with Skylar.

216 · KIMBERLY RAE JORDAN

More people had begun to arrive, among them, Blake and Amelia. Her gaze followed them as they walked into the coatroom, only to reappear a couple of minutes later.

Blake wore black pleated slacks and a cream long-sleeve shirt with a green paisley tie. Amelia wore a dark green dress similar in color to Charli's, which also complemented her dad's tie. Charli figured that Jackson's mom had helped choose their outfits.

When Amelia spotted Charli, she smiled and waved. Charli smiled back, not surprised when the pair headed in their direction.

"Hi, Charli," Blake said, his gaze warm as he smiled at her. "Exciting day."

"For Kayleigh and Hudson, for sure."

"And Layla," Skylar added.

Charli chuckled. "Yeah. I think Layla is almost as excited as Kayleigh."

"Are you Miss H's sister, too?" Amelia asked, peering up at Skylar.

"Yes," Charli said. "This is my youngest sister, Skylar. Skylar, this is Jackson's cousin, Blake, and his daughter, Amelia. Amelia is in my class at school."

Skylar smiled at Amelia. "Is she a good teacher?"

Amelia didn't even hesitate before saying, "She's the best. I love her."

Charli's heart warmed at Amelia's words. "I love you too."

And that wasn't a lie. She loved all her students, but maybe Amelia had become just a bit more special to her.

"Your dress is beautiful," Skylar told her. "Do you like getting all dressed up?"

"I do. Aunt Julia helped me pick out my dress, and then she came over to do my hair. Dad only knows how to do ponytails, so we needed help."

Glancing up, Charli found Blake watching her, an affectionate look on his face. Her heart fluttered in a way that might have been alarming had she not known the reason for it. She didn't like that Blake could make that happen with just a look.

"We should probably find seats," Skylar said.

"Can we join you?" Blake asked.

"Sure," Skylar answered before Charli could say anything. Not that she would have said no.

The four of them passed the wedding planner, who was directing everything. She smiled and nodded at them, not looking as stressed out as Charli would have been had she been in charge.

For all the formality of the wedding outfits, the process of finding seats was surprisingly casual. Skylar and Amelia led the way down the aisle, which meant Charli ended up walking with Blake. Even without trying to, her siblings continued to conspire against her.

"Are you sure it's okay if we sit with you?" Blake asked, keeping his voice low. "I won't be offended if you say no."

Charli glanced over and gave him a quick smile. "It's fine."

Her brothers had already found seats, and there was room in their row for them. Skylar went in first, followed by Charli. She expected Amelia to sit next to her, but after a brief quiet discussion between father and daughter, Blake came into the row first and settled on the seat next to Charli.

"She wants to sit on the aisle so she can see Ciara, Layla, and Peyton," he said with a laugh.

"Not Kayleigh?" Charli asked.

"Nope."

"Poor Kayleigh. Upstaged by her nieces and nephew."

The string quartet on the stage began to play a classical piece of music, and the pews behind them filled. The sanctuary wouldn't be packed, but it also wouldn't look empty in photos, what with most people sitting toward the front.

"The décor is amazing," Blake commented. His voice was low, but Charli was near enough to hear his words.

She leaned a little closer as she said, "Hudson's stepmom insisted on paying for all of it. Kayleigh told her the colors she wanted, and Candace took care of everything."

"Whoever she hired did a great job," Blake said. "Really represents the season."

Charli had always assumed that if she got married, she'd want a spring or summer wedding. But now, seeing how beautiful the colors were for Kayleigh's autumn wedding, she was reconsidering. And she thought that maybe a winter wedding might not be so bad either.

Although, a wedding was the last thing she should be thinking about. She didn't even have a boyfriend, so dwelling on what she wanted for a wedding was a waste of time.

In the months following Blake's disappearance, she'd still imagined a wedding in her future. However, as time had passed, and she went on dates that led nowhere, she'd let the dream die.

Unfortunately, the rash of weddings over the past few years had brought to mind how much she'd once longed for one of her own. Now, the sisters who'd never dreamed much about their future weddings the way Charli had were either married or going to be married.

It took away from the joy she should be feeling that day, and it seemed like a dream—or rather a nightmare—that she was sitting beside the reason her dream had died.

No. That wasn't fair.

She could have gone on to marry someone else. It had been true that dating as a single parent was challenging, but she could have persevered. She just hadn't been interested in putting in the effort to find someone who was willing to take on the responsibility for a single mom.

When she saw Hudson's dad and his wife come down the aisle and settle on the front row, Charli realized she'd gotten caught up in her thoughts. She needed to stay in the moment instead of drifting into the past and allowing its negative emotions to cloud the specialness of that day.

Hudson and the pastor stepped out onto the stage, Hudson looking very handsome in his charcoal gray tuxedo with a vest. More than once, Kayleigh had commented that the man was born to wear a suit, and it had never been more evident than right then as he waited for his bride. He looked at ease as his gaze remained on the back of the sanctuary.

Turning a bit, Charli looked back and saw Gareth walking their mom down the aisle. She was beaming, but Charli could see the emotion on her face. It probably wouldn't take much to push her over into tears.

Once her mom was at her seat, Gareth stepped up onto the stage, taking his place beside Hudson and the pastor. He was in a charcoal gray suit as well, with a burgundy tie that matched the one that Hudson wore.

Next came Hudson's step-siblings, Xander and Sabrina, then Layla appeared with Hudson's other brother, Jayden. The pair were close in age, but Jayden was taller than Layla. He didn't look as thrilled as Layla did about walking down the aisle. But he still escorted her like a gentleman.

"Oh boy," Charli muttered when she saw Layla glance up at Jayden, her smile making her face glow.

Blake turned to her. "What's wrong?"

Without thinking, she said, "Layla is too young to be giving boys smiles like that."

As soon as she spoke, Charli held her breath, hoping Blake wouldn't ask her how old Layla actually was. That was a question she never wanted him to ask, because she had no intention of answering it.

Blake chuckled softly. "It's worse if the boy smiles back."

She wasn't sure if that was true. Maybe in the moment, but Charli knew the pain of smiling at boys, and having them ignore her. She hoped that wasn't what Layla would experience in the years to come, because that hurt, too.

Once Layla and Jayden had reached the front, they separated, each going to sit on opposite sides of the front pews. Since the kids would probably get antsy during the ceremony, only the older teen and adult members of the wedding party were on the stage.

Next came Janessa, followed by Peyton and Ciara. Peyton helped Ciara carefully toss the rose petals onto the aisle for Kayleigh to walk on. The pair looked adorable, and she heard many chuckles from the wedding guests.

Her gaze dropped to Amelia, who was twisted in her seat, watching the pair walk past her. She'd clutched her hands under her chin, a gesture Charli had seen her do frequently when she was really drawn to something.

Blake reached out and rested his hand on her back, and Charli wondered what he was thinking. She was glad Amelia had a dad who so clearly loved her and cared about her wellbeing.

With an ache that was starting to feel all too familiar, Charli looked over to where Layla sat next to Peyton on the front row with Charli's mom, Jay, and Misha. Would he be that way with Layla? If he knew?

Layla glanced over her shoulder and smiled at Charli, her happiness helping to ease some of the ache in Charli's heart. Layla might not have a dad, but she was still happy in the life they had together.

When the music changed and everyone around her got to their feet, Charli stood as well. Since she already knew what Kayleigh looked like, she watched Hudson instead.

Charli didn't need to be told when Hudson spotted his bride because his expression changed. His smile grew, and his love for Kayleigh was clear for all to see.

Charli had to swallow hard and blink rapidly to keep her emotions at bay. On that day, her sister would gain everything Charli had ever wanted. But instead of the jealousy she'd usually felt toward Kayleigh, all Charli felt was a deep sadness. Like her heart was weeping for her lost dream.

But regardless of her feelings, she needed to focus on the joy of the moment. Later that night, she could sort through all the emotions that the events of that day had dredged up inside her.

Unfortunately, Charli knew that the rollercoaster of emotions from that day weren't over yet.

CHAPTER TWENTY

Blake couldn't remember the last time he'd been at a wedding. Certainly not since he'd joined the army.

Before that, he'd attended a few, back when he'd still been part of his family. Those had been extravagant affairs, with hundreds of guests in attendance, in cathedral style churches. Churches that most the guests had probably never attended regularly the way Kayleigh and Hudson attended this one.

From the moment the pastor welcomed them, Blake could see that this wedding was going to be different in another way, too. Since Hudson and Kayleigh attended the church, the pastor knew them, and everything he said contained bits of that knowledge, making the ceremony that much more personal and meaningful.

Is this what their wedding would have been like if he and Charli had gotten married in Serenity?

Blake wasn't sure that it would have been.

Though he'd attended church during the time he'd been in Serenity thirteen years ago, he hadn't been involved beyond going to the Sunday services. Part of the reason had been that it was summer, and most of the programs were on hiatus. But even if they'd been in session, he probably would only have attended the ones where Charli would have been present too.

Blake still only attended Sunday school and the morning service each week, though Jackson had been encouraging him to join the men's Bible study. He'd been using Amelia as an excuse for not going, but he knew—because she'd told him—that Julia would come stay with Amelia so that he could attend.

Maybe it was time to take her up on that offer.

Blake glanced over at Charli, wondering how she was enjoying the wedding. Though her attention was on the pastor as he gave a small challenge to the bridge and groom, her expression was unreadable.

It wasn't hard to imagine why she might not be all smiles that day, unlike other members of her family. If Charli's dream was still to get married, weddings might be hard for her. He felt the weight of being responsible for how she might be feeling.

"Hudson and Kayleigh have chosen to write some personal vows," the pastor said. "Hudson, you can go ahead."

"Kayleigh, it's so amazing to be at this point in our relationship. There was a time when I didn't think we'd ever get here, but I'm beyond thankful for how God has guided us. Having you in my life has made me strive to be a better man. Spending time with you has given me a glimpse of what our future could be, and it's a future I want with all my heart. I look forward to walking this road with you, hand in hand, as we traverse the ups and downs of life together. Whatever you do, wherever you go... I will be there at your side. Always and forever. I love you, Kayleigh."

From where he was seated, Blake could see Hudson's face. The man's smile as he looked down at his bride was full of love.

"Hudson, I wasn't looking for love when you walked into my life, but that didn't stop love from finding me. And I couldn't be happier. The love we share has been such a wonderful thing, and I'm so thankful for it.

"Watching you grow in your faith has been such a blessing, and it has encouraged me to continue to seek God in my life. I'm grateful that you've been willing to give God first place in your life and in our relationship, and I can't wait to see how He guides us in the years to come. Thank you for giving me your heart and know that you have mine in return. Now and forever, I love you so much, Hudson."

As he listened to the couple say their vows, Blake realized that the love they shared had a maturity to it that his and Charli's hadn't. Not that that really meant anything. Young love wasn't necessarily doomed. He only had to look at his aunt and uncle to see that.

Would their love be different if they fell in love again, with twelve years of maturity and experiences under their belts?

They had both changed, but over the past several weeks, Blake still saw much about Charli that he admired and was drawn to. Unfortunately, he was pretty sure that she didn't feel the same way.

"May I please have the rings?" the pastor asked with a smile directed toward the pew where Charli's parents sat.

Peyton got to his feet and climbed the stairs, then held out a small box. The pastor opened it, removed its contents, then thanked the boy.

Once Peyton had returned to his seat, Hudson and Kayleigh exchanged rings, then a woman Blake recognized from the church worship team got up to sing as the couple lit a candle together, then moved with Janessa and Gareth to a small table to sign papers.

Finally, the couple stood facing each other in front of the pastor once again. When the pastor announced that Hudson could kiss his bride, the congregation cheered and clapped as he took Kayleigh into his arms.

After a lingering kiss, the beaming couple turned to face the congregation, and the pastor said, "Dear family and friends, I present to you, Mr. and Mrs. Hudson St. James."

Music swelled as the couple made their way from the stage and up the aisle to the doors. The rest of the wedding party followed them out, then both sets of parents also walked to the exit leading into the foyer.

"All of them were so pretty," Amelia said as she sat turned in her seat, gazing at the back of the sanctuary. "I can't wait to get married."

"Oh, Berry, you've got a few years to go before that can happen."

"I know," she said, swiveling back around to look up at her dad. "But maybe I can be in a wedding like Layla before then."

"Maybe." He couldn't make her any promises since he didn't know whose wedding she'd be able to be in. Maybe Jackson's, if he ever got to that point with a woman. "We'll just have to wait and see."

Amelia smoothed her hands over the skirt of her dress. "Will I be able to talk to Layla?"

Blake glanced over at Charli, who nodded. "Yep, for sure."

"We're all supposed to meet at the park for photos in the garden," Misha said. "So we're on our way now."

"These family photos are madness," Charli muttered. "Especially when people don't listen to the photographer."

"I know," Jay agreed. "But Mom wants these pictures."

Charli got to her feet. "You'd think that now that we're adults, the process would be easier."

As the others around them got to their feet and began exiting the rows, Blake also stood up and took Amelia's hand.

"Did you like the wedding, Amelia?" Charli asked as they walked together.

"It was soooo nice. I loved Layla's dress and the bride's too."

When they reached the foyer, people were milling around the area as others lined up to shake hands with the bride and groom. Layla hurried over to them, a big smile on her face.

She gave Amelia a hug, then said, "You look beautiful, Lia."

Blake had never called her that, but whenever Layla did, Amelia beamed.

"Thank you." Amelia looked down at herself, then reached out to touch Layla's dress. "You look beautiful, too. Your dress is so nice. Do you have makeup on?"

Layla gave her mom a quick smile. "Yep. Mom said I could wear a little bit."

"And just for the wedding," Charli added. "Remember that part."

"Yeah." Layla sighed. "I can't wait until I can wear makeup all the time."

"Stop trying to grow up so fast," Charli admonished her daughter. "Besides, you're beautiful without it. It's old people like me who need it to cover the circles under our eyes."

"You're not old, Mom," Layla said. "And you look beautiful today."

Blake had to agree with Layla. Charli looked very nice in her dress, which was nearly the same color as Amelia's.

"Well, a lot of that is thanks to having my makeup done professionally," Charli said with a laugh.

"Are you ready to go?" Skylar asked as she joined them. "Mom is rounding everyone up."

Charli sighed. "Yeah. I guess so."

"Are you going to be at the reception?" Layla asked Amelia.

Amelia looked up at Blake. "Are we?"

"Yes. We'll be there."

"Yay," Layla said. "I hope we can sit together."

Amelia reached out to take Blake's hand. "Me, too."

A few minutes later, they watched all the Halversons move toward the doors leading out of the church, and Blake fought against the disappointment he felt at not being part of the group. He should have been, but he had no one to blame but himself that he wasn't.

They had over two hours to kill before the reception, so they had time to go back to their apartment for a bit. Blake took Amelia by the coatroom to pick up their coats, then they left the church.

There was a bit of a chill in the air, but the sun was out. So as long as people weren't in the shade, it was probably tolerable. He didn't think he was acclimated to the weather in Serenity just yet though, because shade or sun, he still found it chilly.

Once home, Blake had Amelia change out of her dress so it wouldn't get wrinkled or stained since she wanted some berries. He put on an episode of her favorite show, then sat down with his phone.

But rather than engaging his mind, however, all he could think about was the wedding. Not necessarily Hudson and Kayleigh, but just the reality of sitting next to Charli at a wedding.

They may have been sitting side by side, but there had been so much distance between them. Distance that he wasn't sure how to bridge.

He'd known that he was responsible for losing Charli twelve years ago, but it was only recently that he'd been faced with the devastating loss it had truly been for him.

In the weeks and months following his enlistment, he'd been too caught up in his new life to really experience the heartache that followed the breakup. In boot camp, he'd been put through the wringer physically, leaving him with no time to dwell on what had happened. He'd fallen into bed each night exhausted, which meant he'd fallen asleep quickly and hadn't had time to nurse his broken heart.

Now, he was being faced with the result of his actions twelve years ago. The only thing that could have possibly made the situation worse would have been if he'd returned to discover that Charli was married.

Of course, knowing that she had wanted to be married, made him feel selfish to be glad she wasn't. Because there didn't appear to be much hope of a second chance for them, he should be kind enough to hope that she'd find love with someone else.

With forty-five minutes to go before the reception, Amelia got back into her dress, and they headed out to the resort. When he got there, Blake didn't see any of the Halversons, but Jackson and his parents were waiting in the hotel's foyer.

"Is the bridal party here already?" Blake asked.

"Not yet," Jackson said. "Gareth texted that they were on their way, though, so they should be here soon."

Julia and Robert stood in a group nearby, chatting with people Blake recognized from the church. A few minutes later, Wade showed up, and after glancing around, he made his way over to them.

"Hey there, Amelia," Wade said, holding his hand out for her to slap.

Wade was always good with Amelia, which was probably because he had a daughter of his own, though she was much older than Amelia. Jackson was good with Amelia too, but interaction with her didn't seem to come as naturally to him.

Jackson's phone chimed again, and after a glance at it, he said, "Gareth said they're pulling up."

Over the next half hour, the bridal party arrived, as did more guests. Charli and Layla disappeared with the family into the large ballroom.

A short time later, Blake and Amelia followed Jackson and Wade through the receiving line, then they were shown to their assigned table.

The ballroom had been beautifully decorated with the same colors as at the church. The large round tables had burgundy table clothes, and the centerpieces were made of greenery, candles, and flowers in fall colors. The chair covers were the same reddish-orange-y color as Janessa's dress.

The large floral displays had been brought over from the church and stood near the long rectangular head table that was situated in front of the tall arched windows, that looked out over a forest of bare shade trees and evergreens. The lights in the ballroom had been lowered, and with the help of a ton of fairy lights, cast the room in a cozy glow.

The ambience brought a sense of intimacy and warmth to the large space. It was amazing what some money could do. His mom would definitely approve of everything, since she was so aesthetically oriented.

Each seat had a place card with a name written in elegant script. At the table he and Amelia had been taken too, he found his seat was between Amelia and Charli. Layla was next to Amelia, with Peyton on her other side.

Jay, Misha, Aria, Skylar, and Will were also at the table. The rest of the family were either at the head table or at another round table.

Blake hadn't thought he'd be at a table with the family, but it seemed that even at this event, some matchmaking was going on. He might have thought it was for Amelia's benefit if not for Charli's assigned seat being next to his. They could have put Will next to him. But no, someone had put Charli there.

"This is so beautiful," Amelia murmured as she stood next to the table, gazing over the ballroom.

Since no one else was sitting at their table yet, Blake remained standing as well. He searched the people until his gaze landed on Charli. She stood talking to a man that Blake didn't recognize. They seemed to know each other well as they interacted with an easy familiarity. The sight gave him a sick feeling in his stomach, so he looked away.

Even though they'd gone for dinner, she hadn't seemed to be interested in any contact beyond that one evening. He hadn't pushed too hard so far, and he wouldn't. However, right then, he wanted so much to once again have the easy, fun, loving times that he and Charli had shared.

He'd accepted that things were over for them—or at least, he'd thought he had. It was becoming fairly clear, however, that perhaps he hadn't. Being at this wedding definitely wasn't helping the situation.

"I need to sit down," Misha said as she, Jay, and Peyton joined them.

Jay held the chair for his wife, then took the seat beside her.

"Where's Ciara?" Amelia asked as Blake helped her into her seat.

"She's with her grandma," Misha told her. "My mom said she'd been at the most important part of this day, which, for her, was the ceremony, so she was more than happy to stay home with Ciara and Timothy."

Blake was beginning to think that he might have been happier at home, too. But he was there now, so he couldn't exactly walk out. Plus, he was pretty sure that the slight stubborn streak Amelia possessed would rear its head if he suggested they leave.

Layla and Peyton ran over to the table and, after searching for their names, dropped into their chairs. Gradually, more and more of the seats filled up, including the ones at their table.

Blake saw Charli headed toward their table. As she neared, Blake got to his feet and pulled out her chair. She gave him a quick smile and thanked him as she sat down. With her arrival, their table was full.

"That picture taking was... stressful," Charli said with a sigh as she leaned back in her chair.

"I have to admit, the addition of little ones has made getting everyone looking in the same direction and smiling, a bit more challenging," Jay said. "I'm not sure how Mom used to do it when we were all young."

"With threats, as I recall," Charli told him.

Jay chuckled. "True. Lots of threats and a few bribes."

"I don't remember threats," Skylar said.

"That's because by the time you came along, us older kids got the threats and you little ones got the bribes," Charli told her.

"Yeah," Jay agreed. "Mom would tell the older ones that we had to stay still, look at the camera and smile, or else. She would get pretty ticked off if she finally got the little ones to smile and one of us big kids wasn't smiling or looking at the camera."

Blake enjoyed listening to the siblings interact with each other. He'd certainly never had such lighthearted conversations with his sisters, and that thought made him a little sad.

He wondered if now that they were all older and had had years to find their own paths in life, if he and his sisters could have better relationships. Blake knew nothing about their current lives, but he hoped they were happy wherever they were and whatever they were doing.

Gareth's voice came over the speakers, asking for people to find their seats. Gradually, the chatter of voices quieted. The pastor then joined Gareth at the mic and led them in prayer for the meal.

"What's on the menu?" Will asked once the prayer was over. "Does anyone know?"

"If I know Hudson, it's going to be steak," Charli said.

"Not just any old steak, but probably the *best* steak available," Jay added.

"We already know they serve superb steak here at the resort," Blake said, more than happy to reflect on the evening he and Charli had eaten steaks together. "I don't think I've ever tasted better."

"Is that what you and Charli had on your...uh... dinner?" Jay asked.

Charli frowned as she glanced over to where the girls sat. Thankfully, they were busy chatting with Peyton and didn't seem to be aware of the conversation among the adults.

"Yes. That's what we had."

"When are you going to have dinner again?" Aria asked as a server began to bring the first course to their table.

Blake glanced at Charli but stayed quiet as a server set an elegantly plated salad in front of him. He hoped that Amelia would eat the salad. But when he looked at what the server set in front of her, he realized the kids weren't having a salad.

Each of them had been given a plate with an assortment of cut vegetables and a tiny bowl of dip. That would definitely work better for Amelia. She might not eat the cauliflower, but the carrots and broccoli would be gone.

Blake felt a brush along his arm and looked over. Charli had leaned toward him, but her gaze was on the kids and their food.

"Kayleigh said she'd have different food for the kids, so I'm glad to see that she came through."

"Salad isn't Amelia's favorite food, but she likes veggies and dip."

"Layla's the same," Charli said, sitting back in her seat. "Though sometimes she doesn't care for raw vegetables, either. We'll see which way it goes tonight."

"So they're not going to be served steak?"

"I don't think so," Charli said.

"For Amelia, that's probably a good thing. But what a disappointment for me.

Charli gave him a quizzical look. "Why a disappointment?"

"Well, there's no way she'd ever eat an entire steak. I was hoping to eat her leftovers."

Charli laughed, and Blake smiled at the sound of her laughter.

"I don't think Kayleigh even thought about that when she decided to order a different menu for the kids."

"Ah well. I guess I'll survive."

"You know you can always order a steak from the restaurant," Charli told him.

He shrugged. "I think I'll just wait for a special occasion. Wouldn't want to get bored with steak. If that's possible."

When Charli smiled again, Blake felt a warm sense of satisfaction. He knew that he'd caused her a lot of pain, and probably a boatload of tears, so to know that he could still bring a smile to her face, made him feel that perhaps all was not lost.

It was probably—definitely—a bad idea to harbor any sort of hope that he might get a second chance at a future with Charli. However, he couldn't bring himself to extinguish that little flicker of hope in his heart.

A year ago, he never would have imagined where his life would lead him. Back then, he'd accepted his role as father, though his interactions with Amelia had been limited. He'd been confident that his future would always include a commitment to the army, moving wherever they told him to go.

Now, everything was different, and he couldn't find it inside himself to regret the changes that had been forced upon him.

He loved being a father to Amelia, even if there were times that he felt inadequate to parent a little girl. And though he'd faced a huge career change, where he'd landed wasn't so bad. In fact, he really enjoyed his work at the garage.

So maybe it was selfish to want more. But he did. He wanted those dreams he and Charli had talked about so much during their time together.

He wouldn't get a chance at those dreams if he didn't at least try to take a shot at seeing if she'd give him that second chance.

When the server set a gold-edged plate with a beautifully plated steak entrée on it in front of him, Blake realized with a bit of humor that his mom would probably be shocked that Blake was at the wedding of the son of one of the wealthiest men in the US.

She was all about appearances, and being in attendance at the wedding for Alexander Remington's son would have given her something to brag about for years. And it would have given her and Blake's dad the hope that they could sweet talk Alexander into furnishing his hotels with their company's furniture.

Blake had lived most of his adult life without the excessive wealth he'd grown up with, and though he'd enjoyed the wedding, it brought back memories of being surrounded by people caught up in their wealthy status. That hadn't been the case of those attending the wedding that day.

Honestly, if it weren't for Hudson's suits and expensive watch, Blake would never have suspected he was as wealthy as he was. Hudson was the type of man Blake's father would have wanted for a son. A successful businessman, working for his father's company.

That alone should have made Blake not like the guy, but he just couldn't manage it. Hudson was down to earth and didn't seem to feel that his wealth made him better than everyone else. Not even a veteran trying to provide for himself and his daughter the best way he knew how.

Though Blake wished that he could give Amelia a nice home with a yard right off the bat, he hadn't given up hope that he might still be able to do that one day. But until then, he would do his best to provide her with a safe home where she would always know she was loved.

And maybe one day, if God willed it, he wouldn't be doing those things for Amelia by himself.

CHAPTER TWENTY-ONE

The perfection of the meal at the wedding reception did not surprise Charli. She was sure that the hotel always strived to provide high caliber food and service for anyone using their facilities. However, there was no doubt they'd gone above and beyond at this event to provide a memorable experience for two such valued employees and their guests—one of whom happened to own the whole resort.

This would have been exactly the type of wedding she would have hoped to have. Back in the day. Now, she could see how unrealistic and unachievable it would have been, given her lack of wealth.

She would have had to go into debt to be able to afford it. And while she might have been willing to do that twelve years ago, she no longer was, thanks to having matured over the years.

Charli hadn't thought much in years about what sort of wedding she'd like, considering her current situation in life. However, as she looked around, she knew that she'd want something a lot smaller and more intimate than Kayleigh's.

She'd come to understand that while a wedding was an important moment in a couple's journey, it was just a few hours... just a day. It was the marriage that followed that was most important. There was no way she'd go into debt for a wedding because it would add financial strain to a new marriage.

Even with that financial restriction in place, Charli was confident that she'd be able to find ways to make a wedding special while also keeping it within her budget. Of course, the man she was marrying would have a say in what they wanted for the wedding.

When Blake's face came to mind as she considered who she might plan a wedding with some day, Charli looked over at him.

If she'd just met him for the first time, would she have fallen in love with the man he was now?

They were both different people from who they'd been twelve years ago, but the more time she spent with him, the less she could deny that she was still attracted to him.

Would the draw she felt toward him be enough for her to ever consider rekindling their relationship? Or would the memory of the hurt he'd caused keep her from taking that risk?

"How's everyone doing?" Gareth said into the mic. "Are you having a good time?"

There were cheers and clapping from the guests.

"I'm glad to hear that. We're going to have Kayleigh and Hudson cut the cake, and then, while we all enjoy some dessert, we're going to have some fun. It's especially designed for the single men and ladies in the crowd. So prepare yourselves."

"Are they going to toss the bouquet?" Layla asked. "If they do, are you going to try for it, Mom?"

"Probably not."

"Please go for it, Mom," Layla pleaded. "You didn't even really try at Auntie Nessa's wedding. Skylar caught it."

Charli glanced at Skylar in time to see her frown. She'd been much more excited about trying for the bouquet at Janessa's wedding than she seemed to be now.

"We'll see."

Charli didn't want to do it, but she also didn't want to disappoint Layla. Perhaps she could take part by just joining in, but not actually trying to catch the bouquet.

"Can we go watch them cut the cake?" Layla asked.

"Yes. But make sure you're not in the way."

"Do you want to come with me, Lia?"

When the little girl nodded, the trio got up and made their way over to the table that held an elaborate cake. A cream-colored fondant covered the layers, along with an abundance of sugar flowers in the colors of the other floral displays in the room. The cake was a masterpiece, and Charli didn't want to think about how much it had cost.

"Are you okay with Layla calling Amelia Lia?" Charli asked once the kids had left the table.

She'd heard Layla referring to Amelia that way for a few days, and she wanted to make sure that Blake didn't prefer she not call her by the nickname.

"Yep." Blake smiled, the skin crinkling at the corner of his eyes. "I actually think it's kind of cute, and Amelia seems to like it."

There were times when Charli saw the girls together that she felt strongly that she should tell Blake about Layla. The girls would probably be thrilled to discover they were sisters.

But the other things that needed to be considered weighed more heavily on her, and they were what kept her from revealing the secret she'd kept for so long.

"I sure appreciate Kayleigh and Hudson including me and Amelia today. She was so excited. I don't think she slept much last night, and then she was up early, but it looks like she's having a blast."

"So is Layla. I thought she might get bored, but she's having fun."

"Kayleigh has set the bar high for Amelia's expectations of what a wedding should be."

"Well, hopefully she'll have lowered her expectations by the time she gets married. Or she gets engaged to a wealthy man. I'm pretty sure much of this is due to Hudson's stepmom's efforts."

"Really?" Blake glanced around. "I just assumed that Kayleigh was responsible for it."

"Kayleigh chose the color palette, then let Candace and the wedding coordinator take over. They ran all their plans by Kayleigh, but Kayleigh said that she had no issues with anything Candace presented to her."

It had kind of surprised Charli how hands off Kayleigh had been when it came to those details, as she tended to worry over everything. It had certainly led to a less stressful time for Kayleigh, which was always a good thing.

Charli leaned to the side to allow the server to place a beautifully plated dessert in front of her. Behind the young woman came another server to offer her coffee or tea.

Once she had a cup of coffee, Charli spent a few minutes sipping it before diving into the dessert. She wasn't sure why they were having cheesecake when there was also wedding cake to share, but since she loved cheesecake, she wasn't going to complain.

The first taste was creamy, sweet, and slightly tart. The cheesecake was Turtle flavor, so the topping was a mix of chocolate, caramel, and chopped pecans. In other words... divine.

She had just finished her last bite when Gareth spoke over the mic again, calling for all the single ladies to gather on the dance floor.

When Charli looked over at Skylar, her sister lifted her hands and shook her head. "Nope."

"Mom!" Layla appeared in the space between her and Skylar. "You've got to get up there."

"I really don't think I need to."

"Please, Mom!" Layla pleaded. "Please!"

Charli rolled her eyes. "Okay. Fine. But don't get upset if I don't catch it."

"I won't. Promise."

"C'mon, Skylar," Charli said. "Join me in the madness."

"Nope."

As Layla moved back a bit, Charli leaned down to Skylar and kept her voice low as she said, "You don't have to try to catch it. I'm just going to stand there."

"Charli. Skylar. My darling sisters." Gareth called out for them over the sound system. "Get yourselves up here."

With a sigh, Skylar stood up, and Charli got to her feet as well. She glanced at Blake to find him smiling.

"Are you planning to go for the garter?"

Blake shrugged as he got up. "Maybe. There'll be lots of competition, though. Probably more than you'll have for the bouquet."

He followed them to the dance floor but stayed on the sidelines as she and Skylar joined the other women gathering there. It appeared that Blake was right. There would definitely be more single men than women, which weirdly wasn't how it seemed to be out in the real world.

Kayleigh stood holding a smaller version of the bouquet she'd carried for the ceremony, a smile on her face as she looked out over the group of women. When their gazes met, Charli narrowed her eyes, hoping to convey to Kayleigh how much better her life would be if she didn't even attempt to throw those flowers in her direction.

Instead of looking like she'd received Charli's message, all Kayleigh did was smile more broadly and give her a wink before moving her gaze on to the other women.

The tossing of the bouquet was a moment of fun. After all, it was just a simple bundle of flowers. Nothing that actually meant anything.

Except it did.

Charli was smart enough to understand that the only reason it meant anything this time around was because Blake was there. If he hadn't been there, she would have participated, and if she'd somehow managed to catch the bouquet, she would have just joked about it.

Blake's presence cast the bouquet throw in a different light. At least for her.

Truthfully, it was casting the whole wedding in a different light. It had awakened a part of her life that she'd happily allowed to lie dormant.

"Is everyone ready?" Gareth said. "Let's do a count for Kayleigh. After being a cheerleader, she does well with a count. Right, Kayleigh?"

Kayleigh gave him a thumbs up, then turned around to face the head table. Gareth led the countdown, and as they reached one, Kayleigh flung the bouquet over her head. Right... at... Charli.

As it sailed toward her, Charli took a step to the side, allowing the flowers to fall to the floor right between her and Skylar. She looked down at the bouquet but didn't have the time to do anything before Layla dashed over and plucked it off the floor.

"Here, Mom." She shoved it at Charli so forcefully that Charli had no choice but to take the bouquet. Layla's smile was beaming as she stepped back. "I'm so glad you got the flowers."

"Well, it looks like Charli has the bouquet, thanks to a little help from her daughter. Way to go, Layla. Quick thinking there."

Layla turned her smile on her uncle and gave him a wave. "It was Mom's. She just didn't react fast enough."

"Well, I'm glad she didn't give it to me," Skylar muttered as she moved closer to Charli. "My condolences."

Charli gave a huff of laughter, then sighed. "I guess I should have told her that she wasn't allowed to interfere."

Skylar slid her arm through Charli's as they moved away so the men could take their place for the garter toss. Hudson had joined Kayleigh on the dance floor, bringing a chair with him.

Kayleigh sat down on the chair and edged the skirt of her gown up enough that he could remove the garter from her leg. After Hudson had the garter in hand, he got into position, facing away from the group of men. Kayleigh stood beside him, though she faced the men.

As Gareth counted him down, Kayleigh pulled Hudson down to whisper in his ear. When the count reached one, Hudson tossed the garter over his shoulder. It headed in Blake's direction, and unlike Charli's reaction to the bouquet, Blake actually made an effort to catch it.

And when he did, there was plenty of cheering—most of it from Charli's siblings. When Skylar laughed, Charli crossed her arms and gave her sister an exasperated look.

"Mom!" Layla exclaimed as she pointed at Blake, who was heading to where they stood. "You both caught what they threw."

"We certainly did," Charli agreed.

She didn't want to dwell on it, but she had a feeling that she wouldn't have a choice since she was pretty sure Kayleigh and Hudson had manipulated things—probably at Jay and Janessa's prompting.

They were oblivious to the backstory of what had gone on between her and Blake. And because of that, they'd think it was great that they were the two who had caught the bouquet and garter, especially since that had been the siblings' intention. To encourage them to continue to spend time together, one-on-one.

If this had happened back when she was twenty-one, Charli would have thought it was great. She would have seen it as a sign.

Now, though...

"Can I have that, Daddy?" Amelia asked when he joined them.

"I think I'm going to offer it back to Kayleigh," he said.

"You don't have to do that," Charli told him. "She bought it specifically for the toss."

"I could use it as a headband." Amelia took it from Blake. "I think it will be cool."

Charli noticed she didn't try to put it on her head right then, which was good because she probably would have messed up her hair.

"I'm going back to the table," Skylar murmured. "Since the show's over."

They all trailed after her as Gareth let them know that Kayleigh and Hudson would be sharing their first dance. Charli was glad for the distraction, so that she didn't have to think too much about what had just happened.

They angled their chairs to face the dance floor. The overhead lights dimmed further except for the ones above that section of the room. Hudson led Kayleigh onto the floor, then twirled her around before she settled into his arms.

As their song started to play, they began to slowly drift around the space. It didn't surprise Charli that they didn't have crazy moves or anything because that just wasn't Kayleigh's or Hudson's style. Instead, it was an elegant, intimate moment during which those watching were made to feel that Hudson and Kayleigh had forgotten that they were all there.

Hudson bent his head as Kayleigh looked up at him. They were definitely lost in a world of their own. One filled with love, devotion, and a bright future.

All at once, Charli felt beyond exhausted.

CHAPTER TWENTY-TWO

Charli was ready to go home. She wanted to swap out her fancy dress for her favorite pajamas and curl up in her bed. And in the privacy of her room, she could stop trying to keep her emotions hidden. Her very messy emotions.

She was happy for Kayleigh and Hudson, just like she was happy for Will and Janessa, Jay and Misha, and Gareth and Aria. But she was also sad for herself. So incredibly sad.

For years, she'd thought she'd mourned the loss of her dreams when Blake had broken up with her. But perhaps she'd just mourned the loss of him, because that day—watching Kayleigh marry Hudson—had dredged up her sadness of lost dreams.

Although, had it been the day? Or had it been Blake's presence as a part of the day?

It had been her choice not to pursue a relationship over the years, and the desire to reach for her dreams of a marriage and a large family had died. Or so she'd thought.

When the music faded away, the lights brightened a bit, bringing the mesmerizing moment of the dance to an end. Emotional tension had gripped Charli's chest, and she took a deep breath to try to loosen it.

"That was soooo pretty," Layla said, clearly entranced by everything happening that day.

She'd been in other weddings. Most recently, Janessa's. However, she was older this time. It seemed she was falling in love with the idea of love and all the romantic things she'd seen that day. Just another way she took after Charli. She'd been very similar at that age.

"Your siblings sure are persistent," Blake said as the kids left the table to play around on the dance floor, joining other guests there.

"Some of them definitely are," Charli murmured in agreement.

"Not me," Skylar said, lifting her hands, palms out. "And I don't think any of the non-resident family members are in on these manipulations."

"True." Charli glanced over at Jay, who suddenly turned his attention to his wife.

"Want to dance, sweetheart?" Jay asked.

"Yes. I think I would."

As the couple left the table, Charli let out a huff of irritation. "He likes to stir the pot, but then he doesn't stick around to taste the stew."

Blake chuckled. "He probably already knows what it tastes like."

"It's spicy with my irritation."

"You do know they thrive on your irritation, right?" Skylar asked.

"Yeah. I know." Charli wished she could brush it all off with a lighthearted dismissal, but she had never been that good of an actor. Their manipulations were messing with her emotions in a way that they were totally unaware of, and because she didn't want to explain it all, she had no choice but to deal with it.

"Try not to let them get to you," Skylar told her, then gave a small laugh. "Look at me. Handing out advice like the older sibling."

Skylar was right. She needed to just ignore them.

Charli glanced over at her sister and saw Skylar had pulled out her phone. Frowning, Skylar got to her feet, then said, "I need to go to the bathroom."

Staring at her phone, she walked away, leaving just Blake and Charli at the table, since Aria had long since abandoned them for Gareth. Surprisingly, Charli didn't feel as uncomfortable being alone with him as she might have when he'd first started hanging out with them, but she also wasn't completely at ease.

"Would you consider going out on another date?" Blake asked, leaning close. He kept his voice low, like he was worried someone might hear.

She stared at him, taking in his familiar face and the way it had changed over the years. Where he'd once kept his face clean shaven, he now sported a light scruff that Charli's hands itched to touch. There were lines at the corners of his eyes, a reminder that they both were older. "To what end?"

"What do you mean?"

"Why do you want us to date?" Charli asked, the memory of the heartache she'd experienced at his hands making her bolder than she might have been otherwise. Of course, she should be saying no instead of asking him why.

Yet again, she asked herself if she was willing to give him another chance. Did she want to take the risk of being hurt again?

"I know I hurt you before, and I am so very sorry for that." Blake's expression had sobered, but he kept his gaze on hers.

Charli had always thought she'd never be able to forgive Blake— even though she knew that would be what God wanted her to do— and yet, here she was, considering that very thing. But there was a big difference between forgiving him and agreeing to date him again.

Silence stretched between them. But when Blake's gaze lowered to the cup of coffee he'd wrapped his hands around, Charli didn't get the feeling he was waiting for her to reply. So she didn't. Mainly because she didn't know what to say.

"I've never felt about anyone the way I felt about you. I knew that what we had was special." He glanced up, his gaze meeting hers for a moment. "But I didn't know just how special it was until I'd thrown it all away."

Hurt sliced through her as she recalled how she'd felt following the breakup. Being abandoned that way had made her feel like Blake had tossed her aside. It was a rejection that had shattered her heart.

The only thing that soothed the hurt a little was the fact that he was aware of what he'd done and the hurt he'd caused her. And he was sorry for what had happened.

"I know I don't deserve it," Blake said, looking up again, but this time, his gaze stayed locked with Charli's. "But I'd really like a second chance. Is there any chance you'd give me that?"

And there it was.

The question that had been plaguing her since their dinner... their date... now needed an answer. Could she forgive him and give him the second chance he wanted?

Charli stared into his familiar gaze, the hope there filling her with warmth. Memories of all the times he'd looked at her like that before.

There was a huge part of her that very much wanted to take the chance. No one had ever made her feel as loved as he had. But also, no one had ever hurt her as much as he had.

It was a huge risk.

"How would we even date without getting the girls' hopes up?" she asked. "I could probably take the risk of another heartbreak, but I can't risk Layla having her heart broken. She's at the age where if she found out we were dating, she'd get her hopes pinned on a future with you and Amelia in it."

"How do single parents date?" Blake asked.

"Very carefully," Charli said. "Also, they're not usually trying to date someone in their friend circle."

"So you've managed to date as a single mom?"

Charli wasn't stupid enough to believe that he didn't have an ulterior motive in asking that question. "A few times. In the end, I didn't find it worth the effort."

"If you're not sure about dating, would you be up to talking with me?" Blake asked. "Like phone calls or texting. That way, we don't have to sneak dates in until we're more certain about things."

That was how it had all started the last time. Phone calls, texting, video calls. The first eight months of their relationship, they'd communicated entirely through their phones. And now she was considering doing it all over again.

If what they were contemplating doing had the same start, would it also have a similar end?

The battle between her heart and her mind waged fiercely at that moment. Her heart desperately wanted another chance at the future she'd once desired more than anything. Her mind, however, screamed that there was no way that it would work out. That hurt was inevitable.

Hope or hurt?

Safety or risk?

Which could she live with?

Which would she live to regret?

"I can't promise anything," she told him, hoping her voice wasn't trembling the way her insides were. "I can't promise this will become what we once had."

"I understand that. But we'll never know if we don't try. We're more mature now, and I think we can learn from what happened before."

Though she wasn't sure it would lead to where Blake hoped it would, Charli found that she couldn't say no to him. Couldn't say no to her own heart.

She was going to take the chance.

Against her better judgment, she was going to take the chance.

The only thing that briefly gave her pause was the relationship between Layla and Blake that neither of them knew existed.

If things worked out the way they hoped they would, Charli could then trust him with the information that Layla was his. If it didn't work out, he never needed to know.

Hopefully, he'd understand why she hadn't been willing to share that information with him sooner.

But what if he didn't?

Her head was a mess, but she had to give him an answer. Unfortunately, she didn't think there was one completely right decision. The thought crossed her mind that maybe she needed to take the time to pray about it. But she didn't want to.

"We can try spending time together on the phone."

When Blake's face lit up, Charli felt her heart skip a beat. It had been forever since he'd smiled at her like that. And it was hard to consider that her decision was anything but the perfect one when she saw that look on his face. His blue alit with emotion and anticipation.

"Do you have a preference for time?" he asked, apparently determined to accommodate her as much as possible.

"Evenings are best," she said. "After nine, but before ten."

Rather than complain that she was limiting things by giving him just an hour, Blake nodded. "I can work with that. It's after Amelia's bedtime, but before I need to be in bed myself."

"Yep, that's why that time works for me."

Before they could discuss it any further, Jay and Misha returned, with Lee, Zane, and Wilder following them. They'd been sitting at another table for the meal but joined them at their table now that the guests were wandering around.

The servers had cleared the table of all plates and silverware, though they continued to fill their cups with coffee or tea as requested. At one point, they had some short speeches from Janessa and Gareth, then Kayleigh and Hudson spoke as well. Once they were done, the couple circled the room, talking briefly with their guests and accommodating photo requests.

Skylar had returned to their table as well and was once again seated beside Charli.

"When are you going back to school?"

"Tomorrow," Skylar said. "I took Friday off, but I need to be back for Monday."

"Will you be back for Thanksgiving?"

Skylar hesitated for a moment before she said, "Probably. We'll have to see how it's going."

"Is everything okay?" Charli asked, feeling like something had happened. Unfortunately, with her there for just a short time, they hadn't had time to chat.

Skylar stared over to where their parents were talking with Cole and Gareth. "Yeah. Everything is fine."

Charli wasn't convinced. "You know you can talk to me if you ever need to. Just because you're not here doesn't mean you can't call me."

Looking back at Charli, Skylar gave her a smile. "I know."

"Don't just know... do."

"I will."

Charli hoped Skylar was just dealing with the adjustments of being away from home for college. Though she wanted to press her sister, a wedding reception was hardly the place to hold that conversation. Of course, it hadn't exactly been the place to hold the conversation with Blake, either.

She'd give Skylar a call in a week or two, just to check up on her. Sometimes a struggling person wouldn't make the call to chat but would talk if someone else called them. Charli hoped that would be the case with Skylar.

Finally, Gareth announced that the bridal couple would be leaving. The guests stood and clapped as Kayleigh and Hudson walked out of the ballroom together, waving as they left.

Charli knew they planned to spend the night in one of the cabins at the resort, then they were flying off the next day for their two-week honeymoon somewhere warm.

Once Kayleigh and Hudson had disappeared, the guests gradually left as well. One big difference between this wedding and the other Halverson weddings was that they weren't required to do any clean-up now that the wedding was over.

The same people who had set everything up were taking care of clearing it all away. Though Charli had happily helped her other siblings where needed at their weddings, she did enjoy the fact that they could just put their coats on and leave without feeling like they should stay to help.

As they walked out to their cars, Blake fell into step beside her, while the girls and Peyton skipped ahead of them. Jay and Misha walked along with them, while the rest of the family were straggling out of the hotel behind them, heading toward the parking lot.

Cole, Lee, Zane, Wilder, and Skylar were spending the night at the family home, and all of them would be leaving the next day. She wasn't sure if any of them would make it to church before they left. Christmas was about the only time they all went to church together anymore.

Charli gave each of them a hug, holding Skylar tightly for a bit longer. "Call me."

"I will."

"You'd better." Charli gave her another quick squeeze, then headed to her car where Blake stood with the girls.

"We'll see them at church tomorrow," Charli said when Layla asked to go for ice cream, since she didn't want the evening to end. "So you can hang out then. It's been a long day, and it's late."

Layla sighed as she gave Amelia a hug, then climbed into the back seat of Charli's car.

Charli turned to Blake, a bit uncertain of what to say. There was suddenly a lot she wanted to tell him, but it wasn't the right time or place to say even a portion of it.

"I had a great time today," Blake said. "And I never imagined I'd say that about a wedding, but there you go."

"It was a good day," Charli agreed. "But I have a feeling a lot of us are going to crash tomorrow. Layla's excitement had her—and therefore me—up really early."

"I'm sure. Amelia is already up later than her bedtime, so who knows what tomorrow will be like. She'll probably need a nap."

"She won't be the only one, I'm sure."

Charli was more reluctant than she'd thought she'd be to leave Blake. But when Layla opened her car door to ask how much longer until they left, she finally said good night.

Layla was clearly tired because she hardly said a word during the trip back to the house. That was fine with Charli, as her thoughts were caught up in the wedding and the time she'd spent with Blake.

She wasn't sure if she'd made the right decision in agreeing to pursue a relationship with him. And even though she knew it had been manipulated, her catching the bouquet and Blake the garter had uncovered a little bit of hope that she hadn't realized still existed in her heart.

So she'd set out on a path that was shrouded in uncertainty. And anticipation warred with worry and the fear that she'd made the wrong decision. The last time they'd been in the early stages of a relationship, all she'd experienced was the excitement and anticipation.

Now, however, she was more jaded. More aware of what could happen.

Hopefully, she and Blake would use the experience they'd gained over the years to work harder at making the relationship a success. Charli was willing to do her best, but the wariness that lingered in her mind couldn't be ignored.

As she sat on the edge of her bed, still dressed in her wedding finery, Charli prayed that she hadn't just set herself up for heartbreak.

CHAPTER TWENTY-THREE

Blake walked a tired Amelia into church the next morning, then helped her out of her jacket in the coatroom. There were times when she would sleep in, but there were also times when, even if she went to bed way past her normal bedtime, she would wake up early. Which was what had happened that morning.

Usually, she was much more eager to get to church and go to her Sunday school room. But that day, she held Blake's hand and slowly walked beside him as they went downstairs, instead of tugging him along like she normally did.

"Good morning, my dears," Julia greeted them as they walked through the door into the small classroom. "How are we today?"

"I'm fine," Blake said. "But little Miss Berry is a bit tired this morning."

"Did you have fun yesterday, Amelia?" Julia asked as she took Amelia's hand and led her over to the table set up in the middle of the room.

Blake watched her for a moment, waiting until Amelia looked at him to give her a smile and a wave before he left the room. He nodded to people he met on the stairs as he went back up to the foyer, then made his way to the sanctuary for the adult Sunday school class.

He stepped into the large room, then moved to the side to check who was there already. Usually everyone sat on one side of the sanctuary for the lesson, since the leader used a smaller podium set on the floor instead of on the stage.

It didn't appear that any of the Halversons had arrived yet, so Blake made his way along the outside aisle to an empty pew a little over halfway down, stepped into the row, and sat down.

He took a deep breath, then blew it out, trying to focus on what he was there for. Yes, he was excited to see Charli, but he knew he needed to not let that be a distraction.

Blake was determined not to repeat the mistakes of the past, which included not allowing his motivation for attending church to shift. He had to remember the importance of the changes he'd made in his life over the years. Changes that made him a better man than he'd been twelve years ago.

He was just glad that Charli had given him the opportunity to show that, and he didn't want to mess it up by being distracted from the thing that had helped change him.

There was a time and a place for dwelling on the second chance Charli had given him, and that wasn't during the church service.

"Morning, Blake," Jay said as he and Misha joined him in the row.

"Good morning." Blake shifted in the pew. "You recovered from yesterday?"

"Yeah. We tossed Peyton into bed and crashed ourselves. Unfortunately, Ciara went to bed at her normal time, so she was also up at her usual time, which was... early."

"Amelia was up early too," Blake said. "And she's dragging today."

"We're not usually the first ones of the family here, so I have a feeling a lot of them must be dragging."

They chatted for a bit, and it was with just minutes to spare before the service started that the others arrived. Charli came down the center aisle with Will and Janessa trailing after her. She scooted in and sat down next to Blake.

"Made it," she said with an exhale and a tired smile. "Whew."

"Busy morning?"

"Late start."

"Welcome, everyone," the leader said as he stepped up to the podium, putting an end to their conversation. "Let's say a word of prayer before we begin."

Unlike the service, the Sunday school class dove right into the lesson following the prayer. They'd been going through the book of James, and Blake was enjoying it. The last time he'd been part of a book study had been when he'd been deployed. Unfortunately, he'd had to leave before it was finished.

At first, he'd found it a bit odd that the army chaplain had chosen to do an extended study of a book or passage of the Bible since people on the base were constantly coming and going. There was no guarantee someone would be there for the entire study. However, he'd since realized that he didn't need to be there for everything in order to find value in the part he was present for.

Those lessons had also been less in depth than the Sunday school ones, but Blake had come to realize that, like him, many who chose to attend the services and the Bible studies were young in their faith. Not everyone, of course. The ones who were more mature in their Christian faith had often helped to mentor others.

As the leader began the lesson, Blake unzipped the case that held his Bible and notebook. Charli also pulled her Bible and a much fancier notebook out of the large bag she'd brought with her.

So far, his favorite verses that they'd studied had come from James 1. They were a reminder that the trials he faced in his life had a purpose, and that the refinement of his faith was in direct response to how he handled the trials that came his way. He knew that his faith had strengthened as he'd taken on the full responsibility of parenting Amelia.

Blake wondered what Charli was getting from the lessons. Maybe someday they'd be able to talk about their spiritual walks. He'd been able to have some deep conversations with his Christian friends, especially when on deployment.

Looking back, he was so grateful for the Christian men who'd helped him find his way to God. Jackson and his parents had tried to do that when he'd spent time with them, but it had taken a near death situation to open him up to committing his life to God.

He should have been on the helicopter that had crashed, but he'd been pulled off it at the last minute. When it had gone down, killing everyone on board, Blake had realized how close he'd come to death, and his perspective on life had changed completely.

All that followed had brought him to this moment in Serenity, and he couldn't be happier.

When the class ended forty-five minutes later, no one rushed to stand up. The kids knew enough to head upstairs once their classes were over, so their parents didn't need to go get them.

"How are you today?" Blake asked as he turned to Charli.

"Trying to figure out why I'm so worn out when I didn't really have much at all to do yesterday." She leaned back in the pew, her shoulders slumped. "But otherwise, Layla and I are fine. How about you and Amelia?"

"I'm fine, but Amelia is really dragging."

Her brow furrowed over her soft brown eyes. "She didn't sleep well?"

The concern in Charli's voice for Amelia warmed Blake. He didn't think it was just because she was her teacher. If they were ever going to make a relationship work, they'd both need to take on a role in the life of the other person's child.

"She slept okay, but she woke up too early."

"Maybe she'll take a nap this afternoon," Charli said. "It's the perfect day for a nap."

She was right about that. When they'd left the apartment earlier, they'd been greeted by a gray, moody day. Hopefully Amelia would see it as a favorable nap day the way Charli did.

Charli was dressed for the season in an oversized dark reddish-orange sweater and a pair of fitted black pants. She looked cozy and comfortable, and in Blake's opinion, completely huggable.

But it was definitely not the time or place to be thinking about that.

When the kids joined them, there was some shuffling in the pew, with Amelia ending up next to him and Layla and Charli on her other side. Peyton sat with his parents, though, at the moment, he was talking to the little boy who kneeled on the pew in front of him.

Blake put his arm around Amelia, and she leaned against his side, folding her legs up on the pew beside her. He'd thought she was tired. However, seeing her so low energy made him wonder if something more was bothering her.

Lifting a hand, he put it against her forehead. She didn't feel warmer than usual, so he figured there wasn't anything to be too concerned about.

He wasn't as certain of that, though, when she refused to go to the children's service and stayed curled up next to him. Charli and Layla gave her a concerned look, but then Layla and Peyton headed off.

Partway through the sermon, Amelia slumped heavily against him, and Blake realized that she'd fallen asleep. He lifted her onto his lap, keeping his arms wrapped around her. It meant he couldn't open his Bible or take any notes, but it felt important to make sure Amelia was comfortable.

She slept right through to the end of the service, and even after they'd been dismissed, Blake stayed sitting with her asleep on his lap.

"Is she just tired?" Charli asked. "Or is she not feeling well?"

"I'm not sure." There were times when Blake really felt out of his depth as he parented Amelia, and when she was sick was when he felt the most like he didn't know what he was doing.

Charli reached out and touched Amelia's forehead. "She looks a little flushed."

Blake brushed a hand over her head. "I think I should get her home. And hopefully if she can rest for the afternoon, she'll feel better."

He carefully got to his feet, adjusting Amelia to rest against his shoulder. He followed Charli and Layla out of the sanctuary, then headed to the coatroom.

"Let me help you with her jacket," Charli said. "Which one is hers?"

Blake showed her without letting go of Amelia. It took a little maneuvering and help from Charli, but eventually, they were able to get jackets on both him and Amelia.

"Do you need anything?" Charli asked as she briefly rested her hand on Amelia's back. "Were you planning to go out for lunch?"

"I hadn't thought that far ahead, to be honest," he said. "But I do have food at home, so we'll be fine."

"Well, let one of us know if you need something," Charli told him as they walked to the doors.

Blake would have loved to spend the afternoon hanging out with the Halversons, but it was important for Amelia to be comfortable and for him to do what was necessary to make her feel better.

At the truck, he settled Amelia in her seat, but she woke up as he was buckling her in.

"Daddy?" she asked, glancing around. "Where are we?"

"We're at the truck. Church is over, so we're going home." He leaned into the truck so he could see her more clearly. "Are you feeling okay?"

She stared at him for a moment and frowned. "Just tired."

"When we get home, you can go back to sleep. Okay?"

Nodding, she squirmed in her seat, settling low in her jacket.

When they got home, Amelia changed into her pajamas and crawled into bed. Blake was worried, but she said she was only feeling tired, though she didn't want anything to eat. Not even her favorite berries.

Once she'd fallen back asleep, Blake changed into a pair of sweats and a T-shirt, then went to the kitchen to make something to eat because even if Amelia wasn't hungry, he was. Thankfully, his aunt had taken pity on him and brought over some containers of food a few days earlier, so he pulled out the one with lasagna in it.

The apartment was quiet, so while the microwave heated his food, Blake found the TV remote and turned it on. He switched to the sports channel, figuring that would at least give him something to watch while he ate since he didn't have Amelia to keep him company.

Sometimes the quiet of the apartment, even when Amelia was awake, was hard to take. He was used to having buddies around, providing constant noise and companionship.

Now that it was just the two of them living together, with neither of them very chatty, they often used the television or music to fill the silence.

Once the food was hot, he took his plate and a glass of water to the couch and set them on the coffee table. His mom would have had an absolute fit if she'd seen him eating while sitting on the couch. But she wasn't there, and likely never would be, so he'd do what he wanted in his own home.

It was actually quite rare that they ate in the living room. Well, at least meals. They mostly just ate snacks on the couch or at the coffee table, but he wasn't too uptight about that.

He wanted Amelia to feel comfortable in every corner of their small home. Unlike how he'd felt in the mansion he'd grown up in.

That had been one of the things that had drawn him to Charli back when they'd been together. She'd talked a lot about the home she longed to create for her family. It had been everything his own hadn't been.

Even the apartment he'd stayed in while in college had been decorated by his mom, and because his parents were paying for everything, Blake hadn't felt like he'd could change it into what he would have preferred.

After he finished eating, Blake put his dishes in the dishwasher, then checked on Amelia before returning to the couch. He stretched out, propping his head on a cushion. And even though the television was on, it didn't keep him from falling asleep.

Blake didn't know how long he'd been asleep when a knock on the door woke him. It took him a moment to realize what it was, and he groaned as he pushed up from the couch. He walked to the door, stretching his arms above his head.

Expecting it to be a neighbor or someone selling Girl Scout cookies or something else, Blake ran a hand through his hair as he pulled the door open. He hadn't even thought to check through the peek hole to see who was there because security wasn't something he was terribly worried about in Serenity.

However, if he'd checked, he wouldn't have been so surprised when he saw Charli and Layla standing in the hallway.

"Hey," he said, aware that he probably looked a bit disheveled, considering he'd just woken up.

"Hi." She gave him a smile. "Hope we're not disturbing you."

"Not at all." He stepped back and motioned to the living room. "Come on in."

Charli put her hand on Layla's back to guide her past Blake.

"Have a seat," he said, glad that he hadn't left his dirty dishes sitting on the coffee table.

"How's Amelia?" Charli asked as she and Layla sat down on the couch. She set the bag she carried onto the coffee table.

Blake dropped down in his recliner. "She's been sleeping since we got home."

"Can I go check on her?" Layla asked.

"Sure." Blake wasn't worried about her waking her up. In fact, he kind of hoped she did, so Amelia could get something to eat. "Her bedroom is the first door on the right. The door's open."

Layla got up and hurried to the hall that led to the bedrooms.

"I brought you some soup," Charli said, leaning forward to tap the bag. "Along with a few other things."

"You didn't have to do that, but I sure appreciate it."

"Will's mom made the soup," Charli told him. "She swears her chicken noodle soup will cure what ails you. We always have several containers in the freezer since she keeps us well stocked."

"I'm sure that Amelia will enjoy it."

"She's not a fussy eater?"

"Not normally, but she didn't even want berries when we got home from church. She'll normally eat them whenever possible."

Layla came back out and sat down next to Charli. "She's still sleeping."

"I really hope this is just a case of her being overtired."

"Will you be able to take time off work if she's still sick tomorrow?"

"I think it will be fine, but I should probably text Stan to give him a head's up. I just hope that if she is sick, she hasn't infected anyone else."

Charli shook her head. "Don't worry about that. If someone else gets sick, that's just life, you know. I always say that it seems like the only thing a child willingly shares are their sick germs."

"What do you do when Layla gets sick?"

"Grandma comes and stays with me," Layla volunteered.

"Yep. My mom watches Layla if she's sick when I need to work. Misha's mom stays with Jay's kids if they get sick."

"That's good that you have that support. I don't think my mom would ever offer to stay with a sick child. I'm not sure she even stayed with us when we were sick. Usually. she just left us with the housekeeper."

Layla frowned. "That seems... sad."

"It is," Blake said. "You're lucky to have such a great mom and grandma."

"I love them," Layla said with a beaming smile, so like her mom's. "They're great."

Charli put her arm around Layla's shoulders. "You're pretty great too."

"Daddy?"

Blake looked over to see Amelia coming out of the hallway. She came over to him and crawled up into his lap before turning to look at Layla and Charli.

"How are you feeling, Berry?" he asked as he touched her forehead. She felt warm, but not overly so, and it probably had to do with her being bundled up in bed.

"Not so tired now."

Blake was glad to hear that. "Are you hungry?"

She nodded. "Can I have berries?"

"How about you have a little soup first, then you can have berries?"

Amelia appeared to consider that for a moment, then nodded. "Soup's good."

"Charli and Layla brought some soup for you."

"Do you mind if I warm some up?" Charli asked.

"I don't mind," Blake assured her, especially since he was reluctant to move Amelia off his lap just yet.

Charli got up and grabbed the bag before going to the small kitchen that was just steps away in the open plan space. He told her where to find the things she needed, while Layla and Amelia chatted.

262 · KIMBERLY RAE JORDAN

When the soup was ready, Charli carried it to the table. Blake set Amelia on her feet, then followed the girls over to the table. A few moments later, Charli joined them with a plate of cookies.

"Did you bring those too?" Blake asked. "Or do I have a cookie-making elf in my cupboards?"

"Ooooh, I hope you have an elf," Layla said, her eyes going wide. "That would be amazing."

"Layla," Charli said with a laugh. "Considering you put all these cookies into the container to bring it over here, I think you know there's no elf."

"I do." Layla sighed. "But wouldn't that be the greatest? To have an elf living in your cupboard that would make you treats?"

"I'd like that," Amelia said. "Daddy and I try to make cookies sometimes, but they've not been very good."

"You definitely make better ones when you make them with Aunt Julia."

"It takes time and practice to learn how to bake well," Charli said.

"Even I still need Mom's help sometimes when I'm baking," Layla added.

Amelia leaned close to her bowl and took a careful taste of the soup. "Did you make the soup too, Miss H?"

"No. Will's mom made it. Do you like it?"

Nodding, Amelia said, "I love it. The noodles are nice."

"That's good. I put the rest of the soup in the fridge, so you can have more later if you're still hungry."

Blake had a feeling that Charli was there because of the encouragement of others, maybe even just Layla wanting to check on Amelia. But he didn't care about the motive behind her visit. All that mattered to him was that she was there.

They were in an awkward position once again, trying to build a relationship from a distance even though they weren't distant. But

Blake understood why Charli wanted it that way. She was protecting the girls, and he appreciated that.

Still, he would enjoy any time they got to spend with each other,
even if it was in a non-dating way. Such as sitting around his table
with their daughters.

"Do you usually get your car tuned up before winter?" Blake
asked.

Charli gave a huff of laughter. "Trying to drum up some business?"

"You know it." Though really, he just wanted to make sure that
she was safe while driving once winter hit.

"To answer your question, yes, I usually do take my car in."

"Well, maybe I can help you out," Blake said. "Come by the
shop in the morning, and if you're willing to bring Amelia with you,
you can take my truck to school. I'll work on your car during the
day, then you can pick it up when you're done at school."

"That would work out great," Charli said. "If you're sure it's
convenient for you."

"It's not a problem at all," Blake assured her.

"Will you put on winter tires at the same time?"

"Do you already have some?"

"Yep. They're in the garage at the house."

"If you want, I can swing by tomorrow and pick them up in the
truck, so you don't need to try to get them into your car. Then I'll
do the work and switch the tires on Tuesday."

"That would probably work for me."

"I'll check the schedule at work tomorrow—provided Amelia
isn't still sick—and if it's not a good time, I'll let you know."

Charli stared at him for a moment, then gave him a small smile
and a nod. "That would be great. Thanks."

There wasn't much Charli needed him for, but making sure her
car was running safely was one thing he could do for her and Layla.

He was just glad that she was willing to let him do it.

CHAPTER TWENTY-FOUR

Charli wasn't sure why she hadn't fought Janessa harder when she'd made the suggestion to take soup over to Blake and Amelia. During lunch, Layla had mentioned that Amelia wasn't feeling well. Janessa had immediately latched onto that news, and the next thing Charli knew, they were on their way to Blake's.

She'd been surprised and worried when Blake had answered the door because he looked like they'd woken him up, so she'd wondered if he wasn't feeling well either. Also, Amelia had still been sleeping.

But now that Amelia was awake and eating, Charli felt like maybe she really had just been overtired. Layla went through periods where she needed more sleep, and if she didn't get it, she eventually crashed. It was possible that it was the same for Amelia.

Charli wasn't sure what to make of Blake's offer to take care of her car, but she appreciated it. Her car's maintenance was one of those things that she tended to put off because she hated dealing with it, even though she knew it was necessary. Usually, her dad or one of her brothers prodded her into getting it taken care of.

Once Amelia finished eating her soup, she and Layla went to her room and found a game to play. They set it up on the table while Charli and Blake watched them.

"The Game of Life?" Charli asked.

"Kids' version," Blake said. "Amelia loves it."

Charli watched as the two girls bent over the game board, discussing which mover they wanted to play with. Seeing them together always left her with such mixed feelings.

At first, it had been hard to see Amelia, knowing that she was the result of Blake being with someone else. Amelia was in his life because he had walked away from Charli and the promises he'd made to her.

But now... Now, she struggled with the knowledge only she had about their situation. Well, she and Jackson.

However, as much as she wanted Blake and Amelia to know about that connection, she couldn't bring herself to reveal it. There was still too much uncertainty in how things were going to develop between her and Blake to make herself and Layla that vulnerable.

The girls' gameplay was lively enough that she and Blake talked little beyond interacting with them about what was happening as they played. It was nice to be with him without feeling the pressure of having to find things to talk about.

They'd never had a problem with that thirteen years ago when they'd been long-distance. Whether it was voice or video calls or text messages, their conversations had always flowed easily and had lasted more than just a few minutes. Back then, she'd probably talked more than he had, but he'd shared enough that she'd thought she'd known him.

Now, though... she didn't know what to say to him. There was so much she *wanted* to say, but she was still worried about sharing too much with him too soon.

He'd had a soft side that she'd only seen when they were alone together, but now he showed it to the world each time he interacted with Amelia. Even right then, Amelia had Blake playing along with her, doing the tasks together that the game required.

Had he shown this softer side to Amelia's mom?

Charli knew she shouldn't compare herself to someone who wasn't part of Blake's life anymore. Blake had come back to Serenity. Maybe back to... her. Charli wasn't sure about that yet. However, the more time she spent with him, the more she wanted that to be the case.

When the game ended, Charli decided they should probably leave. Layla protested a little, but she helped Amelia clear up the game, then went with her to her bedroom to put it away.

"Thank you so much for coming and bringing soup for Amelia," Blake said as he got to his feet.

"Soup for you too," she told him. "There's still enough there for both of you."

He grinned, the skin at the corners of his eyes crinkling. "And cookies too?"

"Plenty of those as well."

"Well, thanks for all of it, but especially the cookies. We have tried to make them, but sadly, most of what we bake resembles a hockey puck."

"Keep practicing," Charli told him. "We're not born knowing how to bake. Well, maybe Denise was. I'm convinced that she was born knowing how to cook and bake. She is ah—may—zing."

"Yeah. I've tasted enough of her food to definitely agree with that observation."

"Julia's another one who might have been born knowing how to do it all."

"Well, if she was, it was because she also got my mom's share of that particular gene. Or if my mom actually has that natural ability, she's never chosen to share it with the rest of us."

"My mom tried her hand plenty at cooking and baking, and there were times we wished she hadn't."

Blake chuckled. "That's how I feel about my cooking most days. I'm just grateful that Amelia isn't a fussy eater, or she'd probably starve."

Charli turned as Layla and Amelia reappeared. "Ready to go?"

"Yeah," Layla said, though clearly not enthused by the prospect.

"Hopefully, I'll see you in class tomorrow, Amelia."

Amelia nodded. "I'll be there."

Charli hoped Amelia really did feel better, because she was sure that it would stress Blake out if she was truly sick.

"If it's okay, I'll swing by tomorrow after I pick Amelia up from school."

"Actually, I have a staff meeting immediately after school, so I won't be home until around four-thirty or five. Would that still work?"

"Yep. That would be fine."

Blake opened the door, then stood with Amelia leaning against him as Charli and Layla walked past them out onto the landing. Before they headed for the stairs, Charli turned back and said, "If Amelia's still not feeling well tomorrow, be sure to let the school know."

Blake nodded. "I will, but I'm hoping that call won't be necessary."

"I do feel better, Daddy," Amelia said as she looked up at him.

"I'm glad to hear that." Blake smiled at her as he gave her ponytail a little tug. "Hope that's still true tomorrow."

After saying goodbye, Layla took Charli's hand as they walked toward the stairs. It wasn't until they were partway down the stairs that Charli heard their door close.

"I'm glad Amelia is feeling better," Layla said as they walked out of the building.

"I am too."

Once they were in the car on their way home, Charli said, "Why do you like hanging out with Amelia?"

When Layla didn't answer right away, Charli looked in the rearview mirror so she could see her face.

"I don't know," she finally said with a shrug. "When we first met her, I felt bad because she didn't have any friends. But then, she ended up actually being nice."

"Does she let you boss her around?" Charli asked.

Layla snickered. "Maybe?"

"Probably," Charli corrected, though she really hadn't seen Layla being overly bossy with Amelia.

"Why did you want to know?" Layla asked.

"Just curious," Charli said. "You seem to have fun hanging out with her."

"She's kind of like how Peyton was when he first came. Only she's not my cousin."

No, she's your sister.

That wasn't something Charli was ready to reveal to her yet, however.

"I also feel sorry for her. She doesn't have a mom. I mean, I don't have a dad, but since I'm a girl, it's better that I have a mom. Peyton had a dad, and now he has a mom. I'm just trying to be a girl friend in her life." Charli looked at the mirror in time to catch another of Layla's shrugs. "Kinda like an older sister, even though we're not related."

Charli's stomach knotted at Layla's words.

Over the years, she'd gotten to where she'd rarely thought about Blake being Layla's father. Her family had, for the most part, stopped asking her about it, and it was rare that Layla would bring it up. But now... it was in her thoughts so much, and even when she *wasn't* thinking about it, something would inevitably happen to bring it to her mind.

The secret felt toxic in a way it never had before.

In the past, it had felt necessary to keep that information from everyone. If Blake had been someone no one had known, perhaps she would've shared his identity as Layla's father. However, his connection to Jackson and his family had made her feel like she couldn't reveal who he was.

When they got home, Layla followed her into the kitchen. "Would you let Auntie Nessa braid your hair?"

"What?" Charli turned to face her. "Why?"

"I want to learn to French braid," she said. "But I need someone to show me how to do it."

"I suppose if Janessa agrees, I'm fine with it."

"Thanks!" Layla ran out of the kitchen and then up the stairs.

She wasn't sure what Will and Janessa were up to, but usually Sunday afternoons were pretty low-key. Sometimes they sat on the landing on the second floor, where there were a couple of couches and a fireplace. Since Aria had moved out, the second floor was basically Will and Janessa's space.

Charli poured herself a glass of water, then grabbed a cookie from the container on the counter. As she ate it, she stared out the window that overlooked the backyard and its plethora of trees, many of which had only a few leaves left clinging to their branches.

It was hard to believe they were almost at the end of October. She needed to put up her fall decorations. Maybe she'd dig out a few after she got her hair braided.

Layla had always enjoyed decorating for Christmas, especially the tree. However, she usually left the fall decorating to Charli. Maybe this year she'd be more interested in helping.

She heard steps on the stairs, and soon Janessa and Layla joined her, with Will following behind them.

"I hear that I'm going to be braiding your hair," Janessa said.

"That seems to be what Layla wants."

"Let's do it in the living room," Janessa said. "You can sit on the floor in front of the couch, then Layla can sit next to me and see what I'm doing."

It took them a couple of minutes to get situated, but soon Charli was seated with the coffee table pulled close so she could reach her water and the second cookie she'd picked up before leaving the kitchen. Janessa's legs pressed against Charli's arms, with Layla perched beside her.

"So first, we'll brush through her hair to make sure there aren't any tangles."

Charli found it soothing to have her hair brushed, so she had no trouble sitting there while Janessa fussed with it. Layla had learned how to do a simple braid earlier that year, but Charli still had to do French braids for her.

As Janessa braided her hair, Charli flicked through her social media apps on her phone. After a brief hesitation, she looked up Blake on one of them, then sent him a friend request.

"That's so pretty," Layla said, and Charli felt her run her fingers down the braid. "How old were you when you learned to braid like this?"

"I can't even remember." Janessa laughed. "Probably around your age, though. Kayleigh taught me how, though I never really did it on myself. I got most of my practice on your mom, Kayleigh, and Skylar. Oh, and you."

"Can I try now?" Layla asked.

"Sure. Let me take this out."

Janessa worked quickly, and soon the braid was out, and Charli's hair was ready for round two. After Janessa shifted over, Layla took her place behind Charli.

"Learning how to do this on someone else is easier than on yourself," Janessa said. "It will take you longer to do it on yourself."

"I know," she said. "I want to learn to do it on other people."

"Your friends?" Janessa asked.

"Yes. But mainly on Amelia. She said she wanted braids like mine the last time I had them, and her dad doesn't know how to do them."

Charli closed her eyes because of the emotion that surged through her at Layla's words. She loved her daughter so much. She was blessed beyond reason and so very grateful that Layla had a heart for others.

Charli couldn't say that had always been the case for her, especially after Blake had disappeared. But over the years, God had softened her heart as He'd presented her with situations, both at school and in her family, that had touched her heart and given her a new outlook.

"We should get you one of those mannequin heads that I see people using to do hairstyles on social media," Janessa said. "Then you could practice whenever you want."

Charli liked that idea, so she looked to see what she could find online. She found one that wasn't too expensive, figuring that if Layla put it to good use, she could get her a better one later.

"Maybe if I'm good at this, I can become a hairdresser," Layla said as she carefully followed Janessa's instructions. "Do you think I could be a hairdresser, Mom?"

"You can be whatever you want," Charli said, which was her usual answer. "If you really enjoying doing hair, it's always a possibility."

"First, I have to learn how to do this braid," Layla muttered. "It doesn't lay flat like yours, Auntie."

"Practice, sweetie. Practice."

Charli tapped the button to put the mannequin head into her cart, then checked out, glad to see it would be there in two days. She wouldn't say anything about it until it arrived.

"And if you really like to do hair stuff, maybe Kayleigh could teach you how to do Black hair like mine and Ciara's."

"Really? Would she teach me?" Layla asked.

"I think she might if she has the time."

Layla continued to mutter her way through braiding Charli's hair with help from Janessa. Finally, she patted Charli's head.

"All done. But it's not very good."

Charli lifted her hand and ran it over the braid, feeling the bumps, but also feeling very proud. "For your first try, it's great."

She kept the braid in for the rest of the day, only taking it out after Layla was in bed, and Charli was getting ready for bed herself.

She had changed into her pajamas, removed all her makeup, and was doing her skin care when she heard her phone's text alert. She'd left her phone in her bedroom, so she went and got it.

Blake: *I wanted to thank you again for coming by with Layla. We ate the rest of the soup for supper, and it was great.*

Charli sat down on the edge of the bed as she tapped out a reply. *I'm glad you enjoyed it! I'll be sure to tell Will's mom. How is Amelia feeling?*

Blake: *She seems to be doing fine. No other complaints, and she was able to stay awake until her usual bedtime. Guess it was just too much excitement and then not sleeping well last night.*

Charli was glad to hear that because they were moving into that time of year when colds and the flu started popping up among the students at school.

That's good! Hopefully she'll still be fine tomorrow.

Blake: *I tell you... parenting Amelia when she's sick is terrifying. I always worry that it's worse than she's saying, and that I might miss something serious.*

Charli understood his worries, since she'd experienced them herself—every parent probably had. Thankfully, she'd been surrounded by people who supported her through those times. Having doctors to call on was a real blessing. And perhaps she could offer that support to Blake.

You know that if you ever have questions or concerns about anything health related, you can call Gareth, Misha, or Janessa. Or if you don't want to go to them directly, let me know and I'll get hold of them.

Blake: *Thank you for offering that. It would probably help me not stress so much when Amelia seems off. All I want is to take care of her in a way she wasn't cared for during so much of her life.*

It was hard not to admire that quality in the man. And maybe she didn't need to fight that admiration. After all, she'd agreed to these conversations with him, with the possibility of them turning into something deeper.

And she was coming to the place where she could accept that she wanted that possibility to become more of a reality. It was scary for her, but maybe this time around, they had a chance of making a relationship work.

She's very fortunate to have you.

Blake: *I'm fortunate to have her because she's brought me back to the place I always wanted to be.*

But would Amelia be enough to keep him in Serenity?

Would Charli be enough to keep him there?

She wasn't so sure about that, considering that she hadn't been the first time around.

Serenity seems to agree with her.

Blake: *Yes, she really loves it here. Doesn't seem to miss Texas at all. For which I'm very glad.*

Charli could only hope it stayed that way after winter descended on Serenity. Coming from Texas, northern Idaho's winter was going to come as something of a shock, she was sure.

Blake: *I'd better let you go. Ten o'clock is quickly approaching. Thanks for the chat!*

See you tomorrow.

After they said goodbye, Charli gripped her phone and prayed yet again that she wasn't making a mistake in allowing Blake and Amelia into her and Layla's life.

She knew that she could survive if Blake walked away again. She'd already suffered one heartbreak at his hands, and she'd lived through it.

What she didn't want was for Layla to be heartbroken if things didn't work out. And that would only be worse if she knew who Blake and Amelia truly were to her.

Charli felt trapped, but she knew the longer she put off telling Blake, the worse breaking the news to him could end up being. She hoped that he'd understand why she was reluctant to reveal Layla's relationship to him. After all, he'd walked out of her life without even giving her a chance to talk with him.

As she sat on her bed, Charli closed her eyes and prayed, asking God to give her wisdom on how to handle everything. That she would somehow get control of her emotions, and not make her decisions motivated by fear.

And more importantly, she prayed that Blake's heart would remain open and understanding when he finally found out about his relationship to Layla.

CHAPTER TWENTY-FIVE

When his text alert went at lunch on Monday, Blake pulled it out to check the message.

Charli: *I forgot that I have a meeting after school, so I'll be about an hour later than usual getting home. Will that still be okay?*

Yep. That's definitely fine.

Blake was still in shock that Charli had agreed to have regular contact with him again, with the possibility of something deeper developing. He hoped and prayed that it would, but only time would tell.

Charli: *Have a good afternoon.*

You too. See you later.

He stared at his phone for a moment, then slipped it into the pocket of his coveralls.

"Everything okay?"

Blake looked at his co-worker. "Yes. Why?"

"You just looked a little shell-shocked."

That was a pretty apt description, Blake realized. However, he wasn't going to share the reason he'd looked that way. He didn't plan to talk to anyone about what he and Charli were doing until she told him that she wanted people to know.

Though he wanted to shout it to the world, Blake understood why Charli was being cautious. The reasons to keep things to themselves were different this time since there were kids involved. She was protecting Layla from the possibility that it might not work out, just like he was protecting Amelia. He didn't want Amelia to be disappointed, especially since she was praying for this very thing.

Blake was praying about it too, but his confidence that God would grant him a second chance wasn't very high. It was entirely possible that at the end of the day, Charli would decide that the hurt he'd inflicted on her in the past was just too much to get over. He was braced for that, even as he hoped for more.

After lunch, he went back to work on the car Stan had assigned him that morning. Blake was glad that the job was something he could do in his sleep because his attention was only about fifty percent—if not less—on what he was doing.

When the end of his workday arrived, Blake stopped by Stan's office to let him know he'd finished the car, then he left the garage. Once at the school, he quickly found a parking spot. He usually arrived a few minutes early, so he sat in his car, reading through an email from the only one of his closest friends who had kept in contact with him.

Thomas had left the army recently, and their communication had picked up since then. Being done with the military had become one more thing they had in common.

Thomas had been a Christian since he was a teen, and Blake appreciated his spiritual maturity. He had been glad to hear that Blake had settled into a Christian community that supported both him and Amelia.

They usually sent text messages back and forth, but occasionally, Thomas would send a longer email. Most of those came when Thomas wanted to share something deeper that was on his mind, something embodying a spiritual lesson he'd learned and wanted to pass on to Blake.

Thomas was a father of four, so Blake appreciated the time he took to keep in contact with him. He knew about Blake's history with Lauren and how he'd come to be a single father. What he hadn't yet told Thomas about was his past with Charli, but Blake figured it was only a matter of time before he needed some advice regarding that.

This particular email shared about Thomas' struggle to adapt to civilian life. The man was frank about what he was feeling, knowing that Blake would be a safe place for him to spill his guts.

There wasn't much advice Blake could offer the man, but he could sympathize and pray for him. Thankfully, that seemed to be enough for Thomas.

After reading the email, he had enough time to tap out a quick reply before he had to pick up Amelia. Once that was done, he climbed out of the truck, then wandered down the sidewalk to the walkway leading to the steps at the front of the school.

Parents were not allowed inside the building. But soon, aides guided children out of the front doors, Amelia among them.

"Hi, Daddy!" she called as she ran up to him.

Blake scooped her up and gave her a hug and a kiss on her forehead, giving the aide, who'd come out with Amelia and others from her class, a nod. Turning his attention back to Amelia, he said, "How was your day?"

"It was great," she replied as he set her back down on her feet.

Hand in hand, they walked away from the school. This time of the day had become more interactive as Amelia had started to share spontaneously about her day without him having to ask her a bunch of questions.

Slowly but surely, what she shared began to include the names of kids in her class. He was so happy that she was making friends beyond Layla and Peyton. They were still the two she preferred to spend time with, and he didn't blame her for that, but at least she had a few kids at her school that she liked to spend time with.

When they got home, he set her up with a snack, then went to take a quick shower. Even though he'd be handling dirty tires later, he still didn't want to show up smelling like grease.

While he'd been in the army, he hadn't been as meticulous about keeping his hands, especially his nails, free of the grime that had built up on his hands during the course of a shift. But since having Amelia, he made sure to work the grease off his hands.

And now with Charli, he didn't want to come near her with dirty hands. He felt like he had enough figurative dirt on them from what he'd done to her in the past.

They had a bit of time before Charli would be home, so after he was done with his shower, Blake went through Amelia's backpack. He emptied her lunch bag, grateful to see that she'd eaten almost everything he'd sent with her that day. It was such an improvement over the start of school, when she'd hardly eaten anything while at school.

"What are we having for supper?" Amelia asked as she leaned against the counter.

"I was thinking maybe we'd get some burgers and fries."

Amelia smiled. "Cheeseburger?"

"Yep. If you'd like."

"Or nuggets," she said, a contemplative look on her face.

"Maybe we can each have a burger and share some French fries and a small order of nuggets." He doubted she'd eat her half, but he could finish whatever she didn't.

"Perfect."

"Perfect," Blake agreed as he held out his hand for a high five. She didn't leave him hanging and gave his hand a smack.

They didn't go out to eat too often, since his budget didn't really have room for it. However, since they would be out during their usual dinnertime, he'd make an exception that night.

When he pulled up to Charli's house a short time later, Blake spotted Charli's car in the driveway. Without delay, they both got out of the truck. A gust of cold air greeted him as he closed the door and walked around to join Amelia on the sidewalk.

Amelia headed up the steps to the front door, then waited for Blake before pressing the doorbell. When the door swung open, Layla stood there, a big smile on her face.

"Hey, Amelia," she said, as she moved to the side so they could step into the house.

When Amelia quickly removed her jacket and boots, Blake said, "We won't be here very long, so don't get too caught up in anything."

"Okay," Amelia said with a nod, then followed Layla as she ran toward the back of the house.

Blake stood there for a moment, uncertain what to do now that he'd been left alone in the foyer. He didn't really want to take off his outer wear, since he needed to go back outside to transfer the tires from the garage into his truck.

The house was quiet, and he didn't know if Charli was even aware that he was there. Shoving his hands into the pockets of his jeans, he shifted his weight from one foot to the other as he glanced around.

Though the house was big, it didn't feel empty. The home that Charli had had a hand in creating was warm and cozy. Just like she'd told him she hoped to have one day.

"Hi, Blake."

Blake turned at the sound of Charli's voice. She was walking toward him from the direction where the girls had disappeared.

Though his heart raced at the sight of her, it also pained Blake that she didn't greet him with the unabashed joy she once had.

Returning her smile, he said, "Hey."

It looked like she'd changed after school. He doubted black leggings and an oversized dark red sweater that reached almost to mid-thigh was an outfit she'd wear to school.

"I see the girls are already in Layla's room."

"Yep. They ran off pretty quickly."

"Do you want to take off your jacket?" Charli asked as she came to a stop near him.

"I figured I'd keep my stuff on so I could transfer the tires."

"Okay. Did you want to come through to the garage?"

"I'm going to back the truck into the driveway, so I'll just meet you there."

After Blake stepped back onto the porch, Charli gave him another smile, then closed the door. Blake jogged down the sidewalk to the truck.

He got behind the wheel, then maneuvered the truck so that he could back up the wide driveway beside Charli's car. The garage door in front of Charli's car was open, so he walked into the large space.

Cars were his passion, which meant he also liked the spaces they inhabited. This garage had been painted white and was super clean and bright. It was a large space with room for two cars as well as some storage and worktables along the sides and back. There was a car parked on the other side, which he assumed belonged to Will or Janessa.

"The tires are over here," Charli said, gesturing to where three wheel racks stood. When Blake joined her at the tires, she tapped the ones on the rack nearest to the door of the garage. "These ones are mine."

Blake ran his hand over the tread. "They look good. How old are they?"

"This will be my second winter using them."

"Good."

He lifted the first one off the rack, then carried it over to the truck and placed it in the bed. When he turned, Charli was trying to pick up one of the other tires. Hurrying over, he said, "Hey. Let me do that."

"Are you saying I'm too weak?" Charli asked as she stepped away from the tires.

Blake glanced over, relieved to see that she wasn't saying it in anger or defensiveness. "Nope. Just don't want you to get messed up. My clothes are more used to collecting dirt."

"That's not what you wear to work, is it?"

"It is, but I wear coveralls over them. But while my clothes are made for rougher work, yours are not." Blake lifted another tire and headed for his truck.

He was settling the tire into the truck bed when another car pulled up behind Charli's. Will climbed out from behind the wheel and called out a greeting, which was echoed by Janessa when she appeared from between the two cars.

"What are you doing here, Blake?" Janessa asked as she and Will headed toward him.

"I'm picking up Charli's winter tires to switch them over tomorrow when I winterize her car."

The three of them walked into the garage, where Will said, "Do you need a ride to work tomorrow, Charli?"

Blake hefted another tire up and headed back to the truck, leaving Charli to answer that question.

"No. Blake has offered to let me use his truck while he works on my car." Blake grinned as he dropped the tire with the others, happy that she wasn't trying to hide that they were *choosing* to have contact with each other. "And I'll take Amelia to and from school."

"Wow," Janessa said, like Blake knew she would. "Look at you two having conversations, even when you're not being forced to."

Blake grabbed the last tire and carried it to the truck. Once all four were positioned correctly, he closed the tailgate, then pulled the cover over the tires, and locked it.

"What are we having for supper?" Janessa asked as Blake joined them.

"Spaghetti and pasta sauce."

"Oh, you always make plenty of that," Janessa said before turning to Blake. "You and Amelia should stay for dinner."

Blake hesitated, looking over at Charli. She didn't look upset or frustrated with Janessa's invitation, which was progress, as far as Blake was concerned.

When she didn't protest, he took encouragement from that and said, "Sure. That would be great. Although Amelia's probably going to be torn about it."

"Why's that?" Charli asked.

"I told her we'd be having burgers, nuggets, and fries for supper. But I think she'll be equally happy to spend more time with Layla."

"Well, let's head inside," Charli said. "I need to check the food."

Blake followed the others inside as the garage door rumbled down into place. He took off his boots and jacket and left them in the mudroom, then stepped through the short hallway into the kitchen.

He'd gotten a light whiff of spicy tomato sauce and garlic as he'd stood at the front door earlier, but the aroma intensified in the kitchen.

The girls were there as well, and they were setting the breakfast nook table. It was quite a bit smaller than the dining room table, but there was plenty of room for the six of them.

Amelia always helped to set the table at the apartment, so she didn't need too much instruction from Layla. The way the group moved around each other made it obvious that everyone pitched in to help regularly. He offered his help, but he was waved away.

Soon enough, however, they sat down around a table filled with food. Janessa said the prayer for the food, then they filled their plates.

The food was great, but the company was even better. He was glad—and relieved—that Charli seemed to have no issue with him and Amelia crashing a meal in her home yet again.

Blake sat at one end of the table with Amelia on one hand and Charli on the other. Will sat opposite Blake, between Janessa and Layla. Conversation flowed easily between all of them, and there was a lot of laughter as well.

This was what he was working toward with Charli. This was what he wanted in his and Amelia's future. He didn't know if he deserved it. He didn't know if it was truly God's will. But he was going to give it his full heart, moving forward until the door slammed in his face.

Twelve years ago, he might not have had the strength and determination to fight for what he wanted. Now, however, he knew what he'd lost, and he was willing to work as hard as he needed to in order to achieve it.

But if it came to the point where he needed to walk away, he could do so knowing that he'd given it his all. That he hadn't let the fear of being hurt keep him from trying his best with Charli.

Once they were done eating, the girls went off to Layla's room.

When Blake offered to help clean up, Janessa said, "That's a great idea. We'll leave you two to it."

Charli gave a huff of laughter. "Yeah. Off you go."

"Are you sure?" Will asked, glancing at the back of his wife as she left the kitchen.

"I'm sure," Charli assured him as she made a shooing motion with her hands. "It's fine."

"Well, then." He gave Blake a grin. "See you around."

"Let's load what we can in the dishwasher," Charli said once it was just the two of them. "Then you can wash, and I'll dry and put away the rest."

Blake nodded, then began scraping plates into the garbage before handing them to Charli.

"Do you have to load the dishwasher a certain way?" Charli asked.

"Doesn't everyone?"

"Probably, and if you asked a hundred people how they do it, you'll probably get a hundred opinions."

"A hundred? As far as I'm concerned, there's just one."

Charli chuckled as she put glasses on the top rack. "I agree. There's just one."

As they joked about the differences in the way they placed the dishes in the dishwasher, Blake found himself laughing and smiling more than he had in recent months.

Loading the dishwasher had never been his favorite chore, but that day, he really didn't mind it. In fact, he was rather enjoying the task because being with Charli made it interesting and fun.

Once the dishwasher was full, there were still a few dishes to finish up by hand. Charli started the water flowing into the sink and squeezed some detergent into it.

"You can adjust the water to whatever temperature you can handle."

The warmth of the water actually felt good as he washed the large bowl the spaghetti noodles had been in. When he was done, Charli took it from him and rinsed it under hot water before drying it and putting it away in the pantry.

"Do you think we could take the girls out to do something one of these days?" Blake asked. "It would mean we could hang out, too."

Charli met his gaze as she took the next bowl from him. "What did you have in mind?"

"How about ice skating?" Blake suggested. "I'd definitely be watching from the sidelines, but I think the girls would have fun. Especially Amelia, since she loves it so much."

"I'll check on what time the community arena has open skate."

"Really?"

"Sure," Charli said with a shrug. "I think the girls will enjoy it."

"Will you invite Peyton too?"

She shook her head. "Peyton isn't a fan of ice skating. He went once and spent most of the time sitting on the ice, so I doubt he'd be interested in joining us."

"As long as you don't think he'll be upset."

"It'll be fine."

Since she knew Peyton better than he did, Blake had no reason to not believe that would be the case. Just the fact that she was willing to go along with his idea made him feel excited and a little hopeful.

Both emotions reminded him of how he'd felt the last time he and Charli were in the beginning stages of their relationship. He hadn't felt those same emotions this deeply with anyone else he'd dated, and he'd never been devastated when any of those relationships had ended. However, what he was pursuing with Charli now had a high chance of leaving him broken-hearted.

And yet somehow, even that possibility didn't sway him. His determination was present in abundance this time around.

His time in the army had done what his life before that hadn't. It had taught him how to work hard, and he was more than willing to work hard for Amelia and their life. He was also more than willing to work hard for a relationship with Charli.

And it looked like maybe he would get that chance.

CHAPTER TWENTY-SIX

Charli gripped Layla's hand tightly as they hurried across the short distance from the parking lot to the front doors of the arena. They'd gotten snow twice already that week, and it was snowing yet again. Now that they were into November, the colder temperatures had definitely arrived, bring with them shorter days.

There were only a few cars in the parking lot, so it didn't look like the rink was going to be too crowded. And from a quick glance around, it didn't appear that Blake was there yet.

It was a relief to step into the foyer of the arena and escape the bite of the icy wind. Layla quickly opened the second glass door and led Charli into a large open space. It was brightly lit, with a canteen and a place that had a limited number of skates for rental, since most people in the area who liked to skate had their own.

Amelia had her own pair of skates and had been taking lessons along with Layla. She would still need help on the ice though, so Charli went over to the rental place.

"Hey, Randy," Charli said, smiling at the man behind the counter who had been in school with her and was now the father of one of her students that year. "How's it going?"

"Really well. How about with you?"

They chatted for a couple of minutes before she said, "I'm going to need a skate trainer."

Randy's brows rose. "I'm pretty sure I've seen you skate before. Do you think you've forgotten how?"

Charli laughed. "It's not for me. We've come so Layla can skate with a friend, and the friend is still a novice, so it's for her."

"Okay. That makes sense." He got her sorted with a skate trainer, and she carried it over to where Layla sat on a bench, taking off her shoes.

"Why aren't you skating, Mom?" Layla asked as she shoved her foot into one of her skates and began to lace it up.

"I haven't skated in a very long time, and I don't feel like changing that at the moment. Plus, I don't think Amelia's dad skates, so I'll keep him company while we watch you guys skate."

"Amelia said he's never skated in his life."

"Not everybody is interested in skating," Charli said as she kept an eye on the entrance. Though this wasn't a date for her and Blake, Charli still felt excitement for the evening, and she was looking forward to seeing him again.

"Peyton hates skating, and he said Uncle Jay doesn't really like it either."

"Yep. Some of us prefer to watch from the sidelines."

"There's Amelia and Blake," Charli said as she spotted the duo coming through the second door.

Amelia waved, then ran over to them, while Blake moved more slowly, carrying Amelia's skate bag in his hand. He wore a pair of jeans and a black leather jacket with a scarf tucked into the neck.

"Hi, Layla," Amelia said with a huge smile on her face. "I can't wait to skate!"

"Me, either."

The little girl sat on the bench beside Layla and took off her boots. As Blake went down on a knee in front of Amelia, he gave Charli a quick smile.

With smooth movements, he helped Amelia put her skates on, then laced them up the way he'd learned how to since Amelia had started lessons. Layla could tighten her laces to a certain point, but then Charli had to finish them. When she got to that point, Layla turned and lifted her skate with a purple plastic guard protecting the blade onto the bench next to Charli.

288 · KIMBERLY RAE JORDAN

Once the girls' skates were ready, they all moved together through the door that led from that area into the part with the rink. The temperature was definitely colder in this part of the building, but it was tolerable as long as they kept their outerwear on.

There were rows of seats around the ice, since they also used the arena for hockey games and ice skating lessons. However, she and Blake stayed right at the boards, standing side by side as they watched Layla skate beside Amelia as she gripped the skating trainer with her gloved hands.

"How are you doing?" Blake asked as he rested his arms on the boards in front of him.

"I'm good. Glad it's almost the weekend." Charli glanced over at him. "How about you?"

"It's been a good week. But yes, I'm glad it's Friday tomorrow too."

They'd continued their nightly conversations, and Charli felt herself falling deeper and deeper into her feelings for Blake. Whether it was a long or short conversation, she left each one with a growing confidence that they might really be able to move beyond their past to build something in the future.

"Layla really is a good skater," Blake said, his gaze on the girls as they circled the far end of the arena. Thankfully, there were only a handful of other people on the ice with them. "She's looks like a natural out there."

"She's been skating for a lot of years, but she started out just like Amelia. All of us did. As long as Amelia sticks with it, she'll improve quickly, I'm sure."

"She has been really determined to do her best with both her skating and ballet. Not even complaining about being sore after all the falls she's endured."

Charli smiled as she watched Layla stick close to Amelia, even though a couple of kids from her class were there skating as well.

She smiled and said a few words to them, but she stayed with Amelia as they continued their slow path around the ice.

"Hi, Dad!" Amelia called out as they reached where Charli and Blake stood together.

"Hi, Mom!"

Charli and Blake waved back at them, and Charli was glad that she'd agreed to Blake's suggestion that they all hang out together like this.

The only thing marring her complete happiness in these moments with Blake was the secret she held from him. From everyone. He wasn't aware that the two girls he kept an eye on were both his daughters.

Soon. Soon she'd reveal it.

Just... not yet.

Blake's arm brushed hers as he pointed to where Layla was skating backwards in front of Amelia. "That's amazing."

Charli ignored the pang of guilt. "She was so proud when she learned how to skate backwards. It's a skill she loves to show off."

"I can barely *walk* backwards, let alone skate backwards."

"It's not something I can do well, either. Layla's already better than I was at her age."

A teenage couple glided by with smooth strokes. The guy had his arm around the young woman's shoulders, and their heads were close together. They shared smiles, totally caught up in their own little world.

"It feels like I was never that young," Blake said. His voice had lowered to a point where it was barely audible over the music that was playing for the skaters.

Charli nodded, her gaze still on the pair. She hoped that if the teens were planning a future together in their conversations, it would be a smoother road than the one she and Blake had traveled.

"It does feel like a lifetime ago," Charli said as she moved a bit closer to Blake. "But when I was their age, you wouldn't have found me skating with a guy."

"Were guys back then not interested in skating?"

Twelve years ago, Charli had chosen to be very vague with Blake about her relationships—or lack thereof—with guys while in her teens. She'd been embarrassed to admit that not dating hadn't been her choice. Rather, none of the guys she'd liked had liked her back. And clearly there hadn't been any guys that liked her enough to approach her.

"Oh, they were interested in skating. A lot of the guys played hockey, so they were plenty comfortable on skates." She hesitated. "They just weren't interested in skating with me."

Blake shifted to face her, resting his arm on the top of the boards. Charli could feel his gaze on her as she kept watching the girls.

"Well, if I'd known how to skate back then, I would have been happy to skate with you."

Even though she was standing close to the ice, Charli's cheeks heated as she glanced over at him, butterflies in her stomach. "I think I would have liked that."

"I'd skate with you now, but I don't think it would be the experience we'd like it to be. Do they have adult size skating trainers?"

"They might," Charli said with a chuckle.

"Unfortunately, I'm not sure my fragile ego and pride could take having to use one of those."

"You could get Amelia to teach you," Charli told him. "I think she'd love that."

"Oh, I'm sure she would."

The song changed, and *Jingle Bell Rock* started to play through the speakers.

Blake's brows rose as he looked out at the ice. "Christmas music?"

"Yep. Lots of people in Serenity believe that Christmas and Thanksgiving can co-exist."

"Do you?" he asked. "I've only seen Thanksgiving decorations at your house."

"Yeah. I do. You'll see a few Christmas decorations gradually show up, but I'll go full-out Christmas on the day after Thanksgiving."

"I'm going to have to buy a bunch of Christmas decorations because I didn't really have any in Texas."

Charli put her hands into the pockets of her jacket as she leaned sideways against the boards. "Why not?"

"I'm not sure. I guess I never saw the sense in decorating just for me, especially since I was often deployed over the holidays."

"Do you want a real tree or a fake one?"

"I hadn't really thought about it, to be honest. I figured I had some time before I'd have to make any decisions about Christmas stuff."

"We usually get a real tree, so if you want to come along to the tree farm, you're more than welcome."

"Does everyone go?"

"Not everyone, but a lot of us do. Misha and Jay, of course. Will and Janessa usually tag along, even though they're not getting a tree. Depending on how cold it is, Gareth and Aria might bring Timothy."

"Sounds like fun. I think Amelia would love that."

"It's not just cutting down trees at the farm," Charli said. "They have sleigh rides, Santa, hot chocolate, and mini donuts. It's an experience."

Blake smiled. "And being with you and Layla will make it even more of an experience."

Once upon a time, she would have stepped close and leaned into his embrace. And she'd have done it with the confidence that he wanted her close and that he'd wrap his arms around her in return.

It hadn't been something they'd been able to do much in public, and even now, they still had to keep any moves of affection hidden. Well, they didn't *have* to. It was her choice, and though Blake supported it, she was pretty sure that if given the opportunity, he'd love to share with the world that they were dating.

There was a part of her that wanted to throw caution to the wind and embrace their relationship publicly the way they hadn't been able to the last time. And that part of her was definitely growing.

"When do you usually go get the trees?"

They waved at the girls as they skated by again, then Charli said, "If the weather is agreeable, the day after Thanksgiving."

"You're not a Black Friday shopper?"

"No." She shuddered. "I get any deals that day online. No crowds fighting over stuff for me."

"I've never done it either. Not worth the hassle and frustration."

"Picking out a tree is much more fun."

"And it will last until Christmas?"

Charli nodded. "As long as you take care of it, it will."

"I'm going to need some detailed instructions or a video to tell me what to do."

"We'll make sure you know how to take care of it," Charli assured him.

"I'd appreciate that."

"Daddy, can I try to skate without this thing?" Amelia asked as she and Layla slowly stopped in front of them.

Blake leaned over the boards. "You might fall."

"I always fall," she said as she gripped the boards in front of Blake and gazed up at him. "I'll be okay."

"If you're sure."

"I'll make sure she's okay," Layla said.

Blake considered it for a moment, then nodded. He moved around Charli to the opening onto the ice and took the skating trainer from Amelia. Coming back to Charli, he set the trainer next to the boards.

"I can't believe how strong she is," Blake said. "She is so willing to take on these new experiences in a way I never would have thought she would."

"It took her a little bit to find her footing here," Charli agreed. "But since she has... wow."

Watching Amelia blossom from a bud into a full bloom had been wonderful. Though she still wasn't the most outgoing kid in the class, she was much more interactive with Charli and with her classmates than she'd been at first. It was a testament to Blake's parenting that she was thriving despite a huge upheaval in her life.

"You're doing great, berry," Blake called out as the pair skated past them.

Even with the distraction, Amelia managed to look over at them without wiping out. And the smile on her face? It was amazing, and it matched the one on Layla's face.

"I know you probably wish I hadn't come back," Blake said, turning his attention to Charli, his blue gaze serious. "And I'm sorry for how that made you feel, but when I see Amelia like this, I know I'd have to do it again."

"I understand, Blake," Charli assured him. "I've seen how Amelia has blossomed here. I would never ask you to put my comfort above what was best for Amelia."

"*You* are part of what has been best for her. I'm so glad she ended up in your class. As soon as I realized you were her teacher, I knew she'd be in good hands."

Her heart skipped a beat at the seriousness of his statement. "Really?"

"Of course." He smiled, the corners of his eyes crinkling. "Your passion for kids and the career you wanted was something I always loved about you. I hadn't experienced a super affectionate and attentive mom growing up, so seeing how much you wanted to be a mom who loved and cherished her children was just one more thing I found attractive about you."

His words filled her with warmth, reminding her of how it had felt to be with him twelve years ago. How supportive and understanding he'd been of her and her dreams. Until he wasn't.

"You didn't think I might have changed?"

Blake shook his head. "That passion was so deeply ingrained in you that I was certain it was something you'd always have."

He seemed so certain that he knew her so well, even now. She didn't have that same confidence because, after the way he'd ended things with her, Charli had wondered if she'd known Blake at all. Over the years, she'd accepted that, for whatever reason, at the end, Blake had chosen to act differently from the man she'd known.

It was hard to see that he had now become the type of man she'd thought he would be while they were dating. That person didn't match the man her mind had developed him into over the past twelve years.

Her gaze lingered on the teenage pair as they neared again, moving past the two girls. This time, the guy was skating backwards as the pair held hands.

"I made it once by myself, Daddy!" Amelia called out.

"Good job," Blake replied.

"I'm going to try another time around."

Blake gave her a thumbs up, then watched as the girls headed off for another lap.

"Have you prayed about... this? Us trying again?" Charli asked, surprising Blake, if his lifted brows were anything to go by, as much as she surprised herself.

He stared at her for a moment, then said, "I didn't at first." His gaze went back to the ice. "I wasn't sure that God would think I deserved a second chance."

"But you're praying about it now?" she asked, needing clarification of what he'd said.

"I am because I decided that I want to make sure that this is what God wants for us." Blake paused again, staring at the ice, though Charli didn't think he actually saw it. "I want us to have a relationship. I want us to have a future. So yes, I'm praying and asking for wisdom in how I approach this with you." He glanced over at her. "Are you praying about it?"

"Like you, I didn't pray right at the start," Charli admitted. "But that was because I still didn't know if I wanted us to succeed or not."

Blake shifted to fully face her, a reserved expression on his face. "And you know now?"

Nerves fluttered wildly in her stomach. Could she commit to something with him again? In her heart and mind, she was committed already, but for some reason, it felt like such a risk to voice it.

"Don't hurt me again," she murmured, her voice tight with emotion. "Please."

Blake's expression softened, and he reached out to take her hand, his movement hidden by the boards. "I will try my absolute best to never hurt you like I did before. I know we might have moments when we hurt each other, but I'm not going to walk away again. Never."

Could she trust him? Gripping his hand tightly, she searched his face for the assurance she needed. But even though she could see the determination in his eyes, she knew that life could deal them some blows.

Especially since there was still a secret between them.

Would they be able to weather those storms?

"Daddy! I didn't fall again."

Blake gave Charli a quick wink before turning his attention to Amelia and Layla. He kept hold of her hand with his since the boards blocked the girls' view of their hands.

"You're doing so good, Berry," Blake told her. "Are you getting tired?"

"Nope!"

Blake chuckled as Amelia pulled Layla along. "I must admit, I'm so glad the girls get along well. It makes things between us easier."

That was something Charli had thought as well. She just wanted to make sure that the girls didn't get hurt in all of this, too. Blake wasn't the only person she was keeping the truth from.

Charli moved a step closer to Blake, so they could continue to hold hands as they faced the ice. Blake laced their fingers together, rubbing his thumb against hers. It was something he'd done when they'd held hands before, and the emotion already simmering beneath the surface threatened to overflow.

They continued to stand there for the remainder of the time the girls spent on the ice. Their conversation didn't return to their relationship, but Charli had a feeling that they'd be discussing it again later. And she would be happy to do that.

Once the girls had had their fill of skating, they changed out of their skates, then, after returning the skating trainer, they left the building. Since they'd already decided that they'd go out for dinner, they climbed into their vehicles and made their way to Serenity's one family diner.

It wasn't super busy, and they were quickly shown to a booth. The girls each scooted into the booth, taking up seats opposite each other against the window. After Blake and Charli had joined them, the waitress approached the table.

"How're you doing, Charli?" the middle-aged woman asked with a warm smile.

"I'm good, Lynne. How are you?"

"Doing just fine." Her gaze traveled to the others at the table, greeting each of them. "So, what can I get you to drink?"

Over the next several minutes, they looked over the menus. They'd been to the diner often enough that Layla and Charli had no problem deciding what they wanted, but it took Blake and Amelia a few more minutes.

"I'd like pancakes with blueberries, please," Amelia told Lynne when it was her turn to order.

"Do you want whipped cream on them?"

Amelia glanced at Blake, who nodded, then she smiled at Lynne. "Yes, please."

Layla also ordered pancakes with whipped cream, but she got chocolate chip ones. Both girls ordered chocolate milk. Blake asked for a double bacon cheeseburger and fries, while Charli opted for lasagna and garlic bread.

Charli knew they were taking a chance going out for dinner all together. Especially to someplace like the diner, where there were people who knew her and would happily share that news with their friends.

But maybe it was time to finally take their relationship out of the shadows. It had been hidden so much, both then and in the past, and Charli knew it wouldn't flourish if it stayed a secret.

"Is this a special occasion?" Lynne asked when she returned with their food, clearly fishing for more information.

"We went ice skating," Layla said. "Amelia and I have been taking lessons, and we wanted to go skating together."

"Oh, that's fun," Lynne said, and Charli was glad that Layla had volunteered the information.

"We had a lot of fun," Amelia said. "But Daddy and Miss H didn't skate with us. Daddy doesn't know how."

"And my mom doesn't like to go skating very much."

"I haven't been skating in a long time," Lynne said. "But I'm sure you girls had fun."

When someone at a nearby table drew Lynne's attention, they said a prayer for their food and began to eat. Charli and Blake didn't talk much as the girls chatted up a storm about everything from their skating and ballet lessons to what they wanted for Christmas.

Charli found that she was really looking forward to the holiday season. She always did, but this year had the potential to be something even more special.

Since it was a school and work night, they didn't linger long over their meal. Blake insisted on paying, which made Lynne's eyes light up with interest, and then they left the diner.

The girls said goodbye to each other before climbing into the vehicles, out of reach of the cold air.

"Is it okay if I still call you later?" Blake asked, keeping his voice low.

"Yes."

He smiled. "Great. I'll talk to you in a bit."

Charli returned his smile, then got into her car and turned it on. She wasn't able to dwell much on what had transpired earlier between the two of them because Layla had plenty she wanted to talk about.

Charli waited for her to ask about her and Blake, figuring she'd observed their close interactions. But apparently, she'd been too focused on Amelia and their skating to notice anything to question.

By the time Blake called shortly after nine, Charli was feeling restless with anticipation. She wanted to talk about things, but as soon as she heard his voice, her nerves had her letting him take the lead in their conversation.

"Thank you again for agreeing to my idea to take the girls skating," Blake said after she answered. "Amelia wouldn't stop talking about it."

"Layla had fun too," Charli said as she slipped an earbud in so she didn't have to hold the phone.

"I enjoyed spending time with you, too."

Smiling, Charli went into the bathroom and put the phone on the counter. "It was a lovely time."

There were a couple beats of silence, then Blake cleared his throat. "We didn't really have a chance to finish our discussion earlier."

Charli dumped some cleanser on the cotton pad she held. "No. We didn't."

"Can we talk about it now?" he asked. "I'd really like to."

Though nerves fluttered in her stomach, Charli said, "I'd like to as well."

"So... do you think you want to give us a real shot?"

He was getting straight to the point.

Yes or no.

Yes or no.

It felt like a point of no return.

And maybe it was.

But if this relationship was going to work, she had to also look at it as the first step to forever.

Yes or no.

"Yes."

CHAPTER TWENTY-SEVEN

"Are you okay, darling?" There was concern in his aunt's voice, which wasn't surprising, given what she'd just told him.

"Yeah." He ran a hand through his hair as he stared out the window of the apartment, absently noting that it had begun to snow. "Yeah. I'm fine."

He was far from fine, and he was sure his aunt knew that, but thankfully, she didn't challenge him on his statement.

"I'm going to text you Selena's number and leave it up to you whether or not you call her." Julia hesitated. "But I think perhaps you should. I understand why you haven't had contact with your family for so many years, but you don't want to have regrets later for your lack of actions now."

Blake was all too familiar with regrets, and he really didn't want to add to the ones already present in his heart. "I'll think about it."

"Rob and I will be praying for you," Julia assured him, her voice gentle. "And if you need to talk, give either of us a call. We're here for you and Amelia."

"Thanks. I appreciate that."

After they said goodbye, Blake turned from the window and tossed his phone onto the couch, ignoring it when the text alert went a few seconds later.

He was glad that Julia had waited to call him until after Amelia was in bed. Blake wasn't sure if it was a good or bad thing that, even at her young age, Amelia was very perceptive. She would have likely picked up on the fact that he was upset.

And yes, he was upset. The very opposite of fine.

Though he wanted to spend time thinking over his family history, Blake knew that if he didn't rip the bandage off and call his sister right then, he probably never would.

He reminded himself that he was an adult now. Independent and able to take care of not just himself, but Amelia as well. There was nothing they could offer him that he didn't already have in his life.

Exhaling roughly, he picked up his phone again and opened the text from Julia. He copied the number into a contact, adding Selena's name. Not that he really wanted to have any contact info for his family saved, but that was a juvenile reaction. One he would have acted on twelve years ago. Now, he needed to be mature in his dealings with them.

Selena was the middle child, sandwiched between their older sister, Nicola, and Blake. Because she hadn't been as determined to step outside the role their dad had for her, Selena's relationship with their parents hadn't been as stressful as the one Nicola and Blake had with them.

Nicola had wanted to run the company. Blake hadn't. But their dad hadn't cared about what either of them wanted. That meant that Nicola had resented Blake, hating that he was being handed the job on a silver platter, simply because he was a man.

"Hello?" The sound of his sister's voice momentarily froze Blake's vocal cords. "Hello?"

"Hi, Lena," Blake said. "It's Blake."

"Blake!" She sounded excited and happy to hear from him. "I'm so glad you called. Julia said you might not."

"I considered it," Blake admitted. "And if it had been any other family member but you who'd called, I might not have."

"I understand." And from the tone of her voice, it sounded like she might be telling the truth. "How are you doing? Julia wouldn't give me any information about you and what's been going on in your life."

Yet again, Blake appreciated his aunt's discretion. She might have felt that he should get back in contact with his family, but she hadn't manipulated him or given away any information about him.

"We've moved back to Serenity," he said.

"We?" Selena asked. "You have a family now?"

"Yes. I have a daughter named Amelia."

"No wife?"

"Nope. Never married. I ended up with sole custody of Amelia after her mom passed away."

"I'm sorry to hear that." Selena hesitated, then said, "What are you doing for work?"

"I'm working as a mechanic at a garage here."

"Maybe don't tell Dad that," she said. "He might have another heart attack."

And now they'd arrived at the whole reason Selena had contacted Julia. "How is he doing?"

"He is beyond frustrated," Selena said. "Which is worrying Mom, of course. And since he can't go into the office, he's hounding Nicola like crazy, which is making her mad."

If someone had asked him how his family would react to a medical crisis involving his dad, Blake would have said it would play out exactly as Selena had just described. "I'm sure the doctor has told him he needs to relax and focus on his health instead of the business."

"You bet," Selena said. "So he fired that doctor."

"It sounds like he hasn't changed at all."

"I wouldn't say that." Selena sighed. "If anything, he's gotten worse."

And that also didn't surprise Blake. "I'm not sure what you think I can do."

"It was touch and go for him for a while," Selena said. "I thought you might like to see him again. Just in case."

Blake frowned. Was this some sort of manipulation to get him back to California? When he asked Selena, she said, "Honestly, I doubt Dad would care either way, but I think Mom would love to see you again, especially if she knew she'd get to meet another grandchild."

"Is she a more devoted grandmother than she was a mother?" Blake asked.

That got another sigh from Selena. "I wouldn't say that exactly, but in her own way, she spoils my kids."

"How many do you have?"

"Just two. My husband is quite adamant that we don't need more. And Mom has told me more than once that two is a better number, particularly since we have one of each."

"So she's basically saying that she wished they hadn't had me?"

"I think she was saying that if I'd been a boy, they would have stopped at two, so if anyone should be insulted, it should be me."

"How old are your kids?" Blake asked.

"Eric is ten. Bonita is eight. How old is your daughter?"

"She's also eight."

"That's perfect! I know my kids would love to meet a new cousin close to their ages."

"Does Nicola have any kids?"

"Nope. She isn't even married, though she does have a long-time boyfriend. I'm not sure that they'll ever get married, and she definitely doesn't want kids."

That didn't surprise Blake, and he had to admit he admired her for not giving into the pressure to marry and have kids if that wasn't what she wanted.

"Do you think you could come for Thanksgiving?" Selena asked.

His immediate response was to say no, but he hesitated. "I'm not sure. What would it look like if we came?"

"What do you mean?"

"Where would we stay? Would Amelia be present at the dinner with me? Stuff like that."

"You can stay with us," Selena said without hesitation. "I know it wouldn't be great for you to stay with Mom and Dad. And since I'm hosting Thanksgiving this year because of Dad's medical situation, I'll make sure that the kids are with us. That way, if they get bored, they can go to the playroom and watch TV or something."

As long as Selena followed through on that, it might actually work. "Just so you know, Amelia has been through a lot in her life, so anything that might make her uncomfortable will make me walk away. Like seriously, I would not hesitate to pack up and leave."

"I get that," Selena said. "Until I became a mom, I never understood the importance of protecting those who—through no choice of their own—we brought into the world. So I will do what I can to help you do that with Amelia."

"And your husband?"

Selena gave a huff of laughter. "Oh, he's not a fan of Mom and Dad and how they parent. He's helped me to become a better mom, and he's a very hands-on dad in a way our dad never was."

Blake was glad that someone else had managed to rise above their parents' style of parenting.

As he listened to his sister talk about her family, Blake found the temptation was strong to immediately agree to join them for Thanksgiving. But he knew better than to make an impulsive decision when his family was involved. Seeing them again would open a door he wasn't sure he wanted to walk through.

"Do you think you'll be able to come?" Selena said after a few more minutes of conversation. "I'd really love to see you and meet Amelia."

Blake dragged a hand down his face. "I'm not sure. Julia has invited us to join them."

"Well, if you don't come for Thanksgiving, maybe you can come for Christmas."

That was a solid no. There was no way he wanted Amelia to spend Christmas with his family. For some reason, he wanted to be in Serenity to celebrate that holiday. Hopefully with Charli and her family.

So, if the choice was between Christmas or Thanksgiving, he definitely would go for Thanksgiving. The other plus to going for Thanksgiving was that it couldn't be a long visit. They could fly there on Wednesday and leave on Saturday or Sunday.

"I'll let you know," he said, refusing to make a commitment either way right then.

"Thank you for calling, Blake. I know that you probably weren't thrilled to talk to me, so I really appreciate you being willing to have a conversation. I hope I'll get a chance to see you soon."

After he said goodbye, Blake slumped down on the couch, confused by the fact that he was actually considering Selena's request. There was no reason for him to want to spend time with his family.

He hadn't felt like he'd been missing anything over the past twelve years of not having them in his life. He'd thought more of Charli and Jackson and his family than he had of his own. And he'd certainly never imagined the day he'd be able to introduce Amelia to them.

So now he had a decision to make. Would accepting Selena's invitation be opening the door for more stuff that he wouldn't be interested in? Would he be able to back away from them if he wasn't happy with how things went?

He hoped that Selena really was true to her word. In the past, she had been the best of the worst, and it seemed like maybe that was still the case.

A glance at the clock showed that it was almost nine-thirty. He'd been preparing to call Charli when his aunt's name had popped up on his phone screen, and now he needed to talk to her more than ever.

He'd spoken to Charli each evening since the night they'd taken the girls ice skating, and it had been wonderful. The conversations had been so much like the ones they'd had years earlier at the start of forming a relationship, and he was no longer trying to contain his hope.

When she'd asked him not to hurt her again, hope had flared brightly, and he hadn't wanted to squash it. Instead, Blake had wanted to shout it from the rooftops.

However, he had accepted that if this was going to work, he had to go at the speed Charli was most comfortable with. So far, she'd asked to wait until after Thanksgiving to share the news with their families. It meant a few more days of just phone calls, but he was okay with that.

He couldn't fault Charli for her caution, but he planned to take every opportunity she offered him to prove that he was worth her taking a risk. Even if it was just showing her through words during their conversations how much he cared for her. Soon enough—hopefully—he'd be able to show her in other ways without worrying about raising people's suspicions.

Thinking of Charli made him smile, and since he was still within the hour that they reserved for talking, Blake tapped on her contact info, placing a call to someone he actually *wanted* to talk to.

When Charli answered, the warmth of her greeting washed over him, fanning the flames of his hope to greater heights.

"I'm sorry I'm late." He relaxed back into the couch, stretching his legs out in front of him. "Julia called to let me know that Selena had contacted her to share the news that my dad had had a heart attack."

"What?" Charli sounded shocked. "Is he okay?"

"Depends on who you ask. Selena said Dad was very uptight about the restrictions and life changes the doctor told him he needed to make, so he fired him. He seems to feel he's fine and doesn't need to listen to anyone else."

"Sounds like a bit of a nightmare patient."

"Not a *bit*, he's just a straight up nightmare. He's been a nightmare in a lot of ways to a lot of people." Including him.

"Is he going to take it easy at all?"

"I don't know," Blake said. "I'm not sure that's a concept he understands, so I kind of doubt it. Selena asked if Amelia and I would come for Thanksgiving."

There was a long stretch of silence before Charli said, "Are you going to go?"

He wondered what had given her pause, since they hadn't planned to spend Thanksgiving together. Julia hadn't asked, so much as demanded, that Blake and Amelia come to their home for Thanksgiving dinner.

"I'm not sure, but I'm considering it. I let Selena know that if we did come, there would be some boundaries in place, particularly where Amelia is concerned."

"Was she agreeable to that?"

"Yes. She has two kids of her own now, and it seems that's given her a different perspective. It sounds like her husband isn't a fan of my dad, which means he must be a pretty decent guy."

"It might be fun for Amelia to meet her cousins," Charli said, her voice oddly flat.

"As long as they're nice. I won't hesitate to leave early if they act at all in a way that's detrimental to Amelia."

"You're not worried about being around your parents?" Charli asked.

"Not really. There's nothing my dad can hold over my head to make me do what he wants me to."

"I suppose that's true."

She didn't sound convinced of that, and he wasn't sure why. Blake could understand why she wouldn't view his family—particularly his dad—with any fondness. *He* didn't view them with any fondness, but they were still his family.

Blake felt like the trip home for Thanksgiving could be a good testing of the waters for possible future interactions with his family. If it went poorly, then that would be it. He could move on with his life, not looking back on the relationship with his family.

All too soon, ten o'clock neared and Blake braced himself for the end of the call. The hour always seemed to speed by, and that night, with a shorter-than-usual time, it felt like they'd barely talked at all.

He kept waiting for Charli to end the conversation—because he never was the one to do that—but it was almost twenty after ten before she said she needed to go. Once the conversation had moved on from his family, Charli seemed to relax, leaving him to wonder what she wasn't saying about his plan to see them again.

Maybe it was just a general reserve about him dealing with his family again, and to be fair, he also had a significant amount of reticence himself. But as he had more time to consider the situation, the more Blake thought that he needed to do this. He had a strong desire to prove to his family that he had found contentment and joy.

They might look at the life he and Amelia had and conclude he was a failure because he didn't have a loaded bank account or a fancy house, and he was driving the same truck he'd had for fourteen years.

However, he chose to measure success in his life by how well he managed the blessings God had given him. Namely, Amelia and his job. And hopefully, Charli and Layla.

As long as he provided Amelia with love, security, and a safe environment, and did his job to the best of his ability, he wasn't worried about anything else. Sure, it would be nice to have a bit more money in the bank, but he hadn't had to access as much of his savings as he'd thought he would have to with the move.

So, while he might like a bit more financial security, especially because of Amelia, he wouldn't trade the contentment he'd found for it.

After he'd gotten ready for bed, Blake settled under the covers with his phone to look up flights, knowing that if the trip cost too much, the decision would be made for him. Thankfully, Stan had already told them that the shop would be closed on both Thursday and Friday, so he wouldn't have to ask for the time off.

If he could find a flight that left late enough in the afternoon on Wednesday, they could head straight for the airport in Spokane once he was done with work. Amelia was going to be off school for the week, but Blake hadn't had to worry about childcare. Julia had anticipated that, and she had a bunch of things planned to do with Amelia. Though Amelia might have preferred to go to Layla's, she also really loved spending time with Julia.

The flight availability plus the cost was surprisingly within the schedule he wanted and what he could afford. Did he dare book the tickets without taking more time to think about it?

No. He really shouldn't.

Blake decided to sleep on it, partly because he was still pondering Charli's reaction to what he'd told her. He wanted to spend a little time thinking that over, too.

After setting his phone on the nightstand, Blake turned off the lamp, then he spent some time in prayer. The chaplain on one of his deployments had told him to not hesitate to ask God for what he needed. Right then, he needed wisdom and guidance with regards to his family and to his budding relationship with Charli.

He hoped that God gave him wisdom quickly since he couldn't put the decision off for too long, or he might not be able to get a flight at all. So come morning, if he felt at peace about booking the tickets, he would.

Blake wished that Charli and Layla could go with them, but he was smart enough to know that wasn't possible. He needed to make this first trip on his own. Well, on his own with Amelia.

They weren't far enough along in whatever was going on between them for it to make sense for Charli and Layla to accompany them. Plus, he couldn't ask her to abandon her own family for the holiday. If he did decide to go, it would be just him and Amelia.

It was his prayer that he and Charli would have the opportunity in the future to spend the holidays together. And for the first time since coming back to Serenity, Blake felt like that future was a real possibility.

CHAPTER TWENTY-EIGHT

Charli lifted the serving bowl containing the mashed potatoes for their dinner, then carried it to the large dining table that had been set up with enough seats for everyone who planned to be present that day. Since their parents liked everyone to make the effort to be home for Christmas, they didn't press for their attendance at Thanksgiving since being home for both holidays required a lot of travel and time off work for some of them to take over a short period of time.

That meant that a few were missing. Lee, Zane, and Skylar had opted to not return to Serenity for the few days around Thanksgiving. Cole, however, had come home. He and Adrian had driven back, arriving late the night before. And Wilder was there, having stayed after Kayleigh's wedding, ready to take on his ski instructor job at the resort once again.

Of the three not there, Skylar's absence was the most perplexing, and Charli could tell that her mom was concerned as well. Because this was her first year away at school, Skylar hadn't missed any significant event with the family yet. Charli had a feeling that one or both of their parents would be going to visit her after this weekend to make sure she was okay.

"I was surprised that Blake went to visit his folks," Gareth said as Charli set the bowl on the table. "Considering what happened the last time he did."

Charli didn't say anything in response. Mainly because she had lots of thoughts and emotions regarding Blake's decision to go to California.

She was afraid if she started talking about it, she'd reveal far more than she wanted to. Her reaction would be out of proportion to what people knew of her and Blake's interactions.

Though they acted friendly when others were around, Jackson was still the only one who knew about their past, and no one knew that they were talking every night.

"I don't think he would have gone if his dad hadn't had a heart attack," Jay said. "He wasn't exactly excited about going."

"Jackson says his parents are real pieces of work, especially his dad."

Charli had no idea how the visit was going. She'd gotten a quick text late the night before saying that after a couple of delays along the way, they'd made it safe and sound.

The last few days had been a challenge for Charli. As soon as Blake had mentioned that he was thinking of going to visit his family, dread had settled into her stomach.

It had been hard not to dwell on what had happened the last time he'd gone to see them. This time, however, he'd made no promises to her. They weren't at that point in their relationship.

Sure, they'd been talking every day—much like they had when they'd been long distance—but the conversations didn't last long and hadn't yet reached the depths they had in the past. However, things between them were the most comfortable they'd been since Blake's return to Serenity. And each conversation seemed to bring them closer and closer to one another.

And as an added bonus, whenever spiritual things came up, they could actually have a conversation about them. Unlike the last time they'd dated. Back then, she'd been alone in her faith. Now, they shared that faith, and that connection added a new dimension to things that she really liked.

Charli was glad that Blake had been willing to take it slow as they went through the process of getting to know each other again.

She just hoped that this time he spent with his family didn't change things for them.

She'd already prepared herself to not hear from him for the next few days, however. It wasn't really fair to expect him to contact her each evening like he had been doing while he was in Serenity. But there was a part of Charli that felt like it might be a sign of how he really felt about things between them if he didn't contact her at least once a day while he was gone.

Charli was certain that if she'd been the one to leave, she would have made sure to contact him regularly. She didn't expect an hour-long conversation every day while he was away, but a quick check in with each other would be nice.

Of course, she could be the one to contact him. But if he didn't reply to her texts, it would almost be worse than if he didn't contact her himself.

Being ignored or being forgotten?

Which was worse?

She'd already experienced being forgotten, so she wasn't eager to go through that again. But she didn't exactly want to be ignored, either.

Tangling herself up emotionally with Blake again was bringing her insecurities to the surface, and Charli had to battle not to let them overwhelm her.

She reminded herself that Blake had pursued her, asking for this second chance. He had initiated things between them, so she must be important to him. What they were building was important to him.

"He did ask me to pray that he'd be able to hold his tongue and that Amelia would be okay while they were there," Jay said. "I got the feeling that he wanted to get there, so that he could get the visit over with and come home."

Charli knew from the conversations they'd had that week before they'd left that he wasn't looking forward to it. That was the one thing that gave her hope that this wouldn't end up the way his last visit had. Though she knew it was unlikely he'd abandon her and Serenity, the fear was still alive and active in her mind.

Having been burned once...

"Can anyone tell me why Skylar didn't come home?" Cole asked as he joined them. "I messaged her, but she didn't answer me. And she hasn't replied to any of Adrian's texts for ages now."

"Did they break up?" Charli asked, grateful for something to focus on besides her own issues.

Cole frowned. "I'm not sure. Adrian said he hadn't broken up with her, but she seems to be ghosting him. And me too."

"What's ghosting?" their dad asked as he walked in carrying a platter of turkey.

"It's when you stop talking to someone without giving them a reason," Cole told him. "You just vanish like a ghost."

"And Skylar did that to Adrian?"

"Yep."

Charli wanted to sympathize with the guy because she felt like Blake had ghosted her back when she'd hadn't been much older than Adrian. Even though Blake had sent one last text to break up with her, he'd then disappeared.

However, Charli also knew her sister, and she was quite sure that Skylar wouldn't ghost the man without good reason. Which made her wonder what had happened.

The conversations she'd had with Skylar over the past month had been vague when it came to Adrian, but maybe it was time for Charli to push for answers. She resolved to call her soon and not let her get away without sharing what was going on.

As they gathered around the table once it was loaded with food, Charli couldn't help but wonder how things were going for Blake and Amelia. Though she didn't want to lose Blake to his family permanently, for his sake and Amelia's too, she hoped that things were going well.

Amelia was the most important thing in Blake's life, and Charli knew that if the little girl was struggling, he'd stress over it. Charli didn't want that for either of them. She really hoped that Blake called or texted so that she'd know for sure that they were okay.

The Thanksgiving dinner was noisy and a bit out of control, but that was usual for their family gatherings. The best part of the chaotic atmosphere that day was that her distraction didn't draw undue attention.

While there were times Charli had wished for a smaller, calmer family, when she was lost in her thoughts, she was glad that she could hide within the chaos. She also avoided conversation by diving in to help clean up once the meal was over.

The only time she was forced to talk was when they'd all gathered in the living room, sitting wherever they could find free space, and their dad had started off their annual "What I'm thankful for" time of sharing. Knowing that it was coming, Charli had rehearsed what she'd planned to say, and she was sure she wasn't the only one who had done that.

"I'm thankful most of all for Layla." She gave her daughter a smile. "But I'm also thankful for my students and the great year we're having."

She was also thankful for Blake and Amelia, but she kept that to herself. Hopefully next year she'd be able to share that with everyone.

There were still a few hurdles to overcome on the way to them finding happiness together. But she was hopeful that this time, they'd be able to achieve what they hadn't been able to before.

Her feelings for Blake were growing at an alarming rate, and she wasn't even trying to keep them shoved down anymore. There would definitely be a lot of hurt if things didn't work out.

Charli could pretty much predict what each of her family members were thankful for, and people had learned not to prattle on and on during this time. Even the newest members kept their sharing to a couple of minutes each.

When everyone was done, their mom and dad spent a few minutes praying for all of them. There was comfort and security in the traditions her family practiced, and Charli wished she could share them with Blake and Amelia. Jackson and his family probably had traditions too, but she wasn't sure if Blake had established any with Amelia yet.

With Blake and Amelia in her thoughts again, Charli pulled out her phone. She tried not to be disappointed when there was no message, but it was hard when she was already missing Blake so much. Too much.

Gareth and Aria were the first to leave when Timothy began to fuss. It wasn't long after they'd left that Ciara threw a tantrum, letting everyone know it was past her bedtime, which meant Jay and Misha were the next to head out with the kids.

Knowing Layla wouldn't want to stay once Peyton had left, Charli also prepared to leave. She and Layla hugged everyone who was still there, then left the big house.

"Do you think Amelia is having a good time?" Layla asked when they were on the road home. "She didn't want to go."

Charli wasn't surprised to hear that. "I hope she is. She's meeting her cousins for the first time, and I'm sure they'll be nice to her."

Charli didn't actually feel as confident about that as she was leading Layla to believe.

"I wish I could talk to her," Layla said. "Just to make sure she's okay."

"I don't know what their schedule is like, but if Blake messages me about her, I'll see if you can."

"I hope he messages you."

That made two of them.

Once at the house, Layla ran off to change into her pajamas, while Charli followed a little more slowly, taking a detour through the kitchen to put away the leftovers her mom had sent home with them.

"I get to stay up late, right?" Layla asked when Charli found her in her room.

"Yep. Ten-thirty, but you have to stay in bed," Charli told her. "Go brush your teeth. I'll be there in a few minutes."

While Layla finished getting ready for bed, Charli went to get changed as well. As the minutes ticked past nine o'clock, a knot of anticipation tightened in her stomach.

She was glad for the distraction of Layla's bedtime routine. After saying her prayers and tucking her in, Charli left her daughter with her nose in a book and returned to her room.

Any other night, she might have gone to see if Janessa was around to chat, but Charli stayed in her room. Just in case.

When ten o'clock came and went without a text or a call, disappointment replaced her anticipation.

In an effort to distract herself, Charli curled up beneath her comforter with her tablet. She opened the app where she currently had a book on the go, but it didn't capture her attention the way it usually did. Maybe reading a romance wasn't really helpful when it kept making her think about her own romance with Blake.

Finally, she set her tablet on her nightstand and turned off the lamp. After a moment's hesitation, she picked up her phone and stared at the screen.

Should she message him?

She didn't want him to feel pressured to talk to her if he was focused on his family. But she missed him. It was tempting to leave all the contact up to him, because then she wouldn't have to make herself vulnerable to hurt.

However, if she was truly going to give this second chance a real shot, she had to meet Blake halfway. If Blake could make her feel special by sending her a message, then perhaps he'd also feel special if she sent him a text to let him know that she was thinking about him and Amelia.

With that, Charli brought up her text conversation with Blake. She didn't allow herself to think too much about what she should say before tapping out a message.

Happy Thanksgiving, Blake. I hope you and Amelia are having a good time. Layla and I miss you both.

After a moment's thought, she added two heart emojis. She wasn't sure that Layla actually missed Blake, but she was certainly missing Amelia. And Charli missed Blake, so her statement was true.

She pressed the button to black out the screen, then set her phone on the nightstand, refusing to stare at it, waiting for a response.

It took her awhile to fall asleep, but when she woke up the next morning, the first thing Charli did was pick up her phone and check the notifications.

Smiling, she flopped back onto her pillows and tapped the screen to get to Blake's message.

Blake: *Happy Thanksgiving to you too! Sorry I didn't reply last night. Amelia and I are sharing a bedroom, so I'm going to bed earlier than I might usually. Also up earlier than usual because of that. We miss you and Layla too.*

Charli glanced at the time on the screen and saw that it was nearly nine.

How are the two of you doing? I bet you're enjoying the warmer weather. They're saying we might get some snow later today.

Normally, she'd be rushing to get ready to go find a tree on the morning after Thanksgiving. But when the others had realized that Blake wouldn't be able to join them, they'd decided to change the plan and go Christmas tree shopping on Sunday afternoon, so that Blake and Amelia could tag long.

She hadn't told him that yet.

Charli wasn't sure if she should expect a response right away. But she was in no rush to get out of bed, so she propped herself up on her pillows and began to scroll through her phone.

The knock on her door had Charli looking up from her phone. "Knock, knock, Mom."

"Come in, sweetie," Charli called.

The door slowly opened, then Layla appeared with a tray in her arms. "Breakfast in bed!"

"Oh, that's lovely." Charli set her phone on the nightstand as Layla approached the bed. "Did you do this yourself?"

"Nah. Uncle Will and I made it together. He's taking a tray up to Auntie, too."

Charli helped her settle the tray on the bed, smiling when she saw that there was enough for two. "This looks delicious."

"I wanted pancakes," Layla said as she climbed under the covers next to Charli. "And Uncle Will said Auntie did too."

They shifted around so that they both had access to the plate with the stack of pancakes. Layla had brought two forks and knives, and there were small bowls with toppings, along with a creamer pitcher with some syrup in it. After they prayed for the food, they prepped their pancakes, then dug in.

When her phone's text alert went, it took all her willpower not to snatch it up to see who had sent the message. It was entirely possible that it was from a sibling or one of her parents.

"Your phone went, Mom," Layla said as she lifted her glass of chocolate milk.

Charli glanced at her, then leaned over to pick it up from the nightstand. She fought the urge to smile when she saw the message was from Blake.

Blake: *Weather is nice. We're doing okay. Amelia wants to go home, so I'm glad we have tickets for tomorrow. Probably should have just gotten them for today.*

"Blake says that Amelia wants to come home," Charli told Layla. "I texted him earlier to see how they were doing, since I thought you'd like to know."

Layla looked up from her pancakes with a frown on her face. "You don't think they'll move there, do you? Amelia said she really likes it here. Better than where they lived before."

"I don't think Blake is planning to move there," Charli said, hoping she wasn't wrong. "They just went to spend a few days with his family."

"I hope they don't go for Christmas. I want to spend Christmas with Amelia."

"We'll have to see." Charli didn't want to commit to anything until she and Blake had a conversation about it.

What she did know was if they were going to spend the holiday together, she wanted it to be with them having gone public about their relationship. Although the very idea of that brought flutters to life in her stomach.

Layla gestured to the tray. "Take a picture of this and send it to Uncle Blake for Amelia to see."

"Here." Charli handed over her phone. "Take it the way you want it."

Layla took the phone from her and proceeded to take several photos, each from a different angle. When she was done, she looked through them before she showed Charli which one she wanted her to send.

Layla and Will made breakfast in bed for Janessa and me. Layla wanted me to send a picture for Amelia to see.

After she sent the picture, she set the phone down and picked up her mug of coffee. "Good job. Everything tastes great."

Layla beamed. "Uncle Will didn't even have to help me very much."

Though it felt like Layla was growing up too fast, Charli also really liked her at this age. They could hold meaningful conversations, but also still have a lot of fun together.

There was a meaningful conversation she needed to have with Layla soon. Preferably before she and Blake went public with news of their dating.

"Would you have a problem if I dated someone?" Charli asked just as her daughter took a bite of pancake.

Layla looked up at her, eyebrows raised and chewing as fast as possible. After she swallowed, she said, "You want to date someone?"

"Maybe?" Charli said, then let out a little sigh. "Yes. I want to date someone."

"Who?"

Charli hesitated, knowing that she was at the line that once crossed, there would be no going back. This was what Blake wanted. He'd agreed to take things slow because it was what *she* wanted. He'd be happy to hear she'd talked to Layla about it.

"Blake."

Layla's mouth dropped open as she stared at Charli. "For real? Did he ask you on a date?"

"We've already been on one date, and we've been talking to each other a lot."

"Does anyone know?"

"Janessa and the others know we went on the date because they set it up. But you're the only one who knows we've continued to talk after the date."

A smile filled Layla's face. "He's nice. I mean, Amelia loves him, so I think he must be a good guy."

A few months ago, Charli wouldn't have been so inclined to agree. However, seeing the man he was now, and having heard his explanation for what had happened, she was willing to let go of their painful past to try to build something in the future.

"He is a good guy," Charli agreed.

"Amelia is going to be so excited you're dating. She told me she was praying that would happen."

"Really?"

"Yep. She's praying that we can be a family."

Charli wondered if Blake was aware of what his daughter was praying for. It seemed that they both had a similar desire for a future for them all to be together.

"And how do you feel about that?" Charli asked.

Layla took another bite and chewed it, a considering look on her face. Charli also continued to eat her pancakes, not rushing her for a response.

Finally, she said, "I think it's okay. I'd like to have Amelia as a sister. And I guess Uncle Blake would be a good dad."

Dad... The word made Charli's stomach twist.

Ignoring the relationship between Layla and Blake wasn't a long-term solution, but it seemed to be what she was most inclined to do. Telling them who they were to each other was a huge, irreversible step that she was wary to take just yet.

She probably shouldn't have agreed to date Blake without telling him about Layla, but it was too late to go back now. All she could do was move forward, and hope that when the moment was right, she'd feel at peace about revealing her secret.

CHAPTER TWENTY-NINE

Blake breathed a sigh of relief when he and Amelia finally walked out of the airport in Spokane. The air was colder than it had been in California, but he didn't care. He was just glad to be close to home.

He pulled their suitcase with one hand while he held on to Amelia with the other. They made their way to where he'd parked the truck before they left, and Amelia eagerly climbed into her seat.

"I can't wait to get home," Amelia said once he was behind the wheel.

"Me, too, Berry. Me, too."

"Can we see Layla and Peyton tomorrow?"

"If they're at church, we'll see them."

Physically, Blake would have liked nothing better than to spend the whole day vegging out at home. However, like Amelia, there was someone he wanted to see.

He hadn't had a lot of contact with Charli over the last few days, and he'd missed their nightly talks. Unfortunately, Amelia had been loath to let him out of her sight, and Selena hadn't seemed to want to either, which had meant chats with Charli just hadn't been possible.

"Do we have to go back for Christmas?" Amelia asked after they'd been on the road for a bit. "I heard Aunt Selena say she hoped we would."

Blake glanced at her in the rear-view mirror, then focused back on the road. "Do you want to?"

"No." She spoke without hesitation. "I want to stay home."

"Did you really hate it that much?"

"I didn't... *hate* it, but all of it was different. Fancy."

He wasn't sure Selena would want her home décor to be called fancy. She'd probably prefer elegant.

Selena's home had been large and filled with furniture that Blake was certain came from the latest offerings of the family furniture company. Thankfully, his sister had opted for comfort and practicality rather than the showroom their home had been growing up.

"So, do we have to go?"

Blake wasn't sure if they'd be able to spend the actual holiday with Charli and Layla, but he knew that he'd rather spend Christmas with just Amelia than go back to California for Christmas.

"Nope. We're not going to go."

"Yay!"

Blake grinned at Amelia's response. He wasn't stupid enough to believe that this was their first and last visit to California, but nor did he think they'd be spending the most important holidays with his family.

For the remainder of the trip, Amelia talked to him about the Christmas program the kids were putting on at the church, as well as the one at school. They'd already started practicing at church, and Amelia was excited to have a speaking part.

It was a such relief to see her putting down roots, and in doing that, becoming more confident in herself. And that was part of the reason he'd never consider moving to California. Not even for the well-paying job offered by his dad, who'd gone behind BI's back to extend it.

Of course, the other part of why he wouldn't be leaving Serenity was Charli. And he couldn't wait to see her at church the next day.

Gray clouds obscured the sun when Blake and Amelia left the apartment the next morning to go to church. They'd had completely sunny days for the time they'd been in California, but Blake was still glad they were in Serenity. The cold outside couldn't touch the warmth that existed inside him. The warmth of contentment and even joy.

The only thing that would make life better would be if the relationship between him and Charli was official and out for the world to know.

When they reached the church, they took off their jackets, then headed downstairs to the Sunday school rooms. His aunt was waiting in the room and greeted them with hugs. Blake gave her a quick rundown of what had happened with his family.

"You'll have to tell me more later," Julia said.

"I will," Blake promised. "But just know that we are both very happy to be home."

Julia beamed at him. "I love hearing you say that. We're so happy to have you here."

When the arrival of more children interrupted their conversation, Blake said goodbye to Julia and Amelia before returning upstairs.

His heartbeat thumped rapidly in anticipation of seeing Charli again. It had been late by the time they got home from the airport and Amelia was settled, so they hadn't been able to talk yet.

Once inside the sanctuary, he looked around but didn't see Charli there yet. He headed down to one of the rows they usually occupied and took a seat.

Faces were becoming more familiar. Like the man sitting in the row in front of him, who he recognized from having worked on his car at the garage.

It wasn't long before the rows around him began to fill.

"Hey, Blake," Jay said as he stood at the end of the row.

Greeting the man, Blake got to his feet and shuffled down to make room for the others. Jay didn't immediately follow him. Instead, he motioned for Charli to precede him as she joined him and Misha.

She did so without complaint, and as their gazes met, she gave Blake a quick smile.

Something settled inside him at the sight of her, and he was happy when she chose to sit next to him, leaving only an inch or so between them. He'd moved right to the far end of the row, so he didn't have anyone sitting on his other side.

"How are you doing?" Blake asked.

"I'm good. Especially now."

The boldness of her response made Blake smile. "I feel that way too."

"By the way," Charli said, leaning close. "We're going to get our Christmas trees this afternoon. Want to come?"

Blake lifted his brows. "I thought you were going on Friday."

"We were, but once we realized you weren't going to be able to come with us, we decided to wait."

Unexpected emotion choked Blake for a moment, and he had to swallow before saying, "In that case, we'd love to join you."

"Perfect."

Charli seemed much more relaxed than she usually was when they were around her siblings. Had something happened over the past few days?

"Come by the house for lunch after the service, then we'll go to the tree farm," she said as the Sunday school teacher stepped up behind the small podium.

"Sounds good."

In fact, it sounded *great*. He was more than ready to spend the afternoon with people he and Amelia had come to really care about. Particularly Charli and Layla.

Sunday school and the service were a comforting familiarity, and as he listened to announcements about the weeks ahead, Blake found that he was looking forward to being part of the congregation for the Christmas season.

Once the service was over, he told Charli that he and Amelia were going to run by the apartment to change into more appropriate clothes for wandering around a Christmas tree farm. Amelia was flying high once she heard the plan for the afternoon and hurried him along.

"You don't have to speed, Daddy," she said. "Just go *fast.*"

"That's the very definition of speeding," he told her with a chuckle. "I'm going as fast as I'm allowed to."

Clearly that wasn't fast enough for her, but they made it home in good time. And for once, she was ready first. He'd made sure that they were both dressed warmly enough, including knit caps, scarves, gloves, and boots, before they headed over to Charli's.

"I can't wait," Amelia said as she scrambled out of the truck once he found a spot to park behind the other cars at the house. "This is going to be so much fun."

Blake smiled as he followed her up the walk to the large house. He was looking forward to it as much as Amelia was.

Layla had the door open by the time they reached it, and the two girls greeted each other enthusiastically. Blake stepped into the foyer and shut the door behind him. Warmth and the aroma of food wrapped around him as he took off his jacket and boots.

After he'd hung up both his and Amelia's jackets, he was drawn to the kitchen where people were gathered. His gaze immediately found Charli who was in the middle of removing something from the oven.

She'd changed out of her church clothes into a pair of fitted jeans and a green sweater. Blake wished he could give her a hug, but he had to settle for discreetly admiring her from across the room.

"Ready to get a tree?" Will asked as he clapped Blake on the shoulder.

"I guess so. I've never done this before, so don't know exactly what's happening."

328 · KIMBERLY RAE JORDAN

"No worries. We've got some pros in the group. They'll help you out."

"Amelia is really excited," Blake said as they joined the women at the counter. "Is there anything I can do to help?"

"Not really," Charli told him with a smile. "We're doing lunch buffet style today."

The counter was set with a pile of plates and silverware, along with the food. There was a basket with buns and some small platters with deli meat, cheese, and cut up vegetables. He'd smelled something rich and hearty when he'd walked in, but it appeared it wasn't for this meal.

"We're just having sandwiches now, but I have a couple of crock pots of stew on for after we get home later." She gave him another smile, her brown gaze soft. "I hope you and Amelia can join us."

Like he would ever turn down an invitation from Charli. "I think that can be arranged."

"Do you have decorations for your tree?" she asked as she scooped some dip from a plastic container into a glass bowl.

"I don't, but I thought maybe I'd take Amelia shopping tomorrow after school to get some."

"I might have some you can have as well. I've collected a ton of them over the years."

"That would be nice," Blake said. "I really have no experience with Christmas decorations."

"No need to worry," Janessa told him as she bumped his arm. "We've been decorating Christmas trees our whole lives. We've got you covered."

Jay and Misha's arrival increased the noise level significantly as the kids greeted each other excitedly. Ciara also expressed her delight at being around everyone by shouting hi to each person as she walked around the kitchen. She was such a cute little kid.

Blake didn't have a lot of memories of Amelia at that age since he'd been deployed for a good chunk of that time, plus Lauren hadn't always been cooperative about him seeing her. It saddened him as he watched Jay scoop Ciara up, making the toddler squeal with laughter.

But then his gaze went to where Amelia stood with her friends, and the joy on her face helped to ease that sadness. He might not have been able to be a present father when she'd been younger, but he was going to be there for her now and in the future.

The next hour was taken up with eating the meal Janessa and Charli had prepared, and then cleaning up. When it was time to go, Charli and Layla ended up coming with Blake and Amelia instead of taking their own car.

Having them there with him and Amelia felt so right.

"It really looks like it might snow," Charli said as Blake followed Will's vehicle.

"Wouldn't that be appropriate for this outing?" Blake asked.

"As long as it's not too cold and windy, snow isn't a big deal."

"Are we cutting down our own tree?" Amelia asked.

Charli shifted, angling herself so she could see into the back seat. As she leaned on the armrest between them, her arm pressed against Blake.

It was a bit ridiculous how he treasured those brief moments of contact. It wasn't a sexual thing. It was the connection. The proof that she wasn't avoiding him. That being close to him wasn't objectionable to her the way it probably had been when he'd first come back.

"We can have them cut down one of our choosing, but they also have a section of already cut trees that people can choose from."

"It's more fun to look for the perfect tree," Layla said. "Colby told me this morning that they went yesterday, and he and Aaron found the perfect trees for their houses."

"Can we find our perfect tree and cut it down too, Daddy?"

"Sure, Berry." Blake smiled at her in the mirror. "We can do that."

Maybe some Christmas in the future, instead of needing a tree for each of their homes, they'd need it for just one. Blake hoped he wasn't getting ahead of himself, but it was the future he wanted more than anything right then.

Once they reached the Christmas tree farm, the enthusiasm of the kids was infectious.

Quite a few people were already there, wandering around the large farm. As they walked down a wide path, Will and Jay led the way with the kids, while Janessa and Misha followed them.

Blake fell into step beside Charli, wishing he could take her hand. Such a simple thing, but he really wanted the freedom to do that or to put his arm around her shoulders.

Hopefully soon.

"This is an awesome tree," Amelia said as she stopped to stare up at a huge tree.

"That's not the tree for us, Berry," Blake told her before she got her hopes up too high. "We don't have a tall enough ceiling."

"Yeah. Mom would say it's too tall for our house, too," Layla said.

"Aunt Selena's house would be big enough for this tree."

Blake nodded. "That's true. I think the ceiling in her foyer would have room for a twenty-foot tree."

Amelia stared at it for a moment longer, then turned back to the path. "I'll look for a smaller one."

Charli laughed as they fell back into their formation. Further down the path, they met another group. They all stepped to the side to let them pass, but when Charli moved, she lost her balance and grabbed onto Blake's arm.

He instinctively covered her hand. "You okay?"

She tipped her head up to meet his gaze. "Yeah. I just stepped onto an uneven patch, I guess."

Their steps slowed for a moment, as neither released the other.

"I think I found a tree," Amelia announced, drawing their attention from each other and breaking the moment.

Blake turned his attention to where Amelia stood next to a tree that was about his height. It was only as he stepped toward her that Blake realized that Charli still had a hold of his arm, and he hadn't moved his hand from where it covered hers.

She gave his arm a quick squeeze, then slowly slid her hand from beneath his.

Though he was afraid of what he might see on Charli's face, Blake couldn't help but look at her. Rather than look upset, she smiled at him.

When Charli had said she was ready for them to go public, he'd assumed that they'd have a conversation about how they'd do that. And he'd also envisioned them making an announcement at one of their family get-togethers.

Apparently, Charli had decided to just drop a few hints and let people come to their own conclusion. His thoughts went to Layla, wondering if she'd observed the interaction between them.

When he looked at her, the young girl gave him a quick smile. Had Charli talked to her about them being together?

Blake felt a little lost, so he decided to focus on their purpose for being there and marched over to where Amelia stood. "Which tree do you like?"

Behind him, he could hear mutterings of conversation, but it wasn't loud enough for him to understand anything. This afternoon was turning into something far more important than just getting a tree.

Amelia reached out and touched the branch of the tree in front of her. "This one, Daddy. I think it's perfect."

"Let's look at it from all angles, okay?" Blake held out his hand, and when Amelia took it, the two of them circled the tree.

"It's perfect all around," Amelia declared. "Can we get it?"

Taking a deep breath, Blake looked over at Will. "So, how do we get this chopped down?"

"I'll go find one of the tree choppers," Will said. "Be right back."

Blake hadn't talked to Amelia about what was going on between him and Charli for a couple of reasons. First, he didn't think she'd be able to keep it to herself. Second, he already knew how she felt about Charli, and that there would be no protests from her about them dating.

When he glanced at the others, Jay, Misha, and Janessa were pretty clearly gloating. For once, though, Charli didn't look annoyed by it.

Hope burst into a blazing inferno at that point.

Was this moment for real?

"Can I tell Amelia?" Layla asked her mom, keeping her voice low enough that Amelia wouldn't hear her as she circled around the tree again.

"That's up to Blake," Charli said.

When Layla looked at him, Blake didn't hesitate to nod. Amelia would probably love to hear about the answer to her prayers from her best friend.

"I knew you were meant to be together," Janessa crowed. "And I was right. I can't wait to tell Kayleigh."

Charli gave a huff of laughter. "You didn't know anything of the sort."

"Well, the bouquet and garter do not lie."

Will returned right then with a man dressed like a lumberjack who greeted them all gruffly, then turned his attention to the kids. It didn't take long for the tree to be chopped down, and with the help of a younger man, the lumberjack transported their tree to the front, where they'd pick it up later.

They still had two more trees to find, but Amelia's shriek of excitement distracted them from that goal for a moment.

"Really, Daddy?" she asked as she ran up to him. "You're dating Miss H?"

Blake picked her up, so they were eye to eye. "Yes. Is that okay?"

She wrapped her arms around his neck and pressed her cheek to his and whispered, "It's perfect."

Blake had to agree. It did feel perfect.

After he set her back down, Amelia looked over at Charli and grinned before she rejoined Layla and Peyton, and the trio led the way once again.

This time, as they walked side by side again, Blake held out his hand to Charli. Giving him a smile, she took it without hesitation. Though they both wore gloves, having her hand in his felt amazing.

"That was a bit of a surprise," he murmured as they followed the others.

"Do you mind?"

"Not at all. I was just taken off-guard."

"I figured it was probably better to just... do it. I didn't want to overthink things."

Blake gently squeezed her fingers. "I sure missed you these past few days. Not being able to talk to you every night was hard."

Charli nudged her head against his shoulder. "I missed you too. I'm glad you're both back."

"I don't think we'll be going back to California for a while. I'll tell you about it during our next call."

"I look forward to hearing all about it."

The next hour was filled with laughter, smiles, hot chocolate, mini donuts, and a visit with Santa. Amelia was beside herself with happiness, which made Blake even happier than he already was.

Charli stayed close to Blake, and for the first time ever, they were able to interact in the way they'd wanted to twelve years ago. Being open with her family felt right, though he didn't know if

Charli planned to let people know that this was part two of their relationship.

He would be fine if they kept that information to themselves, but that was probably a selfish thing. If they didn't know about the mistake he'd made in breaking up with Charli the way he had, he wouldn't have to see their disappointment in him.

Once the kids were worn out, the adults retrieved their trees. The guys put them in the back of Blake's truck, then everyone head back to the house.

They took the tree Layla had chosen into the house, where Jay showed Blake how to deal with unwrapping and setting it up, since he'd never done it before. That way, he'd know how to set theirs up when he went home later.

Jay also gave Blake a few things that he called the "real Christmas tree starter kit," which included a stand that he could put water in to keep the tree alive.

Once Jay finished his instructions, Blake pitched in to help get the food set out on the counter, doing whatever Charli asked him to. The time they spent together that day was a clashing of past and present for Blake.

They'd talked to each other about one day making it to this point in their relationship, and now they were there. He just hoped the pain of the breakup was well and truly in the past.

Though Blake wished their time together could last forever, he and Amelia ended up leaving around seven because there was school the next day.

Before they left, Charli hugged him tightly, and as Blake held her, memories assailed him. But then he centered himself in the moment. This was now. He needed to stay in the present, and the relationship they were building together.

As their embrace ended, Charli promised to call him later, then bent to give Amelia a hug after Layla had. Though Blake might have enjoyed a quick kiss as part of their goodbye, he didn't want the first kiss they shared after so long to be in front of an audience.

Once home, he and Amelia worked together to prepare for school the next day. As she sorted out her backpack, she let him know just how happy she was that he and Charli were dating. It was kind of cute, but Blake cautioned her not to tell anyone at school.

He didn't know if a teacher dating a student's parent was an issue, so he didn't want to draw attention to it unless Charli felt it was okay.

Amelia had just gotten into her bath when Blake's phone rang. When he saw Jackson's name on the screen, he almost didn't answer. However, he wouldn't be able to return his call after Amelia went to bed because by then he'd be talking to Charli.

"Bro!" Jackson exclaimed. "I'm so relieved that Charli finally told you about Layla. I understood why she didn't want to tell you when you first got back, but I'm glad she finally did. Layla is a great kid."

Blake's heart stopped when what Jackson was saying sank in, but then it began to gallop at a frantic pace. Disbelief, then anger, swirled in behind the moment of shock.

Charli should have *told* him. Maybe not right away, but definitely before she agreed for them to date.

She should have told him.

"Blake?"

Hearing Jackson's voice in his ear, Blake muttered, "Gotta go."

Before his cousin could say anything more, Blake ended the call, then stood there in the hallway, phone clenched in his hand. He tried to process what he'd just learned, as the times he'd interacted with Layla recalibrated in his mind.

How was he supposed to deal with this new information?

What was he supposed to do?

"Daddy?" Amelia called from the tub.

Blake looked at the open doorway to the bathroom. He could be the father Amelia needed because he was a *good* father. And he could have been a good father to Layla as well.

If he'd only had the chance.

CHAPTER THIRTY

Once everyone had left, Layla headed off to her room to choose her clothes for the next morning and get her backpack ready for school. Charli made their lunches for the next day, then put it all in the fridge so they could just grab it in the morning.

Janessa and Will had gone up to their room once everything was cleaned up. They'd decorate the tree another night that week. It was a multi-day process with letting the tree settle for a day, then putting the lights and the decorations on the next evening.

If they'd gone on Friday, like they'd originally planned, the tree would be already decorated. But Charli wouldn't trade that day for anything.

She hadn't originally planned to reveal their relationship the way she had. But in that moment, it had felt right. She'd wanted to experience that day with the man she had fallen in love with again.

And it had been amazing.

Walking hand-in-hand over the snow-covered paths had been what she'd dreamed of doing one day, and it had been everything she could have wanted. They'd ridden in a large wagon to go see Santa and had shared a bag of mini donuts as they drank hot chocolate.

Janessa had taken pictures of them that were now on Charli's phone, waiting for her to pour over them. The one of the four of them was going to become her phone's lock screen.

It had been perfect. And that perfection had carried through the meal they shared with her family and their daughters.

Charli paused in the doorway of Layla's room, watching as she set her backpack on the chair at her desk. Her clothes for the next day hung on a hanger on the back of that chair. She'd already changed into her pajamas, which told Charli that Layla planned to curl up in bed and read until her bedtime.

"Got everything ready for tomorrow?" Charli asked as she walked into the room.

"Yep." Layla dropped down on the edge of her bed, then scooted back and wrapped her arms around her legs. "Amelia was so happy that her dad is dating you."

Charli smiled as she sat down beside her. "And you're still okay with that?"

Layla nodded. "You both looked happy together. That makes me happy, too."

"I'm glad." This had changed things. Made the future she'd once dreamed of more of a reality.

They talked for a few minutes before Charli said, "Are you going to bed already?"

Layla stretched out to grab the book sitting on her pillow. "I'm going to read until sleep time."

"Want to pray now or later?"

"Let's pray now," Layla said. "I've already brushed my teeth. That way, I can read right until bedtime."

Charli held Layla's hand as she prayed, thanking God for helping them find good trees, and also thanking him for Charli and Blake dating. Charli was so pleased that Layla was happy about that.

When she finished, Charli gave her a kiss. "See you in the morning, sweetheart. Sleep well."

At the doorway, Charli waited for Layla to switch on her bedside lamp, then she turned off the overhead light. They blew each other kisses, made hearts with their fingers, then Charli pulled the door closed as she stepped into the hallway.

She went back into the main part of the house to make sure everything was locked up and all the lights were turned off. With

Layla already settled in bed, Charli decided to go to her room as well to do a few things before Blake called.

Going back into their part of the house, she shut the door that closed off their rooms from the rest of the main floor.

She was in her walk-in closet when she heard her phone ring. Pulling it out, she looked first at the time on the screen, thinking it was early for Blake to call.

But then she saw Jackson's name on the incoming call. He'd no doubt heard about her and Blake. Was he going to ask when she planned to tell Blake about Layla?

Because she didn't have an answer beyond *soon*, Charli was tempted to ignore him. But in the end, she tapped the screen to accept the call.

"Charli." Her name came out rough. "I'm so sorry."

"Jackson? What's wrong?"

After a long pause, he said, "I called Blake. I didn't realize you hadn't... I mean, I thought if you had agreed to date, you'd already told him..."

Charli swallowed hard against the panic that churned to life inside her. "You told him about Layla."

"Not in so many words, but I assumed he already knew, so I think he figured out what I was saying. I'm so sorry."

Charli ended the call before lowering her phone to her lap and clenching it in both her hands. She stared unseeing at the wall, dread robbing her of every bit of the joy she'd felt that day.

Maybe he wouldn't be mad.

Maybe he'd understand.

Maybe he'd be willing to have a conversation with her.

Tears blurred her vision.

But maybe he would be angry with her. So angry that what they'd started to build would be torn down once again.

Charli didn't know what to do. Part of her wanted to call him and get everything sorted out as soon as possible.

But a far, far larger part feared what he would say to her.

She'd been stupid to think that waiting to tell him was the better thing to do. Stupid and scared. It had been a head in the sand approach to the situation that was now coming back to bite her.

When her text alert went, Charli startled, and the phone fell onto the carpet at her feet. The phone was face up, but she wasn't able to read who the text was from before the screen went dark.

It could have been a text from Janessa or one of her other siblings.

Maybe even one of her fellow teachers.

Charli's shoulders slumped. Clearly, she was still on the path of delusion.

She should probably be relieved if it was Blake, that he hadn't called her. Reading a text was better than having him yell at her. But putting off reading the message would not change what it said.

With a shaky sigh, Charli slid off the bed to sit on the floor. She picked up the phone, then paused. She wanted to pray that if the text was from Blake, that he wasn't mad at her. But that felt selfish. Like she thought she deserved to escape his anger.

But she didn't.

She didn't deserve his understanding.

With a sick feeling in her stomach, Charli turned her phone over and over in her hands. Finally, she stopped with the screen facing her and tapped the screen.

The notification showed that the text was, in fact, from Blake. It expanded before she was ready to read it, but she couldn't tear her gaze from the words.

Blake: *I'm not going to be able to talk tonight.*

Tears spilled over, making the words blur. Her heart hurt so badly in her chest that it was hard to take a deep breath. This pain was as self-inflicted as if she'd stabbed herself.

With trembling fingers, she opened the app to respond to him. Ignoring the situation wasn't going to make it go away. She was learning in the worst possible way that sticking her head in the sand would never lead to a good outcome.

Okay.

She didn't know what else to say. He might not know that Jackson had called to tell her what had happened. But her one word response would probably clue him in.

Bending her head forward, she pressed the edge of her phone against her forehead, her shoulders hunching as her mind raced.

She didn't know what to do. Her perfect day had taken a horrible turn. She'd had just a few short hours to enjoy something she'd always wanted. Now... now it was gone.

There wasn't even a flicker of hope in her heart that Blake would forgive her for this. Regret, self-recrimination, and hopelessness dominated her thoughts as she sat there, wondering what she was supposed to do now.

Finally, Charli pushed up to her feet and went to the bathroom. If she was going to get through the next few days at work and around her family, she had to get hold of herself and her emotions.

But she wouldn't be able to do that until she'd let herself cry out her pain.

After she'd turned on the tap, Charli poured some of her favorite bath oil into the water. She watched it fill for a minute, then removed her clothes and stepped into the tub.

Lowering herself into the water, Charli spent a few minutes trying to breathe away the huge amount of emotion that filled her. She couldn't believe she was shedding tears over Blake *again*. Except this time, she had no one to blame but herself.

Never before had she wished for a rewind button as much as she did right then. She should have realized that this moment was inevitable, and by letting her family know they were dating without telling Blake about Layla, she'd invited all of them to witness the heartache resulting from her bad decision.

As she sat in the warm water, Charli tried to think of all the possible outcomes from Jackson's inadvertent revelation. And for each of those outcomes, she figured out how she'd need to react.

The bath water had begun to cool by the time Charli came to the realization that there was no way she could account for every eventuality. But the one thing she could do was prepare herself mentally for the next day.

She'd been able to keep her heartache from her family twelve years ago, and she was going to have to do it again. Until she and Blake had a chance to talk, she didn't want anyone to know what had happened.

So the next morning when she crawled out of bed, Charli refused to dwell on what had transpired the previous night. She focused on the things she normally did on a school morning.

After making sure Layla was awake, she fixed her hair and makeup—applying a little more under-eye concealer than usual—then she dressed in her outfit of choice for the day. On her way to the kitchen, she checked to make sure that Layla was almost ready.

Even though her heart wasn't really into music that morning, Charli turned on her usual playlist, then gathered the ingredients to make some French toast.

"Good morning, Charli," Will said as he walked into the kitchen carrying two mugs. He always came down for coffee for the two of them first thing in the morning, but his second cup would be in a to-go mug.

"Morning." Charli gave him a quick smile before focusing back on the egg mixture she was beating. "Ready for another week at school?"

"As ready as I ever am for the first day back after a few days off in a row."

Layla joined them, setting her backpack on a chair at the breakfast nook. She wasn't a morning person, so aside from giving Charli and Will quick hugs, she didn't say anything.

As Charli lifted the first piece of bread from the egg mixture and put it on the hot griddle, Layla got the parts of her lunch from the fridge and put them into her lunch bag. Once that was done, she added it to her backpack and zipped it up.

She then poured herself a glass of milk and carried it to the table. In between flipping the pieces of French toast, Charli sipped her first cup of coffee for the day.

"It's Monday," Janessa groused as she walked into the kitchen, dressed for her day at the clinic. "And I'm tired."

"Me, too," Layla said, speaking for the first time.

None of them in the house really loved mornings, though Will seemed to be the most alert of them all. Usually, however, by the time they left the house, they were all sufficiently awake to face the day.

As she handed off plates to the others to eat, Charli tried not to think about what Blake might be doing. She had no idea if—when—they'd have the time to hold a conversation, especially if Blake wanted it face to face.

Once they'd all eaten, Will loaded the dishwasher while Charli and Janessa put their lunches together. It was all very normal.

However, Charli didn't breathe a sigh of relief at no one having picked up on her mood until she parked in her spot at the school after dropping Layla off at the middle school.

She took a moment to collect herself, knowing she was going to have to interact with Amelia soon. Though she might not know how Blake was reacting to the news, Charli was pretty sure that he was keeping his emotions under wraps too, hiding them from Amelia.

Gathering up her things, she got out of her car and headed for the school. The day ahead promised to provide her with enough distractions to get her through the next several hours. Then she'd have to deal with the rest of her day.

"Good morning, Miss H," Amelia said with a beaming smile as she walked in.

The smile that came to Charli's face in response didn't feel as forced as she'd thought it might. It was possible that Amelia's enthusiasm for them dating might be enough to make Blake think twice about ending things between them without a serious talk.

It dawned on her then that she was in the position Blake had been in when he'd wanted a conversation about their breakup when they'd seen each other again after twelve years apart. She hadn't been inclined to give it to him then, so she needed to understand that he might not want to talk to her yet.

The tables had definitely turned. But where Blake had had inexperience and immaturity as an excuse for what he did, she certainly did not. She'd simply allowed her fear to hold her back from making the right decision.

It was a relief to have a bunch of rambunctious kids in class that day, since it required her to focus on them. They demanded every bit of her attention, and then some.

All too soon, though, the day with her class came to an end. Thankfully, she still needed to attend a meeting before she could go home. It was just one more distraction that she'd definitely take.

When Denise dropped Layla off at the elementary school, she stayed in Charli's classroom while Charli went to the meeting, reading a book or playing on one of the class's tablets.

The meetings rarely took more than an hour. All the staff were eager for the meeting to be over quickly, so no one dragged anything out. The principal was prompt in convening the meeting and did a good job of moving the agenda forward.

For once, Charli wouldn't have minded if the meeting had run long. Since they had to discuss the upcoming Christmas program, it did run a bit longer, but only by about ten minutes. Normally, she would have been excited about the discussion, given how much she loved Christmas. But that day, her excitement was overshad-owed by what was going on with Blake.

"Ready to go, sweetie?" Charli asked when she stepped back into her classroom.

"Yep!" Layla already had her jacket on, so she just slid her book into her backpack. She didn't normally bring her library books to school, but on Mondays, she'd take one if she was really enjoying the story and wanted to read while she waited.

As they left the school and drove home, Layla told Charli about her day. It took effort to keep her thoughts on what Layla was shar-ing.

"The science fair is happening in January, so we're supposed to start thinking about what we want to do."

Charli grimaced. Science at the elementary level was fine, but overall, it hadn't been her favorite subject in school. Maybe she could prevail on Gareth or Will to help her out. They'd both had more of an interest in the subject than she'd ever had.

Blake had also told her one time that he'd liked science. And if she'd revealed the truth sooner, he could have been the one to help Layla.

She felt like she was floundering, uncertain of what was to come. But until Blake talked with her, she had no idea what to do.

Would he demand a paternity test? Or would he just take her word for it, even though she'd essentially denied that he was Layla's father?

When they got home, the house was quiet since Will and Janessa hadn't gotten home yet. Will had a teacher meeting on Mondays as well, so on those days, he usually took Janessa to work, then picked her up.

Charli changed out of her work clothes, then returned to the kitchen to start supper. Layla had also changed, before settling at the island counter with her backpack.

As she prepared chicken pieces for baking, Charli helped Layla with any questions she had about her homework. It was so normal, and yet it felt like her world had shifted off its axis. Blake probably felt the same way.

Meanwhile, everyone else was moving through their day like nothing was wrong. It was disconcerting, especially when Will and Janessa came home.

They pitched in to help with dinner, and Charli tried to keep up her part of the conversation as they shared about how their days had gone.

"Everything okay?" Janessa asked as she helped Charli clean up after they'd eaten.

Will was seated at the breakfast nook, nursing a cup of decaf as he graded papers. Layla had finished her homework and gone to her room to take a shower.

"Yeah."

"I would have thought Blake and Amelia would come for dinner since you're official now."

"We know we can't spend every day together. The girls still need their schedules during the week." Charli bent to put the plates into the dishwasher. "But we've been talking on the phone every night after the girls go to bed."

"So you're making it work, huh?"

Charli gave her a quick smile that felt so brittle she was sure it was going to crack and Janessa would call her on it. "We're trying."

"Well, I'm happy to hear that." Janessa handed her the platter from the chicken to add to the dishwasher. "I knew you two would be perfect together."

Charli wasn't sure about perfect, but if they hadn't managed to mess things up—twice!—they might have had a pretty good life. His mess up had cost them their first attempt at a relationship, and it was entirely possible that hers had cost them their second.

Maybe they really weren't supposed to be together.

346 · KIMBERLY RAE JORDAN

That thought hurt a lot, and she had to blow out a quick breath to try to ease the pain in her chest.

"I hope the road to your happily ever after is a little smoother than ours was," Will said from the table.

Oh, if only they knew how bumpy it had already been. And she could only imagine what her family was going to say when they found out about Layla and Blake. Because they would find out. It was inevitable now that Blake knew.

He was probably going to insist that Layla be told, and Charli wouldn't fight him on that. But once Layla found out, they'd have to tell everyone else, too.

As nine o'clock neared once more, Charli sat on the edge of her bed, her phone clutched in her hand.

She couldn't continue in this limbo. She had to know where they stood.

With trembling fingers, she tapped out a message to Blake.

Can we talk?

Her heart pounded as she waited for a response, wondering if he was going to ignore that request the same way he had twelve years ago. There was no hope for a relationship if they couldn't figure out how to communicate through these rough patches.

Life wasn't always going to be smooth sailing, so if they hoped to build a future together, it was absolutely necessary that they figure this out.

Although, maybe Blake would bail completely on their relationship after what she'd done. But even if he did, they'd still need to co-parent Layla, which meant they had to learn how to communicate for her sake.

Blake: *Not yet. I need some time.*

Charli's heart sank, and she had to blink against the tears that threatened to fall. Would he ever forgive her for keeping this secret? Would he understand why she had?

At that moment, she was pretty sure that the answer to those two questions was *no*. She couldn't force him to talk to her, so all she could do was wait and deal with this on his terms.

Okay.

There were a lot of things she wanted to tack on to that, but none of them seemed appropriate to say through text messages. Especially the apology she was desperate to give him.

CHAPTER THIRTY-ONE

"It seems you two have a communication problem," Thomas said after Blake had spilled his guts about everything that had happened. Not just recently, but also twelve years ago. "I understand backing away for a short time, especially if you can't trust yourself to respond well. However, the longer things drag on, the harder it can be to overcome the challenge."

Blake ran a hand through his hair, then dragged it down his face. It was nine-fifteen on Wednesday night, and instead of talking to Charli, he was on his phone talking to his friend, Thomas.

The anger he'd felt on Sunday night had eased somewhat, but now it was sharing space inside him with hurt. He wanted to understand why she hadn't told him about Layla once he'd asked for a second chance. Had she planned to keep that a secret from him forever?

Why had he been so willing to accept Charli's word that Layla wasn't his?

Everything he'd known about Charli twelve years ago should have told him that she wouldn't have slept with someone else so quickly and easily after he'd broken up with her. He'd accepted it because it made him feel better about ending things. That if she'd been able to move on so easily, he hadn't hurt her too badly by breaking up with her.

"I don't know what to say to her."

"Tell her that," Thomas said. "Be upfront and honest about how you're feeling. And encourage her to be the same way. It might hurt to hear her reasoning, but you need to. From what you've said, she tried to have a conversation with you when you broke things off with her originally. So, it seems to me she did attempt to tell you."

And that was why his anger wasn't directed entirely at Charli. In fact, a lot of it was aimed at himself. This was just one more consequence of the poor choices he'd made twelve years ago.

His anger at Charli was because she'd agreed to a relationship—a future—with him now, without telling him that Layla was his daughter. She should have told him as soon as she'd made that decision, if not before.

"Forgiveness is key here," Thomas said. "She needs to forgive you for your actions twelve years ago, and you need to forgive her for this. It's the only way you'll be able to move forward."

Blake exhaled heavily. She'd wanted to talk on Monday night, but he hadn't been in a good frame of mind at that point. Not that he was any better right then, but at least he'd gotten to where he was willing to listen to advice on how to handle the situation.

Jackson had texted him several times as well, also asking to talk, but he'd ignored him. He didn't know why Jackson seemed to be the only person aware that Layla was his daughter. Except maybe he'd put two and two together when Blake had told him that he and Charli had been together twelve years ago.

Too bad he hadn't put two and two together for himself.

"Thanks for listening and helping talk me through it all."

"I think you already knew what to do," Thomas said. "But I'm happy to have been able to help. I'll be praying for you."

"I appreciate that."

"Be sure to keep me updated."

Blake promised that he would, then Thomas prayed with him before they ended the call. He slumped back against the couch and stared up at the ceiling.

His mind sorted through his options for his next step. Talking had to happen before anything else, and since Charli already wanted to talk, they were halfway there.

He sent a message to his aunt to see if she'd stay with Amelia a couple of hours the next evening. When she replied she could, he sent a message to Charli.

Can we talk tomorrow night?

As he waited for her response, he wondered where they could go to talk. Neither of their places were really conducive to holding the private conversation they needed to have.

Charli: *Yes.*

Now what did he say? They could just talk on the phone, but he knew this was a conversation they needed to have in person. It was time.

They should have had a face-to-face conversation twelve years ago. He denied her that, and it was possible that she'd deny him this. But if their budding relationship was going to survive, it was time to hash everything out.

More than anything, he wanted to know *why* she hadn't told him about Layla once they'd agreed to date. He just needed to know why.

Is there somewhere private that we can meet to talk? I don't think this is a conversation to be had in public.

Charli: *I agree. I'll ask if we can use the clinic. They have a lunchroom that might work.*

That sounds good.

Charli: *I'll let you know when I've got it sorted out.*

Blake sent her a thumbs up, then set his phone aside. The pain in his chest had been a constant thing for the last few days. He hoped that their conversation would help ease it and give them a path forward.

He still loved her. When he'd returned to Serenity and discovered she was single, Blake knew that if she gave him the opportunity, he was going to try to win her heart again. And now here he was, trying to figure out how to keep moving forward with her.

The only bright thing in all of this was Layla. He had two daughters... It was utterly amazing. And Amelia was going to be absolutely thrilled to discover that the girl she'd claimed as her best friend was actually her sister.

Would Layla be as happy?

He had no idea how Layla was going to feel about this news. Amelia was already praying that Charli and Layla would become their family, so she would accept both of them, no problem.

But would Layla be willing to accept him as her father? Or would she hate him for how he'd treated her mom?

Blake rubbed his chest as the pain pulsed more deeply in his heart. He didn't want to think about Layla rejecting him, but it was possible she would.

When his text alert chimed, he picked his phone back up to read the message.

Charli: *Gareth said it's fine for us to use the clinic tomorrow night.*

That's great. What time is good for you?

They spent a couple of minutes figuring out the best time, then Charli said goodnight and went silent. Blake stared down at his phone, wishing it was already the next night.

All he could do between now and then was pray that the meeting would bring about a result that would draw them together as the family he longed for them to be.

The next evening, just before eight, Blake pulled into the parking lot behind the clinic.

Julia had happily come by to stay with Amelia and put her to bed, if necessary. When he'd told her that he was going to meet Charli, she'd given him a hug and told him how happy she was that they were together. He didn't correct her, hoping that it would still be true after they talked.

Charli's car was in the parking lot, so after saying a quick prayer that God would guide their meeting, Blake got out of the truck. The night was cold and crisp, which hastened his steps to the back door.

Thankfully, the door was unlocked. He stepped into the building, grateful for the warmth that surrounded him as the door closed, cutting off the cold.

He stomped on the mat, knocking off any snow that might have gathered on his boots. There was snow everywhere in Serenity now, gathering in slowly growing mounds across the ground.

"Blake?"

Lifting his head, Blake saw Charli standing a little further down the hallway. She wore a pair of jeans and a baggy, dark green sweatshirt. As he stared at her, Blake gathered his wavering determination and resolved to do what he had to in order to fix their broken relationship.

Straightening, Blake said, "Hi."

Charli's smile was tight as she gestured behind her. "The lunchroom is over here."

As he headed toward her, Charli turned to lead him around the corner and through an open door. The area wasn't super big, but there was room for a small kitchenette, a table big enough to seat eight people, and a corner with two loveseats and a coffee table.

It was decorated in warm tones with the walls being a light sand color. The couches were a dark blue, while the tables were made of a lighter wood. There weren't any windows in the room, but several large landscapes hung on the walls, which kept it from feeling too boxed in.

The space was probably a relaxing place for the employees. Unfortunately, it did nothing to help Blake relax.

"Would you like a cup of coffee?" Charli asked as she gestured to the counter where a couple of coffee machines sat.

Would he be there long enough to drink a whole cup of coffee? "Are you going to have one?"

She turned to stare at the coffee makers. "Yeah. I think I will."

"Then I will as well."

Blake hesitated a moment before joining her at the counter. "Do you want cream or sugar?"

"Just cream, please." She opened a drawer that had a large selection of single serve coffee pods. "Decaf?"

"Yes, please." Blake went to the fridge at the opposite end of the counter and pulled out the container of cream and took it to where Charli was watching the dark liquid stream into a large mug.

When it finished, she pulled the mug out and set it in front of Blake, then prepped a second cup. Blake lifted the mug and took a long inhale, relishing the familiar aroma.

"We can sit on the couches," she said after she'd doctored her coffee and returned the cream to the fridge.

Silence stretched between them as they took their first sips of the coffee, but it didn't last.

"I'm sorry I didn't tell you about Layla sooner," Charli said as she stared down at the mug cupped in her hands.

"Why didn't you?"

Her gaze flitted to his briefly before dropping to her mug once again. "I did try when I first found out I was pregnant. That's why I wanted to talk. But once I realized how easy it had been for you to walk away from me, I knew I'd be raising our child by myself. And so I have. Yes, my family has helped me. However, at the end of the day, the decisions for her care fell to me."

Blake didn't like to be reminded of that, but he nodded, because he understood it was his own fault that had happened.

"When you came back..." She lifted her mug and took a sip, still not looking at him. "When you came back, I didn't know what kind of man you were. I didn't know if I could share parenting responsibilities with you. I needed to protect Layla."

"And once you agreed to date me?" he asked, trying to keep his tone gentle and not confrontational. "Once you realized you could trust me? Or at least I assume you trusted me, since you agreed to us dating and allowing me into Layla's life."

Charli's head bobbed. "I did trust you. But by then, I wasn't sure *how* to tell you. It felt like it was just easier not to say anything."

"Did you not think I would be a good father?" he asked.

She was quiet for a moment, then she finally looked up at him. "I didn't know. When we talked about having kids one day, you told me that you wanted to be a good dad, but you weren't sure if you'd know how. You said you didn't think your dad had been a good example of a father."

Blake had forgotten that conversation. As he recalled it, he said, "And you told me that you'd help me be the father our children would need."

She blinked rapidly, her lips tightening as she stared at him. When she spoke, her voice was soft and choked with emotion. "Yes. I did. But it seems that you didn't need me because you're a great father to Amelia."

"I wasn't for the first few years of her life," he admitted. "I let Lauren dictate everything, which meant that I only saw Amelia for short periods of time. After Lauren died and Amelia came to live with me, I had no idea how to be a full-time dad. The adjustment was a struggle for us both, but I try to always let my love for her dictate our interactions."

She gave him a small smile, but it didn't reach her eyes. The sadness he saw there touched a corresponding emotion within his own heart. The last bit of the anger he'd felt when he'd learned about his relationship to Layla slipped away.

Finding out he had a daughter should have been a happy time. And it still could be, if they could work out how to move past this.

"Where do you want to go from here?" Blake asked, hoping that this had just been a blip in their relationship and not the end of it.

Charli took another sip of her coffee, keeping both hands wrapped around the mug. "Where do *you* want to go from here?"

Fair enough. If she needed to know where his heart and mind were before she answered, that was fine. He would take the risk and lay it all on the line.

His mind went back in time to the promises he'd made to her. He remembered the joy and love in Charli's gaze as they had talked. So full of hope for the future they'd have one day.

This was not the road they had planned to travel to reach their future. That didn't mean they couldn't still have a future together. A different—better—future.

Blake looked at the woman sitting across from him, and for a moment, he saw the young woman she'd been twelve years ago. But he also saw the woman she was now. And that was the woman he loved.

"I want a future with you and Layla. I want Layla to know that I'm her father. I want to raise Layla and Amelia together with you." When Charli's beautiful brown eyes widened, Blake swallowed against the sudden flare of nerves. "I love you, Charli. I want everything you're willing to give me."

Charli finally moved her hands from her mug, but it was only in order to cover her face with them. When Blake heard her begin to cry, he got up and went around to sit on the chair next to her.

Blake hesitated for just a moment before he wrapped his arms around her. When she sagged against him, her shoulder pressing into his chest, Blake knew he'd done the right thing.

He rested his cheek on the top of her head and just held her. Tears weren't something he'd shed a lot of over the years, but the charged emotion flowing between them made his eyes sting. His heart wept right along with hers.

His sorrow was for the lost years. For the mistakes he'd made along the way.

As the emotions began to ebb, Blake took a deep breath to loosen the vise around his chest. Charli held onto his arm with both hands, and Blake could feel her taking measured breaths.

"Do you forgive me?" Blake murmured. "I really am sorry for what I did twelve years ago."

Without hesitation, she said, "I do forgive you."

The knot inside him loosened at her words. Blake waited for her to ask if he forgave her, too. Instead, she lapsed into silence as she huddled against his chest.

Right then, Blake felt like he had the world in his arms. He hadn't thought he'd ever be able to hold her like this again. "I forgive you too."

"You shouldn't," she said, her voice so low he almost didn't hear her. "I don't deserve your forgiveness after what I did."

"You did what you did because of what I did," Blake told her. "If I hadn't ended things the way I had, or if I hadn't ignored your attempts to get hold of me, you would have told me. Bad decisions can set off a train of unfortunate results. I accept that."

"But I could have told you sooner," she said.

She could have. That was true. But she hadn't. So he was left with the choice of holding onto that anger and hurt and losing the relationship with Charli, or letting it all go and embracing the future he wanted.

"Yes. You could have," Blake agreed. "But I don't want to dwell on that anymore. I want to focus on the future and what God has planned for us."

Hopefully that would be a future together, but that was up to Charli.

"Do you really want to be with me?" Charli asked, her voice low and tremulous.

"Yes." Blake said it forcefully, needing her to believe him. "I wanted that before I knew Layla was mine, and I still want it now."

It was important that she understood that he didn't feel that way just because he'd discovered Layla was his daughter. That definitely wasn't true. Knowing that was just an added incentive to make this work. If that was what Charli wanted.

Charli tipped her head back, and their gazes met. Her eyes were still damp with emotion. "I love you too. And I want that future with you and Amelia. I want us to be a family one day."

One day *soon*, Blake hoped. But he'd take the promise of a future with her, no matter how long it might take.

Blake couldn't keep the smile from his face, and Charli smiled back, the tide of emotion slipping away from her eyes.

His love for Charli flooded him, and Blake whispered, "Can I kiss you?"

Rather than answer, Charli lifted her hand to the back of his neck. When their lips touched for the first time in twelve years, Blake had the most intense feeling of being home. Of being right where he was supposed to be.

He cupped her cheek, savoring the softness of Charli's skin as he gently moved his thumb over her cheekbone. Blake didn't know how to pinpoint what it was about Charli that drew him more strongly than any of the other relationships he'd had in the past, but he didn't fight it.

When their kiss ended, they shared another smile, and this time, Charli's fully reached her eyes.

"I've missed you," he told her. "So much. Twelve years is a long time."

Charli shifted closer and rested her head on his shoulder. Her fingers drifted down his arm to intertwine their fingers. Blake sandwiched her hand between his, relieved that the tightness in his chest was finally gone.

"I never wanted to admit it, but I've missed you a lot too," Charli said, her fingers tightening around his. "Even though I tried not to dwell on it, the sadness was there. I never thought I'd have this with you again."

"Neither did I."

Though Blake had asked for a second chance, he didn't necessarily look at their current relationship as a continuation of their previous one. They'd missed the years of maturity that they would have experienced alongside each other if they'd been together.

They were getting to know each other again, learning what had changed and what had stayed the same about the other person. He couldn't allow himself to focus on the past. It was time to embrace the future.

CHAPTER THIRTY-TWO

After they'd had their moment at the clinic, Blake and Charli had a serious discussion about how to move forward with the girls, mindful that it was no longer just the two of them in the relationship. There were now more relationships to consider.

They decided to wait until Saturday afternoon to give the news to the girls, with the plan to talk to the girls separately. Then, depending on their reception of the news, they'd get together for dinner.

Friday night, they joined the others for pizza. Because the secret about them dating was now common knowledge, they didn't bother to hide it anymore.

And soon, everyone would know that Layla was Blake's daughter.

Charli didn't plan to hide that information once Layla knew and had had a chance to process it. Once she had done that, Charli was prepared to share the news with everyone else.

It was time.

"You did really well with your lines today," Charli said as they headed home after the children's program rehearsal on Saturday morning. "And Amelia did well with hers, too."

"She was a bit scared to be by herself, so I'm glad Mrs. Clarke put us together."

"This will be your last year in the program," Charli told her. "Are you sad about that?"

"Yeah. A bit. But I can start doing stuff with the older kids at church. It will be kinda weird not being with Peyton and Amelia, even though I'll still have other friends in the older group."

When they got home, Charli could see that Will and Janessa were there. Will's car sat in the driveway, and she saw Janessa's car in the garage when she pulled her own car in.

"I want to do something fun," Charli said as they took off their boots and jackets in the mudroom.

"Like what?" There was skepticism in Layla's voice that spoke to her lack of confidence in her mom's definition of fun.

"Let's have a picnic in my room." Charli went to the pantry to grab a tray, then set it on the counter. "Come help me get the stuff ready."

She'd prepped everything she wanted for their picnic earlier that morning, and it included all of Layla's favorites. Stuff for ham and cheese sandwiches. Baby carrots with dip. Her preferred potato chip. And for dessert... brownies.

Once they had all the food and some drinks on the tray, Charli carried it to her room. She'd laid out a blanket on her carpet in front of the small fireplace before she'd left earlier.

"This is cool, Mom," Layla said as she sat down on the blanket.

Charli put the tray down in front of her, then went to work starting a fire. "I'm glad you think so."

As they sat on the blanket together, Layla said a prayer for their food, while Charli silently prayed, asking God to prepare her daughter's heart for what was to come. She'd rehearsed a bunch of different ways to tell her, but she was still nervous.

Layla did most of the talking as they ate, skipping from topic to topic. She touched on the books she'd read recently, then moved on to some drama with her friends at school. They seemed to have a lot more of it now that they were in middle school.

Of course, they were about to have their own little bit of drama.

"I have something I want to talk to you about," Charli finally said as they ate their brownies.

Layla paused, holding her half-eaten brownie in front of her mouth. "What's wrong?"

"Nothing is wrong." She hoped Layla felt the same after she heard the news. "We've talked a few times about what happened when I got pregnant with you and what happened with your dad."

"Yeah. But you haven't really told me much. Certainly not who my dad is."

"I didn't think he'd ever be part of your life, so it was irrelevant who he was."

"Are you finally going to tell me?"

Charli nodded.

"Why now?" Frowning, Layla lowered her brownie. "What's changed?"

"He's come back into my life, and he wants to get to know you."

Layla didn't seem as excited as Charli had thought she might be. "Is he nice?"

"Yes. He is."

"I don't know," Layla said. "I haven't thought about my dad in a while. And now there's Uncle Blake and Amelia. Will him coming back into your life mess things up with them?"

Charli gave her a smile. "No. It won't." She took a deep breath. "Because Blake is actually your dad."

Layla's eyes widened as her mouth dropped open. "For real?"

"Yes. For real."

"Is that why he came back? He found out about me?"

"No. He didn't find out about you until just a few days ago."

"You told him?"

Charli grimaced, but she was honest with Layla about how Blake had found out. And then, deciding that Layla was old enough to know most of the details, she shared a little more about what had happened twelve years ago, as well as over the past week.

"He already has Amelia," Layla said. "Why would he want another daughter?"

"Do you *know* our family?" Charli asked.

Layla nibbled on her brownie. "That's different."

"How?"

"Grandma and Grandpa planned to have all you kids. So they love you all."

"I didn't plan to have you," Charli said. "Do you think I don't love you because of that?"

Layla's brow furrowed. "You love me."

"Yes. I most certainly do. And I know that Blake loves you, too."

"Are you going to get married?"

"Yes. I want that, and so does Blake. He wants the four of us to be a family."

"You both already know that you want to get married?"

Charli sat for a moment, then pushed up to her feet, choosing to ignore how much more effort it took these days. She went into her walk-in closet and retrieved the box she'd put there. Carrying it back to the blanket, she sat down and opened the lid.

"This is all the stuff I kept from twelve years ago." She lifted out a small box and opened it. Seeing it again brought forth a lot of feelings and memories. But the overriding pain wasn't there anymore. "Blake gave this to me before he left."

Layla took the box and stared at the ring. "It's pretty. Is it an engagement ring?"

"No. It was a promise ring," she explained. "It was Blake's way of saying that he believed in the future we had talked about having together."

"But in the end, it didn't mean that," Layla said, her gaze still on the ring.

Charli couldn't argue with that, but she also didn't want Layla to view Blake in a bad way for the mistakes he'd made. "No. It didn't."

"Do you wish it had?"

It was a bit of a surprise that Layla hadn't assumed that, of course, Charli would have wanted things to work out the way she'd planned. She hesitated, checking to see if her heart lined up with what she needed to say.

"No," Charli said with all truthfulness. "If things had happened that way, Amelia wouldn't be here with us. We need to accept that things are the way they are and focus on the future. Not the past."

Layla closed the box and held it out to Charli. "Do I have to call him Dad?"

As she took it, Charli shook her head. "I'm not going to force you to treat him differently from how you already do unless you want to. Blake understands you need some time. We just wanted you to know the truth."

"And you're going to tell everyone else, too?"

"Yep. It's time I was honest about everything that happened." She wasn't sure how she was going to tell her whole family, but she should probably start with her parents. And then Janessa. The rest could find out via the family gossip chain.

"Are you going to tell Amelia?"

"Blake is telling her right now," Charli said. "We hoped that you would be okay with the four of us hanging out together this afternoon. But if you don't, that's fine too."

Layla looked down at her hands. "I've always wanted to know who my dad was, but I didn't think you'd ever tell me. So... I stopped praying and thinking about the situation."

"Do you wish I hadn't told you?" Charli hadn't even considered that Layla had changed her mind about learning who her father was.

"No. I'm glad you did. He's nice. I mean, my dad could have been a murderer."

Charli gave a huff of laughter. "True."

"So... we can go hang out with them."

With that decision made, Layla picked up another brownie, and Charli let her.

Once they were finished with their dessert, they cleaned up the picnic. In between trips to the kitchen, Charli sent a text to Blake.

Conversation with Layla went fine. She's a little shy about immediately seeing you as her dad, but I know she'll come around. Do you still want us to hang out? Layla would like to.

They'd just finished cleaning up the last of their lunch when Charli's phone chimed. She draped the cloth she'd been using over the tap, then dried her hands before picking up her phone.

Blake: *I'm glad she was receptive. I have no problem giving her all the time she needs to adjust to the news. And yes, we'd love to hang out.*

Charli smiled when a heart emoji appeared. *Great! We'll be there in about half an hour.*

Two more emojis appeared. The heart eyes one and the kissy face one. She sent those two back to him and tacked on a heart.

"He makes you smile."

Charli looked up to see Layla watching her. "Yeah, he does. Just like you always make me smile."

"Well, not always," Layla said with a smirk. "I don't think I do when I argue with you."

"Thankfully, you don't do that too often." Charli gave Layla a tight hug, smiling when her daughter hugged her back.

Her pre-teen might flip a switch when she turned thirteen, but she'd enjoy these little fun moments they shared until that happened.

"I told Blake we'd be there in half an hour," Charli said. "So let's get some games that we can play there."

"Are we taking snacks?"

Charli grinned. "You're my mini me."

Layla struck a pose, and they both laughed.

"You go get the games," Charli said with a wave of her hand toward the basement stairs. "And I'll get some snacks."

As Layla headed to the basement, Charli found a container and filled it with some of the sugar and gingerbread cookies Denise had made and decorated, along with a few of the brownies. She also grabbed the remainder of the carrots and dip since she knew Amelia liked that snack too.

After a moment's hesitation, Charli grabbed a bag of chips as well. As she was putting everything in a bag, Layla reappeared with one of her backpacks and showed her the games inside it.

Janessa and Will came downstairs as they were putting on their boots and jackets. Janessa had her purse, so Charli assumed they were on their way out also.

"We're going to see Timothy," Janessa said. "Where're you off to?"

"Blake's," Charli told her. "We're going to play some games and hang out with the girls."

Janessa's smile was beaming. "That's great. I'm sure you'll have fun."

Charli had no idea how Janessa was going to take the news about Blake and Layla. She'd probably be mad at Blake initially, but she'd get over it. Hopefully.

They all walked into the garage and headed for their respective cars. Once they were gone, Charli got an alert that the security system had been armed, courtesy of Janessa, no doubt.

When Blake opened his door a few minutes later, Charli's heart skipped a beat at the smile on his face. He gestured for them to come into the apartment, then shut the door after they did.

"Layla!" Amelia let out an excited yell as she ran over to them and flung her arms around Layla. "We're really real sisters."

Layla laughed as she hugged her back. "Yep. We are."

When Charli glanced at Blake to find him watching the girls with an affectionate smile, she skirted around the pair to join him. He transferred his smile to her as he slipped his arm around her waist, and she leaned against him. She still had her jacket on, so she wasn't as close to him as she'd like to be.

"They're amazing."

Charli definitely agreed.

When the girls parted, Layla unzipped her jacket, so Charli did the same. Once they'd removed their boots and jackets, they went to the table in the dining room.

Layla showed Amelia which games they'd brought, and the two of them chose one for the four of them to play. Charli was glad that Blake wasn't trying to force Layla to act any differently toward him. She was sure he wanted a relationship with her like he had with Amelia. But just like he'd gone at Charli's speed for their relationship, he was going at Layla's speed for theirs.

They spent the afternoon playing games and eating snacks. When supper time came, they decided to order some food from the best Chinese restaurant in Serenity. Amelia initially wasn't too sure about the menu, but Layla convinced her to give it a try and explained the dishes she liked to the younger girl.

By the time they'd decided on the order, it seemed that Amelia was on board with what they'd ordered.

They had a great time together, and Charli was so grateful that Blake had been willing to move past what had happened. He hadn't had to. He could have chosen to end things between them and just focus on Layla.

They'd both made mistakes over the years. But she believed that Blake really was a man of honor that she could depend on.

And he proved it again when he insisted on going with her to talk to her parents the next afternoon.

Janessa had agreed to watch the girls, assuming Charli and Blake were going on a date. Peyton had come home from church with them and was also spending the afternoon with the girls. There were plans to decorate cookies, watch movies, and play games.

As they walked hand in hand from his truck to the front door of the family home, Charli said, "I'm so nervous."

He stopped walking, turning her toward him. He took her hands in his and said, "Nothing your parents can say will make me change my mind about you. About us. I believe in our love, and this is another step towards the future we want. Do you believe in us?"

"I do. I love you," Charli assured him, going up on her toes to press a kiss to his lips. "Let's do this."

"Hi, darling," her mom said as they stepped into the foyer. She gave Charli a hug, then turned to Blake. "It's good to see you, Blake."

"You, too."

"We're in the family room," she said.

Once they'd taken off their winter wear, she led them through the house to the cozy room at the back corner of the house. Her dad straightened from where he was building a fire and turned to greet them.

Her mom gestured to the couch and loveseat. "Let's have a seat."

Charli pulled Blake over to sit on the loveseat, while her parents settled on the couch. The fire crackled, spewing out aromatic warmth. She always loved having a fire, and it helped to settle her as she clung to Blake's hand and dove into their difficult past.

It didn't take long for the comprehension to dawn on her mom's face once Charli revealed their past relationship.

"You're Layla's father," her mom stated, pinning her gaze on Blake.

Blake nodded and without any hesitation, he said, "Yes. I am."

"And you didn't want to be part of her life?"

"He didn't know, Mom. He broke things off before I realized I was pregnant, then didn't reply to my message asking to talk once I knew."

"That doesn't reflect well on you." Her dad addressed his comments to Blake.

Charli opened her mouth to defend him, but Blake gave her a quick glance, then gently squeezed her hand.

"I agree. It doesn't," Blake said, his voice calm. "I regret that decision and the hurt it caused Charli. I have apologized for what I did, and Charli has forgiven me."

"Just as Blake has forgiven me for not telling him about Layla when we first began to talk seriously."

Her parents shared a glance, then her mom said, "Does Layla know?"

"Yes. We told her and Amelia yesterday." Charli smiled. "They were both thrilled to find out they are actual sisters."

"I'm sure," her mom said with a chuckle. "Layla has wanted a sister for a long time."

"Amelia has been praying every night that Layla could be her sister, even before we told them about our relationship."

"So what are your intentions, Blake?" her dad asked.

Charli fought the urge to cover her face and groan, but she understood why he was asking. If Layla had been in her position, Charli probably would have asked the same question.

"I plan to marry Charli and build a family with her."

Charli smiled at him, then looked back at her parents to see how they received his comments.

"And you also want that, Charlotte?" her dad asked her.

"I absolutely do. We've talked about it, and that is something we both want. It's what we planned for twelve years ago, and it's what we want now."

"And it's not just because of Layla?"

"No." The confidence in Blake's voice was unquestionable. "I didn't know about Layla when I asked Charli if she'd give me a second chance."

"You didn't want a relationship just so that you're not a single parent anymore?"

Charli frowned at her parents, thinking that the third-degree was getting to be a bit much. Had they grilled Hudson or Will like this?

"Knowing that she was a great mom was definitely a bonus, but the biggest thing for me is that I love her. I know she'll be a wonderful wife to me, and an amazing mother to the girls, and I'm going to try my best to be a wonderful husband and father. The three of them deserve my best effort, and I plan to give it to them."

Her dad stared at Blake, the moment stretching out. But then he smiled, his expression warming. "I'm glad to hear that."

Blake squeezed Charli's hand again as he turned to her. "I'm all in and ready to go the distance."

Charli felt like her heart would explode with the love she had for Blake. She thought of the promises of the past. The broken promises. And it surprised her that she was so at peace about trusting Blake after what had happened.

But she wasn't going to question why. Instead, she was going to accept that for whatever reason, her heart wasn't cautioning her. God had given her peace in a situation where peace didn't seem likely.

As his gaze held hers, Charli hoped he could see everything that was in her heart for him. "I'm all in and ready to go the distance, too."

Christmas music played in the kitchen as Charli pulled the corn-bread muffins out of the oven. As she set the pan down on the rack on the island counter in front of him, Blake said, "Everything smells great."

"Hopefully it all tastes good too."

With just two days until Christmas, the girls were at Jay and Misha's for the evening, decorating gingerbread houses, while Janessa and Will had gone over to Gareth and Aria's.

Blake and Charli had initially been planning to go out too, but then Skylar had asked if she could come over to talk to Charli. She'd said she was fine if Blake was there too, so now they were going to be spending their evening hanging out with Charli's little sister.

"Are you sure you both are okay with me being here?" Blake asked, wanting to give Charli one last chance to spend the evening with just Skylar. "I don't want to impose on your sister time."

"It really is fine," Charli said, smiling at him in a way that made his heart skip a beat. The joy in her gaze made her even more beautiful. "Skylar said she was fine with it, too. That it would give her a chance to get to know you."

"I'd like to get to know her too, since the last time I saw her, she was like seven years old."

Charli transferred the cornbread muffins to a basket. "That's crazy to think. Sometimes twelve years ago feels like an eternity, and then other times, it seems like just yesterday."

"I have to consciously keep from thinking about how much time has passed, so I don't start feeling like it was wasted time." Knowing that Amelia had come from that time helped him to not feel like it was wasted.

"Yeah. I understand that." Charli moved around the island to where Blake sat on a stool.

He shifted on the stool and drew her to stand between his knees, his hands resting on her waist. Charli gripped his forearms, her smile softening.

"We just have to make the most of the time we have from this moment forward," Blake said.

"Exactly." She leaned forward to kiss him.

They'd had a talk about the physical side of their previous relationship, and they'd both agreed to set boundaries. Even though she loved being close to him, they were going to do things differently this time around.

"Love you," Blake said when the kiss ended.

Charli smiled. "I love you too."

The sound of the doorbell had her giving his arms a quick squeeze, then she turned away from him and headed for the front door. Blake stayed in the kitchen, letting the sisters greet each other privately.

The days since they'd decided to go public with their relationship and also reveal their past had been a mix of good and not so good. Blake, Charli, and the girls had spent quite a bit of time together, and that had been a lot of fun. The anger her siblings had expressed toward him had been in direct contrast to the acceptance by her parents and his aunt and uncle.

He could only hope that the happiness they shared would win the siblings over. Charli had assured him that would be the case, and since she knew them better than he did, Blake was willing to be patient and let them process their feelings. After all, if he'd been in their position, he'd probably have reacted similarly.

When they came back into the kitchen, Charli had her arm around Skylar. The younger woman was carrying a large purse in one arm. Skylar was wearing a bulky sweater and loose sweatpants. It was an outfit that Charli favored too, when she was dressing for comfort.

"It smells delicious," Skylar said as she approached the island where Blake sat. "Hi, Blake."

Blake got up as he greeted her. Then they all worked to get the food on the breakfast nook table. Once they were seated, Blake said a prayer for the food.

As they ate, Skylar talked about how school was going. She didn't seem to be very excited about being away on her own.

Blake had been thrilled to go away to college and expand his horizons without his parents hovering over him. Skylar didn't seem to feel that way about her own experiences at college.

After they'd eaten their fill of chili and cornbread muffins, Charli brought out a selection of Christmas baking. Skylar declined coffee but asked for milk instead, which didn't surprise Blake, as he'd discovered that Layla also liked to have milk with her dessert. Amelia wasn't as big a milk drinker, usually just with her breakfast.

Skylar took a sip of her milk, then held the glass next to her chest with both hands. "Would you two do something for me?"

Charli narrowed her eyes at her sister. "Is this something that will make Mom and Dad wish they could ground me?"

"I don't plan for them to know."

"That doesn't reassure me, Sky. What's going on?" Charli demanded, worry on her face.

"I need you to adopt my baby."

Charli's mouth dropped open, and Blake saw a variety of emotions cross her face. Shock. Worry. Resignation. "Baby?"

"Yes. I'm pregnant, and I want you to adopt the baby."

Charli glanced at Blake, then looked back at Skylar. "Tell me what happened."

Skylar took another sip of milk, her gaze dropping to the table. "Last summer, while Cole and Aiden were home, all Aiden could seem to talk about was how the girls liked the athletes. They were throwing themselves at the guys on the basketball team. I guess I just worried that they were going to give him something that I couldn't, so we started sleeping together."

"Did you not use birth control?"

Skylar shrugged. "Most of the time. I'm not sure what happened, but I found out in August that I was pregnant."

"When are you due?"

"March. I'm almost thirty weeks."

Blake's gaze briefly dropped to Skylar's stomach. She did have a soft look to her, but Blake had just figured she was built more like Charli, who had a curvier figure. Still, hiding a pregnancy for that long was pretty impressive.

"Does Aiden know about the baby?" Charli's question brought a scowl to Skylar's face. "Cole said you haven't been talking to him."

"Yes. Aiden knows about the baby."

"And he's okay with the adoption?"

"I don't know, and I don't care." Skylar's expression hardened. "When I told him I was pregnant, he told me he'd give me the money for an abortion."

Charli sighed. "Oh, boy."

Blake wondered what his reaction might have been if Charli had actually been able to tell him about her pregnancy. He didn't think he'd have told her to get an abortion. He'd known even then how much she wanted children and valued the lives of the unborn, so telling her to get rid of the baby would probably have ended things between them.

"As soon as he said that, I knew we were over." She took another sip of milk. "But I can't keep the baby."

"Are you sure?" Charli asked.

When Charli asked the question, Blake realized he didn't know if she'd considered giving Layla up for adoption. Though he knew adoption could be a really positive thing, selfishly, he was glad that she hadn't.

"I'm sure," Skylar said. "I've had a lot of time to think about it. I can't keep the baby, but I also don't think I could give it up to a stranger."

"Why me?"

Skylar gave her a small smile. "You're a great mom. I want the baby to have that."

"Misha and Jay are great parents, too. So are Gareth and Aria."

"I know. But you're my first choice."

"I won't be the only one adopting this baby," Charli told her. "You know that Blake and I are dating. We plan to get married, so he'll be adopting the baby, too."

Skylar's smile grew. "I know. Finding that out reinforced my decision to ask you to take the baby."

"How are you going to keep this from everyone?" Charli asked. "Mom and Dad already suspect there's something wrong."

Skylar sighed. "I know. Realistically, I probably won't be able to keep it from them."

"I know it will be hard to tell them," Charli said, her expression sympathetic. "But the more support you have, the better."

"I'll think about it."

"Also, Blake and I will need to talk about it. I can't make this decision for both of us."

Blake could have told her that he was on board with it right then. But he knew they did actually have to talk it over, just the two of them.

It was a bit weird to be on this side of the situation, but Blake was witnessing the stress of finding oneself with an unplanned pregnancy. It made him sad that he hadn't been there to support Charli through hers.

"I'd like to have this settled before I go back after Christmas. Not knowing what to do has been the hardest thing. I just... I just need to know what's happening as I head into the final trimester."

"We'll talk about it and let you know."

"Thank you for at least considering it." Skylar set her now empty glass on the table. "I think I'm going to go."

Charli didn't argue as she got up and walked Skylar to the front door. Blake followed them, and once Skylar had her coat and boots on, she gave Charli a hug.

"Love you," Charli murmured as she hugged her sister. "Call me if you need to talk. You know I'll understand."

"I will."

After Skylar left, Charli turned to Blake, and he wrapped his arms around her. "That was... a lot."

"It was," Charli agreed.

They stood in the foyer for a moment, then Charli said, "Let's go drink more coffee, eat cookies, and talk."

"Sounds like a plan."

Back in the kitchen, Blake made them fresh cups of coffee while Charli cleared away the rest of the table, leaving only the plate of cookies and some napkins.

As she sat down at the table, Charli looked across at Blake. "So."

"So," he echoed. Watching her closely, he said, "Let's do it."

Charli's eyes widened. "Just like that?"

"Just like that," Blake said with a nod. "It feels right. Helping Skylar in that way after your experience."

"A baby is a lot of responsibility, though, and I don't think we're in any position for me to stay home with the kids."

Blake sighed. "Unfortunately, that's probably true."

"I'm sure Mom and Denise will help where they can." Charli stared down at her coffee.

Blake reached across and rested his hand on hers, waiting until she looked up before he asked, "What are your concerns?"

She gave him a quick smile. "I have a lot, to be honest."

"I have a question for you." When he hesitated, she nodded for him to go ahead. "If Skylar had come here tonight to tell you that she was pregnant and giving the baby up for adoption, what would you have done?"

"I would have told her that I'd take the baby."

"Skylar's pregnancy isn't going to change, and you have no control over that. All you have control of is your decision at this moment."

"Our decision," she reminded him.

"Yes. Ours." Their futures were now intertwined. Whatever path they took forward, they'd be taking it together. "We should pray about it, though."

Holding hands, they each took turns praying about the situation with Skylar, asking for comfort for her, and wisdom for them as they took on this new responsibility. They also prayed for peace for everyone involved.

"You know I'll support you whatever you decide," Blake said when they finished praying. "There is one other thing you might want to think about, though."

Charli's brow furrowed as her hands gripped his more tightly. "What's that?"

"It might be better for us to go through the adoption process as a married couple." He paused. "Which means we'd have to get married sooner rather than later."

She appeared to consider that for a moment. "Would that be a problem?"

"Only because I don't want to deprive you of the wedding you've always wanted to have," he said, recalling the times she'd talked to him about the wedding she wanted, which had been a lot like Kayleigh and Hudson's. "We wouldn't have much time to plan anything like what you wanted."

After sitting quietly for a moment, Charli said, "I don't want a big wedding anymore. We have more important things to spend our money on. Unfortunately, I think the girls have pretty high expectations."

Blake chuckled. "Yeah. They do."

"But I think we could make it work. We can still make it special, even if it's not very elaborate."

"Yeah. I think we can."

With the decision made, their conversation immediately turned to future plans. Including a wedding and a new baby. They were each going to jump from small families of two to a combined family of five.

The girls were going to lose their minds over the news that they were expanding their family even more.

"One thing I will insist on with Skylar is that she tell our parents. She's going to need them after she has the baby. And I don't want to have to lie to them because they'll want all the details once they hear we're adopting."

"And your siblings? I can't imagine Janessa, Jay, or Gareth letting you get away without telling them everything."

"Thankfully, not having a lot of details about the parents giving a baby up for adoption isn't uncommon. We'll just tell them the truth. We were approached about adopting a baby from a woman who wasn't able to keep it and after praying, we decided to say yes."

By the time they left to pick up the girls, they had a plan for getting married. It would confuse most people, but as long as Skylar told their parents about her pregnancy and her request of Blake and Charli, they would understand why they were having a quick and scaled back wedding, and that was the most important thing.

~*~

Charli looked at herself in the mirror, and for one brief moment, her heart longed for the wedding dress of her young self's dreams. Instead, she wore a cream-colored dress that she'd found on Amazon. Bought from there, because of two-day shipping.

It had a fitted lace bodice and long lace sleeves with a flared satin skirt that reached mid calf. It wasn't ugly, and it looked wedding-ish.

The dress and the wedding ceremony were a part of a means to an end. Not just the adoption, but also the marriage. They represented the two things she'd always wanted to be. A wife and a mother. And not just a wife and mother, but a wife to Blake and a mom to two beautiful girls and a yet unknown baby.

So sacrificing a fancy dress and an expensive wedding in order to gain so much didn't really feel all that much like a sacrifice after all.

"No regrets?" her mom asked as she joined her at the mirror.

It was just the two of them in her mom and dad's room, so they could speak freely.

"I know you wanted a wedding more like Kayleigh's," she added.

"That's true," Charli said. "Once upon a time. However, I've discovered I want the marriage and the family more than the wedding. So, no. I have no regrets."

"Thank you for doing this for Skylar," her mom said, her gaze shiny with unshed tears. "Your dad and I will do what we can to help you and Blake."

Skylar had waited until the day after Christmas, right before she planned to go back to college, to tell their parents about what had happened. As expected, Skylar's news had gone over as well as Charli's had twelve years earlier.

Charli still wasn't sure if her parents blamed her for being a bad influence on Skylar, and she didn't plan to ask. However, she did wonder if Skylar seeing the obvious proof of the decisions Charli and Jay had made when it came to the physical aspects of their relationships had made it easier for her to make that decision with Aiden.

She hoped that wasn't the case, but perhaps that was a conversation she needed to have with her sister. However, that was for a different time.

That day was for her wedding.

It was New Year's Day, and the pastor at their church had agreed to marry them. All the siblings that didn't live in Serenity—including Skylar—had left already, but they'd be attending via video chat.

Amelia and Layla were wearing matching dresses in dark green, and Janessa had agreed to be Charli's matron of honor, even though she wasn't as enthusiastic about Blake as she'd once been.

While her parents had been willing to accept her and Blake's past relationship, her siblings had taken a bit longer to accept and adjust to the news.

Jay and Gareth had been the first to let go of their anger over how Blake had treated Charli in the past. Janessa, however, still had moments when she'd glare at Blake, but those moments were becoming fewer and further apart. And Charli hoped that with Janessa agreeing to stand up with her, she'd let it all go completely.

Jackson had gone from being profusely apologetic for spilling her secret to Blake to gloating and taking credit for them being together. Charli rolled her eyes whenever Jackson went on and on about how he was responsible for their happily-ever-after.

It was especially important for Janessa to get over her anger at Blake, since they were all going to be living together for a while.

Since she and Janessa had purchased the house together, Charli would need to pay her for her half if she and Will decided to move out. She didn't mind them all living together. The house and its rooms were large, and they were well soundproofed, so Charli wasn't worried about a crying baby bothering the people on the second floor.

Layla was already planning to share her room with Amelia, so they'd do that until the baby's arrival. Once the baby had joined their family, the girls would have to move to the second floor. Whether they'd share a bedroom or not at that point would be decided closer to the time.

They had three months to make that decision.

They hadn't told anyone about the adoption yet. They'd wait until closer to Skylar's due date, just because it might be too much to spring on everyone. Though she'd had plenty of questions from her family about the rapid wedding, most had accepted it when they'd stuck to their story of it just being time to move ahead after twelve years apart.

Because that was also true. Even without the adoption looming, Charli was confident that they would have gotten married sooner rather than later.

"You look beautiful, Mom," Layla said as the girls came into the room.

"Even if it's not a fancy wedding dress?"

Layla smiled at her, then came to give her a hug. "It's perfect."

When they'd decided to get married so quickly, she and Blake had sat down with the girls to let them know. They hadn't exactly explained *why* they were doing it beyond saying that they'd waited a long time to get married and didn't want to wait any longer.

"You and Amelia look beautiful, too," Charli said, glad that the dresses she'd found on Amazon for them and Janessa fit so well. "Is everyone ready?"

"Yep," Janessa announced as she joined them. "Everyone is sitting down, and Blake is pacing."

"Dad's excited," Amelia informed them. "This morning he said he couldn't wait."

Charli smiled. "I can't wait either."

When her dad appeared, Charli knew it was time.

The ceremony was being held in her parents' large living room, which had been set up with chairs from the church. Everyone had pitched in to help set things up the night before once they'd finished their family New Year's Eve party.

They left the bedroom and made their way to the large opening that led into the living room. Kayleigh had said she'd help facilitate what they wanted, so when she spotted them, she motioned at Hudson.

Immediately, string instruments began to play the song Charli had chosen for them to walk to. They hadn't had time to hire anyone, so they were relying on Hudson's phone and the Bluetooth speakers in the living room for the music.

Soon, it was her and her dad waiting to step into the entrance. He smiled down at her as he offered her his arm. "Ready to get married?"

Everyone kept asking her that like there was any chance that she wasn't. "Never been more ready."

"Then let's do this."

Charli couldn't keep the smile from her face as they stepped into the living room and her gaze found Blake. He, the pastor, and Jackson were in front of the large Christmas tree that stood in the bay window.

At her request, her parents had left the Christmas decorations up, and there was a fire crackling in the large stone fireplace at the other end of the room. The couches and other chairs had been moved out to make room for the folding chairs, which had all been set up in a semi-circle facing the tree and window. There were candles warmly glowing throughout the room.

As her dad guided her down the aisle they'd created with the chairs, Charli kept her eyes on Blake. This was the moment she'd once dreamed of. Her younger self probably would have wept at how long it had taken to get there. But right then, all that mattered was that they'd finally made it to the altar.

Handing off her small bouquet of four red roses and baby's breath to Janessa, Charli turned to Blake and took his hands. His wonderful hands that represented so much to her. In the calluses was his determination to work hard to provide for his family. In the strength was his promise to hold and protect each of them.

But under all of that was his gentleness, which was present in a more profound and deeper way than it had ever been before. It had been that, more than anything else, that had convinced her that it wasn't too soon to get married after reconnecting such a short time ago. She trusted him to take care of her, the girls, and the baby soon to join their family.

The pastor, having heard their story during a meeting with them earlier that week, reminded them again of the verse in Ecclesiastes 3 that said *He has made everything beautiful in its time.* It had certainly taken time, but Charli believed that what they had was beautiful, and it was only going to get more so with time.

When they spoke their vows, Layla and Amelia stood with them, listening as Charli and Blake pledged their love and made promises of forever to each other, before God and family. Happiness radiated off the girls, and it was matched only by the happiness Charli felt and could see in Blake's eyes.

Christmas night they'd told them about their plan to marry, and Layla had run off, making Charli worry about how she was receiving the news. But before they could discuss what was going on, she returned, clutching a familiar box.

Layla had shoved it at Blake and said, "Promises kept."

Blake had stared at her for a long moment before looking at Charli and then down at the box. He'd slowly opened it, then sat with his head bent.

Charli had reached over and covered his hands with hers, waiting until he looked up at her, sadness in his gaze. "Layla's right. Promises kept, Blake. We made it."

Since her gaze held his, she'd seen the moment the sadness faded away.

"Promises kept," he'd agreed, then he'd slipped the ring on her right hand, though it fit a bit more snugly than it had the first time he'd done that.

And after making new promises to each other, he slid another ring onto her finger, and this time, she had one for him too. The rings had also been hurriedly purchased off Amazon, just until they could get what they wanted later.

Once the rings were in place, the pastor instructed them to share their first kiss as husband and wife. Charli went up on her toes to meet him halfway, smiling into the press of his lips against hers. The kiss lingered for a moment, then they stepped apart.

"Today is the first day in our forever," Blake said as he gazed down at her with a smile. "I love you, Charli."

"I love you too. And I can't wait for what's to come."

They kissed one more time, then they turned to take the girls' hands and face the group gathered there.

When the pastor presented them as Mr. and Mrs. Blake Madden and their daughters, Layla and Amelia, their families cheered and clapped. There was slightly less decorum in their reaction than there might have been at the church.

Charli smiled at everyone, thankful that each of them had come to support and celebrate with them. And she knew that they'd be there to support and celebrate with them when their family grew in a few months, even without knowing the relationship they shared with the baby.

Though she would have had a happy life with just Layla, Charli was grateful to be able to experience life with Blake and Amelia. Big changes were coming, and not all of them would be easy, but rather than be worried, Charli was excited, and she knew that Blake was as well.

And even though it had taken them far longer than they'd planned to reach the point of getting married, Charli had decided to let go of all regrets, and she knew Blake had too. They had two beautiful, healthy daughters, with another baby on the way. They had careers they loved. And most of all, they had their faith in God and their love for each other, both of which would be the foundation on which they'd build their future.

They shared the belief that God had brought them back together after years apart, and they knew that He would walk them through the ups and downs to come.

Promises kept.

~*~ The End ~*~

ABOUT THE AUTHOR

Kimberly Rae Jordan is a USA Today bestselling author of Christian romances. Many years ago, her love of reading Christian romance morphed into a desire to write stories of love, faith, and family, and thus began a journey that would lead her to places Kimberly never imagined she'd go.

In addition to being a writer, she is also a wife and mother, which means Kimberly spends her days straddling the line between real life in a house on the prairies of Canada and the imaginary world her characters live in. Though caring for her husband and four kids and working on her stories takes up a large portion of her day, Kimberly also enjoys reading and looking at craft ideas that she will likely never attempt to make.

As she continues to pen heartwarming stories of love, faith, and family, Kimberly hopes that readers of all ages will enjoy the journeys her characters take in each book. She has no plan to stop writing the stories God places on her heart and looks forward to where her journey will take her in the years to come.

Printed in the USA
CPSIA information can be obtained
at www.ICGtesting.com
LVHW090031200624
783498LV00011B/800

9 781988 409771